Angelo Loukakis has worked as a teacher, scriptwriter, editor and publisher. He is the author of the fiction titles *For the Patriarch*, *Vernacular Dreams* and *Messenger*. His non-fiction titles include a children's book on Greeks in Australia and a travel book on Norfolk Island. His collection of short stories, *For the Patriarch*, was winner of a NSW Premier's Literary Award.

Also by Angelo Loukakis

For the Patriarch

Norfolk: an island and its people

The Greeks

Vernacular Dreams

Messenger

The Memory of Tides

Angelo Loukakis

FOURTH ESTATE • *London, New York, Sydney* and *Auckland*

Fourth Estate
An imprint of HarperCollins*Publishers*, Australia

First published in Australia in 2006
by HarperCollins*Publishers* Australia Pty Limited
ABN 36 009 913 517
www.harpercollins.com.au

HarperCollins*Publishers*
25 Ryde Road, Pymble, Sydney NSW 2073, Australia
31 View Road, Glenfield, Auckland 10, New Zealand
77–85 Fulham Palace Road, London W6 8JB, United Kingdom
2 Bloor Street East, 20th floor, Toronto, Ontario, M4W 1A8, Canada
10 East 53rd Street, New York NY 10022, United States of America

National Library of Australia Cataloguing-in-Publication data:

Loukakis, Angelo, 1951– .
  The memory of tides.
  ISBN 978 0 7322 8067 3.
  ISBN 0 7322 8067 2.
  1. World War, 1939–1945 – Veterans
  – Australia – Fiction.
  I. Title.
A823.3

Cover and internal design by Natalie Winter
Cover Images: Tree (200285008-001), the Donkey (ngs4-2750)
and the Woman (rh728-1856) © of Gettyimages
Typeset in Adobe Caslon 11.5/16pt by Kirby Jones
Printed and bound in Australia by Griffin Press on 70gsm Bulky Book Ivory

5 4 3 2 1   06 07 08 09

To the memory of my mother and father,
Nikolaos and Maria, who each fought the battle
in their own way.

Prologue

Since yesterday morning there had been nothing but silence. Communication was cut off. The two telephones at the village of Arkadi, in the post office and in the mayor's office behind it, had stopped working. As the only other phone in the area was located at the monastery a few kilometres further south, a messenger was sent there to seek news: he came back to report that their phone was dead too. The Germans had descended in the north of Crete on 20 May, having given every sign of doing so since they overran the mainland. Here was the first, dreaded hint they might also be interested in this otherwise forgotten corner of the island.

The fighting that had begun on the north coast, not fifty kilometres from here, might as well have been on the moon for all its immediate impact. In Arkadi, the usual dreamy silence heralded each dawn, the cocks still crowed with first light. There were goats to be milked, chickens to be rounded up and fed, fields and groves to be tended, bread to be baked. Reports were heard, plenty of those, of the first few days of struggle. Some successes, they were told, then came news that somebody's cousin had died in Hania, someone else's uncle in

Rethymnon or its outskirts, a brother of somebody else, a friend of a friend.

As her apprehension grew, Kalliope Venakis decided that if she couldn't keep it at bay she would at least keep it quiet and not add to the general gloom being spread about by such as her uncle and other of the village naysayers. Today she had tried to stall her fears for an hour or two by climbing up Gerovouno to collect some wood. She had no enthusiasm for going as high as the old mills, but could see them above as she gathered a few small pine branches and some cones, fallen the previous winter, and made a bundle to tie to the side of her donkey. She waited, watched patiently while Aristotle (Uncle Mattheos' little joke, the name) began chewing on some coarse stubs.

Perhaps in such times even a poor donkey had a lesson to teach. The past winter, from the end of 1940 and into the beginning of this year, had been harder than most, even if it was a winter whose ills were shared with all the people of Greece, island and mainland. Patience was certainly needed in life, to deal with the bad as much as to allow for the good things to come. As to the possibility of good, that was clear for anyone to see on this flowering hillside in southern Crete so bathed in pleasant afternoon sun. The world renewed itself, things came back.

Question was, how much more patience Kalliope could find. It was five years ago that she and Andreas and their friends had last climbed this same hill together. Impossible to believe it had been 1936, the year they had finished school, and not yesterday. *I am not alone*, she had thought back then. Not when there was Marika, joyous and trusted Marika, the person who made her laugh and could brighten any day. Or gentle Manolis who would never be bowed down, despite the cross of a brutal father. Or their brilliant Yannis, so determined and proud. And not when there was Andreas, their champion of Venizelos and democracy, representative government, peace for all. Strong and passionate Andreas, her favourite and dearest of the boys.

And it was here on Gerovouno that Andreas had taken her aside to say they were no longer children, to tell her that he loved her, and finally what was in his heart. That he dearly wished to marry her. That his plan was to make his way out of his prison, the village of Arkadi, and go to a place where he could find a better way of life, for himself, for her, for their children to come. A place like Australia.

'Will you come with me? Tell me you will ...'

Why hadn't she simply said yes there and then? To that young man, to a new life elsewhere? Too late now. Andreas was there in Australia, she here, and a war stood in between. But not only that, as if that was not enough. With each passing year, keeping faith with the dreams they might have once dreamed had become ever more difficult. She had learned some truths they didn't know when they were young: that a cost attached to everything, that not everything was available to be freely given according to will or desire.

Kalliope looked for consolation — and there was some, in the myriad and deep beauty that the passage of a few months, the journey from winter to spring, had brought forth on these fabled slopes and valleys. There were mountain flowers and herbs, daisies and wild thyme all around. She turned her gaze northwards, towards those impenetrable ranges, towards where she knew chaos and death had taken hold. Turning to face south again, she told herself she should have gone higher today. The view from here was pleasant enough, but from further upland and again looking south, she would have had a restful view as far as the sea.

She was content to stand still and feel the cooling air of this calm spring afternoon. There was no reason to give into despair; no calamity had yet occurred for her own people. And whatever did happen, whatever her anxiety, she would be active in her fate, in all their fates. For this was a promise made not only to herself but now to others. She had vowed herself to the fight and would fight whichever way she could.

PART ONE

1

The Glory that was Greece

That the war had not gone to plan in Greece was for Vic Stockton a matter of personal experience. As he sat under a carob tree in the noonday heat, waiting for the water ration to come round, Vic wondered whether it had all gone to blazes because of the element of surprise. But no one could honestly say that a full-scale Nazi assault on this country had been entirely unexpected.

What ordinary flesh and blood could do about that now in this quarter — the rugged backblocks of Crete — was a question to which he knew the answer: nothing at all. Their resistance to the German onslaught had ended. Along with the other men here, he was very tired, experiencing a fatigue close to exhaustion. The task now was to try to keep going across a difficult terrain. The aim was to stay out of harm's way until such time as they could be marshalled and withdrawn from the south coast.

In these few moments of rest, Vic reminded himself that he and the others in his little mob had survived to date, and under direct fire. On the run, they had got away from the enemy earlier today; they were well out of the Germans' sight by now. It would be extremely rotten luck not to make it through in one piece. Things had been a lot worse. And he and Stan Weller, currently propping himself up around the other side of this same tree, were already veterans a number of times over — not only of fights on the Greek mainland but of battles at Bardia and Tobruk and Derna.

The brass might call it a strategic withdrawal but Vic knew for a fact that there were currently several thousand men in an arc south from Hania and Rethymnon packing whatever kit they could, under whatever cover could be mustered against the rapidly building and tactically grouping Germans, and all were considering their fate. They were in retreat and without radio contact: the Battle of Crete, such as it was and had been, was over. 'Battle' was not the right word, for it assumes some contest was possible; but it had not been. For the Germans, Crete had proved no more than an exercise. Kurt Student had been allowed to try out his philosophy of airborne attack was all — a mad Nazi general with a passion for aeroplanes and dropping soldiers out of them.

That part of the German campaign could be proclaimed a failure; Vic had lost count of how many live targets he and everyone else — not only every soldier, but every Cretan man, woman and child, every *yaya* or *papou* in possession of a shotgun, hunting rifle or pistol — had killed as they tumbled from their planes. But it was a failure long past. The Germans had weathered the ferocity of the local counterattack and then their assault started in earnest; by the end, hundreds of Luftwaffe planes had been landed and thousands of men and their gear had been disgorged. Whatever Vic and his mates or anyone else had done to try to stop it, the invading bastards had become the new owners of the place. For the men with Vic now heading south towards Sfakia, the fighting was over, or so he hoped — for his own sake and that of the rest of this miserable group of eight.

They had been among the last on this stretch, hiking slowly to conserve energy, when they had spotted an abandoned truck off the side of the road. With an idea to repair and use it, they set to work. They were still at it after everyone else had disappeared ahead — even after the official rearguard had caught them up and pressed past, full of warnings about their falling behind. But they had argued the truck would be a boon if it was made mobile, that once it was going it would take them no time to regain the others, and that the vehicle could carry some of their remaining weapons and supplies, or else men who were too ill or weak to go on over this tough terrain. All well and good except that, after repairs and a mile or so travelled, the engine was not firing on all cylinders and was having trouble with anything like a serious rise.

The brief stop for water was over, and Vic got up to put his shoulder to the rear of the truck again. The thing was becoming more a liability than an asset, that was clear; they had spent so much time on it they could no longer see any of their own troops in the distance ahead. But as did everyone else, Vic continued to push as hard as he could, trying to get some purchase up and over a steep, gravel-strewn, dried-up creek bed, trying also not to consider his own chances in this mess.

Vic looked across at Stan leaning into the job of the truck, and thought again of Bardia and what they had gone through there, though they had somehow managed to stay alive. North Africa had been grim and brutal, while judged a military triumph. Once on the Greek mainland, there was a different feeling: Greece was an ally, its old glory might be brought to life once more, it was worth the trouble. What was it that Menzies, or was it Churchill, had said about their contribution? 'A great risk in a good cause,' or somesuch. Whatever the reasons, they had towed their equipment and artillery up to northern Macedonia where they waited to start all over again, engage the enemy in battle once more. On their way up through Attica and Boeotia heading north, they had seen the hills and the sides of the roads covered in broom and camomile; it was spring after all. In every village there were people smiling at them, waving, men and women giving them food and gifts, crossing themselves on their behalf as they headed north to fight the good fight. They had tried their hardest, fought where and as best they could, but met the inevitable; barely weeks after establishing their initial positions they were routed.

They had been sent on to Crete, it was said, because a permanent holdout was intended to be set up on this island, a place where a Greek government-in-exile could be formed, after which would follow the campaign to eventually regain the mainland. It was a big island with a large population, it would be hard to take, there was plenty of room. That had been the official story. But what each and every soldier knew, even if some were clearer about it than others, was that this whole bloody show in Crete, too, was doomed. Had been pretty much from the outset. From the first day when the airfield at Maleme was lost, the actual fighting had lasted only ten days — and then it was a matter of when to start the retreat. Vic didn't know what was worse — the chaos of getting on boats at Piraeus and the fear of getting blown out of the water on the way down to Crete, or what had happened since they got here, including this desperate scramble.

As he continued to shove he tried to redirect his thoughts, knowing that what he was feeling at this moment might go by the name of self-pity. On the other hand, he wondered, what emotion might be deemed more appropriate while you were trying to escape a formidable enemy? He hoped he might be forgiven that, considering the number of times he had pulled a bloody trigger. He never thought of himself as a coward, but not as a hero either — and what were the odds of a bloke like him surviving? Especially now as they stood listening to the unmistakeable drone of a Stuka, invisible in the cloud cover but there somewhere in the north-western sky.

The reality of a plane was worrying enough, but it wasn't so much the possibility of them getting blasted from the air, it was one of the other truths about planes that was now weighing on all their minds. That when they weren't dropping bombs or on recce, German planes were usually flying cover for troops on the ground. And the thought of encountering the krauts once again, and maybe in serious numbers, was just too much to let in under the circumstances. So, for now, what else was there but to press on and try to be cheerful?

When the truck was more or less mobile again, lumbering forward after a fashion, Vic whistled and called Stan's name. He turned and came over to walk alongside his mate for a while.

'They reckon we've got deserts back home, Stan. But I don't reckon any of this qualifies for the Garden of Eden, do you?' Vic said.

'Dunno about that. Eden's round the corner, haven't they told you … ?'

Soon they were heading up a pitted, narrow road that wound over a barren hillside. Though it looked exposed for the next two miles or so, they might be able to turn down into a more wooded valley and find shelter there. From what they had seen of this island, with its high, bare ridges dividing and enfolding all sorts of little hollows, fertile plateaus and green corners, it was a reasonable expectation. They had to take such a circuitous route to avoid the larger, more open plains. The Amari triangle below Rethymnon, the flattest and therefore quickest way south, would have been ideal, but unfortunately the Germans knew that too.

'Tell me something,' Vic said. 'Am I hearing birdies?'

Stan looked ahead to where their lowly transport was grinding along, in bottom gear, and as slowly as possible to conserve fuel. He grimaced and replied, 'Naooo … not unless they're motorised these days — Christ! What do we do?'

Vic took a few further steps, seeming to need the momentum for thinking purposes. He looked quickly ahead at the rest of the men who, also having heard the sound in the distance, apparently had no plan but to pick up the pace and trot more quickly in the same forward direction. Then, as the significance gripped, a couple took off and ran alongside the truck to get the driver's attention. Their battered vehicle quickly came to a stop.

Vic was with Stan when their sergeant jumped out of the passenger side of the truck and waved to them to come forward.

'Hello, there might be a plan,' Vic muttered as they headed up.

'How much do you want to put on it?'

They had barely time to group when they realised it was not one vehicle, but a number, and maybe half-tracks as well. And more: against the hellish bass of heavier engines something lighter played, probably the two-stroke beat of motorcycles. Vic felt the familiar jolt of adrenaline, that old injection of juice where you really had none and that came with the anticipation of action, of something physical being required. Marvellous how being given an order, told to propel your body in some direction, towards some end — before you had time to assess it as stupid or sensible — helped you manage the otherwise intolerable.

They were ordered to ditch their own vehicle or to attempt to make it as scarce as possible, then to take cover. They scanned this bare stretch; the nearest place where you might hide a truck looked to be a good mile away.

'Where'll we put it?' someone asked.

'Up ahead,' the sergeant replied, 'or if they get here too quick tip it over and get away from it. All right? We can muster after they're gone.'

Vic turned slightly to Stan and said softly, 'So how much do you owe me?'

As the noise behind them rose rapidly in volume, it was blindingly clear that the truck would have to look after itself.

Vic looked around and saw a cloud of dust less than half a mile behind them. 'Shit, come on! That way!' He grabbed Stan by the arm and they ran quickly to the back of the truck to retrieve their rifles and half-empty, mostly useless kitbags. They tore straight down the exposed eastern slope to their left, obliquely in the direction of the advancing Germans, but with the idea of making the only cover available — a few straggly olive trees lining another slope in the distance.

As they ran, they were surprised to see some of the other men race back up to the vehicle they were supposed to abandon, with their sergeant either in pursuit of them or having fallen in with this change of plan. 'Mad bastards,' Vic muttered to himself. 'They'll never get away.'

Vic and Stan reached the relative safety of the trees and flattened themselves on the ground behind the fattest trunks they could find, waiting and watching as furtively as they could.

Three transports went by, two pulling artillery pieces, then four motorcycles with outriders.

'Never do things by halves, do they?' Stan said.

Immobilised, they continued to wait but, no more than a minute later came the sound of rifle and light machine-gun fire. This was a kick in the guts like no other.

'God, no … God, no …'

In anger and pain Vic and Stan jumped to their feet again, not knowing what else they might do. Going back up, they knew, would mean their certain end too.

The sound of shooting came to an end; the whole thing had not taken two minutes. Then the German engines started up once more.

'Gone soon. Maybe we can get back up there then?' Stan said hopefully, his face flushed bright red behind the dust.

Vic shook his head at the thought of what they would find. This was too much, too bloody much.

Still paralysed, both men expected to hear the motorcycles roar off any moment. They watched stunned as, instead, one of the riders got off and stepped to the side of the road. They saw him raise his hands to his head.

'Glasses …!' Vic gasped, pulling Stan back to the ground. Both had anticipated, without saying as much to each other, that they would stay to bury their mates. With the Germans halted and a scout scanning the area, even such ordinary decencies might not be possible.

But then, stroke of luck, something in the opposite direction seemed to take the attention of the rider and his cohort. Vic and Stan watched as the party of Germans turned around and stepped away to the other side of the road. Without another word, the two Australians got to their feet and quietly took off in the opposite direction, ducking from one tree to another for cover. Nothing more could be done, they knew, than to get the hell away from this barren place and its tragedy, and as quickly as possible.

2

News from the North

The sun had begun to drop, it was time to come back down off Gerovouno. Kalliope tugged at Aristotle, but for the moment he would not be turned from his own occupations. In the wait until he was more inclined, she thought again of how she had been approached and the undertaking she had given. It had been one of the mayor's own men who had come to her to ask whether she would assist in the work that would need to be done if the worst came and they were overrun. Surprised as she was, she'd had the presence at least to ask him in turn what would be required of her. He had replied that things were unresolved. Everything depended on what came to pass and when, and there would be rumour and confusion in the meantime. Events would dictate what would finally need to be done and how. Armed combat was unlikely near here but, should Crete be overrun, resistance was inevitable. An effective resistance would take many weeks, months, of organisation, and would probably involve the British and such secret activities as they too were bound to establish. The important thing was whether she was willing to take part and make sacrifices if necessary.

The chief difficulty for her, it was explained, was that none of her family, not her mother, Despina, nor her uncle Mattheos, was to be told anything just yet. 'Your mother is the worrying kind and your uncle merely worrisome,' he had said. She had felt like hanging her head at the words, but then he said, 'It's you we need — later they will know what needs to be known. All right?' If she was to join the resistance, she was also to be joined to secrecy.

Moved that such faith had been expressed in her, and on behalf of others, Kalliope had asked for a few moments to think. In the end she had said, 'Yes, yes, I will.' After which the mayor's man had said only 'Good', that the mayor himself would next make contact, and that she was to say and do nothing in the meantime. To have been considered in this way had given her a kind of satisfaction she had never felt before, just as it had brought a degree of fear; there was no denying either.

Aristotle appeared at last to be done with working the ground. Kalliope tested his willingness by tugging him around in the direction of the village. He may have finished eating but the further question was whether, with the firewood and her own weight, he felt himself too laden to ride — he was always contrary if he sensed that more than one task was required of him. Thankfully he was ready and she was able to begin the descent towards home.

Kalliope looked to the north one last time, still half expecting to see the smoke of battle or at least some sign of what was happening. She tried to imagine what fighting must still be going on along that coast right now, knowing that the mountains between here and the north of the island could hide anything and everything. Those mountains also meant their own village was not on any quick or direct route, although a narrow, part-sealed road had in the last few years joined them more easily to the outside world. There was a strong chance that her own people, she herself, might never be called upon to bear arms; she hoped so. But if they were, it was possible they would not be alone to deal with any direct assault upon them, from what she had heard. Thousands of soldiers from elsewhere had already lent their strength to the fight: men from England, and even from New Zealand and Australia, had been battling the Germans. They had fought in Hania, and around Rethymnon, capital of her own prefecture; perhaps they might one day come to help here also.

Even without them, should the battle come down to the defence of individual village and hamlet, Kalliope believed everyone would do what was necessary. She took courage in their history: Saracens, Venetians, Turks and others had all been seen off. Cretans had been martyrs, men and women, for a thousand years. They had seen the rape and murder of young girls, seen the men of entire villages carried off in slavery to other races. She had read of these things and had heard some of the old-timers who still talked of the Turks, who had been finally driven out as recently as a few decades ago. Slaughters had always been avenged, invaders put to the knife or chased off. Kalliope thought of the massacres of times past, and how it was the blessed dead, her ancestors, who had made possible this world that was her home and the home of her loved ones. As a child at school, she had learned the names of their flowers, the island's birds and mountains and rivers, but she had also learned that whatever they had on this island had ever to be defended.

Kalliope was home in time for an anticipated early evening radio broadcast via shortwave. She joined her mother and uncle at a table in the half-room that was their kitchen and dining area, a small space separated by an arch from Mattheos' sleeping quarters. She sat and wondered at how so very few months could have taken such a toll. What would they learn tonight that wasn't already known? The Greek government had been exiled to Cairo. On the military front, the news these past weeks had been only of disasters, retreats. That the Greeks had shown courage was not at issue but there were few recent triumphs, only setbacks and withdrawals. They heard the announcer begin:

'Men and women of Crete, for five entire months, from October 1940 to this May, the world looked to Greece and felt hope for the first time since the war had begun. No one could believe what they were reading in newspapers and hearing over the wireless. As our enemies threw an apocalypse of blood and death at us and we countered it as nothing less than heroes, it seemed that a final victory over the fascists would soon be ours. But today we know we Greeks must do more ...

'We saw Mussolini's hideous divisions, armed to the teeth, full of naive bravado. We saw them drive their trucks and wagons and, waving their inglorious flags, come down upon us through Albania. They imagined they were on the road to a famous, an easy victory — and we threw them out.

'For all that they hurled at us in the first few weeks, and all that they would throw in the ensuing months, nothing the Italians could do seemed to make any difference. They were astonished at our resistance: we mined bridges and roads, we anticipated every geographic point of entry into our land, we stood to meet them in the remotest mountain passes. And there, upon encountering them directly, we fought like dogs, like lions ...

'We address this to you, dear people of Crete. We remind you that a few short months ago we defeated the enemy and chased him not only out of Greece but deep into the wilds of Albania. We threw him off our sacred soil. Now we must do it again ... The world saw in us an inspiration. And it was Winston Churchill himself who said of our valiant army that it had "revived before our eyes the glory which, from the Classic Age, has framed their native land ..."

'But now, it is our solemn duty to tell you that Crete, great island of our history, is in mortal danger. The barbarous tyrant, our enemy, has secured a foothold on the coasts of the north and to the west and the whole is threatened. Now is the time to again show the world the spirit of sacred Hellas and repel the new usurper ... Organise! Be staunch! Resist! Resist! Resist ...! And we shall, as God is Almighty, overcome once more!'

So it had come to this. Kalliope understood the message beneath those fiery words: the war on Crete, too, was being lost. She looked across the table at her mother and her uncle, both overwhelmed with emotion, her mother dabbing at her eyes, her uncle also on the verge of tears, his jaw jutting out in some personal act of defiance.

Whatever the radio was suggesting of things to come, there was much to be proud of already. A poor agricultural nation of no more than seven million people had achieved great things with precious little; insufficient arms and equipment, impossibly stretched supply lines, with everyone and every available thing — civilian cars and trucks, village mules and donkeys, boy and girl soldiers — called into service. Kalliope had hoped that they could do it all again, had hoped that the Germans were wasting their time and their resources, at least on the island of Crete.

'Well here we go again is all I say!' declared Mattheos. 'Let them come! Victorious once, victorious again we shall be! It will be 1896 once more, you will see! And 1905, and all the other glorious days of our freedom!'

'It is not 1896, *Thio* ... or any other year. It is now,' Kalliope said.

'Ha!' he scoffed.

After Hitler's advance on the mainland through April, when it was perfectly clear that Crete too was to be attacked, the choices had become stark, were widely spoken of in town and village and field: firstly, to prepare to defeat the enemy so that they gained no foothold here; then, if a definite victory was not to be achieved, a staunch defence that would make them suffer to the point of bogging them down and forcing them to question the value of staying on. And then, as Kalliope had learned directly, should such a defence fail the organisation of a fierce resistance.

Kalliope had worried when Manolis went north with the Cretan division to fight against the Italians on the frontiers. She was concerned, too, that Andreas probably knew little about what was going on here. She had not heard from him since last October and could not be sure her letters had reached him in Australia. And what was his fate in that distant place anyway?

She took a deep breath and got up to see if there was any more camomile tea left in the pot. As she filled a cup for herself and her mother, the words on the radio came back to her. What was there to do but endeavour to be brave?

She came back to the table with both cups and sat down opposite her mother. '*Ohi*, mama,' she said, touching her mother's hand as the older woman continued to sob quietly. In this room, with the bluish late evening light still slanting through the tiny window behind her, Kalliope knew that, whatever might be inflicted on them now, other kinds of pain had already visited those who sat in here.

In low moments Kalliope was inclined to feel herself a prisoner, because of her history as a child, fatherless at two, and because of her fate ever since. She and her mother had the misfortune of living with her mother's brother in this, his small house at the first turn of the road into the village, compelled to come here in the year after Kalliope's father died, as the debts he had left meant their own house had to be sold. Andreas had left for Australia before the war. She had fewer friends to call on than in times past. Even though she sometimes felt both abandoned and trapped, the present brutality had brought possibility: in the duties and responsibilities she would be required to undertake, whatever they might be, she would have a chance to do something serious, maybe even to make something of herself.

In her last year at the Lyceum, when it was said she had given the school's best ever portrayal of Antigone, and shown great flair in earlier roles, her head teacher had put her name forward for a scholarship to the drama school in Irakleion. But Mattheos was vehement that she reject the offer. Studying drama was of no value to a young woman, he had shouted; she would be going off to a nest of *poutanes*, loose morals and fast living. Becoming an actress would only bring shame on all of them.

The heat of that moment had passed long ago; she had been a mere student then. And she had not been entirely convinced herself, besides. Today, more adult and unexpected demands had been put before her.

With the broadcast ended, the sound of Sophia Bembo's lusty voice now filled the room; a mournful, liquid voice that sang so artfully of unrequited love and all over a tango rhythm. It was a distraction but not nearly enough. Kalliope needed something more to stave off the peculiar mix of anxiety and anticipation she felt, and rather than busy herself with household tasks, she resolved to write some letters. She had been meaning to write to a favourite teacher, Dido Manikakis, who in the last days before the war had somehow managed to publish a first book of verse. Then she certainly owed Andreas a letter; and, with him, this always meant more than passing on gossip or idle news.

As the music ceased, to be replaced by static, Kalliope got up and turned the radio off. Wiping the last of her tears, her mother went across to the kitchen to wash and soak beans for tomorrow's soup. Her uncle, this small, intense man with his half-comical, half-tragic expression, remained at the table, brooding and nodding his head at nothing in particular, as he went about preparing another of his stinking pipes.

Kalliope climbed the narrow and steep stairs in the corner to the little attic bedroom she shared with her mother. The first letter would be for Andreas. Sad as she had felt when he left in a cloud of heat and torment nearly three years before, Kalliope hoped her feelings for him had not been intensified merely by his absence. He had surely been dealt a bad hand in life, what with that mad mother of his, a father who had disappeared, and having to support himself practically from childhood. She had often felt sorry for him, wished there was something more she could do. Perhaps these emotions added up to what people called love.

She allowed her mind to drift to better days. The previous summer had held small joys, diversions of a kind that were now hard to even recall let alone imagine might come again. Only last August they had taken a summer holiday at Aghia Galini, a few weeks in which it was possible to feel that maybe not all was doom and gloom in their world. Even though she had had to endure Uncle Mattheos' continuous ill humour all year, as every year, even though she had not heard from Andreas in months and the news of war from Europe was growing grimmer with each day, they had been able to have their summer seaside escape in the house of Kalliope's only aunt. She would hold the memory of these better days as a lamp for the future, and they would surely come again.

As the dark took hold beyond her own small window, Kalliope lit the oil lamp on the trunk between the two narrow beds and took out her writing pad, her fountain pen. She sat on her own bed and began to write.

My beloved Andreas,

Forgive me for not having written these past months. Call me a forgetful and silly girl if you like, but you would be wrong. You can't imagine the obstacles which now appear in our path — all our paths, I mean. The war does not go well, but I don't know how much you know, as far away as you are.

I'm trying to be strong, as you would ask, but just to amuse you, you should know that the plan for marrying me off is gathering speed. Predictably the main agent of my destiny in this matter is *Thio* Mattheos. My mother is his helper in the question. I have not mentioned this before but you should know that last summer I was obliged to inspect, and from far too close, one silly boy in particular (who was promoted as a young man, of course) — some offspring of the Kondylis clan, of all people, those unspeakable traitors who dare to support Metaxas. It was almost too much to believe.

Neither Marika nor myself could take it too seriously but at the same time it was not enough to make us laugh out loud, believe me. This is my lot, I suppose, or what others want from me anyway. Needless to say, I made as much noise as I could after he had left — what a nervous and fussy type he was, wound up like a clockwork toy! — even if they try to pretend I am only being choosy or difficult. But there are more important things than this nonsense.

You asked last time about our friends. What can I tell you except that, but for Marika, our friends seem lost to us?

Manolis went north to fight last November, somewhere around Lamia we believe, and of him nothing is heard but the worst feared. Yannis, whom we all once loved so, is living in Austria. It's said he is studying further in medicine, and we hear talk that he argues now openly for the Nazis and tells everyone that Hitler is the answer to the problems of Europe. We can only hope that these are rumours, but that news comes from his cousin in Irakleion, whom I don't think is any sort of liar …

Kalliope tried not to feel bereft as she wrote. She was twenty-one years old now, going on twenty-two, old enough to deal with the temporary absence of friends, or so she would tell herself. Still, except perhaps for Yannis, she was missing them more than ever. It seemed that only Marika was left to support her and to be supported by her. Kalliope would sometimes say that they had already lived one life together in the few years since they had truly forged their bond as friends for life.

When a young girl had recently asked whether she and Marika had been friends 'forever', because of the way they would walk down the street arm in arm, laughing and glancing all round, always together at local events, at church, Kalliope had replied, 'Yes, of course, since before you were even born.'

3

Duty

The night of the broadcast, the local defence committee led by Mayor Kannetakis, sent a message by runner throughout the locality that the village of Arkadi in the Prefecture of Rethymnon would waste no time, now that events had taken the turn they had, and would begin its own preparations. A series of communal working bees was proposed, the first to create an inventory of ammunition and guns and any other equipment that could be put away for later use, should fighting occur even here. No one really expected that to happen but it was agreed, nevertheless, that they should be forearmed.

The next morning Kalliope was up early and getting ready to go down to the grounds of Aghia Sophia for the first of these sessions. She came downstairs to find her mother and remind her of what they were pledged to do, but then had to deal with the usual idiocy: trying to get her confused parent into some sort of order before they could leave. It was never easy. Her mother never knew where anything was, not that she ever had much to misplace in such a tiny house; whether stockings or skirt or bag or comb, their exact location was always a mystery. Their absence was always lamented by an ever-sadder keening about her creeping old age (she was only fifty-two), lack of help, the clutter of modern life, and so on. But today's issue was quickly resolved when the only missing thing, her otherwise empty purse, was thankfully discovered under her pillow.

Having settled her mother, Kalliope cursed under her breath when she saw Mattheos now carefully propped on one knee on his armchair, peering into the old shaving mirror he had hung on the wall behind it, arranging his appearance. Today, he would be dressed formally in suit and hat, commanding and businesslike in his contribution to the war effort. His thinning hair finally arranged to his satisfaction, he then announced he intended taking along his flag, a fragile thing of rice paper that he kept for national occasions. But to retrieve it meant having to dig through piles of papers and memorabilia right to the bottom of his trunk under his bed. This scrabbling about further held up their exit.

Mattheos then ushered them out, flag rolled up under his arm, with pronouncements on their sacred duty and the new world to come once the mighty sons of Leonidas had dealt with the fascist hordes. By the time they left the house, Kalliope felt like screaming.

The walk to the church took a couple of minutes at most. They got there to find that few others had yet arrived — whether because of tardiness or some other reason, the assembling of so few villagers jolted Kalliope. She had assumed everyone would turn up for something so important. Halting outside, Kalliope let her mother and uncle go into the grounds ahead of her and stood still to look through the gates for a few moments. It was hard to accept what they were planning to do here this morning. She was numb at the thought they were readying themselves, as best they could, for the possibility of combat.

How foolish that she and her friends had taken so seriously their harassment around this holy place by the various urgers of good order and discipline those years ago. How minor were their tribulations from today's perspective. But much of their common life had centred on this church, the new-built (as it was then) Aghia Sophia where everything important seemed to happen. It was also acknowledged to be a marvel. In a small village with hardly any large buildings let alone institutions of any sort, Aghia Sophia was the pride of their community.

The church had not long been blessed before beginning to serve a purpose that neither its congregation nor its priests had ever imagined for it. Beautiful, orthodox it may have been in the way it continued to perform its functions and to impress, in every Byzantine echo and dazzling reflection, all who approached or entered. But it was the other side of the lovely Aghia Sophia, the side not immediately visible, that held the greater attraction for Kalliope and her friends; where the southern side of the church met the low rubble wall that marked the end of Mattheos' vineyard was were they had so often congregated to meet and talk and arrange more rendezvous.

Marika was always concerned back then that Kalliope and Andreas should take care not to be discovered, either at the church or anywhere else in this nosy village. Anyone would think they had a population of three thousand rather than three hundred, considering the amount of gossip and treachery that went around. And Kalliope was well aware that her blossoming relationship with Andreas could turn into a matter of life and death.

Kalliope walked forward into the church and lit the candle, placing it in the stand inside the entrance. To be reined in, frustrated by your own people, was one thing, but to be attacked by those from another country far away was something even more horrifying. And that was a nightmare that might not be more than a few days off. Kalliope crossed herself, bowed forward and kissed the icon of Aghia Sophia, crossed herself again, then hurried back outside to find a dozen more people had arrived to begin the day's task.

Mayor Kannetakis and his immediate circle had done some preliminary work by dragging in three large trunks and draping over each of them a sign painted on calico — 'Ammunition', 'Small Arms', 'Rifles'. Kalliope stood by her mother, her uncle having already gone over to join the men, and watched. Shouting them all to attention, Mayor Kannetakis reminded everyone of the plan that he and the local committee had settled on, then began to call for contributions.

Mayor Kannetakis was a tall, gaunt man. He walked in a deliberate, calculating way as he spoke, and generally seemed to be in a lugubrious funk. A man who always looked as if he was expecting the worst. When he said they would need not only to collect but share out what was available, he spoke slowly and loudly, like a junior grade teacher addressing a rebellious class.

After a few moments one old veteran called out that he could spare the trusty *toufeki* he had by his side, left over from a generation ago, and that he had a dye for bullets but no gunpowder or lead. This was all right and a good start, said the mayor; gunpowder was not an issue as one of his own retainers had a supply. Then another man, a young labourer, held out some objects wrapped in waxed paper, saying these were two pistols left to him by his father. There was also some ammunition to spare but he hadn't fired the guns in a while and wasn't sure how they would react. That too was all right, came the response. Every such offer was valued — the important thing was to lay in a supply of weaponry and to ensure that a nominee from each household could access whatever might be allocated.

After the mayor had finished speaking there was a longish silence. Kannetakis tried some reassurance. There was no need for people to feel nervous, he said — nobody was talking military strategy or asking people to take front-line action. This was an insurance policy only, a means of dealing with something untoward, the sort of disaster that was extremely unlikely but one they would have to deal with should it eventuate. By way of a joke he said, 'Come on now, all of you, last Easter enough celebratory guns went off to suggest we could arm an entire brigade! Where have all those arms gone, then?'

The silence continued until a small farmer by the name of Tziganos raised a faltering voice and said, 'Excuse me your worship but if I give over my gun, which is a rabbiting gun, how will I then keep down those pests? Right now they are breeding like God's business and I have been having a devil of a time trying to control them. Only last week I potted sixteen of the mangy little beggars, and believe me, this is no joke when …'

Someone behind him began to snigger; one or two others saw the humour and joined in. The mayor did a fair job of staying patient, difficult as that was. He waited for the noise to die down and it did. But before he could begin again, Mattheos suddenly pushed his way to the front. 'For the love of God! For the love of God!' Then, with a few purposeful strides he joined the official group and turned around to face his fellow villagers.

Drawing himself up to his full height, he shouted with great indignation, 'Which of you is laughing? Which of you is laughing? This is not funny, what we are doing! Anyone who laughs is a traitor and a fool!'

'It's all right, Mattheos,' came the calming voice of the mayor behind him. 'You don't need to get worked up.'

Wheeling about briefly, Mattheos said, 'Oh, but I am involved, your worship. I have to be. As each and every one of us must be in order to save our sacred land. Now is the time for heroes! Now is the time for sacrifice!'

Taken aback, Kalliope had resolved to go forward to retrieve her uncle but Mattheos' voice boomed out to stop her in her tracks. 'And, Your Worship, and those who will not die for their country, well, I say may Satan take them!'

'That's enough, Mattheos,' the mayor said harshly. But it was too late. Young Spyridonas, that unfortunate boy so touched in the head, had unbeknownst to his mother sneaked out from home, and was among them. Hearing the words 'sacrifice' and 'die' and 'Satan', he tore out from the crowd and rounded on the villagers, his head bent forward like some tortured dog, wild-eyed and terrified.

'You see?' he shouted. 'What *Thio* Mattheos says? You see? We will be sacrificed and die and Satan will have us! Satan will have us all! Now do you see? I told you didn't I? I told you Satan would have us!'

There was pandemonium. As Kannetakis and the more sensible came forward to try to grab hold of the boy to calm him down, Mattheos cried, 'Don't pander to him, he shouldn't be here! Where is his mother? You, Spyridonas! Go home! Get away from here! Go home to your mother!'

'I'm here! I'm here!' Spyridonas' unhappy parent shouted as she began trying to gather up her son.

As Mattheos shouted, Spyridonas began to howl and cry all the more. Mattheos had had enough. Exasperated, he moved towards Spyridonas, raising his flag like a weapon and taking swipes at him in the hope of shooing him off.

And at that Kalliope, having gone from mere annoyance at her uncle's inveterate grandiosity to outrage at the stupidity and cruelty also just beneath the surface, moved forward to block his path and to allow Spyridonas' mother to finally take hold of the boy. Her own mother took out her handkerchief to dab further at the swollen cheeks of her confusion and self-pity.

Kalliope braced herself to deal with Mattheos, but the mayor raised a palm in her uncle's direction before whisking her out of the mêlée and leading her towards the church gate.

'Forgive my uncle, *Kyrie* Kannetakis,' she began.

'No, no, forget that, girl,' said the mayor. 'I wanted to speak to you today anyway. Our fight may soon have to go underground. We are told that the English are managing to leave the island by ship, but not all. They will need supplies until they can be moved to safety. Then if we are to fight successfully again, we will need to be in a position to reorganise.'

'Things are not going well, are they?' she said.

'No. Not well at all. But it is our intention to do what we can — for our allies and for us, and until we defeat the bastards who have fallen among us. Your friend Marika, would she help you?'

'*Vevea*, yes, of course.'

'Well, ask her to join us, and if she says yes …'

'She will, I know that.'

'Good, now … the task is to build a supply store for us. This will have to be done quietly, and so that what is put together — food, bandages, water bottles and so on — is substantial, packed well and easy to transport. You will need to find a useful and secret place for it also. Can you do that?'

Kalliope thought for a moment then answered 'Yes, I can do that.'

'Good. Oh, and be prepared to go to the monastery from time to time — they will be working with us. We also know that the English have already had some contact with them.'

'The monastery? But they don't like women, girls, going there. Some of those old monks ...'

'Ha!' said Kannetakis, suddenly squeezing her forearm as if she were a man. 'You will find their attitude has changed considerably in the circumstances! Anyway, their abbot is a good man, we all know that.'

'If you say so, *Kyrie* Kannetakis.'

'I do. But more later. For the moment, do me a favour and please take that excitable uncle of yours home. Never mind me, he has made enough misery for others here today.'

4

A Bit of a Bushwalk

The consolation of having a mate along was not lost on either Vic or Stan. After an afternoon of scrambling as fast as they could, up and over, down and across the ravines and folds of this part of southern Crete, glancing every so often back in the direction they had come from, Vic moved up to tap Stan on the shoulder.

'Cobber, time to sit down somewhere and nut this out.'

'No argument from me.'

They had not long come down off a high ridge from where they had had an occasional clear view of the distant sea to the south, even if no Allied craft had appeared on the horizon. Now they took themselves off into the corner of the small gorge they had been trudging along over the past hour. This was a deep, steep-sided and winding passage, maybe twenty yards wide in parts, maybe narrower, strewn with smooth pebbles, obviously some old dried-up river bed. It felt like a natural route for foot slogging, being too difficult for motorised transport and thus the enemy. They had seen quite a few of these features on this side of Crete and found that they were more frequent the further south you went; this one had appeared a safe enough route for travelling and for the occasional halt.

Vic headed to one side of a bend where there were some scrubby bushes and a few cypress trees for shade, while Stan was perfectly happy to let him lead. Since their encounter with the Gemans they had seen no one and nothing in these wild and apparently deserted parts, but this would count as an extra precaution. They sat down under a tree and Vic looked up at the long line of blue above their heads, forward and aft, the view of sky above this narrow slit in the rock. You would have to be bloody unlucky to be spotted by someone on the ridge above, Vic thought.

'What have you got in mind, Vic?'

'Not a lot. There's got to be a way off this island, that's all.'

'That's a start, I suppose,' Stan replied, letting in some sarcasm.

'Get to Egypt would be the best thing, but North Africa would be just fine, I reckon. Wasn't that the general plan? And only a few hundred miles away, at that.'

They said nothing for a time after that, knowing that a rocket to the moon would have been as likely a possibility. Then, to break the silence, Stan said, 'Boats would be a bit scarce along this stretch, I'd say.'

'Maybe it's not the fishing season yet,' Vic said, knowing that with the Germans increasingly in charge of these waters, anything larger than a trawler was most unlikely to venture out in daylight hours. 'At any rate, the Poms were supposed to be doing night removals, weren't they?'

'That's what was said,' Stan replied.

With dusk approaching, they agreed not to bother looking for food, but to finish the remaining dry biscuits they had between them and then kip down somewhere out of sight. Rest would stand them in good stead for whatever tomorrow held.

They went on further ahead, to another and flatter stretch. In the shelter of a rock overhang they dumped their gear and set up camp. Vic stretched out and pulled his .303 closer so as to use the butt as a pillow. He exhaled a long sigh of the sort you might let go on a holiday at the beach.

'Comfy?'

'Very.'

Stan went to his pack and took out his last few biscuits, then sat down cross-legged next to his mate. 'So what were we looking at Vic, earlier in the day? Libyan Sea? Is that what it was?'

'Presume so.'

They knew all right. As they also suspected the main evacuations by ship had probably already been carried out — if not by now then by tomorrow night at the latest. The Royal Navy could not risk embarking troops off this part of Crete forever. Vic and Stan had been told that the small coastal town of Horon Sfakion, more commonly known as Sfakia — which was where they'd been heading before the disaster — would be the mustering point. But for no more than a night or two — or three at best. After that, and while the Germans had maritime superiority as well as control of the air, it would be just too dangerous.

While Vic was prepared to believe they could, by some means, get off the island under their own steam, neither of them was ready to address the most likely situation: that by now the enemy mongrels had taken full possession of the place, land, sea and air. Instead, as it didn't bear thinking about and there were no other options, they both lay back and in their exhaustion had no trouble finding sleep.

They woke to the screech of aggressive birds, racketing around in the long slit of dawning light above them. Before morning took proper hold, Vic grabbed his rifle and whispered to Stan that he would try to bag something for them to eat, a rabbit or hare or even one of the overhead pests if his arm were steady enough. Game was often about at this time of the day and perhaps he would be lucky. Not having eaten much for a couple of days, they were in sore need of food. Vic found a zigzag way up and out of the gorge and onto the more exposed slopes above. But the hunting expedition was fruitless. None of the barren, rock-strewn ground within a reasonable distance revealed any targets, and the birds had gone.

Vic came back to see Stan squatting on the gully floor, disconsolately raking the dirt by his side. He seemed to Vic to be in a poorer state of mind today than yesterday. Vic resisted the frustration that began to rise in him, the urge to remind Stan that they had evaded the Germans so far. Maybe what had happened to their mates was beginning to bite harder; he could be forgiven if it had. Vic himself was blocking out the memory at every moment it threatened to resurface. The strategy worked only up to a point; it was more useful, he found, to occasionally go home in his head.

This morning, a recollection of yesterday's sight of the sea had led him to thoughts of boats and home, and how he had badgered his old man to let him join the sea scouts when he was a kid. He could see himself even earlier, in that tiny dinghy on the Parramatta River, learning to pull an oar, following his father in the way he threw in a line, learning to fish; then later again, having joined a sailing club at Balmain, the thrill of going out to race in a skiff for the first time — and he wasn't bad either, for someone from landlocked Enmore, even by his own estimation. But he could not linger in the pleasant past forever. Their present situation pulled him back soon enough.

He stood and stared at Stan, looking for acknowledgement. None came.

'Seeming a bit down, there, Stan. Hope you weren't expecting bacon and eggs or something.'

'No, mate. Just thinking.'

'Well, that's no good either ...' Vic said. 'Look, we're bound to come across something handy eventually. You never know, perhaps some of our own blokes even. Might be a big island but it's not that big.'

'I was thinking of that, too. And another thing ...' He gave Vic a quick glance. 'Do you really reckon there's any odds? I mean, to keep heading the way we're heading?'

Vic was surprised, reading in Stan's expression that his mind was already made up on something.

'I don't have any better idea,' he said. 'Maybe you do.'

Stan took his time to answer, standing up again before speaking.

'I reckon this direction is a mistake, Vic. I think we should just try to get to Sfakia. That's where we were originally headed, right? The place where they were going to round us up and ship us out?'

'It was.'

'And wouldn't that be further sou'west from here, not due south, not the direction we first took off in? As far as anyone can tell?'

'No compass, as you know, but the North Star was more or less directly behind us last night. You might be right.'

'So what do you reckon?'

'I'm prepared to follow your nose, you being a punter and all.'

Stan brightened. He was a twenty-year-old former farmhand who had made his way to Sydney for the first time only a year ago in search of work. He'd often deferred or kept his counsel around Vic, not confident that he could influence the older, harder man much. Vic was a fully qualified carpenter, after all.

After an hour's walk, they reached the top of one more ridge in this steeply dissected landscape. Their reward was another view of the sea, some eight miles off as the crow flies. Attempting to establish their bearings as best they could from the relative positions of the sun and the sea, they picked out a path that they thought represented a south-westerly direction, believing that at its end they would find Sfakia. The easy part done, they set off again.

Over the next half day and into early afternoon, Vic Stockton and Stan Weller toiled up and down, trying to avoid the steepest ravines and gorges, stumbling and occasionally scraping a knee on this still difficult terrain. Gaining the top of yet another ridge, they were blessed with the sight of what was obviously a small town on the coast not more than two miles away. They stood together, staring in relief.

'So what else could it be?' asked Vic.

'It's not big, but guess what? It'll do!'

'Too right, mate.'

They started walking towards the town, using as roundabout and indirect a route as possible. Vic had figured that now they were so close, it was unsafe to use anything that looked like a regular path, even a well-used donkey track. They had to assume there were still enemy everywhere.

Late in the afternoon, approaching along another dried-up stream bed that seemed to be taking them generally where they wanted to go, they reached a turn from where they could see a few low-roofed buildings, more like produce or work sheds than houses. Clearly they had reached the periphery of the town. Now, with the possibility of finding sanctuary — or even a means of leaving the island, if troops were still being evacuated from Sfakia, as Stan hoped — came the realisation that they no longer had the freedom of being lost and forgotten. From this moment, every step had to be taken with great care.

They kept moving, slowly and quietly, towards those structures. From ten yards away, the buildings looked unused, locked up. They were dark and all was silence, until a side door swung open and a man came out, wearing a tattered jumper and rough clothes and carrying a work bag.

All three froze. Stan began to reach around his shoulder for his rifle. The man, middle-aged, stubble-faced, perhaps a farmer, saw the action and put his arms up. Vic understood that this fellow was no trouble and waved to Stan to put his rifle back. He then beckoned him forward.

'*Ela*! *Ela*! *Filos*! *Filos*!' he said in Greek as emphatic as he could muster, Come! Come! Friend! Friend! But only when he added the word '*Afstralezoi*' was the message accepted. No longer so fearful, the man began to approach.

'*Ti thelete*?' he asked.

Vic took a guess at what he had said. He didn't have enough of the language to respond in Greek, instead pointed at himself and Stan and then towards the town, hoping the man understood that they sought safety there.

The fellow nodded in a way that suggested he did, but then began to shake his head and wave his arms across his chest. '*Ohi*! *Ohi etho*!'

Stan and Vic stared at him. They had not been expecting such a negative response. Cretans had been usually friendly in their experience.

Vic spread his own arms wide, raised his eyebrows. A 'why' as clear as he could put it without words.

The Cretan again seemed to follow.

'*Germanoi. Polli Germanoi etho. Prepi na figete, i tha sas piasoun,*' he said and drew a finger across his throat.

Vic and Stan looked at each other, each thinking the same. They were too late. Why shouldn't there be Germans here? They were in every other part of the bloody island.

Ever hopeful, Stan said, '*Englezoi?*' and made a gesture with his hand to suggest a boat on the sea.

The man thought for a moment and shrugged. Then, apparently giving the matter further thought, he threw his hands up in the air as if to say, what was the use, how could they, the English or their allies, dare for a vessel in the circumstances?

Before they could fully process what he meant by that gesture, they heard the sound of a military vehicle some way off in the background. The Cretan quickly herded Vic and Stan inside what was evidently a storage shed with grain bags everywhere, then immediately made to leave.

Vic stopped him for a moment. '*Proi?*' he asked in his limited Greek. Morning?

The man frowned then responded.

'*Ah! Na pate etsi … pros to moni tou Kastelli … Kastelli,*' he said, indicating the way they had come. Before they could extract any more detail, he again shook his head and waved his arms, as if to say, 'No more now.' Turning his back on them he paced away, almost at a run, towards the town.

5

The Work of a Thousand Years

Despite the deep tiredness they felt, Vic and Stan managed to rouse themselves at first light. Moving slowly, they were also able to clear out of the shed without making any noise. Outside the door, they found a small cloth-wrapped package of bread and hard-boiled eggs. 'Bless 'em,' said Vic, stuffing it into his sack. 'We'll get to this in a minute.'

Once they were on the outskirts again, it didn't take much figuring to find the track they had used to get to Sfakia. Then, after they'd gone a mile or so, they stopped to eat what they'd been given.

When they had finished, Stan blurted out, 'Well then, what do we do now?'

'What I think is, we keep going till we spot another village or something. What did that bloke say? Kastelli? Didn't that sound like a town to you?'

'Stupid trying to do anything without proper information, my mum used to say. Kastelli could be anywhere or anything.'

'Not much sense getting inland again. Staying on the coast, we've got some show of spotting any transports.'

Vic was surprised that the welcome breakfast hadn't put Stan in a better frame of mind. He himself wasn't in the mood for grumbling, muted or otherwise.

'Vic, I've been thinking,' said Stan slowly. 'If we don't strike anything by tonight, I want to take my chances at Sfakia. I think that's the best bet.'

Vic said, 'All right by me, if that's what you want. Just that I won't be coming with you. You saw how the place was crawling with you-know-what.'

He wanted to leave it at that, but knew that something more needed to be said. Facing Stan squarely he added, 'Listen Stan, I'd like us to do this together. And I can't see the sense in what you're saying.'

Stan bristled. 'So don't then! Maybe I am only an idiot, and you're not!'

'Didn't say that, did I?'

'Yes, well.'

Both knew they couldn't afford to sink into this kind of disagreement at such a time. 'Come on idiot,' said Vic, slapping his mate on the back. 'Let's at least make a start.'

They got themselves down to the coast again. There they began heading east, trekking around rocky foreshores, up and down countless low cliffs and headlands where there was no other passage; they covered maybe ten miles, without seeing either a human being or habitation. By mutual consent, they called a halt around five in the afternoon.

Their only sustenance through the long hours of marching was a little rainwater that had collected in sheltered pools in some of the rocky hollows along the way. They had hardly time to think about what might be done about more food when they heard the sound of planes in the distance. The aircraft eventually appeared high overhead in the western sky — two German Junkers, flying east.

'Shit, what did I tell you, Vic,' said Stan. 'They're flying the way we're heading.'

'Wouldn't make too much of that. Might be only a reconnoitre for all we know.'

The planes passed and they waited in silence for a few minutes, each less happy with the other after their most recent exchange. When Vic was reasonably certain there were no other planes, he began scanning the rise to the north on his left. For once the slope was not entirely barren but studded with low-lying clumps of vegetation.

'Stan, remember the greens we used to see them gathering around Rethymnon?' he asked.

'What about it?'

'I think we're looking at the same stuff up there.' He pointed away behind them.

'So? We've got nothing to cook with.'

'That stuff was soft. Probably wouldn't need to cook it if it came to that.'

Stan said nothing, simply getting up to scrape his boot violently across a patch of ground, supposedly to make a more level place to sit. Seeing his anger, Vic decided not to press the point.

'Never mind. I'll be back with dinner.'

Vic left Stan and went up to check out the vegetation more closely. He was right, it was some kind of ground-hugging, saw-toothed plant, rather like dandelion leaves, the plant the locals called 'rathiki'. He pulled a few leaves off a young-looking plant, then squeezed them in his hands; they were neither soft nor hard.

He put a leaf in his mouth and began to chew. It was bitter but not impossibly so. More important, it was obviously edible.

Vic began pulling up a few of the plants, then called out 'Hey, Stan! Come here!'

Vic was pleased when he saw Stan respond almost immediately, watched as he strode towards him quickly. 'Look Stan, we've eaten this rabbit food before. It's all right, too, if you recall!'

'Cobber, that might be all right, but this isn't. I've had enough.'

Stan's expression told Vic all that he needed to know. He had been expecting this sooner or later, especially after the morning's outburst.

'It's no good,' Stan continued. 'The way we're going, we don't know what's in store. I'd like to be your mate in this, honest, but I say it's wrong. I'm convinced now. We left the action behind and if anything's going to happen by way of an off, it's back there.' Stan pointed back towards Sfakia.

'Mate, you heard what that chappie said back at Sfakia. The place is crawling with krauts.'

'But that's not all he said. As to ships, he was saying maybe yes, maybe no, wasn't he? As if there was still a chance?'

'You're clutching at straws there, Stan,' Vic said.

'I don't care. I'm sorry Vic. But that's it for me. I'm going to go.'

Vic turned away in silence, not knowing what to say, or even whether there was any point in trying to change Stan's mind.

'Vic,' said Stan. He had thrust his hand out. He wanted to shake. 'No hard feelings?'

'No. No hard feelings,' said Vic. 'Do what you have to do … That's what I'm gonna do.'

They shook hands briefly, stood for a while trying to find something else to say. Stan, also stood there waiting, his expression — peeved and eager — suggesting he still sought affirmation for his decision.

After a few moments, Stan said, 'All right. I'm not going to waste any more time, Vic. Think I'll start back before dark. Least, thanks to this bit of a bushwalk I know of a couple of places for a kip along the way!'

If that was the best he could come up with, Vic thought, God help him. Stan said, 'See you in Cairo!' and made a mock salute and Vic gave him a nod and a weak smile in return. He stared after Stan. Saw him retrieve his pack and rifle, watched as he began his trudge away and back to Sfakia. Then, leaving his own gear where it was, Vic began to seek out some more greens to pluck.

He hoped he might thus avoid considering, for a time anyway, the import of Stan's departure, but that was not to be. As he moved around, Vic thought of what the two of them had gone through together in North Africa; it was hard not to in the circumstances. It was at Bardia that they had both been blooded, where he himself had seen his first, worst action, things he would never have believed humans could do to each other. To overcome the fortress, they had had to make a direct assault across flat and stony ground, over an empty field of at least a mile, against a number of fortified and heavily armed strongposts and batteries.

In the worst of the fighting, to advance a thousand yards took all day. Men would stand up to take a run, only to drop straight down again, dead. Vic saw one poor bastard stitched in two by machine-gun fire right in front of him, his upper body cut away from the lower at a line above his waist. Then, by some miracle he and the others arrived at a pillbox, bayonets ready, charging and stabbing terrified Italian gunners who had no idea how to defend themselves, only how to fire their cursed guns.

That battle won, all through the following night, Vic's heart refused to stop racing; all through the night he had retched and retched until his whole body ached and trembled with the effort of it. He would never as long as he lived forget the feel of human flesh giving way so softly as he pushed sharpened and hardened steel into it. After Bardia Vic had cause to wonder if he could be of any further use at all in this fighting game. He had no heart or will for it whatsoever. But like everyone else, he kept going. After all that, after what they had done together, he would more than miss Stan.

On his haunches, a new plant in his hand, Vic reassured himself that he had known worse days and worse moments than this. But, even though his life wasn't in mortal danger right at that moment, he wondered what on earth he'd done to cop this lot. In frustration, in fear of being overwhelmed by the brutal reality he now faced, Vic stuffed some leaves into his mouth, and chewed wildly. At least that way he would let out none of the animal fear he felt welling up inside.

By the time it was dark and the only sound was the wind whistling through the low scrub, Vic returned to where his gear still lay in its own sad little pile. He told himself that whatever happened, he had a plan of his own. And he would follow through on it, tomorrow.

Strolling in the Cretan sunshine was fine, even pleasant on a warm morning in early June, but some idea about where he was actually going would have been better still. On the positive side, he told himself, staying close to the coast he would have no difficulty identifying which way was east.

Vic had thought he might continue in this easterly direction by walking along the beaches, but after a couple of hours, he found there were too few of these and a great many more low, steep cliffs and sheer headlands. Progress became so difficult he gave up this way, to strike out on a vaguely north-east path instead.

He wasn't sure whether seeing almost nobody was a plus or a minus. On the first day after Stan had gone his own way, he came across two shepherds, probably a father and son, who scurried away the minute they saw him, chasing a small flock of sheep ahead of them. On the same day he noticed one old lady way upland, travelling a local trail on a donkey and heading who knew where. She had been too far away to notice him, so far away that he didn't know how to attract her attention, short of firing a couple of shots into the air; but that would only have made her disappear even faster, he'd thought.

Vic presumed that any activity in these parts would be concentrated in tiny villages hidden away to the north of this coastal strip, in the foothills of the *Lefka Ori*, the White Mountains. He further presumed the people living there would not have much reason to come down to the sea unless they were fishermen, who tended not to live inland.

Hungry and tired most of the time, eating only the occasional wild *rathiki* and raw eggs stolen from the nests of some kind of ground-nesting birds, Vic could not make any great pace. In some ways that didn't matter; he had to give himself time to scan distances as he went, looking out for nasty surprises as much as searching for some possibly useful encounter with a friendly human.

Having trudged through a second day and covered some twenty miles in total since departing Sfakia, Vic slept rough again. He had hidden himself away in a low depression under a small copse of trees along the side of a tiny creek. The water was welcome but what he had eaten, unsupported by anything that might have helped to tie his guts together, had the expected effect on his bowels.

On the morning of the third day after leaving Sfakia, shouldering his pack (now containing only a knife and jumper) and his gun, Vic left the shelter of the trees and began trekking up to the higher, barer ground of the next visible hilltop. He had spotted the same kind of small birds whose nests he had previously raided in numbers strong enough to suggest there might be another feed to be had up there. Once he made it to the top and frightened the birds off, however, there was still no breakfast. The nests were empty.

The absence of any other animals, wild or husbanded, he found striking. Not having seen any sheep since his near encounter with the shepherds, he was kicking himself for not chasing after them and securing himself some nice lamb chops, his fear of being given up to the Germans by some traitorous local notwithstanding. But if there was no game or tucker to be had this day, there was plenty of time to observe the scenery. The place was often lovely to look at, spectacular even, although so much of it also seemed tough and harsh — maybe not to those who were born here and knew their way around, possibly not to someone from the bush back home, but certainly to a bloke from Enmore.

Inland as Vic was, he often had little idea of his position in relation to the water. He was thus not expecting, having scaled yet another featureless hill, to look to his right and find once more that the Libyan Sea was only a few miles away. And not too far from its shores on another sloping hillside, what looked like a monastery. Vic had seen two or three on the mainland, and this was the same: a compound of old stone buildings, two or three domed and topped with Greek crosses, all surrounded by a perimeter wall of rubble masonry. A closer view showed that there were two enclosures, each with its own set of buildings; the lower one smaller and in a poor state of repair, possibly even abandoned.

Vic let out a small shout of 'Hooray!' and thought if it's not safe here, it's not safe anywhere. Stumbling in his tiredness, he began to make his way down the slopes towards what he dearly hoped might mean refuge and safety, if not exactly a ticket back to Port Jackson.

Getting nearer, he spotted two monks outside the walls of the main, and functioning, site. They were busy in what looked like an orchard of orange trees. As they had not noticed his presence, Vic had time to take his pack and rifle and lay them on the ground. He went forward slowly over the last two hundred yards of sloping and twisted terrain, down to where the land levelled off and was planted not only with fruit trees but grapevines as well.

In a few moments, the two workers heard his crunching steps and looked up, startled to see this sunburnt apparition. Vic was mightily relieved that they did not run at the mere sight of him. His shout of '*Afstralezos!*', he was also grateful to find, did not immediately offend.

One of the monks put down his brush — he had been painting lime onto the trunks of one of the trees. The other, however, held onto what looked like a hoe or mattock. Vic raised his arms, slowed down even further, and put on as big a smile as he could in his state of exhaustion. He was rewarded by seeing the second monk drop his implement and, with the first, step gingerly towards him. Vic saw a bloke not much older than he, as far as he could tell under that shiny black beard, and an older, middle-aged man. Both wore black cassocks tied around the middle with a thin rope, and both had large crosses dangling on their chests. They seemed to be conferring.

A few yards away, the older monk held up his hand to check Vic's progress. '*Afstralezos?*' he asked suspiciously.

'*Ne, ne,*' Vic replied.

Once again the two spoke briefly to each other, but continued towards him, checking out the remains of his uniform, and the slouch hat. Then, the older man came up to Vic and extended a hand.

At that moment, Vic Stockton felt everything fall away from him. He collapsed at their feet. He began to cry. The monks immediately lifted him up and held him by either arm. They spoke soothingly to him. Had he known more Greek he would have understood what they were saying: Don't be afraid, don't be afraid, God is great, and Christ is our salvation ...

They began to walk the short distance to the monastery and Vic remembered his rifle and pack. He stopped, pointed back and made a trigger motion with arm and fingers, then indicated the ground. The younger one soon twigged and scurried back up to retrieve the remains of Vic's kit.

Still propping him up, his gear now slung over the younger man's back, the two monks gently marched Vic through the gates of the compound. They led him to a small building near the main chapel, past the eyes of other monks in the quadrangle who had stopped to stare.

The younger monk waited outside with Vic while the older went in. After a minute or more, he re-emerged to wave them both into what was obviously an office, full of books and holy pictures. A stout man stood at a desk, an impressive-looking character, Vic thought, older than the two men he had met and sporting a great grey beard.

Vic presumed this was the boss and prepared to tell his story with every bit of fractured Greek he could summon, only to be put off by the abbot gazing gently at him, like some sort of ancient saint, and saying, 'Good morning, sir. What is your name?' He spoke in clear, rather melodious English.

Vic couldn't believe his luck.

'You speak English?'

'I studied English,' the abbot replied. 'Your name?'

'Vic Stockton, sir. Private. Originally 6th Division AIF, and part of the 19th Brigade here.'

'Australian, they tell me.'

'Yes. I am.'

'Good, good … and bad. Because we have some other visitors here, sometimes. They are not Australian. You understand?' He looked stern for a moment.

'I think so. You mean Germans?'

'Germans, yes. You have no one else, young man? You are by yourself?'

'No one else, sir. What did you mean by Australian being bad?'

The abbot bade Vic sit at one of the chairs next to his desk. Never was something so simple as a wooden chair so welcome.

'Bad for you because you are too late. We already make rendezvous with many English, many English and we keep them here, safe, until the submarine came to pick up from the coast. I'm sorry, but you are too late. Gone three days ago.'

Vic slouched forward in his chair, felt like crying once more. The abbot saw his despair and came around to his side, to put a hand on his shoulder.

'And bad because Germans already come here one time and make big trouble. They know we done something but they don't know what. They shoot their guns, to scare us. They take our food. They will come again one day.'

'How long since they were here?' Vic asked the obvious question.

'How long time … ? Only two days before … Now, this *moni*, this monastery as you say in English, we will help you. It is our job. But you can not stay in here, with us.'

In the silence that followed, Vic began to feel panic creeping in. Then the abbot added, 'But we have place for you. Somewhere they don't find you. You can stay there until it is time for you to go.'

'When will that be, do you say, sir?'

'Don't ask me. Ask the British. Or better, ask God. He is the big boss, yes?'

The abbot smiled at Vic, who tried to smile in return. But uneasy thoughts about his ultimate fate seemed to affect the muscles of his face.

The monks who had brought him here came in with some clothes — a work shirt, a pair of breeches and fresh boots of the local variety rather than Australian Army issue — and took him to a rudimentary latrine in which there were a couple of big metal tubs. He had to bucket water out of an adjoining cistern to fill one; but neither that effort nor the coolness of the water and lack of soap mattered at all — he couldn't remember when just sitting still in a bathtub had ever felt so good.

Out in the sun again, Vic was not at all sure that he was effectively disguised as a Cretan peasant. Certainly the monks looked him up and down more than once as they took him off to sit at a table under a plane tree in the quad. They had prepared olives and cheese, bread and water for him and he fell on the food like the half-starved man he was. When he had finished they took him back to the abbot who was waiting outside his office.

'Oh! You look like one of us now,' he smiled, seeing this sandy-haired, freckled young man in baggy breeches and white *stivania* boots. 'So, please, you come with me now.'

Vic followed the abbot and the younger monk across the main yard towards the larger of the two chapels he had spotted from the hilltop earlier in the day.

The younger monk opened the door to let his leader and the Australian go in first. Vic had occasionally entered Greek churches on the mainland, out of curiosity, before things had spun totally out of control. But he had never seen one as rich and enchanting as this. Not much natural light got in here, yet he had no trouble seeing: small and ancient wooden pews on either side, icons everywhere — some ghostly and indistinct, others candlelit, their detail clear and bright.

At the front was something wondrous: a wide wooden screen, whose varnished panels were covered in icons of Jesus Christ and John the Baptist and the Virgin Mary and St George. But there was also a scene of Adam and Eve. Not the apple and the serpent and all, this was about Christ lifting them out of some sort of hell, saving them. And about that, unless he was reading too much into their faces, they seemed mightily relieved. Vic, finding it hard to look anywhere else, thought not of the origin of sin and damnation, but of boys and girls he had seen in the fields of Boeotia from the back of a transport. It was somehow more Greek than Christian.

'It is beautiful, yes?'

'Yes, it is …'

'It is not a normal *iconostasion*. Normal have Our Lord and Aghios Ioannis and the other saints and Archangeli Michaelis and Gabriel, like you see. But this, this one was painted by a great of the great, Michaelis Kastellis. It was new idea for that day.'

'Kastellis? That's a name we heard in Sfakia. I thought it was a place.'

'It is a place, as you say. It is the name that is given to this monastery, in honour of this man and the *iconostasion* you see here. But full name is the Holy and Patriarchal Kastelli Monastery of Saint George the Trophy Bearer.'

'Yes, well ...' Vic said, at a loss as to what there could be to say to that.

The abbot left Vic to go towards that marvel. He knelt in front of the icon screen and kissed the painted feet of Christ, then stood and began to chant and pray and cross himself several times. He then returned to Vic.

'I ask God for our safety — for you and all of our people.'

Vic felt troubled. He wanted to honour what had been said and been done for him already, but didn't know how. He thought it would be foolish, insincere, to try to pray to God in this place, strange and magical as it was. Vic knew he was still fighting God, a battle he'd been engaged in since way before the war; in fact, since Sunday School.

But he owed them something. 'Thanks sir, for that,' he said. 'Oh, and what's your name?'

'I am an abbot. Abbot Nektarios.'

Repeating the name slowly so as not to make a complete hash of it, Vic produced a reasonable enough rendition for the abbot to reply, '*Ne*, like you say, Nektarios.'

As for owing these monks something, he wasn't so sure when, after allowing him further rest, they bundled him, with rifle and sack and a couple of bags of hard biscuits, out of the monastery and began to walk him back up into the hills. It also felt odd to be dressed the way he was — he had hung on to his army clobber, however, and, not wishing to offend, would change back into it when he had the chance.

They were moving somewhat east of the monastery, but still within a reasonable distance and view of Kastelli, when they arrived at a decrepit old shepherd's hut. There the monks left him, saying only that one or more of the local youths would come to bring him some food and water whenever possible. And that the monks, too, would call 'sometimes'. They could do nothing more until they got further news from the resistance which had already begun to take shape in surrounding parts, or the British who were beginning to organise alongside them.

6

The Modern World

Kalliope set out for Andreas' old shop this morning with a small but comforting thought: that in his own small way Andreas had brought a little innovation to their stifling village. In the months after leaving school he had daringly opened a business right next to his family home. Out of his father's one-time stable and storehouse, joined to their home in such a way that it seemed part of the house, he had begun to sell manchester and haberdashery. He had somehow managed to continue a small trade in rugs, mats, fabrics and threads, and thus earn a modest income for himself at a time when regular cash was uncommon in such rural parts. But there had been hardly enough custom passing through Arkadi to allow for opening the shop more than once or twice a week, so Kalliope and her fellow villagers had seen Andreas plying his wares mainly on Friday and Saturday mornings.

For Andreas, who had abandoned the idea of further education for lack of money, it had been an achievement to secure some sort of living this way. Even if some of the other villagers had raised an eyebrow, or made snide jokes about it — as villagers were always wont to do about 'middlemen'. The years before the war had been among the most trying anyone in Greece had faced since the drama with the Turks in 1922. Many who had come to rely on selling produce and crops for cash had found themselves in difficulties when townfolk and merchants stopped buying. Kalliope knew that there were those who saw Andreas as an oddity, as well as an object of occasional insult — a 'trader' who had not gone under — and had tried to defend him. Andreas' argument was that he had had to do whatever he could to support himself and his ailing mother, never mind what a few peasants might have to say on his choice of occupation.

Kalliope slowed as she approached, trying to somehow draw out of this rundown structure some sustenance, perhaps some ghostly vibration of her long-departed Andreas. Her heart went out to him, remembering how he would stand alone inside the now boarded-up doors on those mornings years ago, waiting for business. And she remembered how it had all ended. Today she saw that Andreas' old bedroom window was shuttered, presumably to keep out the heat. There was no sign of anyone being home, and this was good. Kalliope did not at that moment want any contact with Andreas' ancient mother, so she quickened her pace.

She went around the side passage to the back of the former stables, where she knew there was another entrance. The twin wooden doors here were in a worse state than ever, giving way with only a slight shove. Inside, things were much as they had been left — a large old wooden counter along one side, some shelving against one wall, and a number of barrels and bushel baskets. These Andreas had kept for a talking point when he was running his shop, joking that if the ladies of the village stopped buying hankies and doilies, he would turn his hand to wine-making, in the manner of his ancestors, and drown his sorrows.

As she surveyed the dark interior, with its corners and containers and places for storage, Kalliope recalled that the place had a small cellar. She looked around the floor until she found the opening, half-hidden under one corner of the display case, which might prove a greater blessing than the cellar itself. She began to make an inventory of the wooden boxes, pulling out a small crate containing some old, unsold small mats and rugs, all still neatly folded in quarters.

Kalliope took one of the mats and shook it out — an odd-looking thing of weak colours and nondescript pattern. No wonder it hadn't sold. She smiled sadly, reminded of Andreas' idea of female taste — not that he always got it wrong. But it was Andreas who had given her the most pleasure in her life and caused her the most grief — whether he was here or elsewhere. He had been attracted to her and she to him, from their early days in high school. In contrast with his ardour and eagerness, Kalliope had always tried to remain discreet — beyond her circle of trusted friends, anyway — while she attempted to work out the nature of her feelings towards him, and knowing full well what any open affection might cause to rain down on their heads. There were others who, whatever the truth, saw things how they wanted to.

Kalliope folded the mat and replaced it, then in the darkness moved towards the front of the shop. It would be a good precaution, she thought, to pull some of this stuff forward to block any access via the doors that opened onto the street. When Andreas had been running his shop those doors counted as the public face of his enterprise. Terrible to think that they had also been implicated in what he saw as a public humiliation, and the start of his downfall.

That moment had arrived on a chilly afternoon in January of 1937. The friends had come at Andreas' invitation to view some recently arrived stock. They came with goodwill, except for Yannis. By their final year of schooling, politics had so intruded between him and Andreas that they were often irritable with each other. As far as Andreas was concerned, the furnace of Cretan republicanism had thrown up a genuine hero and saviour — Eleutherios Venizelos, the man who had given his all to modernise the country, drag it out of its stifling rural inertia, create opportunity and the chance of enterprise and reward — not only for people like him who had some education, but for those lower down the social scale too. Not everyone agreed, however. The rump of royalists and arch-conservatives would always have their say, and the previous year they had greeted the demise of Venizelos with naked and vulgar satisfaction as nothing less than he deserved. The subsequent installation of dictator Metaxas, they took to be an event almost as significant as the Second Coming.

And yet in these disasters, Andreas believed Yannis saw only some intellectual game unfolding. Yannis spoke of them in terms that seemed to Andreas wilfully contrary, unrealistic, finally jeopardising the future of their people. Yannis never accepted what had happened as the brutal clash of power and interests that Andreas had tried so often to convince him it was, choosing to treat these differences as no more than a subject upon which to exercise his intellect. Then gradually Andreas came to think that Yannis had changed, seriously changed, and for the worse: that he secretly supported what had happened. And soon all could see the tension that had grown between them.

Kalliope and Manolis and Marika had tried, sometimes with humour, sometimes in earnest, to get them to mend their differences, but with little success. The tension began to affect them almost as much. Not wishing to cause any more upset,

Andreas and Yannis had tried to pass over the difficulty when they were all gathered as a group, making jokes about how each fowlyard still needed a rooster and a hen, even when they were trying to peck each other's eyes out. But they also knew their counterpart bore ill-feeling that wasn't easily going to go away.

Kalliope remembered how Andreas had hung out of these Dutch doors a few of the smaller and prettier mats and rugs that had come down from Athens, alongside some folds of lighter fabric for tablecloths and such. The bright colours made for a pretty and cheery contrast to the whitewashed walls and blue doors along this section of the village street, a welcome splash against an overcast winter's day. She had been the first to spot him leaning out of the opening, waiting for them, when along with Marika, Manolis and Yannis had come around the last bend in the lane before his place. They had turned up almost as one but not quite, for Yannis was trailing behind them.

Andreas came out onto the street to greet them but, as Kalliope could recall as if yesterday, couldn't resist a crack.

'So what is eating you, dear Yanni, on such a glorious day?'

Yannis drew nearer then but was reluctant to speak. Political views aside, he had become ever more difficult and superior since he had completed his first semester at medical school the previous year. It was hard for any of them still to consider him an equal member of the band of friends who had, these past six or seven years, made their way together along the tracks and over the fields, through the schools, the pleasures, pains and life of Arkadi and Rethymnon.

Kalliope meanwhile knew very well that had Andreas overheard the theme Yannis had been rehearsing today, he would have been outraged. As for Yannis, he appeared unable to leave things alone, and was challenged by the way she was looking at him then. 'By God,' he had said, and with such exasperation, 'anyone would think I had said something that isn't true!'

Perhaps she too should have left it there, but without willing it she blurted out: 'Some of the things you say, Yanni, should never be said, that's all.' Now Andreas came forward to listen. And that was all it took for Yannis to be away again on his hobbyhorse.

'What do you mean, never be said? All I said was the obvious. Metaxas is right — sometimes people don't know what's good for them and you have to be firm with them — especially with troublemakers ...'

'Look,' Yannis began again. 'Let me illustrate,' he said, all patronising mollification. 'You said, "and me wanting to be a doctor ..." but what does a doctor sometimes have to do? Sometimes a limb has to be cut off, yes, even removed completely from a person's body, in order to save the patient! In the event of a massive infection, gangrene say, or potentially terminal damage of some kind, a doctor is obliged to be cruel in the short term to be kind in the long. It's the same with politics. That's what Metaxas is thinking, I'm sure, with these measures he is taking. That's all I'm saying.'

A long and difficult silence followed, which at first Andreas was inclined to lighten: 'Come on, now. What are we doing here on such a fine day arguing about politics when I have such colourful fabrics to show the girls!'

But Yannis would not have it. He ushered Andreas to one side and said, 'It's what you're doing here, I suppose, that worries me. I really don't know why you threw in your schooling. What have you become instead?'

Kalliope saw Andreas stiffen as he responded. 'What do you mean "become instead"?'

'A merchant! A commercial type! When I always held out greater hopes for you ... And was it not Andreas Coroneos himself who once told me that he would become a naval architect one day, a man who designed ships and boats? Ha!'

Andreas had clenched his fists, hardly able to reply to the insult. For the sake of the others he tried to tamp down his rage. 'It was a child who said that. But you, you insult me. Why? You of all people, with all your privileges ...'

'Money hasn't made me, Andreas.'

'No? Well, that's what allowed you to study medicine. Not having it gives me my fate. And you stand there to lecture me ...'

Yannis cut him off, his own anger boiling up. 'Is that right? You have always been an egotist, only for yourself, like all the other paltry petit bourgeois that have sprung up since '22. But there are better days, I say ... Viva Metaxas!'

The last insult, piled on those he had already endured, sent Andreas into a cold fury. He raised a fist to Yannis, then quickly spun around and raced back into the store. He re-emerged a few moments later, this time with a sacking knife held by his side.

Manolis shouted, 'Andreas! No!', but Andreas walked slowly towards Yannis. Yannis, stunned, held up his hands and backed away. Kalliope, at first unable to make sense of what they were seeing, shrieked, 'Stop!' and stepped forward to intervene, only to have Manolis grab her on the way.

Hearing the terror in her voice, Andreas was restored to momentary sense and threw the knife on the ground, then rushed to tackle Yannis. The two boys scuffled while the others tried to separate them. But even to get hold of them was very difficult. Finally Yannis and Andreas got to their feet, kept apart by the barrier of Manolis, Kalliope and Marika.

'So it's come to this, has it?' gasped Yannis.

Andreas' breath slowly returned, and he became aware of the flushed, terrified faces of his dearest companions, now looking at him as if he were some fearsome beast. Wrenching sobs burst from him as he ran back inside and slammed the doors. Kalliope was in tears, as she, Marika and Manolis threw themselves at the doors trying to gain entry. Neither their weight nor their banging made any difference. They waited an hour and more but he would not come out, shouting that he would not do so until they had gone home and he had calmed down.

After that dreadful incident, Andreas was all steely resolve and silences. He would say only, 'This place is finished for me. And soon for you too, I hope.'

Kalliope returned to the dangers facing her and all who remained in Arkadi. She made a last mental note of the cellar space, thinking it would make a good place for dried produce, nuts and dates and figs, as well as whatever equipment might need to be hidden away. She would tell Kannetakis about it at their next meeting, scheduled for tomorrow, and see when he would like her to start putting things aside. She closed the back door as gently as she could and set off to for Marika's place, a hundred or so metres further on. As her potential partner in these new matters, she would need to be told what was happening.

After she turned the corner into the lane, Kalliope became aware of her footsteps resonating on the cobbles as she passed the Coroneos house. A moment later, there was a new sound — a soft tap on the ground behind her, then another, then one much louder. Before she had time to turn, she saw a stone skitter past on the cobbles. Someone could only have thrown it.

Turning, she was shocked to see Andreas' mother standing in her doorway. She took something from her apron, raised her arm and threw something. Kalliope felt a sting of pain on her chest.

'*Na mi pernas apo tho!*' — Don't you come by here! — she heard Andreas' mother shout. 'Do you hear me? Don't you come bothering our Andreas — he's a good boy!'

Kalliope called back: '*Kyria* Coroneos? Why can't I come this way?'

Andreas' mother took a couple of menacing steps towards her before raising her voice even further. 'You know very well, you dirty girl! I saw you with my boy and you turned his head, and I've heard the stories about you. You leave him alone. No more! Do you hear me?'

'What are you talking about, dear woman? Your son is gone, and gone many years — he lives in Australia now.'

A window opened a few metres away. Old *Barba* Kounelis stuck his head and said, 'What's all this? Who's barking out here?'

'This is none of your business, *Barba*,' *Kyria* Coroneos said. 'You just close your window and never mind.'

Kalliope had become red-faced, rigid with rage. All she could think to do was stand her ground as long as she could.

'This is the last time, do you understand?' said Andreas' mother. 'If I see you trying to arrange rendezvous with Andreas I will slap you and I will tell the *horofilaka* and anyone else I need to, you *poutana*. Do you hear me?'

Kalliope thought it best to concede nothing, answer nothing, and wait for the storm to pass so she could go on her way. But Andreas' mother took this as dumb insolence. Without another word, she bent forward to pick up another stone.

But though Kalliope was tempted to look around herself for an object to throw, she held herself still. She would not be intimidated in this way. Whatever else, the woman was clearly not right in the head. As Andreas' mother continued to stare menacingly at Kalliope, *Barba* Kounelis had called out in a scolding voice, 'Stop it, stop it for the love of God! Stop it or I will call the corporal and he will put you both away!'

The name of the dreaded local agent for law and order was just enough to give Andreas' mother pause. She turned toward *Barba* Kounelis. 'What did I say to you, *Barba*? This is not for your ears.'

'May not be for my ears but you're making sure I hear it like everyone else. Go back inside your house, *Kyra mou*, before something bad happens.'

During this diversion, Kalliope found she could move at last. She took one, then two, then another step away, looking back over her shoulder as she went. But feeling she had achieved some little victory, *Kyra* Coroneos threw the stones in her hand hard on the ground. 'Yes, that's right, go away my girl,' she called. 'And don't ever forget what I told you here today!'

Kalliope walked faster. It was a blessing that no one else had poked their nose into what had just happened; a miracle really, given the amount of noise Andreas' mother had been able to make. Her head was pounding. What had she done to bring such hatred upon herself? She was a grown woman, not some child to be scolded and threatened. And where was Andreas, where had he been through all that? Ten thousand miles away.

Her life, she thought, was a frightening mess. Her eyes began to sting with the threat of tears, as she continued the few hundred metres to Marika's house.

By the time she arrived there it was all Kalliope could do to smile for Marika's mother and return her greeting. Marika hurried her to her room, and Kalliope suddenly fell to her knees on the floor next to her bed.

'What's happened to you?' asked Marika, in fear. 'What's the matter?'

It was at least a minute before Kalliope could speak through her rage. Finally she hissed: 'Unspeakable woman ...'

'Who?'

'Who do you think? Andreas' mother!'

Marika sat on the edge of the bed, keeping one eye on her friend. She had never seen Kalliope as angry or as upset, and could think of nothing to do but stroke her hair and wait.

Kalliope's tears slowed, then ceased. She had moved on from the shame of how she'd been treated and from the unworthy desire to retaliate. Now she felt only the despair of the imprisoned.

They had all talked their fine talk, dreamed their pleasant dreams down the years. But what was there for them in actuality? She stared into the furthest corner of Marika's room, then up at the ceiling — rough-hewn beams holding up even rougher lath and plaster, with cracks and gaps clear to anyone. That was their real life, a thing threatening to fall on her and all their heads any time. There were few comforts, even less security. How many houses in this village? A hundred? A few more? A miserable little place — even if some of the layabouts at the *kafeneion* insisted on calling it 'Little Paris'.

'Little Paris' indeed. In America they were making machines that could see right through a human body, or so she had read in a paper in Irakleion a year or two back. There, too, she had seen a shop display with clothes from Italy; how beautiful, how daring, she had thought then were the dresses and shoes and stockings in the world beyond. For all the bragging the men did, for all the theories they had thrown about, what change had come to Crete, what good had been brought to their lives?

She leaned her head against Marika's knee, calming further as she felt her friend's hand lightly on her hair, and began to allow that these were unworthy thoughts. Somehow she had to find the strength to be the best person she could be, no matter what, including the bad conduct of others, especially in these dangerous days. But it was sometimes very hard. She had never found it easy to brush aside the sense that there were too few adults you could trust to care for you properly, that what they did for anyone, when they did anything at all, was always conditional. And that held for her own mother too.

In an effort to direct her elsewhere, Marika said, 'So what have you learned? Did you at least get inside the place this morning?'

Kalliope raised her head and attempted a smile. 'Sorry, I'm sorry … all these silly tears … Yes, I did get inside. You would be surprised, or maybe not — nothing much has changed in there.'

'Can we use it?'

'We can — so long as by stealth.'

7
Shame

The Germans motored in like so many tidy demons on steel and rubber wheels. Neatly uniformed, smiling, relaxed as you like. But for Provatos, the shepherd, Arkadi would have had no warning at all. Coming down off Gerovouno, he had spotted their convoy a few kilometres distant, making slow progress on the difficult road through these parts, and raced the rest of the way to the village, arriving only minutes ahead of them.

Kalliope stood silently by the side of the lane along with a hundred others, watching as they drove past. She had never experienced such a feeling in her life — as if she was an animal caught in a trap, waiting to discover its fate. To summon all the angels in heaven, arm them in righteous fury and strike these agents of Satan down, that's what she wished. But she knew that no such miracles were available. Endure, be brave, endure, she told herself.

All eyes followed the Germans as they continued on their way to the square near Aghia Sophia — ramrod straight, arrogant and all-conquering. There they halted, assembling their motorcade around the available space in two tight rows on either side.

Kalliope stared at these strange beasts. Who were they? Why had they come? What could they possibly want here of all places?

A poor corner of the earth, a place unlikely to supply anything of use to them. And, as for being their slaves, how much more preferable it would have been to have met in battle and died instead.

But the occupying force expected no trouble in these parts, and they would stand for none, Captain Marius said from the back of his touring car, barking out words that were translated by their unhappy schoolmaster. They would get none, the mayor said in reply, so the captain and his men needn't trouble themselves on that front. Good, said the German captain. He demanded that all the people of this place be called together to be counted and to have their names recorded.

A few minutes later in his office the mayor told the captain that this was a village of simple people, villagers, peasants, innocents who could be relied on to go about their business and not cause any distress or drama to the acknowledged victors and new masters. This was the first and last encounter between old and new authority: hardly had the mayor finished speaking than they took him out into the street, made him kneel on the ground in front of the post office doorway and shot him in the back of the head.

Kalliope was still in the square waiting to be processed when she heard the shot and looked up. She saw a figure on the ground in the distance, heard a female voice shriek the mayor's name. With the realisation and the shock at such a sudden, meaningless act of cruelty, it took a desperate effort not to scream or vomit. Many others cried out, including her mother. But Kalliope understood that she, that all of them, would have to find the nerve to cope with further such tragedies if they had any hope at all of surviving to triumph in the end. The Germans were brutal, their terror was calculated — that was the only message Kalliope was prepared to admit on the first day of their ordeal. Her uncle

Mattheos was still busy cogitating on how best to deal with these monsters, or so he whispered in a tremble as he stood beside her; her mother was too terrified, too lost in fear and upset to do anything beyond shedding tears.

The herding and counting finally over, Kalliope ignored the pleas of her mother and uncle and let them retreat to their house on their own. Unless commanded otherwise, she was determined to stick around to try to pick up something about these men. They were incomprehensible in so many ways, but she would not give up trying to understand them, if only for the sole purpose of besting them.

Kalliope's group had had just enough time in the days before the Germans arrived to smuggle some supplies into the corners and nooks and crannies of Andreas' store, and — vitally — into its cellar. Realising that the enemies would likely turn every place over as they went about establishing control, Kalliope had installed a decoy cache, something easily discovered when the store was entered. For this purpose she used the oldest containers, a few very large *pithoi*, tall and bulbous clay jars that looked practically archaeological but were merely drawn on a traditional pattern and were at most thirty years old. The resistance had guessed right: their conquerors, these shiny gleaming men of steel, these educated men of the modern age, raided Andreas' place in the first forty-eight hours, and then revealed another side.

Germans after all, lovers of all things classical, when they came upon those jars they simply had to stand to marvel at them: were they from the early Classical period? Even older, perhaps Mycenaean? They did not look to be Minoan, not nearly sensuous enough in shape, said one young officer. Not long after, one of their number came outside waving a pistol and rounded up a few old men and boys. Their job was to bring those heavy pots out through the doors and into the street, then carry them, never mind that they were filled with almonds and walnuts in the shell and weighed fifty kilos if they weighed anything, all the way up to their own new quarters, the mayor's one-time office. And with deference to their antiquity, they were not to be rolled along the ground.

The laughing among the troops who oversaw this exercise was only the half of it. Exquisite satisfaction, marvellous confidence written all over their faces; these Cretans were so naïve and stupid that they deserved their fate. How bizarre that they thought they could use such simple stratagems to hide provisions like that! And also that they were so ignorant of their own history and heritage that they would hide nuts in objects of possibly great cultural significance. So confident were the Germans that they had readily outwitted the locals, they didn't even bother demanding the old stables and storehouse be boarded up.

As Kalliope watched the whole tableau play out from further up the lane near Marika's, she wondered whether it might not have been better had the Germans gone to the trouble, that way they might also assume the place was completely out of service, which would have helped rather than hindered her own cause. The thought that they might pay another visit sometime was worrying.

Kalliope's anxiety was not relieved when the mayor's second in command set a meeting to take place there in the middle of Friday night, only a day after the Germans had turned the place upside down. Kalliope arrived first, knowing her way around it better than anyone else, and carrying a small oil lamp. As this was the first meeting since the death of Kannetakis, she was both heartened and a little upset by how quickly they elected a new leader — the mayor's deputy himself, as it turned out, Yorgos Sotiriou — and how swiftly the meeting got down to business.

If they had perhaps been fortunate in not having to try to repel an armed attack on their village, Sotiriou said, the news was still not good. The whole of Crete was now under formal occupation. British troops and their Australian and New Zealand allies, they knew, were lost and wandering over the west of the island. All had agreed that whatever could be done for these men, should be done. It was an honour to help those who had tried to help us, said the new head.

Having assigned tasks to the other four men and two women at the meeting, he got around to Kalliope. Her next job would be to meet and assist an Australian soldier, recently rescued by the monks of the Monastery of Kastelli, who was currently in hiding. Supplies for him, and for anyone else who might fall among them, would be drawn from the steadily growing provision beneath this very floor. The new head stopped to thank Kalliope personally for what she had done so far, then acknowledged all those who were supplying her out of their own meagre resources.

Privately, Sotiriou told Kalliope that the soldier in question, a fellow by the name of Vic Stockton, had been taken to Manolakis' hut, empty since last winter when that old crank of a shepherd had died, and had spent the past few days there. Only the monks knew he was in the hut. Kalliope was more than happy to accept the task of keeping him alive until his exit off the island could be arranged. He was fortunate to have been found in an area where the new resistance had already some strength; fortunate not to have been put in a prison camp, like so many Allied soldiers elsewhere.

Their first brief rendezvous, to establish contact and supply the soldier with a little food, would take place with the knowledge and involvement of the monastery. Brother Thoma had already informed Vic that a young village woman was coming to help him, and had given him her name. Kalliope was told to join the Australian soldier in a hollow in the hills behind the monastery at a rock spring the locals called Vrisses. As it only fed water into a nearby river in winter, Vrisses had been abandoned; dry during the summer months, it was therefore unlikely to be visited by anyone, not even thirsty Germans. It would be unwise to meet the Australian at the hut itself, for a day or two anyway, as a few of the enemy had been seen close by. If Kalliope felt she needed help, she was told she had authority to call upon her trusty Marika.

It was already warm at six on the June morning when Kalliope, who had had at most three hours' sleep, left through the front gate of her house. She did not completely close it for fear of waking her mother or Uncle Mattheos. After walking quietly along the lane to Marika's place she tapped gently on the shutter; her friend, she knew, was awake and expecting her. The shutter opened soundlessly to reveal Marika waving her arms and shaking her head from side to side. In a loud whisper she said she would not be going with Kalliope as her father was expecting Captain Marius early that morning — something about securing a supply of dried figs for his junior officers' use — and that her being absent would attract suspicion.

Kalliope set off again with greater speed, to get out of the village as quickly as she could. The Germans were rarely up before seven, but you never knew. She was soon beyond the vineyards and the groves south of Arkadi and climbing the hills.

From a half-buried pile of stones on one summit Kalliope looked down past the hut and towards the sea — the monastery lay to the right about midway down the slopes and on the other side of the river. She then she turned towards Vrisses, that ancient water source, hidden in folded rocks away in the opposite direction. Kalliope stopped to catch her breath. She had spent better days on the same slopes, days bathed in the kind of sunshine 'as could never be matched in all of Crete or in all of Greece,' as Manolis used to say.

She had some provisions in the satchel held firm across her shoulders by two leather straps. As village supplies were closely monitored by the Germans she had only been able to gather a kilo or so of almonds in the shell from a supply that had been hidden at Andreas' shop, and a canvas sack with a couple of litres of drinking water. These, as well as tobacco from *Barba* Iacovos, their retired postman, hardly seemed enough. She thought to take some tomatoes but few were left; most of their small crop had gone to Marius' men. So she decided to take a detour via the monastery with the aim of picking up something more. There she was in luck: she asked for Brother Thoma and a loaf of bread was spared.

Once on the slopes again and from a few hundred metres off, Kalliope started looking for some sign the man was there. Approaching closer, she made the noise she had been told must be used for these encounters — the harsh baa of the kri-kri, their indigenous mountain goat — as best she could with a dry throat. Within a second or two, she heard the crunching of boots on loose rock and from behind the rocks stepped a tall, thin man in baggy khaki shorts, with an odd-looking hat turned up at the side. This was the first Australian soldier she had ever seen.

Kalliope could see he was no more at ease than she was. Only when he was directly in front of her did he nod a couple of times, all the while glancing around them both. He said something that sounded like '*Efharisto*' once or twice. She began to ease the satchel off her shoulders, but he said '*Ohi*, not here,' rather loudly, and once more scanned their surroundings. Turning away, he rapidly moved ahead, waving to her to follow him.

Kalliope hesitated. This was not what had been decided, nor did she have a clear idea where he intended them to go. But she soon saw he was moving in the direction of the hut, and fell in behind him. She watched him as he walked in front of her. Strange, but not frightening, she would have said. She noticed his fair skin and the lightness of his hair, almost red, grown long and hanging below the rim of his hat at the back. He walked like a young animal, all loose in his limbs, not tired or stiff or measured of gait as the men of her locality, young or old, tended to be. Perhaps they did not have hills to trudge up and down in Australia of the sort that they had in these parts.

A few hundred metres further on, and they arrived at the old rubble shelter where he had been hiding for the past couple of weeks. The door, such as it was, was no longer on its hinges and so he had to lift it out and put it to one side so they could enter.

He stopped, then turned to her and said, 'Kalliope … *ne* … ?'

'*Ne*,' she said, surprised to hear her name repeated in such an odd accent, but pleased also.

'May as well come into my lair,' he said waving her in.

Kalliope was unsure as he stepped aside to let her enter. But there was no point in her standing there, outside and alone, in easy view of anyone on the surrounding hilltops, the monastery, or even further below on the coast. She would not stay long, she thought.

Inside, she saw he had attempted to create some order out of the belongings the old shepherd had left before he died. There was a pot in the corner atop a cinder brazier, and a number of old flour sacks arranged into something like bedding along one wall. Her head almost hit the slats of timber that passed for a roof here, while the Australian, tall as he was, bent quite noticeably in fear of lifting the roof. The whole hut couldn't have occupied more than six or seven square metres of this precipitous slope — and, but for the small patch of even ground on which it sat, would surely have tumbled down the hill years ago.

Kalliope was overtaken by awkwardness about being there. The only reason for her visit was to complete her job and hand over the provisions. She slipped the satchel off at last and left it on the ground between them, lowered her head, and with a small nod began to back away as if to exit. Vic put a hand up, then made small welcoming circles with it to show he wanted her to stay. Only then did he realise the practicalities were against any socialising — there was nothing for her to sit on, for a start.

However, Vic considered himself nothing if not ingenious: he suddenly looked around and in pantomime created the impression that someone had obviously made off with the otherwise splendid furniture she might have expected in here, and that he was shocked. He shrugged his shoulders, sighed, and dropped to the ground in front of her. There, sitting cross-legged, he looked up at her and grinned broadly.

At the absurdity of the performance, Kalliope was able to find a small smile in return. She would not sit on the ground, choosing to lean back against the wall next to the door, her arms folded across her chest for want of something better to do with them. Vic shrugged again, content just to have her company, however long she chose to stay. He couldn't say he found the sight of this olive-skinned, dark-eyed, slim Cretan girl, dressed in a summer skirt and white blouse and with her hair tied in a bun, unappealing.

Kalliope looked down at the satchel that lay between them on the packed earth floor. She moved over to pick it up and was about to hand it to him, but decided to open it instead. Kneeling down, she began to take the food out and place it on the white cloth she had also included. She handed the small muslin bag of tobacco and papers to him directly. He took it from her with both hands, repeating his '*Efharisto*' so many times she looked away in embarrassment. He then rolled the first cigarette he'd had in weeks, finally reaching into his sack to look for the matches he thought were still there. Only they weren't. Kalliope looked into her own satchel again; Iacovos had given her all the makings for a smoke except the means of lighting up. She opened her palms and gave him a look of sympathetic frustration.

'Never mind,' he said, 'maybe when the monks come, the *kalogeroi*, or however you say that …'

She thought she knew what he meant, but also waved a rolling wave with her right hand. '*Ali fora*.' Next time.

After standing up and moving back towards the entrance, Kalliope stood, trying not to look at him, while trying also to think of something to say or do that he might find reassuring. When she couldn't, she gestured that she would leave now, and said, '*Paraskevi*.' Friday.

His limited Greek did not run to days of the week, and he suddenly felt frustrated. He got to his feet.

'*Paraskevi*, what's that … ?' He had an idea it was a day but not which one. All he knew was *avrio*, tomorrow and *simera*, today. 'Look, please don't go yet, no hurry …'

Again Kalliope had a pretty good idea what he was getting at, if only from the way he was pointing to the ground with the fingers of each hand. She shook her head, repeated '*Paraskevi*' one final time and stepped outside. Vic followed her out but she signalled to him to go back inside and then broke into a run.

As Kalliope began marching across the slopes in earnest, she felt light-hearted, elated almost. Things occasionally went right, even in the direst of circumstances, even in the middle of a war. You could make plans, you could carry them out. She felt then, if only for a moment, the surge of her youth and strength. Although her family had no knowledge of what she was doing, although what she had undertaken had its dangers and its limits, Kalliope felt a freedom in this. She put out of mind for the moment how Mattheos and her mother might react if they were to accidentally discover what their innocent little girl was up to — as for their having to be told one day, that was in the hands of her superiors. She was perfectly ready to take orders, ready and willing to repeat in a few days' time what she had done today.

Vic decided you could trust in the silence of these hills, and very deep it was too, broken only by the occasional cry of a bird or small animal. Or, more practically, in the knowledge that there were few roads and it took time and effort to get around this part of the country. Either way, the odds were serviceable. After a few more days of peace and quiet, of sitting in the hut working on a length of wood with his penknife, of long afternoon sleeps Vic was bored enough to try a little risk.

How likely was it, for instance, that the krauts would suddenly appear if he were to take a chance and go the rest of the way down the slopes past the monastery and towards the inviting water below? His fitness was returning, and he did not like this feeling of limitation — too much of this sitting around with nothing to do. He could see how someone might be inclined to give themselves up, no matter how nasty the repercussions.

Soon after daybreak on this mild Friday morning, he stepped outside and surveyed all that he could see from his hut. Even at such an early hour that turquoise blue of the sea was like a charge of electricity. For a change of clothes, he pulled on the breeches and boots he'd been given and began the descent to the water's edge.

He made the trek down and arrived at a lovely stretch of sand, with a small cove of pebbles at one end, and by his estimate a mile or so further east of the monastery. He spent a few moments gazing out over the quiet sea to the south, allowing the general calm to overtake him. Vic hadn't experienced anything like this at least since the start of the Greek campaign, but there was something more. The place had a special air about it; the whole country did, something that even war and poverty hadn't been able to knock out of it. Maybe it was a rocky, tough place in parts, but the Greeks acted like all of it was something special. Treated it the same way. They just loved it, every bit of it, Vic thought.

You could see how the locals felt about the place from the way they tended and cared for land that wouldn't even qualify as scrub back home. Something more than necessity drove them. They would pick a spot under a few trees and lay out a table for a celebration — a few chairs, a bit of canvas strung up to keep out the worst of the sun, and pretty soon you had music and dancing, hooting and hoppa-ing, war or no war, occupation or no occupation. He had seen them do just this with his own eyes, God bless 'em, on the mainland when the fighting was not two hundred miles up the road. This land was theirs and no bastard was going to shift them, especially not a bunch of Nazis. They would see them off in the long run, of that nothing was more certain — which was what happened, Vic supposed, if you really loved your country. He only hoped to count on the same back home.

At the place where the sand met the pebbles, Vic took off his shirt and boots and waded in to the slow lapping of some gentle waves. He stood there, enjoying the coolness for some moments, before dropping down to immerse himself fully, finally head and all. It was the first time in weeks he had felt truly relaxed. He rose again, stretched out and splashed forward a few strokes. All in one, a swim, a bath, and a few moments' illusion of peace. A delight if ever there was one.

Once he'd had his fill, Vic turned and began to wade slowly back towards the beach. This breakout aside, he was conscious of the need to stick to the routine he had been given by his protectors, and would soon again make his way to the hut. First, he would allow himself the pleasure of drying off in the open air.

Choosing a spot a little removed from the water and protected by a tumble of rocks and boulders, Vic lay down to soak up some sun. But as it began to bite too quickly, he decided he should cover up and head for the hut. He put his shirt and his boots back on and started the hike up. He was a fair way above the monastery when he saw a figure appear on the further heights between himself and the hut. Kalliope. Spotting him, she began to wave something, maybe a handkerchief. Wanting to call out in recognition, he suppressed that to wave back at her instead, to encourage her to come down. She was supposed to come today, although he had not expected her to be so early or to find him here.

Kalliope stopped waving and stood still for a time, and Vic wondered what she was going to do. To his delight, he saw her begin to head towards him.

Meeting him at a small rocky outcrop, she returned his smile with one more tentative. He couldn't help himself: he touched her gently on the shoulder, a gesture to which she reacted not at all; then, he nodded vigorously at her, to make sure she understood how satisfied he was that she was here. He only wished he knew he knew more of her language.

'*Efharisto. Kala.* You are *kalo koritsi*, good girl,' he said, not sure what else he could offer by way of greeting.

She smiled more easily at his silly Greek, or rather the enthusiasm with which he blurted it out. She knew he wouldn't understand but decided to reply anyway.

'*Ti kanis etho? Ine epikinthino na fenese etsi.*' What are you doing here? It's dangerous showing yourself like this.

Confronting his bafflement, she spread her arms in a questioning gesture, looked around. This he understood.

'Oh, only a swim, Kalliope. Felt like a swim. Sick of being stuck up there ...' he said, then made swimming motions with his arms.

Kalliope nodded, knowing full well from his still wet clothes what he'd been up to.

He grinned at her cheekily, before pointing towards the water. It took her a moment to understand, but then she shook her head. '*Ohi.*' No.

Vic shrugged and was about to point back to the hut when Kalliope took a small parcel out of her now-familiar satchel and gave it to him. He realised from the smell what it was — some hard cheese. She had also brought a large piece of pan bread.

Smiling and nodding even more furiously, he said 'Thanks, thanks love,' and touched her lightly again, this time on the hand.

Kalliope tilted her head to one side to suggest he should sit to eat. At which he cocked his head too, to say she should join him. He led the way to the cover of some trees. She followed by his side.

They sat facing the sea, she a small distance from him. He began to tackle the food.

'This is good,' he said finally. '*Kalo, kalo.*' Then, after a further time, he added, 'You're a godsend, you are. Can't thank you or your people enough, love.'

His speaking in English unsettled her. If only she knew what he was saying. A few minutes later, frustrated and becoming more agitated, she got up again, making signs they should leave. Vic couldn't argue with her.

'I know, I know. I'll come with you …'

Side by side once more, they began the walk back.

At the start of the steep last section, Kalliope made clear that she should take one path, he another. Vic understood, even if he didn't like it. He nodded resignedly. The Germans to one side, it was important that he not be seen at all by anyone except those in the know, and that included some of the more erratic locals who might gab in the wrong ears. Chief among the villains he'd been warned about, for instance, were the area's rural constables, only too willing to pass on information to their occupying masters in return for favours.

Being seen in the company of this village girl was another matter entirely. It would be naive to think that there weren't parents in the background, a boyfriend or jealous lover. The Greeks were pretty keen to protect their womenfolk, he'd been told. But against reason and sense and caution, he couldn't help himself. He took her hand and squeezed it. To his delight, she squeezed back. Then, pulling her hand away firmly and deliberately, she turned and made off on her own path.

Vic looked at her as she went, expecting her to disappear quickly. But after a few seconds she stopped and turned her head briefly to look at him, then continued on her way. He stared after her, pondering that look. He had seen something like that expression before on this island. It was a glance only, but there seemed to be a great deal in it: fierce resistance, something sad, a wary knowingness, all somehow mixed in. Something special to them, he decided. A Cretan glance. The tenderness, though, the way her eyes signalled compassion and understanding; that he hadn't seen everywhere.

8

Discipline and Dance

Vic Stockton had never so looked forward to another human being's presence in his life. Kalliope was a blessing. Otherwise it was sheer misery to endure this waiting, this expectation without real hope of a moment when some means of getting him away might eventuate. What relief, then, that the time could be boxed off as the three days between each visit from the young woman named Kalliope Venakis. She was a lively girl, a spirited girl, he could see that. He saw it again today, after she had sounded her goat's call again and appeared in the distance, steadily and sturdily climbing up towards the hut.

He welcomed her with his usual '*Kalimera*', as she did him in return. But only when he smiled at her did she return the smile. She seemed not entirely sure of the right protocol between two people in such a situation. She liked the fact that he was humorous and gave a sense that there should be some ease between them. For his part, Vic was pleased that she now felt comfortable enough to simply follow him into the hut and sit on the ground, where once she had hesitated.

Today, as she slipped off the satchel and began unpacking things to hand him, she also began to look at him directly in the eye. This was different, he thought. Next, she took out a small book, which she handed to him. A Greek–English dictionary.

Then she addressed him in a new way. She pointed to herself and said '*Ego gineka*', I am a woman, then pointed again and repeated the words.

She could tell Vic wasn't sure what she was saying, so she reached out to take the dictionary from him, found the word in Greek and handed it back. Vic read the English translation.

'Ah! Woman! Well, I wasn't in much doubt, you know!'

She said it again, '*Gineka*', and this time smiled at him a little shyly, while waving her hand in a way that suggested he try the word.

He did, and it wasn't too bad to her ears.

Now she motioned for the dictionary again.

'*Ke esi prepi na mathis pio polla Ellinika*,' she then said. And you need to learn more Greek. '*Ke ya na mathis kati, prepi na ehoume pitharhia*.' And if you're going to learn something, we will have to be disciplined.

This was all too complicated so he just grinned at her and shook his head.

Fishing around in her bag, Kalliope took out a pad and pencil and began to write, setting down the key words in the first phrase she had spoken. He watched her writing, head bent, pad on the satchel across her knees, legs crossed. He was moved, not least for the efforts she was making.

When she had finished making the list and dog-earing the relevant dictionary pages, she looked up and saw the expression of expectant delight on his face, a look in any man's language. She was baffled at her surge of feeling in response as he turned to leaf through the pages of the dictionary.

In the time he took doing this, Kalliope's thoughts strayed to a different subject. What is it that draws us together, what pushes us apart? Questions that hadn't occurred to her in a long time. The man probably had his own family, his own loves somewhere. If so, where were they and what did they think had become of this son or brother and whatever else he was to others? She looked to see if there was a ring on his finger — there wasn't — and began to wonder: in Australia, did they do things the way they were done here? Betrothals, arrangements between families known to each other, elopements and scandals. There was in his manner a disarming openness. Had she the language, she would have liked to talk to him about these things.

Vic continued to turn pages distractedly. Outside, the sound of cicadas, a wave of that distinct buzzing, could be heard somewhere in the distance. At least he thought they were cicadas — the sound was not exactly the same as he knew from Australia. But it was a warm morning and getting hotter, the kind of weather that always set the buggers off.

He smiled at Kalliope and got up to have a look, indicating that she might like to come too. Thinking that this was some signal to end their session, Kalliope gathered up her things to take with her.

Outside, Vic found it a little hard to believe he was actually listening to cicadas so high up on these sparse slopes. There was nothing like the sorts of trees or shrubs nearby that might host such creatures, he thought. But as he looked down the slopes his gaze settled on the small wood to one side of the monastery, probably the origin of that noise. He thought of something, turned to Kalliope.

'Cicadas, Kalliope. Cicadas we call them ...'

She understood he was giving her a language lesson of his own. '*Tzitzikas*,' she said with a smile. '*Tzitzikas*.'

He repeated the word as best he could, then said. 'Ah yes, but that's only if they speak Greek! How do you know they're talking Greek, not English?'

Kalliope looked confused.

'Oh, don't listen to me, love.' He waved the moment away with a grin. 'I'm just an Aussie idiot.'

The wedding of Georgia, cousin of Marika, and her young blade Vasillis was a few days away, the first such event on their calendar in a long time. Despite the occupation, a few of the natural rites could still be observed around these parts, were a necessity even. Life had to go on, war and all. Perhaps, as *Barba* Yorgos had said, a marriage might be considered frivolous in the circumstances. But some of the wiser heads knew better. There was humanity in this, and not a little defiance either. Such sacrament might also stand as a rehearsal for better days, a chance to show that joy and the chance of children to come might not be beyond the bounds of imagination after all.

Not that the thing could proceed as easily as once it might have done. The German authorities had to be notified of any proposed event involving a gathering of more than a few men, with formal permission needing to be granted. This was achieved through the good offices of the deputy mayor who, along with the priest, had gone to Captain Marius to put the proposition. They were a little surprised when he agreed to let the wedding go ahead, though without the usual feasting and fuss for days before and afterwards. All was to be concluded on the one day and there must be no incidents or stupid behaviour of any kind. And the mere sound of a single celebratory gun shot would, he said, cause him to put a call through to the commander of the main force in the area, garrisoned at Rethymnon. They, as he well knew, would have no hesitation in delivering the 'full consequences'.

The principals had not figured on the Captain's reasoning — that a few ritual shenanigans were always acceptable if they had the effect of pacifying and diverting the peasants for a time. But it was consoling to learn that Marius' men would not attend or supervise the event.

Soon, all invited were anticipating the celebration, the *glendi*, even if it was to be restricted unnaturally to the period immediately after the wedding ceremony itself. In times past the feelings that attached to a wedding would rapidly turn from excitement, to delirium as the day got closer. But now the talk of costumes and dresses and trimmings, of the mothers' competition regarding who would provide which sweets and desserts, was restrained by the sense of tragedy that hung over the event. They were enslaved, and their treasured customs were afforded them by grace and favour, not by right.

The only question that raised any sort of frisson was: just what sort of *cavalliero* was this Vasillis likely to prove, anyway? This was a subject tackled only by the boldest of the young women, including Marika and Kalliope — and never in the presence of their mothers, who always insisted that unwed females could have no useful knowledge of such matters. Kalliope never thought of herself as especially worldly wise, but saw no harm in a bit of delicious speculation with a friend. Marika, on the other hand, was much more informative on the subject, having her cousinhood with the bride as a door to all sorts of intimate revelations. Which, to Kalliope's delight, she was only too keen to share.

It was apparently fact that these two — Georgia Oretakis, aged nineteen, and Vasillis Vrassides, aged twenty-one, daughter of Arkadi's one and only pig farmer and son of a mostly absent sponge fisherman — had already chanced that thing that populated the world, and what's more their luck (or otherwise, depending on one's point of view) had come in. According to Marika, their respective parents did not know about this tender detail, and she was on pain of death forbidden to tell anyone. While it was a pity that Marika never could keep a secret when it came to other people's amours, Kalliope would never pass on such a thing to any other soul. Indeed, when she was first told, she had been so startled that she immediately grabbed Marika by the arm and covered her friend's mouth with her hand, even if she couldn't help a little smile.

In a break with tradition, and to the irritation of Father Constantinos, the empty ground next to the olive oil cooperative had been chosen for the site of the *glendi* instead of the main square near the church; more particularly, the area outside and along the eastern wall of the extraction shed. There had been talk at one stage of using the bride's father's spare barley paddock, the one next to his pig yard, but for sensible reasons that had been passed over. It had been agreed that good man though Oretakis senior was, he and his wife would need help in organising such an event. They were simple people, well-meaning people, but marrying off their daughter was as big a challenge as they had ever faced.

They were fortunate in having the support of their fellow villagers. The efforts of the various branches of Marika's family, with those of their friends and willing locals, meant no shortage of helpers ahead of the day. Kalliope and Marika, for instance, took charge of cleaning up the chosen area — it was strewn with rubble

left over from local building works and overgrown with weeds —
as well as the more pleasant task of illuminating it in preparation
for the greater part of the affair that would take place after dark.
Luckily they were able to access electrical power from the
generator at the adjoining factory, and so the string of coloured
lights they had purchased from a merchant in Rethymnon was
then run along the outside wall before being extended outwards to
be hitched again at a couple of small, nearby tamarisk trees. A
wooden platform was then set up to accommodate the wedding
party and the musicians. Tables were provided by the church, and
chairs would be brought across from the junior school.

Preparing the food and delivering it in time was a gargantuan
task, but just as challenging had been the gathering and storing
of the large quantities of ingredients needed against the strictures
and methodical thieving of the Germans. What could be spared
for the occasion was spared, and then some more. It was no small
thing when a young couple set out on such a path; it behoved the
more knowledgeable and experienced to make it as enjoyable and
special a send-off as possible.

The day before the wedding went well enough. The contents
of the dowry box were viewed by the other young women,
according to practice and to everyone's apparent satisfaction —
but then a complication arose. Spanakis, the only man in the
village who could arrange music and lead a band — he had
played and organised semi-professionally before the war — had
with some trouble put together a troupe as required. This because
most of the younger musicians who had gone off to fight had
either died or were trapped elsewhere, obliging him to call on
some old-timers. With a day to go, however, two of them begged
off through illness. It took an afternoon of phone calls to
Rethymnon, grudgingly permitted under the watchful eyes of the

Germans in the post office, to assemble the final respectable-enough group.

It was around midday on Saturday, while at Marika's house, that Kalliope first heard the musicians tuning up in the grounds of the junior school. From there they would head off to meet with the wedding party, then lead the entire village as well as those who had arrived from other parts, down to Aghia Sophia.

The sense of excitement being what it was, Kalliope couldn't help but become flushed. So stirred was she that at one moment, when a few bars on a *lyra* came floating over the air, the hairs stood up on the back of her neck. She barely had time to give Marika a quick peck before the latter hurried away to be with her family who, being related to the bride, needed to join the wedding party. Kalliope and her mother and Mattheos would follow them as closely as possible, but at a discreet distance. This did not prove possible though, for by the time they were ready, the road was already so thick with people they had to fall in with the crowd where they could.

'So many, who would have thought?' Kalliope's mother asked.

'We are hungry for something other than misery, mama,' Kalliope replied.

The church, large as it was, was still too small to accommodate everyone. The numbers had been swelled by family and friends from other parts. That suited the younger boys just fine — it meant they could ogle and stare at will, talk too, which you definitely couldn't do if you were inside. And the men could smoke, though Kalliope was not too impressed when Mattheos lit up within a few metres of the church gates.

At three in the afternoon, something like an hour and a half after official proceedings had commenced, Kalliope and her mother stood next to each other to one side of the entrance and watched as the couple left the church, duly and properly married. Shouts went up from the assemblage, the church bell rang out — with as frantic and insistent a rhythm as anyone had surely ever heard — and then, to the joyous whooping of the wedding party, the bride performed her traditional dance in front of the church to usher in the next part of the proceedings.

Father Constantinos led the wedding party off. It was customary for the religious to steer the newlyweds to the celebration and to stay for a decent part of the event, presumably so that the young marrieds didn't finish up in hell too soon. The band struck up and a veritable battalion took shape to march to the other end of the village, though not before a brief stop at the bride's new house for the other small traditions, her taking the key and making a cross in honey on the door before stepping over the threshold, her friends scattering the rice and petals inside.

At the olive co-op meanwhile, some of the mothers and their helpers had already spread out the feast. They had arranged plates of *mezedes* on the long tables covered with coloured cloth. For effect, sprigs of olive and cuttings of cyclamen were placed at their ends. The wedding table had been dressed in a beautiful piece of what looked like white linen, a rarity in these parts.

Before the music and dance could begin in earnest, the formalities had to be endured. Kalliope found seats for herself, her mother and Mattheos as near to Marika as possible. The priest made a speech welcoming everyone, wishing the couple well and entreating them to always step on God's illuminated path and no other. Then a toast was offered. With glasses of fiery *tsikoudia* all drank to the health of Georgia and Vasillis and their families. A second toast was then suddenly proposed, if out of order, by the bride's father, who couldn't help himself but asked for God's gift of children 'within a short time'. Marika and

Kalliope exchanged glances, each wondering whether the old boy just might have had a farmer's instinct on the subject.

Spanakis and his makeshift band, consisting of *lyra*, fiddle and mandolin, now had their moment. They took to one end of the platform especially set aside for them and began to arrange themselves on a number of wooden chairs. It was time for the *tavla* repertoire, the 'songs for the table', which they had practised as much as they could in the short time available. And Kalliope thought they weren't too bad as she listened to these tunes of love, marriage, the joy of the hunt; they would disgrace no one. But nobody was prepared to voice the sadly obvious, either: these men were either too young or too old. They lacked the energy and joy of the star players, the real champions of the art, who were now lost.

Feasting continued, and then it was time for dancing, required to proceed in the correct order. First the bride's family stood to hold hands, join in a circle and request *kordylies*, music the band was only too willing to play; then it was to be the family of the groom's turn, then friends of the groom.

Deciding that Kalliope counted as family too, Marika swept her in with the first group. She was keen for her friend to have some pleasurable exercise, Mattheos' eagle eye notwithstanding. Although she let herself be dragged in, Kalliope was not sure at first that she needed to be seen dancing by quite so many of the Oretakis family males, who seemed terribly interested in what she was doing. But among such pleasant sounds, such insistent rhythms, it was easy to forget them. When the *syrto* they danced finally ended, the two girls stood back to one side to catch their breath. Kalliope smiled at Marika, and when she was able to said, 'Not bad for someone who says she doesn't like to dance.'

'It's all so old-fashioned. Enjoyable to a point, but ...' said Marika.

'What do you mean?'

'Look.'

The most prominent dancing men were now lining up to make donations to the musicians, ostentatiously placing coins and notes in the hands of the mandolin player in plain sight of all the guests, each trying to outdo the other.

'Is that not vulgar? I mean, right in front of the bride and groom and everyone?' said Marika.

'Oh, it's only high spirits and showing off, nobody pays them any attention. It's tradition!' Kalliope said.

'And as for the dances … what about the new ones? My God, even in Rethymnon you can get a foxtrot, or a tango, or a polka.'

'Ha!' Kalliope responded. 'So when did we last go dancing in Rethymnon, girl? As for a tango … seen by us once only in a movie, as I recall. It's a miracle to hold such a thing at all, the way things are.'

But Marika was hardly listening. Her high spirits and skittishness had taken her over completely. While the musicians took their break and in the general milling about before the next set, she boldly took two small glasses of *tsikoudia* in one hand and put them behind her back. Without letting Kalliope see what she was holding, she whispered that she should follow her, and led the way around the side of the co-op and out of sight of the other wedding guests.

Marika brought the glasses round from behind her back and offered Kalliope one. Kalliope could not help smiling at the cheek of this.

'I knew you were up to no good. As for another one, I don't know if I can …'

'Oh don't be silly! And didn't I see you raise a glass at the toast along with your mother?'

'Yes, but …'

'*Stin ygeia mas*,' Marika proposed. To our health.

'And to those we love,' Kalliope added, and then immediately swallowed the aniseed-flavoured liquor.

'And who are not with us,' said Marika.

Kalliope looked at Marika and wondered to whom she was referring specifically. She took the remark as a cue. 'Speaking of which, I got another letter from Andreas …'

'You haven't mentioned letters for a while — what's the latest?'

'Again he says it's hard to write — he has to travel around everywhere in the army there.'

'So what else?'

Kalliope looked down at the ground and replied, 'This and that. Also that he wants me to join him.'

'What? What are you saying?'

'Join him, Marika. Go to Australia and get married.'

'Why didn't you tell me the instant you got it?'

'Because, well … You know this is an old theme. Just that he hasn't mentioned it for a while.' Kalliope raised a reassuring hand. 'Look, I can't go anywhere straight away. After the war, who knows?'

Marika began to look very glum. 'Of course, who would not want to start another life, but …'

'Stop fretting, girl! — It will be a long time before I, any of us, goes anywhere. Andreas must know that.'

'It's not that. I suppose … I wish I had someone or something to drag me away one day.'

'But marriage, Marika. It's a big thing.'

'Is it? Really? I mean is it? Look at these two today. They might be as dumb as sticks, but …'

Kalliope didn't like to hear Marika speak like this. 'Shh,' she cut her off. 'Don't call them that.'

'Sorry, I didn't mean … But look, I mean even simple people like them are giving it a try.'

Kalliope understood, as Marika did, that there was much more to such a question for them. They had been drawn into the fight against an oppressor; they were not daughters of the land but young women with some education. They could at least imagine the possibility of somewhere else, something more, better, one day — even if they were in no position now to define that else, more, or better.

'This is for another time, Marika. Let's get back, they will start missing us,' Kalliope said. '*Ela,*' — Come — she said, taking Marika's hand and tugging her playfully. 'Before there's an incident!'

But a moment later, they both noticed a shadowy shape dart across the darkness beyond the shed. They froze, thinking they had been spied upon. Then a few metres from where they stood a man slowly emerged from the shadows and took a step or two towards them. Marika took a startled step back but Kalliope in an instant realised who it was: the Australian soldier. She whispered quickly to Marika. Then she began to frantically wave him away.

Vic responded with a calming gesture, slowly lowering his two palms towards the ground a couple of times. He took another step forward, all confidence and bravado. He pointed to his eyes and then at the celebration in the distance. It seemed he had come down from the hills to take a look. Kalliope shook her head, giving him as stern a stare as she could come up with — allowing that there was something also pleasing in the boldness of what he had done. But whatever she and her friends and allies might think of him, she knew very well that there was probably a traitor and a troublemaker or two in this very crowd. He could not afford to be seen around here at all.

Kalliope was relieved when Vic, as if finally aware of the danger he was creating, appeared to run off into the gloom once more. But he had only disappeared around the back of the building to find a way onto the low roof of the shed. Now he lay flat, bobbing his head up over the parapet to look down at the two women. Marika pointed him out, exclaiming, 'Look! There is our man again!'

And again Vic grinned at them both.

Kalliope waved her arm to get him to lie low again, which he did. But as she turned to scold Marika, her friend surprised her by whispering loudly that Kalliope should wait there and that she would be back very soon.

Vic looked across at the celebration, framed in those pretty coloured lights, and thought it was fantastic. He didn't care for the music particularly — the fiddling was a bit screechy and overwrought, although he found the rhythm appealing. He preferred watching the men doing that acrobatic stuff they called dancing. How these villagers had convinced the Germans to let this take place was one marvel — the expression of defiant joy he could see being enacted not a hundred feet away was another. Like the war had never happened and they weren't under a Nazi yoke at all. This was a tremendous mob, truly, he thought — you'd have to say almost worth the bloody killing and dying for.

Vic briefly considered defying Kalliope and making his presence known — he would have loved to join in, join her — but the game was not worth the proverbial. He had no illusions about what would happen if word got back to the Jerries that these people were harbouring an Allied soldier.

A moment later Marika reappeared with yet another glass of *tsikoudia* in hand. Kalliope was uneasy. 'Oh, for God's sake Marika, you're going to get us into trouble,' she said. 'Stop this, or you will get us killed. It's bad enough that he's here.'

'I thought maybe …' Marika nodded at the glass and in the direction of Vic on the roof.

So outrageous was the idea that Kalliope suddenly let out a laugh. Whether it was the dark, or a letting go encouraged by the fact of this wedding, however circumscribed and strained it might be, or something else, she did not know. After the past months she, too, felt a need to rebel. She took the glass from Marika and boldly strode over to the wall of the shed. She made the sound of the kri-kri and on cue Vic leaned his head and shoulders over the parapet.

Kalliope held up the glass of spirit and Vic reached down, smiling, to take it from her.

'*Sto neo kosmo*,' she said.

And Vic knew exactly what she was saying.

'*Neo kosmo*, all right, love,' he said. 'Cheers!' He took the glass from her, gestured with it as if making a toast, and pulled back behind the edge of the roof once more.

'*Ela*,' said Kalliope. 'We've been here long enough. Let's go,' she said, taking Marika's hand in hers.

They arrived back without attracting any notice, the crowd still large enough for a quiet entrance. Marika saved Kalliope the trouble of pacifying her parents by offering that it was her fault, that she had dragged Kalliope away to talk to a girl from a distant village they hadn't seen in ages.

Now the musicians, emboldened by the reception they had received so far from the guests, made their way back to their places to play again. They had hardly seated themselves when some commotion began beyond the lighted area. The musicians, like others around and near them, turned to that direction, and saw the crowd begin to part. The reason was soon obvious: the Germans had turned up.

Captain Marius, with a small contingent of armed men, came striding through the guests. He was making his way towards the priest and the wedding party. Everyone froze, not knowing what to do. They were powerless, not only because the four soldiers had their rifles slung over their soldiers. The priest and the fathers of the bride and groom were the only ones to react. Expecting serious trouble, they had got up from the wedding table and come around to find out what was happening.

Captain Marius made some sort of reassuring gesture with his hand, as if to say no one should get upset, everyone should remain calm. Then, in full view of the guests as well as the terrified bridegroom, he began questioning Oretakis senior, occasionally nodding in the direction of the table still amply covered with food. At least he wasn't shouting and his men seemed to have no intention of making their weapons ready.

This was not what had been promised; they had been told all could proceed without interference. But Kalliope and Marika both realised there was a more dangerous possible reason for the German presence. An Allied soldier was not fifty metres from Marius and his men.

Kalliope signalled to Marika to stay where she was. Her own heart began to thump as she quietly stepped towards where she had last seen Vic. It seemed to take her forever, her only aid being the shadows beyond the lights. She looked back from time to time, wondering why those Germans had turned up and what they intended. She covered the last few metres to the shed as quietly as she could. Making the contact sound softly, she waited but received no response. She tried once more, again, nothing. Perhaps Vic had spotted what had happened and had got away. But perhaps he was just lying low on the roof. Quickly, she picked up a small stone and threw it over the parapet at the point where she believed he might still be. It landed on something hard. She took that to mean he was not there, although she had no real way of knowing.

Frustrated, not knowing if there was anything more she should or could do, Kalliope walked quietly back to rejoin Marika, who was talking to *Kyria* Venakis and Kalliope's uncle.

'Where have you been, you silly girl?' Mattheos hissed.

'Nowhere, *Thio*,' Kalliope answered quietly

'Don't be upset, *Thio*,' Marika said quickly. 'She was with our dear friend Maria, from school … you remember her?'

'You all have too many friends in my opinion,' Mattheos said sourly, no longer interested in pursuing the matter of Kalliope's behaviour. It was increasingly erratic in his view anyway — comings and goings, disappearances, you never knew where she was any more. He was beginning to think that the young woman was mad, or getting that way.

To everyone's relief the Germans began to move off, leaving as nonchalantly as they had arrived. With their departure, the first notes of a *sousta* were heard. Marika quickly grabbed Kalliope's hand and pulled her over to where other girls were getting ready to respond to the music.

'What happened?' she asked quietly. 'Is he still there?'

'I don't know. I hope he's gone. What was that all about?'

'Ha! You could have predicted it. About food. The Germans wanted to see if we had been holding out on them. They had heard reports we had been keeping food from them, wanted to know where some of our banquet had come from.' Marika gave a contemptuous smile.

'What banquet?'

'Exactly. They are not as hungry as we are, we can tell them; just in case they're suffering from delusions. Anyway, Father Constantinos smooth-talked them and Oretakis, clever man, offered them what was left of one the spit lambs ...'

'They took it?'

'Of course, even if it was more bones than meat! And then he had the idea of handing over a big bowl of *Kyria* Chrissakis' almond biscuits too!' Marika laughed. 'Come on, Kalliope. This is our dance, girl.'

And it was. A dance for young women in pairs, a dance for exchanging confidences and secret knowledge. Slow and rhythmic, just right for two friends.

9

The Sounds of the Past

For Vic, pent up mostly in his hut, the following two weeks held nothing as exciting as that night down in the village. He had afterwards felt very guilty for having gone and intruded himself on that wedding; too late had he understood that he could have put the village people in serious danger. He had luckily managed to get away, clambering down at the first sight of the Germans, though he regretted the necessity; that roof was the best vantage point in the whole area. But had he got drunk, as he had been sorely inclined to do by asking the girls to bring him more grog, or fallen asleep on the roof then woken up unawares, who knew what might have happened?

There had been repercussions of a sort. On her next visit, Kalliope had looked sternly at him and even wagged a finger (while trying to suppress a smile). More seriously, she then handed over a note written in English in an unformed hand. 'You must stay hiding. Not come village or show anybody. This is order.'

He believed the note had come from somebody other than Kalliope, though possibly at her instigation. He'd contemplated asking who had actually penned it, accepting that it would have been someone underground and associated with her, but thought that would be pushing things, given his behaviour. Still, what he had done had been great fun. And when Kalliope handed him a small gift of wedding bombonieri, sugared almonds, as she was leaving, he had concluded she could not have been too worried about what had happened either.

In the days after his big night on the tiles, Vic had spent most of the time looking out through the door of the hut, following the course of nature — or such of it as he could observe — in the immediate area. He passed the daylight hours weather- and cloud-watching, trying to identify the birds circling in the skies beyond and to discern the patterns of their flight. But that was generally during the mornings and evenings; in late summer the temperature still tended to climb, and the middle of each day saw the skies pretty much empty. The highlight of the past two weeks had been another sally down to the coast for a quiet swim. As he only had the rattling cicadas for company in the immediate vicinity of the hut, he more than ever looked forward to his twice-weekly visits from Kalliope.

There was not a lot to do. The worst times were the evenings when the light had disappeared and it was too soon to try to get some sleep. Then Vic would find his thoughts wandering to questions he had no way of answering: of home, of the state of the war in Europe and beyond, of his mates and their respective fates, Stan's in particular. He had heard nothing and had no expectation of hearing, but only hoped that the bugger had been rescued and found some way of getting off Crete to safety. It weighed on him that he had maybe let him go just a little too easily. You were supposed to look after your mates — an idea you heard a lot about back home and something he believed in too, hoping he hadn't been entirely remiss through this miserable stoush. But what could you do if they were stubborn bastards who wouldn't listen, whatever you said?

Vic tried many things to occupy himself with through the lonely days. If he was inclined to feel he had been catapulted onto another planet, as he sometimes did when the night closed in, he would attempt to find connections between where he was and what he knew. Heat, scrub, sheep (weird sort compared to your Merino, however), not a lot of water, that was very similar, not to mention the bloody cicadas … Then the people, they were sort of cynical, sort of not, like your best type of Aussie; they liked a laugh; regarding the important stuff, they fell in love and got married, as he'd seen first hand (but that happened everywhere, obviously), fought if they had to, but were more inclined to sit around and have a beer if it was hot, or more likely a retsina.

One night he got to considering what made you one nationality or another. Never mind that you could see lots of similarities between people wherever they were. Possibly it was just luck where you were born, but people turned out different from one place to another, didn't they? He had wondered what it was that had made *him* who he was. How much was his father, how much his mother, how much the place? That was too hard, but some things were certain: your mother gives birth to you, you're raised somehow or another, and you go on your way. Did they worry about you when you were in a spot like this? What did it feel like to be a parent and be missing your kid?

Vic had an inkling how his parents might have been feeling about him but couldn't pin down that feeling exactly. That night, however, he just hoped he would see them both again. His cranky old man, telling him that mucking around in boats was fine, he liked a bit of that himself, but that if he didn't get a trade he would 'finish up at the bottom of the screaming heap' — a good dad in his own way. His mum, always at him to 'keep yourself tidy', always asking after this or that girl she had noticed him speaking to on the street. Why did they care about what became of him? Something that only a parent knew, he presumed.

Whatever he thought about home or anything else, Vic also told himself this constant mulling over things was a function of too much time to think — you had to drag yourself back to the here and now. And at present, knowing what was going on around you was primary. On the subject of local information, though, there was precious little available currently through the village or his girl helper. Despite that they had made further progress in understanding each other, and he probably had a couple of hundred Greek words by now, communication between himself and Kalliope was not as easy as he would have liked. And even if it was easier, he wasn't sure what these poor people might know or learn that could be of real use to resolving his fate anyway. In their own way, they were as trapped as he was.

So Vic stuck to his routine, did as he was told. On the best reading, one day some opportunity to make an escape might possibly arrive, and he would be told by the resistance what form that would take. But that was on the best reading.

For Kalliope, nothing much was suggesting change either. She still visited the *levendi*, the young brave hidden in Manolakis' hut, although these visits took little of her time each week. Her days were filled with helping Mattheos in his vineyard as required, or trying to grow some vegetables in a patch of their courtyard, just a few marrows, some cucumbers and beans for the table. The courtyard had proved a boon, as it was hidden and there was less chance of their produce being stolen. Since the arrival of these tyrants, food grown in larger plots and orchards had been subject to regular raids and confiscation.

The only other new development was that Kalliope and her mother had begun to knit and sew in earnest. They were competent seamstresses, although Kalliope had never been particularly fond of the so-called feminine arts, much to Mattheos' displeasure. Indeed, her uncle had never been happy that she had continued her education after primary school, and was further annoyed that she showed no interest in the domestic science subjects, far preferring the liberal side of her education, such as it was. She had sometimes baited him by saying that she did not set the curriculum, so it was not her fault that as well as teaching girls their future wifely obligations, and stressing their family and religious duties, her school also required of her some knowledge of Greek language, drama and history.

But schooling had long ended, Kalliope's life had been overtaken by her responsibilities and duties as daughter and niece, and any ambitions she may have had for herself had come to nought. The coming of war had finished them off entirely. An artistic life, the theatre, had never been a realistic possibility. Perhaps to have become a teacher, that might have been something, and she still spent idle moments wondering what that would have been like. The times were what they were, however, and there was only survival — which meant that she and her mother had to make their own mats and rugs and any other soft furnishings that might be needed and for which material could be found. Long gone were the days when they could simply buy what they needed right here in Arkadi, thanks to the efforts of her Andreas.

This morning Kalliope was on her way to collect some scraps from various neighbouring houses that her mother might make up into rag mats. Autumn was approaching and replacements were needed to cover the cold stone floor of their house.

As she approached Andreas' place, she thought to go quietly so as not to attract his mad mother's attention. But she was shocked to see that the Coroneos place was open to the four winds. The door and two windows onto the street had been thrown open, as had the doors to the storehouse and stable, Andreas' one-time shop. She could see straight inside. And there, turning over various empty boxes and crates, looking for heaven knew what, stood Arkadi's two ageing louts and wits, Kostas and Aris.

'Hey,' said Kostas, turning to Aris. 'Remember that time he returned from Athens wearing the same clothes he'd left in? And carting his one and only bag and nothing more? When the sod said he was going to bring back all the latest wares? Then again, where would he have found the money?'

Aris replied, 'Yes well, he always was big on schemes and ideas. And he was definitely one of the parasites among us.'

Kalliope listened, trying hard to keep a grip. She had heard this sort of talk, directed at 'traders' and 'middlemen', before. Her anger always grew, not only because she felt sympathy towards Andreas who, after all, had tried his hardest, but for the fact that the critics were hardly making any sort of useful contribution to the common good. They were either living on broken-down inheritances, or else, like Kostas, were being supported by a government pension, secured through nepotism or some other nefarious means. More important now was that these two idiots not discover what purpose this place served these days — although she doubted that they had or even could.

'You two!' she called. 'What are you doing in there? What's going on?'

Kostas spun around, looking a little guilty. 'Oh, it's only you. Haven't you heard? They've taken *Kyria* Coroneos away …'

'What do you mean "away"?'

With a finger twirling around his ear, Aris responded: 'She's lost it completely. They've taken her to Irakleion.'

'Who?'

'Dr Takiztakis came to check on her last night and found her wandering around with no clothes on, babbling. He called the Germans and they took her in one of their cars not an hour ago.'

'Yes,' said Kostas, 'these Nazis are not all bad, you know … Why, their captain gave a speech the other day, not that I heard it but was told, to say that the unfortunate ill would be dealt with, not merely left to wander around and suffer like wounded animals. If they took her away, I say it shows they are considerate of the suffering. Who said they could not be civilised in their own way?'

Kalliope did not know what to make of this story — these two were not known for their grasp of reality — and so settled for dealing with what she could.

'Forget all that … by what right are you in there, going through their things?'

'Hey, relax, sister,' Aris said, spreading out his hands. 'The Germans threw the place open. They want it cleaned out proper.'

'And we're helping,' said Kostas.

'Helping my foot,' Kalliope spat back at him. 'You have no shame. Get out of there!'

'In good time, girl, in good time,' said Kostas.

Feeling helpless, unsure as to what could or couldn't be done, Kalliope decided it best to move away as quickly as she could. Other than report what she had seen to her contacts — the only good men left in the place as far as she was concerned — she didn't know what else she might do.

10

The Sounds of the Future

Nothing much doing again that morning. Vic stepped out of the hut and went for a slightly longer walk than usual in order to take a piss. He walked far enough to get to the point where he could gaze down at the water, and there contemplated whether he should go to the trouble of a swim again. The breeze was a little chillier than usual — it was Autumn now — and instead thought to make his return into a firewood-gathering expedition. He had lit one or two small fires in the past week, but only at night so the smoke would not be seen from a distance.

With a small bundle of twigs under his arm, Vic arrived at the hut once more half an hour after he had left. There he saw that the panel of nailed-together boards that stood for a door lay to one side. Sure that he had closed it earlier, he began approaching warily when a figure lurched out, startling him — Thoma. The monk was not expecting the sudden encounter and reeled back. The small, red-bearded little man, more Norse in appearance than Cretan, was so frightened he immediately began crossing himself.

Vic tried to reassure him. 'It's all right, mate, it's all right.' The monk came up to him, still in a state of distress.

'*Pou isouna? Pou isouna?*'

Vic got the sense of the question — Where were you? — and pointed down to the sea.

'*Ah! Then xerame. Perimenoume tous Germanous simera! Germanous!*' he said rapidly in his high-pitched voice. We didn't know where you were. We are expecting Germans today!

Vic wasn't clear about the first bit, but he had no trouble understanding those last words. He stiffened, looked around the vicinity.

'*Prepi na figis apo tho,*' Thoma said — You have to leave here — and begun tugging at his sleeve. '*Ele me mena, ela!*' Come with me, come! He grabbed Vic by the arm and began pulling him forward.

While Thoma was tugging at his sleeve, Vic became aware that another figure was making its way up towards them. A few moments later he saw it was Kalliope.

'Wait, wait,' he said. He wasn't prepared to go anywhere until she arrived and he had heard what she had to say.

Kalliope joined them, breathless, and immediately had the same message to impart: '*Germanoi. Prepi na figis.*' Germans. You have to go.

That was the only prompting he needed. He made to duck back into the hut to gather up his things but Thoma was so insistent and so panicky — he still held Vic's arm — that he thought better of it. This might all blow over, he thought, and if so he would find himself back here later in the day anyway; on the other hand, if anything serious was about to happen, nothing he had inside would be of much use. Vic could see no alternative to putting himself at his rescuers' disposal. He presumed they had somewhere in mind for him to go.

It seemed they did. Almost at a run, Thoma led the way along the path to the monastery. Then, at the point where the one track became two, he veered to the main enclosure and led him through the gates. The urgency with which this fellow was hurrying him began to worry Vic. Although he could detect no military or aircraft noise, this did feel like something was developing. What did they know?

Waiting for them outside the smaller of the two chapels, that dedicated to Aghios Nikolaos, was the abbot himself. Next to him stood three men in civilian clothes — sturdy, reliable-looking coots, to Vic's eyes. He presumed they were from the resistance. When he saw the easy familiarity with which they spoke to Kalliope, he was sure.

The boss crossed himself, then took Vic's right hand in both of his.

'My fellow,' he said, 'we have trouble coming to us. They tell us that more Germans are coming this morning from the north. Already they stop some places like ours north to … bang!' He let go of Vic's hand to make a gesture of shooting a rifle.

Vic was impressed that they should have such information here, already, in this isolated place. 'How do you know this?' he asked. 'Do the shepherds call to each other across the hills or something?'

'Shepherds?' The abbot was confused. 'No, no, telephone.'

This struck Vic as impossible. 'You have a telephone here?'

'Of course. What, you think we don't know nothing because we are, how you say, monks? One telephone is here, and one telephone still in Arkadi, the post office. Germans cut this one, but we fix. But this very bad. For many weeks, they leave us alone. Now they think we are doing something against them, who knows? We ask you, please, if you help us, *Kyrie* Vic.'

Vic knew there was only one answer, given what had been done for him. 'Look, happy to help,' he said. 'But I don't know that I can add much. What help, anyway?'

'You are military man. My people here, they don't know about such things,' he replied.

Vic was pleased that someone still thought him useful, even if he and his comrades had been so thoroughly routed.

'So what do you want me to do?'

'Do? Give us idea how to fight them!' Nektarios said. 'But first, we will pray!'

He led the way into the chapel through a low, arched door.

Vic noticed the lettering above the point of the arch and asked what it was.

'This one is for Aghios Nikolaos, Saint Nicholas, my friend. Very old. God been here for us many times in this place.'

Inside was cool and dark, the air smoky and incense-scented. The space was no bigger than a large living room — you couldn't have got more than thirty people in here, Vic assessed. At the other end was the screen, the *iconostasion*, though not as elaborate or beautiful as the one he had seen in the other larger chapel.

After lighting a candle, the abbot went behind the screen to the altar, bowed his head and began to pray or chant, or whatever that kind of vocalisation was called. His voice wasn't loud, it didn't have to be to fill this space with sound. It was eerie but beautiful. The sound got to him, Vic was not ashamed to admit. Old and mysterious.

As Vic stood and listened, he allowed there might be a God, if not for him, then at least for these good and harmless men who had taken him in and had done what they could for him. Certainly none of them deserved to find themselves at the mercy of the mongrels who had invaded their country.

As they moved out of the chapel, Vic could see that war had reared up even here — and in the way Vic remembered it always came to you: with shouts and alarms and a lot of running to and fro. There were blokes everywhere, coming and going from their cells. The abbot called them all to gather around him: the half-dozen senior monks, the resistance men and Kalliope, the juniors, and Vic. Nektarios spoke quickly in Greek to the others, then caught Vic off guard by turning to him to say, 'I tell them you are soldier and we must listen.'

'Hang on, I can't take charge here. I'm only a private.'

The abbot gave him a stern look. 'I said we listen to you first. That's all. We are not babies. If we don't like what you say, we won't do.'

'That's all right, then.' Vic tried to think clearly, conscious of the anticipatory stares directed his way. He replied, 'Look, this is all I have to say, right? We don't have an army here. So don't even think about setting up and trying to win some blasted battle with the Germans. That's the first thing. Situation hopeless equals minimise casualties. OK? What I reckon we should do is all clear out — not give them any targets. Let the bastards have what they want, then come back and pick up the pieces, whatever's left. They're not stupid, they need you blokes probably for what you can give them. So, just for now …'

Vic hesitated, very uncomfortable about trying to give advice to these people. Who was he to be listened to, anyway? This was their land and their lives. Nevertheless, his mum had always said you were allowed to give your opinion if asked. He began again. 'For now, abbot sir, is there any place you can go from here, for hiding? What do these others say?'

Nektarios didn't respond to his last questions but launched straight into a rapid-fire translation for the benefit of those without English, meaning everyone else. That was followed by some parley between the resistance men. The one who seemed their leader, a tough-looking, moustachioed chap built like a brick shithouse and almost bursting out of his too-small dark suit, got into an especially lively altercation with the abbot. Then there was silence as Nektarios bent his head towards Vic.

'The committee people ready to fight, but they have few guns. They ask if you have any.'

'Tell them, yes, I've got one — and five bullets. And tell them they're mad to even think about it. Anyway, what do their bosses say? Surely someone higher up somewhere else has got a plan?'

A quick question brought the response from the abbot: 'They say people here must make decision for monastery — command agreeing with this.'

More excited talk took place, with the abbot seeming to raise his voice above the others from time to time to assert some authority. He appeared relieved next time he spoke to Vic.

'I tell them we must listen to you because you have more experience with fighting them. All right, they say. We go.'

'And now?'

'Now we have problem. We are twenty monks and two more, two help-men. No place big enough for us.'

'What do the committee blokes say?'

'Blokes?'

'Yes, those ones there,' Vic nodded at them.

'They say if we no fight, we can go to Arkadi village.'

'Well, I'd take that as good advice if it was up to me, sir!'

But then, making instant mockery of all efforts at counsel and organisation, they heard the muffled roar of a German transport in the distance.

A general shout went up: 'Go! Scatter!' Vic only registered how incredibly fast events were moving. He saw the monks run to their cells to gather whatever belongings and artefacts were important. Then, in the few minutes left to them, he helped move boxes and suitcases, loaded bundles and bags of clothing and books onto various shoulders, and stood by as the monks trooped out through the monastery gates, bound for the hills and across country to the village of Arkadi, eight kilometres north.

Led by the abbot, side by side with Kalliope and the village men, Vic went upland after them. Working cross-country, they kept a good distance from the track that led to the monastery. Vic thought there was still some possible value in his own hiding place, but Nektarios told him that getting supplies to him there would now be too difficult. They could probably find a cellar or a hole for him somewhere in Arkadi.

But events put paid to theories and plans. Before they had even got as far as Vic's hut, a motorised group could be seen on the track over the furthest rise, forcing them to spread out and seek cover behind whatever tree or rock they could reach. And it was from a grove of carob trees that Vic watched the German unit make its way past them towards the Monastery of Kastelli. This they did not do directly; first there was a swerve off the dirt road towards the rustic shepherd's hut.

Kalliope moved away from the others to be with Vic. She watched in stomach-tightening anxiety as a motorcycle and sidecar unit stopped on its way, the rider and offsider getting off to inspect his hiding place. The offsider must have decided that no risks were to be taken and unloosed a volley of machine-gun shots across the structure at waist height, concentrating on the doorway. Kalliope flinched and without thinking leaned into Vic, who put his arm around her shoulder. They continued to watch as the Germans went in to inspect the hut. Vic was relieved that he'd taken all his gear with him when Thoma had hurried him from the hut earlier. Then came a bit of fun. The soldiers proceeded to unpack and ready a flame-thrower, then set to incinerating the roof and insides. Vic saw one of them unclip and line up a grenade for the *coup de grâce*, but then, small mercy, a second soldier seemed to talk the first one out of it. He could hear the thought: that tiny structure wasn't worth blowing up and would only scatter them with shrapnel.

Vic looked in dismay at the abbot, who had been watching the same scene from behind a tree a few yards away. He shook his head sorrowfully, crossed himself a couple of times, finally extending his arms in a shrug for Vic's benefit. What indeed could anyone do?

But that was only the appetiser. The entourage went the rest of the way to the main gates of Kastelli and blew them in with a bazooka. Then they went in and there was silence for a while. When they came back into view, it was obvious what had kept them occupied.

Carrying out food, barrels of wine and grain, all the provisions that had had to be abandoned, they began loading their vehicles. Vic, Kalliope and Abbot Nektarios watched in resignation as more soldiers emerged laden with furniture, tools — anything deemed useful and transportable.

While they were doing this, a team of other soldiers went to one of the half-tracks and unpacked a number of heavier weapons. These they lined up to concentrate a barrage on the buildings. In turn, the storehouse, the abbot's quarters, the latrine, the monks' cells and various outbuildings were subjected to machine gun, grenade, bazooka and flame-thrower. For some reason they spared the main chapel, but not the smaller one of Aghios Nikolaos.

Vic heard a couple of the men hidden around him begin to cry, to wail and shout in their pain and frustration. Abbot Nektarios was on his knees, bent over and praying with a kind of supplication Vic had never seen before, would not even have thought possible. Whatever higher power he was beseeching, he was being sorely let down.

The resistance men roused the abbot and some talk passed between them. Vic assumed they were saying that what was lost was lost and they should keep heading for the village. There was a further regrouping and discussion: for added safety they should split up, the village men and Kalliope taking one route, the abbot and his troupe another. The fact of that decision seemed to calm people; sensible it was, too, as the bastards had finished their dirty work below, were all packed and had started their engines. There was some small consolation in that, despite the barrage, the monastery walls had mostly withstood the onslaught. To demolish the place, they would have needed some serious artillery.

As far as Vic could tell, the monks seemed far more upset about the assault on their sacred territory than the fact that the Germans might soon be heading in the same direction as themselves. They were not so much in fear of being caught; knowing their way around the treacherous goat tracks and back routes that led from there to Arkadi. Not even those German transports could go where they were going.

But their confidence was misplaced.

Just as the soldiers at the monastery started their transports, the monks heard the distinct sound of other vehicles beyond them on the slopes. Vic knew immediately what had happened. There was another wave of Germans coming; their half-tracks were giving them purchase on the rough ground that lay between the monks and the soldiers. The men spoke quickly with the abbot, who in turn told Vic the obvious: they were caught between two raiding parties. Hardly had he spoken when Vic heard shouts of, '*Achtung!*' from a few hundred yards off. Abbot Nektarios told him to go quickly, to leave, run, make his way without them.

'We will give ourselves up to them. God will look after us. You will see. But you, they will kill you with no words if they catch you.'

At a loss Vic stood transfixed, glancing from the abbot to the men to Kalliope, whom he could see was doing her best to try to stay calm and useful. He was unable to think. He was torn by this as much as by any other test he had undergone so far.

'I can help you,' he eventually said.

'No. You cannot.'

Vic watched anxiously as the abbot and the men turned to Kalliope and spoke rapidly. He saw, as Kalliope began to nod her head, some agreement taking shape.

'I tell you now,' the abbot said. 'You go, down there, anywhere. Go to the water. Or go back to Sfakia … Please, you listen to me.'

'What do these men say?' Vic asked him.

'They say now cannot go to village — go to water. Girl can show you from here.'

Three or four seconds passed before Vic could do as he was told. He tore himself away and, with Kalliope by his side, began a weaving, dodging run, angling away from the two sets of hunters and their quarry. When they were far enough distant to safely catch their breath before another burst, they stopped and waited. For one minute, then two, then three, hoping not to hear the sounds of gun shots. Those men, if any on this rotten stinking planet, did not deserve to die.

Ten minutes passed — long enough for the rest of the party to have been rounded up, long enough for them to have been shot on the spot. Yet there was no sound but the wind from the sea rustling up through the scrub. Vic began to calm down. Perhaps they had remained free? It was possible. Or if they had been mustered, he hoped they were at least to be taken to somewhere they knew, maybe even Arkadi, for incarceration. They surely deserved better than a prison camp.

They set off again for the coast, Vic by now prepared to follow Kalliope anywhere. She knew this place so well that he felt safe enough. She led him to a certain rise and began to point out a path. *'Eki.'* There. *'Pare afto to dromo.'* Take that route. And turned as if to leave him. It was a shock; he felt abandoned.

Then he understood. She would want to go back to her people. But he didn't like this development one bit. He didn't know why. He could probably negotiate the few miles down to the coast from here by himself. But he didn't want to. Given a choice, he would much prefer to have this woman by his side — not that he could think what might happen after he got there. The bigger picture was still a muddle. All he knew was that he didn't want her to leave.

Kalliope saw that he understood what she had to do next. If only she had the language to express what she felt about this. He had become a brother in arms, he was a young man who had done his best. There was no question she trusted him, was drawn to him. But what more could be said or done now? Nothing.

In this mess, there were few thoughts Kalliope could let in, beyond that Vic was probably safe temporarily — and that life was still at stake elsewhere. Events having gone the way they had, she would be needed back home in the next few hours. God knew what was going to happen with the monastery folk. And if these garrison troops got to Arkadi first, as seemed very likely, her mother would be worried sick at her absence.

Now she came to Vic, put a hand on his chest, reached up and kissed him quickly on the cheek. Then before he could reciprocate she stepped back and away from him quickly, waved at him to go, pointed out the route once more.

'Trexe. Fige, fige ...' Run. Go, go ...

She turned away from him and ran.

11
Cicada Tide

On 8 September 1941 Vic Stockton set sail from Crete. Not that he knew what the actual date was, having long since lost track. He went with thoughts of days on the river back home, fishing expeditions long gone, and was cross with himself for not having paid more attention to what he had been told about knots and winds and tides. But his father had always said he was a fidgety sort of kid, wouldn't concentrate hard enough, jumping from this to that. In honour of the old man, he had cast off thinking: *I'll listen better next time, Dad, promise ...*

Vic had left from a rocky, deserted stretch of coastline, with no witnesses to his folly but with an accompaniment of sorts: the sound of cicadas ratchetting away in the woods above. There had been a big mob of them, and he had heard them quite clearly over the small waves lapping along that pebbled shore. It was amusing to think he had beaten this latest retreat to the rhythmic clatter of a bunch of winged insects.

He had timed his departure according to a plan. Weighing the risks, he had decided to go on a warm, balmy and moonlit night. There was a chance of being spotted from upland; on the other hand, he needed to know where he was headed, more or less, as the possibilities of simply being banged back onto shore were too great. He also thought it best to wait for an outgoing tide and enough of a breeze to save rowing. Now it had become apparent the course had to be revised, the only question being the further seagoing abilities of HMAS *Gullshit*.

Back home, Vic had liked to think of himself as a resourceful sort of cove. On a building site, say, whenever there was a shortage of cross-slats for bracing at the regulation thickness of 3" x 1", he would split what lengths there were of the proper stuff into $1\frac{1}{2}$" x 1", and Bob was your uncle. Cross-bracing was never so critical in timber houses where you had good 4" x 2" hardwood framing — more something they drummed into you at Tech without allowing you to question its need. A lot of that went on in life, he had long ago concluded.

He had had plenty of time to ponder what corners might be cut — or whether there were any corners to cut at all — in the lead-up to this voyage. Of the two weeks since the disaster at the monastery, he had spent the first wandering along the coast well to the east of Sfakia, along numerous stretches of shore and little headlands whose names he didn't know and was not prepared to seek habitations or contact to discover. He had caught the odd fish, slept rough, drunk rain and stream water; might have been an idyll, too, if not for his living in dread of capture or worse. But the adventure had had the marvellous effect of concentrating his imagination on just what might be done. And so he'd gone ahead and done it.

Found the bare hull of an abandoned and holey fishing boat beached on a low and rocky spit, something like a breakwater, at the head of a small bay. (A boat with some discarded fishing line tangled in a corner as a bonus.) Got hold of a length of tamarisk branch from a dead tree and fashioned it into a mast using his penknife. Raided an abandoned mill for grain sacks, which he tied together into a rough triangular sail using thread from some of the sacks themselves. Collected a supply of drinking water in a four-gallon olive tin, and three containers of chocolate found washed up on a beach (grim reminder of how many Allied boats had gone down in these seas).

As a last preparation Vic scouted the shoreline for bait, which he found in the form of a couple of not-too-long-dead seabirds — and which he assumed he could preserve well enough by dragging through the water as he went. And then, checking one last time the holes that he had filled in the bottom with lumps of matted seagrass tied around timber plugs (the seagrass would swell and tighten into the spaces, he figured, and rightly so), he launched said *Gullshit* with himself as captain and commander into the briny deep.

Ahead of setting sail, his confidence had grown daily as the plans and possibilities began to multiply in his head. His first thought was to hug the coast, to see whether there were any other lost souls he might shanghai for crew and who could help search for a more serious means of exit. Another plan, with or without companions, was to simply head due south and, assuming luck was his lady, and with a bit of celestial navigation, eventually just bump into Egypt.

After three days at sea working east along the coast, and not having spotted a single other human being on shoreline or on water — he discounted the villain (he hoped German) who had decided to fire on him as he sailed past Aghia Galini — Vic took a bearing from the sun and trimmed sail to attempt the long trip. The biblical trip, had he any animals two by two. Or the journey of Jason, but for want of a few Argonauts. No other choice made sense, indeed no other choice presented itself at all. Not now.

Not since he had concluded he was a madman and thus obliged to take the madman's course.

At night Vic was able to take his direction from the North Star — pity that this time there was no Stan to share the knowledge with. During the day, for determining south, he used the shadow cast by a thin strip of metal cut from one side of a chocolate tin and impaled in a plank. (He hoped the day would come when he could thank his old scoutmaster directly for whatever skills he'd been able to recall to far.) This he continued to do for a further four days and nights, which was as long as the weather held. Beginning on the fifth day the wind blew harder, seeming to come from all directions at once. Later in the day, it settled into a northerly gale.

The job then was to hang on: to the mast, such as it was; to the sail, which he had reduced to half its area so as not to be completely blown over; to the gunwales as the waves lifted and lowered his little fourteen-foot tub, end to end. And above all, to the tiller.

This windstorm pushed Vic to the outer limits. He endured a heavy battering and was bruised on arms and legs as he struggled to keep his hold on the tiller. But he kept it and once there were blue skies and a bearing established, he was heading south again. When the wind died down, Vic opened and ate his remaining two chocolate bars — with the greatest relief and all at once. It was not a sensible thing to do, he knew, but at that moment he could not restrain himself. The chocolate did nothing, however, for the pain he was feeling — his knee had begun to swell and was throbbing intolerably.

Vic then inspected the boat for damage and saw that it had taken a blow or two itself. The three plugs in the bottom had been jolted so often that they were now less than watertight. As the only means of baling was the drinking water tin, there was a very real problem approaching. By Vic's reckoning he had been earlier averaging two or three knots an hour; not exactly blue-water racing standard but good enough to get him the three hundred and fifty or so miles to North Africa inside the ten days of his original calculation. Allowing for the variations — a day of very high winds, a day of being to all intents and purposes becalmed, and the regular breezes in between — that still held.

Vic used his boots to bale water, cut small sections of the sail with his knife for extra plugging, and somehow the boat stayed together through the next days. Its condition even receded a little as the most serious of his problems. With each passing day he was becoming convinced he would not reach the sanctuary he had hoped for, unless his intention had been to wind up in heaven or hell. He began to curse himself for his stupidity. Where in Christ had he thought he was headed, really? What madness had led him to think he could get a tiny boat across hundreds of miles of open water?

After ten days Vic was so hungry he was hardly aware of his pain and could think of little else but food. For some reason fish had become less plentiful the further south he went. He had put out a line the past three days with no luck. The dead bird bait no longer held any attraction for anything at all below the surface. To think he had found it a bit hard at first to cut slices of fish and shove it raw into his mouth … Now he would have no qualms about chewing the sides of the boat itself, or the miserable thing that passed for a sail, if there was any sustenance in them. But with the last attempt of the day to catch something turning into another failure, Vic thanked whoever or whatever that he still had a couple of litres of drinking water left.

*   *   *

On the morning of day eleven, Vic thought he could see the haze of land out on the horizon. If the abbot had put in a good word for him with the bloke upstairs, the old bastard was probably still asleep. It was too late. The boat now began to do in earnest what it had been threatening to do for the past day or so. In a choppy sea, it was starting to come apart. At around midday, a small wave lifted then dropped the bow and that was it: two hull planks split away and the boat began to sink beneath him. Vic jumped over the side and onto a gunwale for the time it took before the boat sank completely. He trod water and contemplated his chances, the one thing he had become very practised at. There was nothing for it but to start swimming.

To conserve what little energy he had, he lay into a side-stroke, making it as steady and slow as he could. Still, it was a good five or six miles to shore. As for the dangers, the thought of being eaten by sharks entered his head as he stroked, as did the idea he might be taken by a giant squid, or even strafed to death by a passing Stuka. Eventually his delirium and fear became so consuming he began to think this was somehow very funny. A cartoon perhaps. *That's it*, he told himself, *I'm living a cartoon rather than a man's life, rather than the life of a living, breathing human being*. An idea he somehow found sustaining.

Vic made landfall in Egypt. His head barely functioning, he was yet capable of feeling amazed. That he was still alive. That he could move at all. He staggered ashore, falling onto a strip of beach backed by sand dunes. On hands and knees and with enormous effort, he dragged himself forward. But it was too much: he soon stopped and forced himself to sit upright, instead of toppling on his face as his body insisted it would have preferred.

His mouth was parched. He noticed for the first time how raw his skin was and how every part of him ached. After a time, something like normal breathing came back to him and he discovered enough energy to stand up again and even begin walking. He would walk along the beach. After all, he was still inhabiting some fantastic comic strip and you never knew where things might lead.

They led right into the path of two fellows in British uniform manning an RAF listening post at the next headland. *Stanley finding Livingstone has nothing on this*, was Vic Stockton's last thought when he fell in a heap at their feet. Saints that they were, they picked him up and dumped him in the back of their jeep. They gave him water, he revived a little. 'You're going to Alexandria, lucky man,' he heard one of them say.

Vic Stockton woke up feeling most peculiar. He did not know that he was in a hospital bed and that an entire twenty-four hours had passed since his two British saviours had brought him in. Groggy, he tried to remember whether the brickie was due on site today or whether he had even called him at all, but couldn't. He gazed down at the clean linen and the pillowcases, unable to make any sense of them. Did they own striped sheets? His mother must have bought these only very recently, must have come into his room and changed everything while he'd been out working today on that pair of semis they were putting up at Flemington. Satisfied with that, he rolled over and went back to sleep.

12
An Artful Love

The stranded *Englezoi*, counting Aussies and Kiwis as well as British, were all gone within a few months. There were rumours of submarines, of fishing boats, even of British destroyers calling at night and removing the scattered remnants of the defence of Crete, the hundreds of men who had neither been caught by the Germans nor shipped out in the first days after the defeat and who had gone into hiding. The rumours were true and false.

By early October of 1941, it was as if they had never been there at all, so little trace of them was left. The village of Arkadi had only ever had responsibility for that one soldier, but sometimes when locals left to go on errands to places further afield, or found themselves trekking along less common paths in distant places, they would come across another stray or two. *Barba* Yorgos himself, on a visit to his brother in a village in the Amari valley, had once practically bumped into a British soldier, bold as you like, taking a shit off the side of a track. Smiling at each other, they had gone about their business. They may as well have been, as Yorgos was wont to say, creatures from another planet, those redheaded and blond and blue-eyed and often tall types. Simulacra from space perhaps, aliens who had been sent to this island for some contest organised by the gods.

But these aliens had allied themselves to an earthly cause, even if sadly in the end they had been unable to prevail. And about them, people over the whole of Crete, this part especially, shared a view: they had done their best, they had died in their thousands and would be loved by true Greeks as just men — and men they were, not boys — for as long as there was memory.

During this time the head of Kalliope's group agreed she could safely tell her family about her activities so far. Kalliope had become very tired of explaining her regular visits to Andreas' shop as going down to the church to see if any help was needed, or her twice weekly journeys to the soldier's hut as walks to the monastery for some exercise. Her contribution was bound to take new forms in the months ahead; further absences would require yet more lies.

'If your uncle acts up, let me know,' their leader had said. 'I don't expect so as, with respect, your Mattheos is better known for his bark than his bite — he will stay quiet, unless I'm seriously misguided.' Kalliope could only support this assessment.

When she did finally tell her mother and uncle, Kalliope was agreeably surprised that there were no hysterics. Her mother had only sat down abruptly at the table, stunned and open-mouthed. Her uncle had immediately set to pursing his lips and nodding wisely — as if he had known all along, as if he was in some way the architect of these good works and, more than that, as if he was somehow responsible for everything good she had ever done.

Kalliope was meanwhile still trying to come to terms with the departure of 'her soldier' as she called him. The resistance was lying low these days, new strategies as to what they should do next were being discussed in other parts of the island. This meant that she, with other low-level operatives in the area, had no immediate duties. Dwelling on the events that had passed, the one thing she returned to more than once, and would kick herself for, was that she had never got an address from the man. But could she assume that he would live out the war, let alone get back to his home? The chances seemed remote.

For those left behind, in and around Arkadi, there was a further reality: living with and dealing with their occupiers. Thankfully, after the raid on the monastery, there was not much troop activity and little violence either. As far as the Germans were concerned, they had crushed the main threat of resistance, the monastery, and more force was unlikely to be needed.

Arkadi had seen its numbers swollen, not just by the monks from Kastelli, but by a few other strays. The monks were kept under guard in the olive oil plant until the Germans seemed to decide that, except for the abbot who was to be imprisoned in an old chicken shed at the back of Corporal Thanassis' courtyard — the *horofilaka's* rural gaol — they had been neutralised and terrorised enough to be let go. Once freed, they were boarded out with various families. Their presence had not made much difference to anyone — used to eating little, demanding little, they were no great imposition. Their constant praying and murmuring was perhaps the only irritation they brought with them.

Captain Marius' contingent, the small number of Germans in charge of Arkadi, seemed very settled. Maintaining their headquarters in the one-time mayor's office and keeping generally to their barracks in the church hall they had little to do with anyone, except for that infamous informer and traitor Corporal Thanassis. Twice a day they would march through the village in formation, then back to their barracks, such as these were. They were well supplied with food and other materials courtesy of their own supply line and what they had sequestered from the inhabitants. So comfortable did they appear to Kalliope that she sometimes wondered if the worst might eventuate and they would stay here forever. But one morning in late October she saw them load up their lorry and make troop and disappear. There was hardly any time for rejoicing, however, as that same afternoon saw another force arrive, of 'macaroni boys' as they were instantly labelled at the *kafeneion*. They were Italian *paesani* and *campagni* from God knew what misbegotten parts of their own abandoned country.

Sorry excuses for soldiers they were, too. Their officer made a figure of sorts in his tunic and jaunty cap and well-knotted necktie but the rest were poorly dressed, unshaven and gave every indication they would rather be anywhere else than here. Could it have been that this part of Crete reminded them too much of some of the places they themselves had left behind? Their demeanour changed little over time; they always looked both confused and furtive. And, unlike the straight-backed, firm-jawed Germans, they did not appear to all be cut from the same cloth but came in all shapes and sizes. They were clearly discards of one sort or another.

It did not take long for the Arkadiotes to understand that, among these newcomers, the common plan was every man for himself. Their leader, Lieutenant Bruno Rossi, had a devil of a time trying to impose order on the fifteen ragtag recruits he had been assigned with which to control this and adjoining villages. Rossi's own puffing and blowing around them suggested that he had little regard for these so-called countrymen of his.

But Rossi was not stupid. In no time at all he succeeded in palming off his strays on detachment to various farmers around the place. If there was little for them to do in the military line, they might as well be put to use helping with whatever else needed to be done, olive cropping or vintnering or growing vegetables. Why not? These men came from rural parts of Italy, Sicily and Calabria. His troop might not have known the difference between a Mauser and a Lee Enfield (except at the business end) but they could surely tell the difference between a grape and an olive. Rossi would probably thus endure fewer complaints from them about lack of food, acknowledging that his crowd were generally less well supplied than the departed Germans.

Having his soldiers off his hands for long periods freed up Rossi for more civilised pursuits. He was keen on history; he also like to draw and sketch. Photography, too was a strong interest; first noted, as many things first were, by the loafers and wits Kostas and Aris, in their capacities as habitués of *Barba* Yorgos' *kafeneion*. With plenty of time available for the art of casual observation, they were there when Rossi went past one morning with a tripod, a large box camera and a small stepladder. They watched as he set up his gear near the old Turkish quarter, where he proceeded to train his camera on something that seemed of special interest to him. As far as they could tell he intended to take a picture of the ancient arch that led into that tiny, cramped and long-abandoned area.

As they watched, *Barba* Yorgos joined them at their table and exclaimed, 'Look at that fool. If anything were to be gained I could sneak up and take his pistol and pop him off right there … that'd be a picture worth taking!'

As time passed and the good lieutenant became more comfortable with these easy-going Cretans, he showed a few of his photos to those friendly boys at Yorgos' cafe. Knowing that such simple folk would probably have very little interest in some of his more avant-garde exercises, he thought to break the ice with a few of his family photos. These he brought along in a shoebox, an object whose appearance sparked the sort of response one could always expect from Yorgos' apprentices, Aris in particular: 'Hello, he's selling shoes now! What is it with these Ities and shoes?'

Seated at the table and supplied with a coffee by the *Barba*, Rossi began passing his pictures around — photos of his '*sorella*' sister, his '*mama*' mother, his '*nonna*' grandmother, his '*sposa*' wife, his '*ragazzo*' boy, and so on. Aris and Kostas did their bit, in turn loudly proclaiming their affirmation and appreciation. It was soon all '*bravo*' and '*bono*' and '*molto bene*' and '*bella*' and '*vera*'. But had Rossi's Greek, and his hearing, been better he might have picked up what his admiring audience was really muttering from the other side of the table. 'Did he know he was marrying an elephant at the time? … The boy is three parts chimp … Why would you waste good film on your mother-in-law?'

At Mattheos' invitation, Rossi turned up one indolent Saturday afternoon at his household with his shoebox under his arm. Invited by that cunning devil to bring along 'any photos that are important to you', and being told Mattheos would be interested in seeing some of his 'historical' work, Rossi was only too happy to spend time with Mattheos and family. It was Marika's misfortune, however, to be visiting Kalliope when Rossi arrived.

Mattheos insisted that they all gather around the table in the small main room for the viewing, urging the young women to bring coffee and sweets for this respected military gentleman. Sent to the kitchen thus, Marika and Kalliope stood quietly waiting for the coffee to boil, unable to avoid hearing Mattheos in the next room. Used to having him play lord and master, they were astonished to learn he could also turn so craven and slavish, producing an obsequiousness that was almost sickening. He was speaking in a broken Italian that made him sound like some sort of mid-Adriatic *karagiozi*, a puppet theatre clown.

Kalliope returned with the coffees, and undertook her own small rebellion by refusing to sit at the table when Rossi began to spread out his pictures.

Again the lieutenant described various members of his family, speaking carefully and slowly, directing his words to Mattheos and waiting while he translated for the others. Kalliope might not have understood the language but she did not miss the exaggerated courtliness and the sentimental note in his voice.

Marika, meanwhile, had not been quick enough to avoid sitting down and so found herself sandwiched between *Kyria* Venakis on one side and Rossi on the other, with the ugly face of Kalliope's uncle directly across from her. After a time, Rossi pointed to her and called her the '*bella signorina*'. It seemed that he had some photos of particular interest to someone as beautiful as she, and he requested permission to show them to her. Mattheos' expression as he translated this suggested there was no 'permitted' about it; Manika was being advised to be obliging.

Rossi moved his chair a little closer to Marika, who obediently began looking at some odd photos of animals behind bars in a zoo, photos of the Eiffel Tower taken from various angles, and portraits of some women, presumably Italian, frolicking on a beach. Kalliope watched her friend being her usual accommodating self, and was reassured in knowing that what Marika thought and what she said or did were often very different things. But the Italian's second looks and long stares were beginning to trouble Kalliope.

After Rossi had left, Mattheos looked as if he had just won some great victory. He straightened himself in his chair, raised his chin and said, 'There! You see? That is the only way to play these people. Excuse my language, girls, but lieutenant my arse … he is not a true lieutenant's buttonhole.'

Astounded that he should now speak like this — he might as well have just announced that Jesus Christ was discovered to be a Turk — *Kyria* Venakis said, 'But what are you saying, Mattheos? You told us he was a good fellow, or anyway not as bad as some.'

Mattheos pointed a finger skyward. 'Ah, yes! But this is my game, you see. I know how to play such as him like I know how to play backgammon …'

Not very well you mean, Kalliope would have liked to retort, but that was not her place; nor could she get a word in when Mattheos was off and away impressing himself like this. Nevertheless, intrigued, for this was the first she had heard of Mattheos' subversive plan — as far as she knew, his only orientation was that of main-chancer — she continued to listen.

'If you work a knave like him right, you never know where it might lead. There may be advantages in that for us; probably there are. I urge you girls, play along with him.'

'What kind of advantages?' Kalliope's mother asked.

'Well, for example, has he not allowed his no-good soldiers to walk from house to house and take our needs from us? From you of late, if I'm not mistaken, some of the knitting you made for sale and dresses you have sewn for others? Our fellow villagers, they too have lost various produce that is of value to them … But if we follow my plan, be his *amici*, his friends, I guarantee we will have no more trouble, and instead over time even some privileges, just you see … What is needed is to show him an artful sort of love, if you get what I mean.'

Even *Kyria* Venakis was troubled by Mattheos' purposes and felt she had to get up to clear her head. As she made to rise,

Mattheos urged her to stay seated; the points he wished to further expand and elaborate could not be hurried. And it was obvious from her puzzled expression, he said, that she wasn't quite understanding it.

Kalliope now signalled to Marika that they should clear the coffee cups and plates. Anything to get away from this nonsense. Arms laden, they left for the kitchen while Mattheos went droning on.

In the village of Arkadi, as in other villages of Crete, the meaning of inevitable was well understood. Had been for centuries, with regard to weather, crops, the making of babies, and any other natural phenomenon you cared to name. That there are certain things that always happen, must happen, was a commonplace. But the old truths were useless when it came to twentieth-century men, city men like Bruno Rossi. They were not always 'natural' in their behaviour, but driven by unnamed forces, blown here and there by their passions or passing enthusiasms. Their motives and behaviour were not always clear; nor could one always make sense of or control them through the mere application of a peasant's cunning, in the way Mattheos had proposed.

Thus had Kalliope tried to explain what she felt about Rossi when, a few days later, Marika told her the lieutenant had approached her about posing for some 'artistic' work he had in mind. In such circumstances, Kalliope said gently (knowing that this man's will would decide what happened), with a man whose inner workings were entirely foreign, and who beyond that stood as their formal enemy, no was the only possible answer. But then, as Marika reminded her, how could you say no to the enemy, the invader of your country, who controls your home and your material destiny?

'At the risk of sounding like my silly uncle,' Kalliope replied, 'maybe it can only be done "artfully"?'

'"Artfully!" But what does that mean …?'

Kalliope saw the searching look on Marika's face, and wished she could think of the right answer.

'You're right. Nothing. It means nothing …'

13

Bitter Waters

Kalliope and Marika had been entirely open with each other in the past, and there was no reason for that to change, not even when some odd Italian soldier had entered Marika's life, or at least was on the edge of it. Marika was perfectly happy to share tales from her sessions as a photographic model for Rossi, and Kalliope, like Marika, couldn't help finding some of his antics amusing. If he had come as one of the oppressors, there was still novelty in such a type — a very different idea of a photographer from the old man who took family pictures in his dusty studio in Rethymnon.

The first time Rossi took Marika on one of his expeditions, he decided that they should go to the old acropolis, that pile of ruined marble blocks on the slopes behind Arkadi. It turned out that he had spotted them on one of his own walks, nature walking being another of his many interests. In those early days, Marika's parents were still fearful of the Italian's intentions, and her father insisted on coming along. This didn't seem to bother Rossi, who loved an audience and was always pleased to show off his knowledge of the the art of photography and its associated technology. On that day, for example, he unveiled his latest acquisition, a Kodak camera that could be folded down into a small rectangular box and kept in his pocket.

But Marika's father, who was getting too old for hoofing it up the hills, had grumbled quietly all the way, not having come up this far in years and reminded of how difficult the climb was. 'You might be some kind of mountain goat, boy, but I'm not … This is murder. Marika, better you get him to shoot me now and push me over the side …'

Marika told Kalliope of that day when they had to wait at the top among the half-buried bits of foundation stone while Rossi took forever to set up his older box camera in a strong breeze. Of how he wasn't sure whether he might be better off with his new hand-held version. Of how he made her stand on a rock for the first photo, her dress blowing about while her father called out to her to keep herself decent, not knowing where to look, sorely wanting to rush up and hold a hand over Rossi's eyes.

Marika described another occasion when the lieutenant brought round to her house an entire album full of the photos he had taken of her in Mattheos' vineyard. The idea was that she should appear in the guise of some typical village maiden, look 'fetching' in a gypsy headscarf which Rossi had supplied, while removing bunches of grapes from the vines and smiling coyly and sidelong at the camera. This of Marika, who had no interest in the agricultural life or its produce, who had recently announced to her friends her intention of finding a rich banker and settling down to a life of ease in Irakleion.

She had bravely shared those photos with Kalliope. How ridiculous they were — the photos, men like Rossi — and how the two of them had laughed.

But after about a month, Rossi announced he wished to try something bolder, more daring, adding that he would explain later. And one day at his base in the *horofilakia*, the Italians' barracks, he took out of his officer's case a book of photographs to show Marika. They were of female nudes.

Marika saw what he was getting at straightaway. She was not worried about herself, she told him, but should her parents find out this would cause great trouble, a scandal, and old rituals of shame and honour would need to be enacted. Rossi didn't seem to be following her — perhaps it was his poor understanding of Greek. She took her finger and drew it across her throat, then in front of his — taking care not to touch him — while saying '*Greco, morto*' in a dark voice. She tried to explain she could help with almost any other style he might want, but not this.

When she made to leave, Rossi came around to block her path. 'Signorina, don't disappoint me, please …' he said. Then, 'Signorina, I have to insist …' She didn't know exactly what he was saying, but she knew what he meant. What could she do, she explained to Kalliope later, but play along with this?

That was as much as Kalliope was told. Marika provided no further reports about what happened after that day. But she did eventually leave an envelope of photos under Kalliope's pillow.

Here were photos of Marika naked in classical poses, but with some little inventive variations of Rossi's own, such as talcum powder to whiten her like marble, or spread-eagled on the ground, or posed as if fallen in mythological battle while someone largely out of sight, Rossi presumably, held a sword over her. Kalliope was stunned to see her friend displayed like this. For a long time she could do nothing but sit on her bed, her stomach churning.

What the photos didn't tell, and Marika had not spoken of, was the steely grip he would put on her as he marched her to some unvisited corner of the woods near Vrisses, this time without her father. Of his pushing and shoving and tugging of her should she show any hesitation in removing her clothes; the interminable time he took behind the viewfinder; the fact that he would even sometimes put his hand down his trousers and move it around in full view of her. And Marika could not tell Kalliope of the last session, where he had forced himself on her, brutalised and assaulted her, before calmly ordering her to get dressed and help him pack up for the return to Arkadi, giving her the tripod to carry as if nothing had ever happened.

Kalliope knew after the earlier, more harmless sessions that, laughter aside, Marika felt ashamed to have been used the way she had. Kalliope had tried to reassure her, telling her that Rossi was a vile, manipulative type. That Marika should not allow herself to be so troubled by the stupidity of such men, that the day would come when the war was over and they would depart and never bother them again.

But these new images, the fact they had been left for her to find, Kalliope took as more than a sign of Marika's pain — though that was bad enough. She assumed that Marika was asking for help, for her to do something. If Rossi had pushed her to such limits already, how much further was he prepared to go?

The next morning Kalliope went to see Marika but she was not home. There was no sign of her anywhere else in the village and it appeared that Rossi was not about either. Concerned for her safety, Kalliope went out to look for her. She had no clear idea of what she could do if she came across Marika compromised in the way those photos had shown — but her mere presence might, she hoped, cause the Italian to desist.

Her first thought was to head up to the same places where these most recent pictures had been taken. She had no difficulty recognising the locations in the photographs, as Rossi was inclined to include plenty of background scenery in his so-called art. There was no sign of her friend and the tormentor when she searched around some of the outlying vineyards. Nor later, when she took the donkey and climbed Gerovouno.

Then she thought she might try the area around Vrisses. This old supply of water for the area, more recently the point of rendezvous with the Australian soldier, was as it always had been, but with one difference. Unusually good early Autumn rains had fed into the long concrete cistern below the heads, and it had been full since early September. So much rain had fallen that by winter there was even an overflow. Kalliope watched those untrapped waters find a course from the cistern into a nearby rivulet, which would itself link with other waters to empty into the sea below the monastery.

She found a spot under a pine tree to one side and gazed across at the cistern. Deep and shaded as it was, the surface of the water did not reflect the blue of the sky but looked instead like some glassy, black sheet. Or it may have been that it was so dirty from the occasional fall of mud and debris from above, it reflected only its own interior. Miraculous in a way that no one had ever succumbed in the days when this water was taken for cooking and drinking, considering it was never cleaned out properly. Perhaps the various degraded spirits that dwelt within were satisfied that they had claimed their share of lives in other ways.

This was the place people came to die, those unable, for whatever reason, to go on. There had been only one such death in Kalliope's lifetime — that of Ioanna, the forsaken Ioanna, daughter of the baker and afflicted all her life with some terrible 'nervous condition' that no one could explain. Unable to swim, she had thrown herself in and ended it all here. Kalliope had been told of one other death, the postman before Iacovos, but he had been a very old man, and that had been decades ago.

A wave of blood surged in her head, began to beat in her temples. Something was wrong here — she somehow knew it. She went to the cistern, stumbling, unable to bear the thought, hoping she was wrong, tired, mistaken, wrong. She was not.

Kalliope lay herself down in the dust, her head on one side, and let out a scream. She heard it as if it had come from some wild beast and not herself. How could this have happened? Why? Why had she not got to Marika in time? She didn't know anything any more.

Kalliope cried for her dead friend, for herself, for Andreas, for everything that had befallen them all. Gradually, there were no more noises to make, and she was able to sit upright. She wiped her eyes on the sleeve of her black cardigan, useless dull thing that it was, and stared at the cuff. Her hand looked like an old woman's.

To think it had taken no more than a few weeks to come to this.

The young Georgiou boy returning to the village via this route heard Kalliope's cries. He had been out chasing hares. He came to the cistern and found her, still sitting on the ground. Looking in, he saw too what Kalliope had seen, Marika's body at the bottom of this water, as if anchored there, held somehow. Kalliope would not answer him when he spoke, but he had the presence of mind to go straight to Arkadi and seek help. Kalliope remained silent when they turned up, silent when they jumped in and retrieved Marika's body, her pockets and apron stuffed with large stones. But when they hauled her out, how she cried again over her dead friend.

Kalliope would not go back with them, insisting against all entreaties that she wanted to stay a while longer. After half an hour, an hour, she had no idea how long, she stood and went down to the edge of that tank. There, looking in, she saw the fluid surface bending lightly in the wind, lapping at the sides. She could no longer control herself, but let the tears come again. She could not, she would not stop herself grieving. This was agony, hurt of the purest kind. Marika who had been her dearest companion, her sister, who knew her better than her own mother. The selfless friend who had held her when she was alone, who had comforted her when sick.

Kalliope hit her fists against the hard sides of the cistern until they were raw and another, more manageable pain took hold. What did she care? They were good for nothing. They had created nothing. They had stopped nothing.

14
Harbour Trades

Kalliope's giving in to Marika's fate was the beginning of a giving in to much else. As the months passed, she realised she had not nearly the reserves of fight and fury left in her as she once had. There were few bright moments, barely anything to lighten the heart in the constrained and fearful place in which she lived. Kalliope continued working for the resistance, along with the other active local members. As their efforts largely consisted of helping with communications to and along the south coast, she wondered in low moments what it, if anything, it was worth. But from time to time news was heard that gave courage to go on.

Along with her comrades, Kalliope would hear of how the Cretan resistance was becoming ever more organised and efficient under the banner of the *Ethniki Organosis Kritis*, the National Organisation of Crete. Although she considered her contribution to be small, Kalliope was proud that their organisation grew stronger all the time, was becoming among the most effective in the whole of Europe. Elsewhere, and with the aid of the British Special Operations Executive, some wonderful sabotage was being achieved. The toll of Germans ambushed, kidnapped and killed grew steadily, and the fear instilled so great that the oppressors began to venture out of the big garrisons or barracks in the towns and cities of the island much more rarely. Kalliope, as did everyone else attending clandestine meetings in Andreas' old cellar, drank in such news, lived for it. And made sure it was passed around to their other compatriots. Only pity was there weren't a few more Nazi devils in their own area upon whom they might wreak serious harm.

One fine day in early April 1942, however, just as Spring began to make itself known, the Germans decided to pay another visit. The villagers of Arkadi had given them no trouble or cause to come calling, the small amount of underground activity remained undiscovered. Kalliope learned at one of her meetings, that the Germans were, however, apparently furious with their Italian colleagues, arguing that they had effectively lost control of the broader area surrounding this village, and were instead holidaying or spending too much time with the local women. Things were not going nearly as well, according to reports, as they had in the great and halcyon days of Captain Marius.

A black staff car pulled up in front of Rossi's headquarters at around 8am. Having driven all the way from their regional command at Rethymnon, a couple of grim and very senior-looking officers got out and entered the building. Immediately, Rossi appeared on the front porch and blew his whistle — usually the signal for his own dozy men to rise from their beds and present themselves for morning parade, such as it was. As usual, they turned up in ones and twos, dribbling in from this and that house, the places whence they'd been comfortably boarded for so long now, since abandoning official barracks. Watching this farce, the Germans grew ever more impatient, and tense, loud words were directed at Rossi. He, in turn, gave orders to his misbegotten recruits, orders which seemed to require them to suddenly go off in all directions with little apparent reason.

But there was. Before long they had rounded up the monks still living in and around the village. When at last assembled, they presented the saddest of sights, their poverty only too obvious in the heavily patched and cast-off clothes they wore, whatever the villagers could spare the monks to replace their worn-out garb. The monks were made to stand in line at the entrance to the *horofilakia*. The Germans appeared satisfied with this, until enquiries were made as to the location of their chief, the Abbot Nektarios. Asked first, the Italian lieutenant shrugged — he did not know his name and anyway there was no abbot that he was aware of, or none he had seen since arriving here himself. If the Germans knew of this fellow, why hadn't they told him? Marius turned on his heels and went straight to the monks in a fury. Their response was silence and surly, downcast looks.

Kalliope and everyone else in Arkadi well knew that Abbot Nektarios had escaped from the village after being caught with the others that fateful day, and was eventually spirited away by boat to Egypt. Kalliope also knew that one of their underground guerillas had been involved. She didn't know who, as it was safer that way. Nektarios was to play a continuing part in support of his beleaguered faith, not only in Rethymnon province but across the entire island, and in helping repatriate remaining Allied soldiers. Such daring, random escapes had been possible when the occupation was not complete and there was chaos and opportunity. There had been much debate at resistance meetings as to what the occupiers knew of the abbot. Nothing apparently.

But Marius was having none of this insolence. Not from the Italians or these rebellious Cretans. Under cover of presumptions about a missing and dangerous religious, as an example to the conquered, and to put some spine into these lousy leftovers of Mussolini's failed imperial adventures, the monks were without another word taken to the wall outside Aghia Sophia. There, in full view of those shocked inhabitants who had heard the commotion and begun to come out of their houses, and with the forced participation of three Italian soldiers chosen by the German officers, whose leader was required to give the order, the monks were machine-gunned to death. Kalliope, like everyone else who was indoors at the time, only knew what was happening when she heard the gunfire and exited her house. And like everyone else, she could not make her way to the scene of this crime because her path was blocked by the remaining Italians who had been posted as guards.

While Kalliope and others who had come out onto the street tried to look past the soldiers to establish for certain what had happened, some of the Arkadiote men were ordered to drag the bodies into the churchyard. Walking slowly among them, a devastated Father Constantinos could do no more than bless them in death and pray for their salvation, while weeping at the unfairness of their fate and the brutality of such monsters as had done this. After the Germans had packed up and left, a few women came in to help the priest's wife dress the bodies for burial. The people of Arkadi had not known the monks as family, but as friends: men who never did harm but who prayed much and were content to help with the work needing to be done in the fields and plots and groves around Arkadi.

Next day, the postmaster took on the task of trying to make contact with their relatives — surely they had brothers and sisters some of them, the younger possibly even mothers and fathers still? Kalliope had gone around the village with him to try to uncover names and addresses. They were not very successful. The life of the monk in many cases had required cutting himself off from a personal past and from family connections. In all, they found relatives for five only of the dead men.

As for herself, had Kalliope needed any more evidence, the events of that day provided it: there was no God, but instead a thousand devils and evil spirits. And that these had for some reason decided on a panegyric at Arkadi, Rethymnon prefecture, and were all trying to outdo each other in sallies of pain and misery. Had they been such great sinners, the people of Arkadi, that they deserved such a fate? Whatever they had or hadn't done, this evil visited upon them in the bodies and uniforms and guns and hatred of an occupying power, had brought too many deaths and too much grief.

Another two years passed, grinding years in which little changed either in the fortunes of the village as a whole or in the experience of the Arkadiotes personally. They remained under occupation — food, money, material comforts of any sort stayed scarce. Reports from elsewhere were far more disturbing than any news from hereabouts. Kalliope would hear stories of villages being burned to the ground, their entire male populations taken away and executed, of rapes and random murders, of terrible torture and cruelties of all kind. But to her relief, to the relief of all, no further acts of violence were committed upon the inhabitants of Arkadi. Perhaps their German masters had decided that, having learned a good lesson, they and the hopeless Italian troops supposedly overseeing them should be left to go about their business. As if they just didn't matter to anyone anymore. But if the Germans thought the Cretans were ciphers, ghosts, nobodies, that suited the Cretans just fine …

By early 1945 it was obvious to all but the most stubbornly belligerent, meaning the Germans, that the war was entering its final phase. Hitler no longer looked as is if he could conquer Europe; outposts such as Crete were hung onto only by fingernails, and everyone was anticipating the endgame, even while they didn't know when that might be.

15

A Promise to Keep

Andreas began to write more often to Kalliope. She had received two or three letters in each of the past couple of years, but since the beginning of 1945 they arrived at the rate of about one a month. Kalliope knew he had been in the Australian army these past few years and was sometimes not in a position to write or send letters. But she always looked forward to hearing from him, if not as anxiously as she had before the war. She was a person with experience now, she sometimes told herself; not nearly as moved or excited as the eighteen-year-old girl she had been when he left. If she had been hardened by the war and the things she had seen and done, more interested today in information and facts than romantic flourishes, she was still pleased to have affectionate communication from Andreas.

His first letters had been full of detail about the marvels and peculiarities of that strange continent Australia. He had gone to the north, as he said he would, and started work with a relative. The labouring, he wrote more than once, was hard and the climate was hot. Yet there were many distractions and entertainments by way of compensation. The animal life was like nowhere else, apparently, with many creatures unknown in Europe, let alone

Greece. There were zoos, he told her, where you could inspect the creatures up close. In one letter he began to describe what a kangaroo looked like, but then gave up in favour of including a postcard with a picture of this odd beast. People there seemed to love the beaches and the sea — Ingham, the town where he first lived and worked, had been quite close to the sea — whereas in Greece holidays for those who could afford them were usually taken in the mountains where the air was supposed to be good for you (a theory she herself wouldn't vouch for). There were many differences, but the critical one seemed to be that a young man could find work and make money.

That had been Andreas' experience, and its fruits had been felt as far away as this village. He had sent what he could as a contribution to some of the essential works and projects around Arkadi that could not be financed by local funds alone. He had, for instance, been able to help towards the cost of re-roofing the primary school, and had once paid for an entire set of readers for the senior year. He had also for a long time sent money to support his increasingly frail and incoherent mother, both when she was still in the village and after she was institutionalised in Irakleion.

Kalliope had dutifully replied to each letter Andreas wrote and made sure that everything meant for his mother was passed on. Kalliope had sent money to the institution where she had been told *Kyria* Coroneos was incarcerated. For a long time she received no reply, and had to assume that it was being used to *Kyria* Coroneos' benefit. But in April of 1945 a new bureaucrat in charge of the institution made contact with Kalliope. He informed her that there was no *Kyria* Coroneos in residence, and no record of her ever having been there; he also asked that she stop forwarding mail as they had only ever returned that to its sender. Kalliope had no idea where these letters or the money had gone, but that was the least of it.

Although she had no way of finding out what had happened to Andreas' mother after she had been taken away by the Germans, Kalliope assumed the worst. She had never trusted the occupiers — why would they have bothered with that poor old woman, who by the time they arrived was wild-eyed with madness and grief, a peasant woman in mourning black given to meaningless shouting and wailing in the street? In fact, what would have stopped them simply killing her?

Then had followed the most difficult letter she had ever written to Andreas, to tell him that his mother had tragically disappeared. He wrote back, full of grief and guilt, to say he had been a bad son, that he should never have left, and how sorry he was for everything that had happened. Kalliope tried to suggest he was punishing himself unfairly for things over which he had no control, nobody did.

More recent letters from him had told of his life and times in the army. How ironic, he once wrote, that he had escaped the uniform of the Greek private only to find himself across the world in the uniform of the Australian private. So much for escaping Hitler's wars. Still and all, he had been lucky enough in not having been sent to fight overseas, which in Australia's case included the jungles of nearby New Guinea. He had been perfectly happy to be a member of a supply unit, loading and unloading ships, labouring at railheads and munitions dumps in the west of Queensland and New South Wales, and even more grateful for what was easily the most unusual and artistic chore of all: painting camouflage colours on the sides of tents and trucks and jeeps, a job he did for many months through 1943.

The war and his enlistment had put some brake on all his endeavours and plans, even while he was still able to earn a soldier's pay. But the letter from Andreas at the war's end was different again. There was more life in it, an enthusiasm Kalliope had not detected in him for some time. He told of his belief that the defeat of the Nazis and the Japanese would lead to a great renewal across the globe — of energy, hope, of building and creating. People would feel safe to make plans again. In that vein, he said, he was anticipating some of his own. New possibilities were beginning to appear for him.

If that letter from Andreas ended on a note of optimism and renewed expectation, the one that followed, in early 1946, was on a higher plane again. 'My dearest Kalliope,' it began.

I write to you firmly and directly to the point. Many years have passed I know since I put this to you, but now I do it again with all the love that is in me for you. A love that has remained with me since the day I left our beloved Greece. As the war is over, I will soon be discharged from the army, a free man once more. And soon, newcomers will again be allowed to migrate to Australia, something that has not been possible during the last few years.

Kalliope my love, I want you to come and join me at last. I want us to marry. Please say yes. Say yes, and when the time comes you will arrive as I did by ship. You will sail through the heads of Sydney into the most glorious harbour in the world. And you will sail into my arms and into my love forever more. We are entitled, you and I, I believe, to our time of joy after all the years of savagery and misery. I have never forgotten you, and I believe you have never forgotten me. Do you remember when you came to my aid the day Yannis finally showed his evil hand to me? You were my defender then. And I want to be yours now. Of course, many matters will have to be attended to first — I know very well it is not easy to do what I'm suggesting. But it can be done where there is a will. Please say you have that will. I do. Write to me immediately.

All my love, Andreas.

Kalliope did not know whether she loved Andreas enough to do as he asked immediately and without demur. But she did know deeply that she needed to stop struggling with what had been, what was past, to give herself over to something beyond her own misery and the world she had known so far. Something of life and joy, something she might believe in. She had once wanted to say 'Yes' to him. But it had been over seven years since she had seen him last. She remembered Andreas as a good young man, loyal to his friends, energetic; she had no reason to doubt he had remained constant in his love of her, both when they were adolescents and ever since. People had always left in past eras to seek their fortunes, a better life in other countries — and from what he was saying such opportunities were soon to be at hand again in Australia. But a plan like this would need time and very great effort to realise.

For the moment she folded Andreas' letter and placed it on her knees, unwilling to put it away, enjoying the feel of the paper, the phenomenon of its existence. She let herself return to that day when Andreas had come to blows with Yannis, remembered by him so long after the event. That he had thought so well of her in a time when she believed she had only failed him — that gave her more courage and faith than he could know.

After that dreadful incident, Andreas had been all iron resolve and silences. Whenever she had suggested to him that things might turn out better were he to stay and with the passage of time, he would only say, 'This place is finished for me. And it will be soon enough for you too, I hope.'

Kalliope recalled how she had exhausted all forms of persuasion in the months before Andreas finally left. She had tried to explain that he was needed in this place and not only by his mother, that better not worse times might lie ahead and he would be in no position to experience them if he were to exile himself across the globe. But all she heard from him was that he felt shamed, cheated, even abused here and there were simply no other options left. And she had also felt deeply hurt, punished, when he said on one occasion that she too should wake up and see their reality for what it was.

Notwithstanding her efforts to get Andreas to remain among them, what she got in return, it seemed, was more confusion and a sense that, for all their youthful comings and goings, the fates were conspiring to separate her from each and everyone she cared for.

So that, when, in the early morning of that day in February of 1938 Andreas finally prepared to leave the village for the port of Piraeus, she believed her only choice was acceptance.

She recalled how they had arranged to meet a short distance outside the village on the road to Irakleion, from where Andreas would be picked up by taxi. There would be no prying eyes there at that time. Andreas had something to tell her, and had hoped, he'd said, she would have something to tell him.

She would never as long as she lived forget the sight of him standing there alone among the roadside weeds, his single suitcase strapped together and by his side. He was dressed in his only suit and wore a hat: a twenty-year-old man who looked ten years older. This was what life had done to him, to them both. She rushed to him and threw her arms around him. He took her closely to him and then there were no restraints. She kissed and kissed him, held him to her body as any woman would.

'I don't want you to go,' she said. 'This is wrong. Why go?'

'No point to go over all that now, Kalliope, believe me … The thing I want to know is, do you love me, and will you join me some day?'

She could find no words to answer him beyond 'I love you'. What else could she have said to him there and then that would have made sense? She was drowning in the surge of emotion she felt for him. It was all so desperate, his plan. And so troubling to her. It was not possible to be sure about anything. The world was crazy and unsafe.

That particular morning, only she and Marika knew where he was headed and they had vowed to him to keep their silence. As for the weather, which had thrown such a grey haze over the mountains to the east, Kalliope had reassured herself it meant nothing unusual or portentous. It always rained in winter. She could hardly believe that almost ten years had passed since that time.

The day after receiving this most recent letter from Andreas, Kalliope sat alone on the front step of her tiny house in this corner of the village. There was no one about and no activity, save for a couple of hens pecking their way past her and up the lane. Last night and this morning, she had tried to reflect calmly on all that he had written and on what she felt, as far as she could determine. She had decided. She could not put her life off forever. She would give herself over to the plan. Kalliope knew herself to be a determined person, as others did too. She had to call upon all her strength when she went to her room and sat to compose the letter she would send to Andreas. If she saw her decision as affirming a new life, which is what she knew she would need to do for it to make sense, to others it was something else. 'A matter of life and death' was how Uncle Mattheos described it when apprised of what Kalliope was up to. (For that she could thank a nosey clerk in the post office at Rethymnon who had often shared a cup of coffee and a game of backgammon with Mattheos whenever the nice old boy was in town and on business.)

Mattheos flew at Kalliope. How could she even think of such a thing, the state her mother was in? For a daughter to abandon a mother was a terrible thing. Andreas Coroneos was a ne'er do well anyway — why him of all people? Then there was what she doubtless imagined to be the insignificant issue of the money required. Where was that to come from, had she considered? Mattheos naturally omitted to refer to any needs of his own that might go unmet should his niece decamp from Arkadi for the other side of the world. Details such as his evening meal, his washing and ironing, and those very nice sweet biscuits she baked once a week and that he enjoyed with his mid-morning coffee.

In the face of such open opposition she could not for the time being do a thing. A year passed and it was 1947. Andreas' impatience grew with every letter. More strength was needed when Kalliope next made discreet enquiries at Rethymnon regarding the rules for emigration out of Greece in the coming year of 1948. And strength yet again when she found herself unable to get away either that year or most of the next. There were too few boats, difficulties with visas and other bureaucratic annoyances. In the meantime she had to endure more ugly behaviour from Mattheos. Again he threatened murder and worse, accused her of selfishness and ignorance.

It was a small mercy that her mother's disapproval was less voluble. In her usual way, she tended first to sighs and tears when confronted with this 'drastic scheme' of her daughter's, as she termed it. Then for a long time the matter was never allowed to come up between them.

It was late in 1949 when *Kyria* Venakis next got a hint that her daughter's intentions had gathered new momentum — she had found some official-looking letter with a British seal on it addressed to Kalliope. She could not let this rest.

They were together one morning in Mattheos' vineyard, tidying the vines at the end of autumn, making small piles of the clippings and cuttings. Her mother bade her leave the rest and go home early — she would finish what needed to be done. 'I'm old,' she'd said. 'Better me that gets tired than you.'

Kalliope said the remark sounded bitter and asked her what she meant. 'It's that you are planning to leave me, girl, I mean, I suppose ...'

Her mother moved closer to her as they stood among the vines, then looked up into Kalliope's eyes. 'I don't want you to go, please, you must know that. I'm not able to give you anything, I never have been able. But I have always loved you, *Kalliope mou,*' she said. 'And you are the pride of all of us. I have no education, everyone knows that. But you do, and your friends, they love you too, don't they? What does it matter if someone like me gets tired instead of you? I want you to stay with me and enjoy your youth and your beauty, and I will do the work, whatever needs to be done, believe me, Kalliope.'

Her mother looked at her imploringly and Kalliope saw that she wished to say more but couldn't find the words. This was as good as a knife plunged into her heart.

'I'll go back,' Kalliope said. She turned away and left quickly, broke into a run. On the way back to the village she felt as if she was being blown along, nothing more than a scrap, a leaf on the wind.

'What friends?' she called out to nobody in particular. 'Where are they? Who are they?' Before the war ended she knew that Manolis had died, that Yannis was for her as good as dead. As for Marika, her fate was still too hard to bear. Andreas, only Andreas was left … Others, the people she knew and moved amongst in Arkadi, had since the war ended become ever more insubstantial. Acquaintances. Fellow villagers tending their fields and sitting in their boxes at night. Faces at church. Not people she could love or care about, or who cared for her.

November 1949, and Kalliope had still to resort to various ruses, subterfuge, and what in other circumstances she would call plain dishonesty, before she could make progress in carrying out her own plan. And this amid further political troubles. On the mainland, an arm of the Greek resistance had come under the control of the communist Greek Liberation Front, EAM, and civil war had begun to rage between left and right. On Crete, where the attitude was more liberal and independent, strife had continued to grow between the old EOK — the National Organisation of Crete — and the more radical EAM. At the end of a barbaric war, after they had all endured so much, Kalliope lacked the stomach for, or even interest in, such manoeuvrings. As for many others in Arkadi, postwar politics held no interest for her, especially as it seemed to make no difference to their living conditions.

But political chaos had the effect of making her escape more precarious. Yet, as Kalliope had committed herself to getting away and had become desperate in that commitment, anything and everything had to be tried. She even had to leave in the dead of night and be transported by produce truck to Rethymnon because she couldn't afford the taxi or the possibility the driver would give her away. At Rethymnon she boarded a bus to Irakleion, seventy kilometres and more than two hours further away, and then had to wait through more night hours in a cold and miserable shed by the docks. And then to board a ferry for the mainland at 1.00am.

When she was finally on her way north, she was relieved this much had been achieved at all. To get on the ferry had taken her own effort and gumption, but she knew that the sea journey to come would not have been possible if Andreas had not secretly got a little money to her. This was done via an old acquaintance who had moved to Aghia Galini but who would occasionally pass through Arkadi on his way north.

Piraeus proved less of an ordeal than Kalliope had expected. She was able to manoeuvre her way through Customs — with a couple of hundred other young men and some women also headed for Australia — and then to board the SS *Oronsay* with relative ease. But, having made it to Aden a few days later, she hardly expected to be stranded for a full two weeks, unable to get off the boat or sail on due to an outbreak of cholera in Colombo, their next port of call. In the cramped quarters of a cabin shared with two noisy girls from Yugoslavia, and with whom no sensible communication was possible, she began to wonder whether even being imprisoned could be worse than this.

They did, however, get moving again. And in February of 1950, Kalliope found herself sailing into Sydney Harbour. Here were sights, sounds, a scent on the air like nothing she had ever known before. The ship passed through those heads and Kalliope marvelled. They were just as lovely as Andreas had said they would be.

PART TWO

16

The Lucky Bastard

Great result whichever way you looked at it, Vic thought. Washed up in Egypt, dried off, patched up, given a bit of a furlough in which to hobble around Cairo and buy a few souvenirs for those back home, then troopship back to Sydney.

A troopship that, unlike so many others, didn't get sunk either. And then, courtesy of a knee they'd told him would take a very long time to heal entirely, if ever, discharged from the army. A bloke couldn't have asked for more. When so many other fellows came home only to be sent on to other theatres, he was the lucky bastard, if ever there was one.

So Vic began life again in Australia from the old home base in the Sydney suburb of Enmore. His mum still lived in one of a pair of semis his father had built (Gran, and Pops while he was still alive, lived in the other) and where there was always plenty of room for her one and only son. Especially so since Dad had died when Vic was seventeen and his older sister Pamela had married and moved out not much later. Vic liked getting back there, in March of 1942, as much because he was back with Mum and felt safe (unless one of the local toughs, of whom there were plenty, came and cut his throat in bed). The shops along Enmore Road, the Jubilee picture palace, the Capitol milk bar, the local high school where he had done his Intermediate may not have had the same pulling power as the Parthenon or the Great Pyramids at Giza, but they would do him. A rundown joint some would say, at any rate not too flash. But a nice quiet place to collect your thoughts and work on the plan to get re-established. And that was the thing uppermost for Vic once he was out and about again.

Funny, but it wasn't as easy as he might have hoped. He knew what was required, what was best, or thought he did. But over the first three or so years, the time it took to see out the rest of the war, there were periods when he just couldn't get motivated. Worse than that really. It was an ordeal just to get out of bed and up and around. Then he would tell himself it was all just a question of attitude and he would take up this or that hobby — stamp collecting for a time, making model planes — to prove that he could master himself whenever he went 'wobbly'. The term was his mother's and she had come up with it after a particularly long stretch when he simply didn't want to leave the house, except to go to the corner shop or the nearby butcher's on an errand for her.

She had no simple explanation, however, for the most unpleasant of those episodes, the time when he hardly left his room and got angry with her whenever she said she really should call the doctor as he wasn't at all well in her view. That dreadful time when she could barely get him out of his bed to change the sheets and he was given over to crying for often what seemed like no reason at all. But if she couldn't see any sense in how he was behaving, nor could Vic. Through the entire episode, which lasted a couple of weeks, Vic felt one minute terribly lonely, the next that life just didn't make any sense — one minute you're shooting and killing men, the next you're going to the corner shop for a pint of milk and half a loaf of bread. His mother kept suggesting that she should call his friends to come and visit, as it was no good his being so on his own all the time. But Vic only grew angry again — shouting that he didn't have any real friends around here anyway, only neighbours, that his father had been his only true friend, and he was dead too — before giving way to remorse and saying sorry a thousand times over to her, and coming to tears all over again.

In the depths of this, Vic finally allowed his mother to call the doctor to see him, and Dr Finemore gave him pills to help him sleep, sleep being, in his estimation, the universal cure-all when a bloke was suffering from 'nerves'.

Vic eventually began to come round, began around midday each day to turn off the radio and drag himself out of bed to spend the afternoon in the living room or kitchen with his mother, peeling a few spuds or taking out the rubbish, making himself handy again. He tried to explain to himself what had been the matter. The fact that the building work he could do was only available in fits and starts made it that much easier to hang back, he told himself. Question of attitude. Blokes need to be fully occupied if they're going to to be of any use to anybody, specially themselves.

At later moments when Vic felt himself sinking into something like that bad low he had experienced, he would accuse himself of being lazy, tell himself to snap out of it. Then he would throw himself into one physical activity or another, to improve his character, if nothing else. During one period he went to McQuillan's boxing gym every other day to 'build up', then later proclaimed that what they needed most was their own backyard vegetable patch, whereupon he planted every square inch of the pocket handkerchief yard they had with cucumbers, tomatoes, lettuces, beans, you name it, only to let it all go to seed before the end of the summer.

Try as he might to force change, come up with something worthwhile for himself, Vic's plans didn't seem to him to amount to much. And so it continued for the next five years and more. He realised he wasn't the only one unable to gouge out sufficient space to set up his own small outpost in the shiny new world that was here already, meant to be on its way, or expected any day now. It was beyond most ordinary people in the straitened times through the end of the war and the years immediately after to achieve a better standard for themselves and, if married, their families. And governments didn't appear to be able to bring about the better times so anticipated, not even in Australia.

Vic sat at home on Saturday mornings and read in the *Sun* of shortages, of rationing still. He could testify to shortages: you were only allowed a limited amount of meat at the butcher's; and, wanting to buy a new suit, he found that the cheapest ones, those he could afford, were all made out of service material offcuts — military blues and khakis and greys. Then there were rail strikes, coal strikes; the place was still having its usual punch-ups between capital and labour, still had as a prime minister a bloke from Bathurst who had once been a train driver and who always got around looking like he was wearing a potato sack. If the prime minister himself had to dress in offcuts, then God help us all, was what Vic thought; though he set no great store in fancy clothes himself, he knew a bad suit when he saw one, and the impression it created. This, while over in Yankeeland the cars were getting bigger and skyscrapers were going up and there was talk even of using nuclear power to make electricity.

Europe, the place of so much of the action during the last stoush, had not only hit the canvas, but some places there had gone down for the count and were yet to get up again. You never heard much news from Greece but it looked like the commies were going to take over in that country, as they had done elsewhere. An iron curtain all right, right across Europe — the price paid for the Russians having been on 'our' side, Vic supposed. At least that was there and not here, although the Reds were playing up a bit in Australia, too. Here for Vic it was more a case of making do, picking up bits of work, odd jobs for this one and that one until the blessed 'postwar reconstruction', that everyone was always promising got seriously under way.

If he was inclined to the occasional bout of grumbling, there was always a corrective available. He only had to think how some blokes had never made it home at all to be reassured that what he did have — his life — was a very great bonus. Plenty of boys had fallen; some unknown to him he had seen die himself, the fate of others he had learned only much later. To this day, and whenever he would allow his mind to stray there — which was not very often, as it troubled him to weigh up his own part in what had transpired — he presumed that one of his own mates, Stan Weller, had been among those who never made it. Cold hard facts like these helped Vic to keep things in perspective.

By the late forties, there were still days when Vic's thoughts would fly back to the war, when he would feel desperately sad about what it had done to young blokes, to everyone really. He had joined a sub-branch of the RSL and begun to go along to meetings in a local hall: but it was one thing to hear of those incapacitated soldiers who, with their families, were doing it tough, or to learn of the plans to try to raise money to do something about it all; the talk of what they were due, however, what the politicians should do for them, what the nation owed, just made him all the sadder.

Vic let his membership lapse after a couple of years, and made it a policy to avoid the formal celebrations on Anzac Day. But he had also made it a point of going down the local to have a few beers on 25 April. There was honour in it somehow, to sit with the other ex-soldiers and shed a quiet tear or two. He would turn up religiously, though with some apprehension as well. The day inevitably wound up with him coming home half-drunk, his head a chaos of flashes from North Africa and Greece and Crete, his guts telling him he might not have done all he should have over there.

It had taken longer than anyone had imagined, or promised, but it happened. Australia was on the up and up. The second half of the century had arrived, progress was in the air. Larger building companies became more common. These put forward bold schemes and ideas for big estates, meaning there was much more work than the small stuff Vic had been used to; they were putting men on and, for a change, keeping them on.

Prestige Homes gave Vic his first solid start after the war; he was signed on by the big boss himself, J.V. Alderton, in April 1950 after applying for a job advertised in the paper. Prestige was headquartered out west, in Parramatta, in nice new modern-looking offices. A mix of sharp curves and long straights, the building always reminded Vic of the funnels and lines of a ship. Only later did he appreciate that there was some architectural story behind it.

Alderton was a character, a little, round chap in a three-piece suit, who looked like a gangster from the movies, maybe Edward G. Robinson. But Vic liked him, and the old boy (he couldn't have been more than fifty but looked older) liked him in turn. He paid what he said he would and he never, to Vic's knowledge, ever shouted at anyone. The only problem with the job, he thought, was the travelling. All right once you got to Parramatta because there you had access to the company vehicles for getting out and about to the various jobs — but the train travel to and from was a bugbear, what with getting up at 5.30am to walk to the station for a 6.15 on the western line, and the whole rigmarole all over again to come home.

Vic worked on himself after getting the Prestige position. He had to stay straight, he knew, to keep a job such as this, so he cut back on the grog and 'kept himself tidy', as his mother always wished. He turned up on time, took his responsibilities seriously. Within two years Vic was considered supervisor material, and he was to be given charge of some quite large projects. Among the early tasks in his new management role was the organisation, including the quantity surveying and site management, of a couple of estates at Penrith and St Marys. He was not much over thirty years of age but had been given, and was seen to be able to handle, a lot of responsibility — not to mention the trouble that went with it. And there was always plenty of trouble.

The thing that went wrong most often on building sites, Vic was happy to tell anyone who would listen, was people. You could rely on a hammer staying true to itself and not breaking (actually, they did break sometimes, but rarely if the thing was made of Sheffield steel, and the best ones were), but you couldn't always rely on men staying true. Some came with fine cracks in them that you didn't see at first but which showed up under pressure. Others came to you whistling one tune, mostly a pretty nice one about what they had done, what they could do, etc, but soon dropped it for some nastier number — usually 'Prestige was a bastard' or variation thereof. But the worst thing was conflict between men. Then, inevitably you would find yourself reaching for that handy phrase 'on for one and all'.

He encountered his nastiest complication on a relatively small job late in 1954. It started out with a bloke, an old German chap by the name of Siegfried Muntz, who'd been running chicken farms out at Leppington for donkey's years and who wanted to subdivide some of his spare land for an estate. Prestige had come in on the deal, but only for the building work, and Vic had control of that side of things. First, foundations were to be dug so that the job could start in earnest. Vic had assembled a team in the usual way, a site foreman in charge of a team of labourers, the latter a new bunch not long off the boat, mostly Poles, with a couple of Latvians and Lithuanians.

Later Vic blamed himself for not thinking far enough ahead and on a sufficient number of fronts. It was not a happy accident, for instance, that the old boy's own home was very much part of the property, was sited in the back corner of the four-acre lot given over to the new houses. The fellow was just around too much, another no-no. Had he not been on site nothing would have happened.

On day one of excavations, Muntz decided to come over. Vic was on site to do the handover to one of his experienced foremen when this sixty-something-year-old marched over to them with a grin on his face, and in a heavy German accent bid them 'Guten Tag'. Those poor migrant bastards who had been picked up for a few days' labouring might not have known much, but there was no question they knew German when they heard it.

Vic registered the looks exchanged between a couple of the Poles. Then another worker began to speak to them in low tones. Vic wasn't able to pick up everything that passed between them — the details only came out during the court case — but he could tell straight off that they were not happy.

Vic knew there was no love lost between German and Pole, but the words that were then hurled at Herr Muntz by one of the Poles, who for his sins knew a fair bit of German, were clearly over the top. He said he hadn't known he would be working for some

Nazi cunt, who for all he knew was responsible for the murder of his own family. If he had, he never would have bothered turning up. And what kind of a country was it that would not only let Nazis in but would let them buy up the land as well?

Muntz was outraged; he had been living in Australia since the early 1920s and had no connections with modern Germany at all. He tried to explain and defend himself, in the face of a loud and aggressive worker and a couple of cheerers on the sideline. Vic and his foreman tried hard to calm things down, but were facing the wrong way when Muntz suddenly leaned forward, picked up a mattock and swung wildly at the head of the offending Pole. Muntz was a thin and wiry type, fit from years of farm work, and unfortunately he connected. The Pole took a glancing blow to the side of the head and was knocked unconscious.

Not even Muntz could believe what he had done. He was so horror-struck that he immediately rushed over to try to help. But his presence only made things worse; Vic and his foreman had a devil of a time trying to stop some of the others from attacking Muntz, calming everyone down, calling an ambulance, the police and head office. The Pole finished up in hospital with a deep cut across his scalp and a dose of concussion. There were charges of aggravated assault and Vic had to spend three days in court. The German was put on a good behaviour bond, but to the company's dismay he pulled out of the development. If *they* were the kind of men Prestige used, Muntz said, he would have nothing to do with the company; he would take his business elsewhere.

That was blokes for you, Vic would often say. Never discount wounded pride — it often hurt more than losing your money. And if there was enough wounded pride about, and it was allowed to get together in a mob, trouble was never too far off. What probably worried him more, though, was how much show and ritual there was in what men did; an idea he'd first formed during the war watching drill sergeants and parade ground nonsense but had found reinforced on the home front ever since. An awful lot of grandstanding went on in life, and the grandstanders were sometimes not even aware that's what they were doing. Putting on a performance, playing a part. But not very well at that — not when you could see right through the act.

Whether it was the strain of those events or something else, Vic felt very bad for a couple of weeks after the court case. One Friday evening, he came in to the city on the western line as usual, but then continued on to Central instead of getting off at Enmore. There, he crossed over to a south-bound platform and caught a train to Cronulla. At Cronulla he phoned his mother to say he wasn't coming home, but not to worry as everything was all right, and that he would see her on Monday. Then he took a room in one of the two pubs near the beach and went out and bought a newspaper and magazines, a puzzle book, and half a dozen bottles of Dinner Ale from the front bar of the pub. With these supplies he returned to the room to do nothing for the next two days.

Vic had got out of bed at home that morning with a strong feeling that everything was most fragile. A feeling that, as during the war, he was in someone's gunsights; not a real threat but some dread you couldn't put a name to.

Once he was outside the house, his nerves just wouldn't settle. The birds seemed louder than usual, as did the noise on the street. He kept noticing some foul smell in the air. On the way to the station to catch the train to work, he had felt like telling everyone and everything to shut up. The train trip to Parramatta hadn't helped his mood: he kept noticing some old codger in an overcoat who kept staring at the calves of a young office girl. He had actually called out, 'Stop staring at her, you silly old coot,' embarrassing himself and everyone else in the process. The girl had blushed, apparently angrier at Vic than at the thought she was being perved at. The bloke himself had given Vic only a hard stare back and turned to look out a window instead.

Since arriving here, he had slept, done crossword puzzles when he was sober, stared out the window for a while, gone to bed both afternoons. All in a pleasant enough location — there was a window that looked out across some parkland over the road, grassy slopes that reached down towards the beach. It occurred to him that the only other time he had been cooped up in four walls for hours alone with nothing to do but gaze at a scenic downhill view towards water was on Crete. Only thing that was missing was a lovely maiden to look after him.

For a long time after he'd had that thought, he continued to sail back to those days and recollections of Kalliope. But it made him feel even odder, as if he was missing her and that place, when he wasn't — he had hardly thought about her or that time for years. He reassured himself that he was far better off in Australia; no bastard was trying to murder or imprison him, even if he did sometimes become very anxious.

Nuts or sane, he had certainly not been able to sort things out, think things through, as he had told himself he would on the train here. Each attempt he had made to imagine some other life for himself, something more than he had managed so far in the years since the war, came to nought. He had been too easily deflected. His head didn't appear to be up to the job.

On this Monday morning, three days later, he sure as hell didn't feel normal. He had a headache from last night's drinking — he also felt sick, had not shaved or eaten or even left his room since the previous morning. He shouldn't make too much of it, he told himself — he had passed the time, filled these two days adrift in a strange room, that was all. The one time he had gone for food, he went downstairs and had a pie in the dining room. Again, normal enough. He was not going nutty; he didn't feel anything like he'd felt in that period when he was supposed to have been suffering from 'nerves'.

Vic undressed to stagger to the shower. He had been wearing his work shirt and trousers for pyjamas this last night when it had been cooler. Dressing again, he pulled on his blue sports jacket and grey slacks, now stained and creased. One last time he went over how rattled he had felt and was still at a loss. The way he had reacted on the morning train — out of all proportion as his outburst might have been — didn't mean much. But the practicalities of getting back into the city and off to work were enough to divert him from any further soul-searching.

Vic tidied himself up as best he could and, convinced he didn't look too bad really, came downstairs to pay his bill to the suspicious woman at the pub office. He left and walked up the road back to the station to wait. What he was going to say to his mother was the looming problem. When he'd called her she had tried to quiz him as to what he was doing, but he had cut her short. She would almost certainly have been concerned about him in the meantime. He would have to go to work this morning as if nothing had happened, but at day's end she would want him to say something. And he did owe it to her.

Vic tried some words as he stood at the station staring down the empty tracks in the direction of Sydney: *Just a chance to clear my head, Mum. Bit of a break in the routine, you know? Sometimes a chap's just got to give himself some thinking time ... Sorry if you were worried, but I'm a big boy, aren't I ...?* It all sounded so lame. Truth was he didn't know what to say, or how to properly explain this disappearance of his.

17
Home Fires

Coming out of a low period, Vic found the passage of time usually had a healing effect. A few days after his 'off' weekend, he was already starting to feel that he was getting back on an even keel. As he also believed in the value of a good pep talk, he made sure he gave himself one of these too. Thing was to drop negative thoughts as soon as they entered your head, not keep chewing over things you couldn't fix or change. But getting a grip again was, as usual, accelerated by a new diversion — on this occasion he took up dancing.

Vic explained to his mother that he had decided to take a few lessons as a way of helping strengthen his bad left knee, which still troubled him whenever he clambered around building sites. But the benefits were more diverse. His confidence grew, and he enjoyed the rhythmic movement so much that he took it further and began to venture out to 50/50 dance nights at the Trocadero. And an incidental but welcome result was that he was also assured of female company on Friday and Saturday nights. The Troc in the city was a great place to meet girls, and meet them he did. Not only could they be great fun on a night out, Vic discovered, girls were sometimes a wonderful lift to the spirit when you were down.

Vic had some joy on the female front, he couldn't deny that. And why not? He had a good and steady job these days, he wasn't an ugly chap, and now he could dance as well. But fun was only fun, and you had to take on some responsibility in life if you knew what was good for you. With his mother getting on in years and urging him to consider his future, he became more attentive to the company he was keeping, and started to evaluate each woman he met as a potential life partner. One young woman in particular caught his eye: Joan Lawford, the daughter of their local newsagent, Bill Lawford. She was a girl with a good sense of humour and, happily, she too was keen on dancing. There were more glamorous specimens than Joan around, granted. One particular knockout, a willowy blonde by the name of Sally Fawcett, worked as secretary to his boss J.V.; he had gone out with her quite a bit in recent months before turning his attentions to Joan. He had even toyed with the idea of steering their affair into something more serious, but stopped before they had marked off two months together.

Not that Sally ever suggested she wanted anything more than a good time. He would have happily admitted — in male company, that is — that Sally was hot stuff. Not at all shy, you might say. But something about her always left him thinking that she wasn't a stayer. His parents' own good and long relationship had taught him the importance of that tenet: marriage was for stayers, not sprinters, and being constant was the 'only recipe for happiness', as his mum had said more than once. He thought that with the right sort of training and encouragement, he would be content to saddle up as the former, rather than the latter. Anyway, at thirty-five years of age and keen not to be a kid any more, he proposed to Joan and was accepted.

Joan had her own view on this fellow who had blown into her life, and she liked what she saw. He had arrived with guns blazing, bailing her up one day in her father's newsagency with a cheeky grin and some idle chatter, which had been entirely beside the point. He had urged her to go dancing with him, and when she did, she saw that he was a natural, stepping and turning with a relish that was rare in men, in her limited experience at any rate. Vic seemed to be energetic and have plenty of ideas; working in the building game seemed to have encouraged his thinking on all sorts of possible schemes. She did like energy in a man — too many of the blokes around seemed to be half-asleep, or doing nothing, or wasting their lives down the pub.

As she began to trust Vic and become very fond of him, Joan began to imagine an appealing future. She tried to think about her own wants and needs and believed that Vic, big-hearted puppy that he was, would be the kind of husband who would let her fulfil them. She had spent her whole life buffeted by the noise and wind generated by her two younger brothers. She was ready to be more than 'big sis'. No more trailing after their footy teams, or being ignored when the boys came home each night to monopolise their parents' attention with talk of their various exploits and triumphs and tragedies, or even being told what time she had to come home from the Saturday flicks, for God's sake, so that their blessed dinner wouldn't grow cold.

Marriage to Vic meant the chance for Joan to have her own life. He needed a bit of retraining, perhaps. Males didn't seem to have a clue around the house for one thing. But that would not be impossible, not if he really loved her, and he said he did. She would help him sort some of his less practical notions. The fact that he was inclined to bend her ear about particular ideas that had occurred to him, did worry her somewhat. In the months after their engagement he had spent an inordinate amount of time on one possible project: buying a caravan park down the coast as a business, or setting up one somewhere, as he figured car and caravan holidays were going to become very popular and wouldn't it be great to get in at the beginning. They could put a manager in and even reserve a caravan for themselves to get away to occasionally.

Joan kept her counsel for a time, but finished up telling Vic that his caravan plan wasn't worth pursuing for lots of reasons. Petrol was too expensive for one, and she didn't think wives would buy the idea of carting the kids and everything else a hundred miles away just so they could cook and clean and wash somewhere by the sea … He had taken some convincing, but she was relieved when she was finally able to turn him round.

If Joan had an inkling that some of her future husband's schemes would definitely need knocking on the head from time to time, she also took heart that Vic listened to her when she questioned something, or pointed out that it would require money which they didn't actually have and were in no position to borrow, even if there was any sense in whatever it was he was proposing. Vic's shortcomings aside — and these did not seem critical — she was ready to take a chance with him.

He may have been a lucky bastard to survive the war, but Vic Stockton thought of himself as an even luckier bastard to be getting married in 1954 to a terrific girl who was pretty keen on him and who was looking forward to settling down and raising his kids. Both nominally C of E, they got married at St Stephens, Camperdown, a nice old Gothic-style dump not three miles from the GPO. It was a wedding with all the trimmings, including a proper reception at the Albert Palais. The venue was on Parramatta Road, heading west, and close enough that people did not have to travel far. That was a good choice for the pair of dancers that they were, what with its proper sprung floor and room for sixty couples at a time if required. They had made quite a few friends, both at the Troc and in local Saturday night dancing, over the past year, and it was a delight to be able to watch their mates go through their paces on the night.

The question of where to live had come up, although Vic hadn't given it much thought. Content as he'd been to move in with his mother, he had assumed that his bride would be all right if they continued living next door. He was somewhat disappointed to discover that Joanie wasn't entirely enamoured of the idea. She had suggested they might want a 'fresh start' somewhere else, maybe in one of the newer areas where they could have a bit more space, for instance. When he pressed her on it, she told him she was interested in somewhere to the south, the flash new suburbs like Sylvania or Oatley or Jannali, where there were some very nice and affordable houses going up. This hung about as something of an issue, but the only one of any substance, as Vic reassured himself, in the early months of their marriage.

And, if Joan didn't want to continue living next to her mother-in-law in an admittedly small house in the old inner city, well, Vic could see she was entitled to her point of view. If it came down to it, he wouldn't have minded a bit more space himself. Finally they decided somewhere near Vic's work would be best — where there were also plenty of newish houses on good quarter-acre blocks to be had.

Thus, in the second half of 1955, Vic and Joan left behind their respective childhood terrains and homes to move into a new brick veneer, three-bedroom house in Wyatt Street, Toongabbie. None of their parents were entirely in support; Joan's couldn't see the sense in going so far out and Mrs Stockton was too old to cope with any sort of change. Vic left her on the basis that, were she to become too ill or old to look after herself, she would come and live with them. This was necessary as his sister Pamela had long ago moved to Queensland with her husband and family and was in no position to help. Joan agreed, so long as the same held for her parents too.

No one need have worried, for Olive Stockton passed away not six weeks after the move. She died on a Saturday afternoon sometime after the first race at Rosehill and before the sixth; one of the local SP's runners came in, as he usually did on Saturdays, to see if she wanted to place a bet and found her slumped at the table with the radio on 2KY in the background and with a form guide in front of her.

Vic felt a little guilty about what had happened to his mother. He allowed it to niggle at him that he had perhaps not done exactly the right thing, leaving her on her own to fend for herself. He was also a little annoyed that Joan offered no opinion one way or the other regarding the wisdom of leaving her back there at Enmore, but then she had hardly expressed any sorrow at all that her mother-in-law had died.

This was to eat away at Vic for some time. Joan had her own reason and later was sorry she had not articulated them. One afternoon in the week before the wedding, Mrs Stockton had cornered Joan in her kitchen and told her that modern young women 'weren't worth a bumper', and that Mrs Stockton sincerely hoped she wasn't one of those, although the signs weren't good. She had added that her son was a 'sensitive boy' who had suffered 'more than most' during the war and he needed to be treated properly. She also stated in no uncertain terms that not having babies 'when and how God intended' was modern folly, and that 'young Joan' would be better off not playing any games in that department. But instead of telling Vic she had been abused by his sainted mother, ironically enough to spare his feelings, Joan had stayed quiet.

Joan saw Vic upset for a number of weeks after his mother died, and as a reaction to her death or because it was his nature to hare off down this or that path, she was none too pleased when he revived his caravan park idea. He did ask if she wanted to go with him on research expeditions, but she resisted. If he wanted to go tearing up and down the coast looking for a potential site or existing caravan park, he could do that by himself and consider it his own adventure. She was of more use keeping the new house going, especially as she was busy sewing curtains and edging tablecloths.

Vic reasoned that while you had to salt something away early, life was short and you also needed to enjoy it while you could. 'This way, what with the work for J.V. and a little business on the side, such as the caravans, I could be retired before I'm fifty, and we could both be leading the life of Riley,' he had explained, trying to stave off her disapproval this time around. He needn't have bothered; nothing likely or affordable presented itself in the few weekends he allotted to the search. Joan was relieved when he dropped the idea, just like that, after coming back late one Sunday afternoon from Kiama, saying his faithful old Austin wasn't up to long journeys any more.

He became more cheerful when Joan fell pregnant a few months after his mother died. Her pregnancy was uneventful, and this was a busy and good time for both of them. Everything was happening at once, Joan sometimes felt. Having finished getting the house in order and properly furnished, she turned her attention to setting up a nursery; at the same time there were greater demands on Vic at work. He was already more or less

J.V.'s right-hand man now and if everything continued as it was, there was a good chance of him being approached to come in as a partner, which he wouldn't have minded at all, as he told Joan.

Baby Jennifer was born in August 1956, a bouncing 7-pound 10-ounce cherub. Vic and Joan were thrilled and took the precious bundle back to the little room they had set up for her, and in the right colours too — Joan had cleverly bought things in both blue and pink. But it was soon apparent to Vic that Joan couldn't bear to be more than six steps away from the baby at any time of the day or night. This was not something he had been expecting and found ever more disconcerting as the months passed. For a long time, it was as if he did not exist for Joan, a situation he didn't like at all.

He mentioned this problem to one of the older family men at work, to be told that this was normal behaviour. Women 'go off' after babies were born, he learned, occasionally for a very long time, and he could forget about sex while that was happening. Vic didn't know whether this was reassuring — at least he had an explanation — or depressing. But it certainly confirmed his experience so far. For almost a year after Jennifer's birth Joan was completely off limits in the bedroom department. He tried hard not to let it bother him, but found he had to occasionally fight off some meaner and more selfish impulses. Still, he would tell himself, Joan was trying hard, and it was not good to get cranky and annoyed just because he wasn't having things his way.

The period of difficulty, the time of strain and distance after the birth, seemed to end when Jennifer found her feet at fifteen months. Vic and Joan drew close to each other once more. Vic was eventually offered a partnership, which all agreed would be a good thing. The bank was happy to finance him into it, and so he took it up with enthusiasm. Soon the fortunes of Vic and his little family flourished, as he was now deriving a small share of profits from Prestige, not just a wage.

Vic's confidence grew to the point of finding he had time and energy to try things beyond his previous compass. He came to the view that his 'show-offy' side, as Joan called it, could do with a bit more of a workout. He had always liked dancing for its own sake; the rhythms and the movements, the little attacks and retreats, the swings and swoops — there was satisfaction in the mastery. It could be a pretty sexy business, he wasn't so stupid as to not know that, and he enjoyed that aspect. But at the same time he realised that he enjoyed expressing himself generally, presenting some other less expected parts of himself through performance. Long ago, before marriage, before children, he had wondered what it might be like to be an actor. God knows, acting was something that went on all the time in daily life. What would it be like to do it for real, so to speak, to play a theatrical part or role, to be someone else for a while?

Vic surprised himself, although not Joan as it happened, by following through on this. He had become aware of a new theatrical group starting up in their area — there was a poster on the council chambers noticeboard near his office at Parramatta — he even took down the phone number of the organiser, a woman named May Bartlett. Might be worth a laugh, he told Joan. But only if she was all right with the idea. She didn't mind, this once; anything that allowed him to expend his excess energy was fine by her. After doing his chores on weekends, Vic was apt to be a caged lion around the house, all restless movement.

He made contact with May, who told him that hers was an amateur group, the only requirement being to turn up to acting classes one night a week, and then to rehearsals for an end-of-year production. When Vic suggested to Joan that she might like to join him on this escapade, her reply was, 'Not on your nelly' — her hands were still full with Jenny, who had just turned two. But when he seemed crestfallen, she did say she wouldn't rule it out entirely for later on.

Starting classes, which were held on a Wednesday evening from 5.30 to 7.30pm in the local scout hall, Vic discovered that May was actually running a sort of school, as well as a troupe intended to put on plays. He was one of about fifteen, all sorts of people, young (or youngish — no one under sixteen was allowed) and old, reasonably sane as well as out and out nuts.

It was a revelation to Vic that so many different types, people you wouldn't imagine would have much in common, could get together like this. From talking to various members over the coffee urn at the back of the hall, he learned that one woman was a retired schoolteacher, there was a schoolgirl who was getting ready to do her Leaving, and there was also a mad little old coot with tufted eyebrows, an old-fashioned waxed moustache and a cravat. This chap May called 'the Professor', out of his earshot and with more than a hint of bemused toleration in her voice. To round off the numbers there were two more glamorous types in their early twenties; two young women who had been signed on for some sort of radio soap opera and who'd been told to take some lessons.

May herself veered more than a bit towards the eccentric. She was round and solidly built with a ruddy complexion and cropped red hair. She also had a tendency to sweat easily; Vic thought she looked as if someone had lit a fire under her which she hadn't had time to put out yet. She had a loud, penetrating voice, too, and always seemed to be speaking over the top of everybody. It occurred to him on the first evening that she would have made a great foreman.

To attend, a small fee was required. That, he didn't mind so much. He was more disconcerted to learn that May subscribed to some high-falutin' theories, not only about acting but about the place of drama in life, and even about art and life. She believed the theatre was the most important thing in the world, or so she said on day one; he could see it meant something (though not in a way he could easily put his finger on) but thought it was far from being the most important thing in the world. He was prepared to sit through a half-hour lecture on the theatre at the beginning of each Wednesday session, which he didn't think was too long. But there did seem to be a lot of talk about 'the Method', and some bloke called Stanislavski. Also a fair bit of blather about various theatrical traditions — British versus American mainly, as Australia apparently didn't have one.

Vic was much happier when they were given little roneod scenes from plays which they were then asked to read and discuss. He liked it even better when, more familiar with the conventions, they were asked to block out the action, take the various parts, and speak the lines. It didn't matter that his memory wasn't at first up to the task of remembering big slabs of speech, as they were allowed to refer to their scripts.

After Vic had gone to a few of his theatre group evenings, Joan noticed that he came home overexcited; why this should be so was a mystery to her, although she also noticed that little Jenny didn't mind. In fact she loved it when her father came marching in, shouting, 'What-ho!' and, 'Where's my lovely?' pretending to be a pirate picking her up and tossing her in the air, to her evident delight, expressed in shouts and peals of laughter. This always seemed to happen just as Joan was getting her ready for bed.

Vic looked as if he was ready to do the same again one night when he came through the door a little before eight, wearing a wicked grin and asking Joan where Jenny was.

'Shh! She's just about ready to drop off. Don't go unsettling her like you always do, will you?'

'No. OK. You're right …'

Joan followed Vic as he went quietly into the nursery. Jennifer was lying on her side in bed, drifting off to sleep. She had only just graduated from her cot and she seemed lost in the gigantic spaces of her new single bed.

Vic looked down on her. 'Hello kitten … Daddy's here to say goodnight. Goodnight, love.'

Their little girl was too tired to do much more than just raise her head slightly, acknowledge her father's presence and give a gentle smile before dropping her head back to the pillow and putting her thumb in her mouth to ready herself for sleep.

'She's gorgeous, isn't she?' Vic said quietly.

'Yes, she is,' Joan replied.

'And all our own work, too …'

A moment passed, and Joan put her hand gently on Vic's shoulder. It was all he needed. He turned slowly towards her, took her waist in his two hands and pulled her close to him. She let him.

18

The Theatre

When Vic had a chance to read through the whole of the play they were preparing for the end of the year — *Our Town* by Thornton Wilder — he couldn't have been happier. He thought it was really 'meaty' and told Joan so the same night he'd finished it, sitting up in bed.

'The play's sort of about everyday life, but there's more to it than that …'

Joan was not too far off sleep but, if she was not sure about this theatre stuff, at least she liked to see him expressing enthusiasm about something. He had been moody in the weeks before taking this on, which she put down to the demands of his work and the child and supporting them all. He was working pretty hard. She made an effort and asked, 'Where does it happen?'

'Well, somewhere in America …'

'America? That's a bit general, isn't it?'

'Let me see …' Vic flicked back to the beginning. '"Grover's Corners," it says. "A small New Hampshire town," wherever that is …'

'So what part have you got?'

'Don't know yet. Been reading the Stage Manager's role ...'

'Stage Manager? That's not a role is it, that's someone who's behind the scenes, or something?'

'It's a part in this play as well.'

'What do you mean, a part as well?'

Try as she might be doing to show interest, something about her questions was making Vic irritable. He knew it was late and she was tired, but there was still something he didn't like in her voice.

'Oh, never mind. I'll tell you about it some other time when you're more awake.'

May still began each session with a general talk on some aspect of the theatre. This made Vic impatient; with the production already planned, he could hardly wait to get to some real practice. May might have reckoned it was important they develop a knowledge of the drama, but Vic was finding it hard to concentrate.

One evening, though May arrived late, she still insisted on the usual structure for the class. But instead of getting straight into her talk, she was fussing around with an easel, trying to pin up some poster while the cast chattered and carried on like so many naughty schoolkids.

'Quiet everybody please! Now look at this ... Here's a picture of Peggy Ashcroft playing the part of Electra. Electra is the main character in the play of the same name written by Sophocles, one of the ancient Greeks. And, as well you know, or should know, the Greeks invented drama ...

'Doesn't she look wonderful? Wouldn't it have been great to see her, eh what? Let me read you a quote from *Punch*. "A haunting revelation of suffering. Miss Ashcroft can tear the heart out of you with a whisper."'

While May droned on, and almost against his will, Vic was drawn to the image of the young woman on the theatre poster. May must have noticed as, mid-sentence, she said, 'Vic, you look pretty distant there. Were you going to say something?'

Brought back, he felt obliged to speak. 'Oh, I was just thinking I knew some Greeks once myself,' he said. 'During the war. They were a great mob, but they had a different sort of drama on their hands in those days. And there wasn't a lot of play-acting going on, I can tell you. Poor bastards had to cop it sweet for a long time.'

Vic heard some titters coming from a couple of the young ones in the row behind him, but only smiled. What he had said, it occurred to him, they must have taken as just the sort of thing an ex-digger would say. He didn't mind — that was who he was. He didn't blame them. How could this lot, or anyone else who hadn't been there, know what the war had been about anyway? *Let them laugh*, he thought. *Kids should laugh.* Had he been concentrating he might have said something more sensible, but while May had been speaking of the ancients and that actress in the poster his thoughts had been elsewhere. The figure in the flowing gown had brought to mind another young woman, whose memory it was not unpleasant to recall, here, today, in this little suburban hall.

Peggy Ashcroft somehow echoed how Kalliope was — erect and defiant, with a candid, direct stare, and somehow shy and vulnerable, all at once. As May spoke, Vic began to wish the girl could somehow materialise, here and now. She was the genuine article, not some Pommy sheila dressed up; she could show these puppies a thing or two. The more he thought about Kalliope, the more real she became. What would have happened had he not decided on his Captain Cook act, but stayed on? He had heard of some who did just that — melting into the populace, going native, living there for years and years. Could he not have just roamed the hills until it was all over? The Krauts had been booted out in the end. Perhaps he could have hung on, seen them out, even found something to do there. He could have gone back to Arkadi, and maybe to her.

Staying with the thought, Vic wondered whether that might have added up to a more satisfying life. He wasn't entirely unhappy with what he had here, but he didn't always feel content either. It was hard to know why that was so. Soul-searching, which he believed he was no good at anyway, got him no further than identifying a restless nature — even while he sensed there was more to it than that.

Vic was relieved when they began rehearsals in earnest. He'd never paid much attention to English at school — although always a good reader and speller — and was easily bored by abstract talk. It was his nature to be impatient generally when a subject was tackled side on instead of directly, which it seemed to him May did too often. He had, he felt, a pretty good fix on *Our Town* anyway — this play told a story where everything that happened was happening *to* the characters, they were being pulled around through life by something other than their own efforts. The Stage Manager was like a puppeteer, like God pulling the strings. Or that was how he saw it. Pity he felt less godlike in his own life.

The production was scheduled for three performances over three nights, beginning on a Friday late in October. As the date drew nearer May insisted they needed two evening rehearsals per week. Vic felt obliged to meet the requirement and thus was away on Wednesday and Friday evenings. These extra absences did not go down well with Joan; she eventually told him that she would appreciate having him home at a decent hour, as she was tired out by the end of each day by the demands of young Jenny and with cleaning and getting dinner ready. Vic dug in, saying that this wouldn't last forever, asking why she couldn't be a little more flexible.

Vic found he needed to spend more time trying to memorise lines. The Stage Manager's role was a pretty big part and he was nervous about getting all the words learned and stored in his head. He had learned a few words off by heart for nativity plays and little sketches at school back at Enmore, but had had no previous experience of learning big slabs of speech.

By the end of the third week of rehearsals, the sight of Vic wandering around at home with a copy of the play in his hand, mouthing his lines silently or out loud, had well and truly got to Joan. Her irritation one evening was such that Vic went outside to practise the words. He was still distracted when he came back inside, which added to Joan's annoyance.

'Vic, you had practice yesterday and you're there again tomorrow ... don't you think you're overdoing it?' she said to him one Thursday night.

'Won't be long now ... nearly over,' he said, trying to pacify her.

'It's *not* nearly over. What about the nights when you're actually going to be doing the thing? I don't know why you had to take this on, Vic, really I don't. Haven't we got enough happening here?'

Vic put the play text on the kitchen table and sat himself down. There was no escaping the challenge in her remark.

'Why get upset? I've never done anything like this before. Besides, thought you might appreciate your old man doing something different. You said as much at the beginning.'

'Don't "old man" yourself … It's just not like you, that's all. Can't understand what you're getting out of this, going off with all those mad types.'

'Mad? They're not mad. I like them. Not afraid to have a go, that's all.'

'Sure they're not just show-offs?'

Vic was determined not to be goaded into an argument. 'I might've said that once, too. Since I got to know them I've found they're just ordinary bods, most of them. Don't you think that's good?'

Joan suspected his new interest in drama was not the real story. Quietly she asked him, 'Well tell me then, so I understand. What *are* you getting out of it?'

'I don't know, Joan. I just don't feel right about things, somehow. I think I need to get something new, something different in my head as well as just this …' Vic moved his arm to indicate the room, but Joan saw much more.

She looked at him for a long time. His head was lower now, and she could see that sandy thatch of his. She was distracted by his physicality for a moment, thought how she had always liked his hair.

But the diversion didn't hold; what he had said, the gesture, was too upsetting. He had put into words something she had begun to detect in him anyway: some kind of unhappiness, unacknowledged, undefined. Joan let some more time pass, trying to be fair to him, not wanting to rush at him.

What do you call it when your husband is there, but not there? He could be hard to take when his mind was so often elsewhere. When he was around, which was rarely of late, he was either all over the child or her, or else entirely switched off and grumpy. In that mode, he would come home from work and go straight out to the shed or the yard to muck around, as if she or Jennifer weren't home at all. Never mind how she or her daughter might be feeling. How much did she really count in his estimation, she wondered. She herself, Joan. There were various kinds of betrayal, weren't there?

'Something new and different..?' She tried not to sound as if she was mocking him. 'You're not satisfied, then?'

Vic put his hands up instantly, defensively. 'Didn't say that! Hey! Come on, Joanie, no need to go on the attack, love.'

Joan did not respond immediately, hoping he might go on to explain himself a little better. He did not.

'Vic, you also said something other than just this … Are you tired of us? Is that what it is? Come on, you can tell me …' she put her hand across the table towards him, hoping that she could stave off her anger and foreboding. She even managed to smile at him. 'Men get tired of home and hearth sometimes, that's nothing new. Is that what's happening?'

'No,' he said, hoping it sounded convincing. Because he didn't in truth know what he thought about her question. Not yet. It was his turn for reticence. He stalled for time to think, though time brought no further enlightenment.

'Look, I don't know what's going on with me. Feeling a bit low, is all. And this is good, you'll see!' He tried to brighten for her. 'It'll be fun! You can come and laugh at me up there on the stage! Oh, and did I tell you, there's going to be a group from work come along? It'll be a hoot.'

Joan looked at him calmly before replying. 'I don't think so, Vic. It's not that kind of a play, is it? It's a bit more serious than that, isn't it? From what I've read, anyhow.' She nodded towards the copy of the play that lay between them.

Vic strived to keep a lighter touch. 'There are a few funny bits in it, I would've said.'

Joan pulled herself together. He was tired from work, what was asked of him there. He was a good provider and kind enough. You couldn't accuse Vic of being the way so many men were — cruel and selfish. She would give him the benefit of the doubt, and maybe try harder herself. Let him have his lark. He might be right. It might turn out to be fun.

Vic hadn't given any thought to the fact that he would need a costume for his part. May herself wasn't one to waste too much time on what she considered a relatively unimportant matter. The play was the thing. The words. Sets and costumes were only critical in kiddies' plays and pantomimes, not proper drama. And if she had drummed anything into her players in the past few months, it was that *Our Town* was proper drama. Its themes were universal, so it made precious little difference whether the actors wore authentic period outfits from New Hampshire or their underwear. This was all very well except that they still had to wear something 'appropriate to the part'. May reminded everyone that as an amateur group they had few resources available, and so making do was the order of the day. And that was where Vic was up to a few days before opening night — rifling through his wardrobe, trying to think what he might have that would suit.

The only idea that came to him was that, as the Stage Manager was a kind of organiser and fixer of things, a tradesman's outfit might not be inappropriate. So, what was wrong with wearing overalls and a tool belt? Pleased with the thought, he even rang May at home to suggest it to her. Her reply was a relief: she thought it made a lot of sense. So that was that. He would look as he had done on building sites, before becoming a collar-and-tie-wearing manager.

The play was to open at 7.30pm on a Friday evening at the Parramatta Town Hall. Vic spent the day at work in a state of distraction, going over some orders for materials ahead of a coming job. He knew his lines by now and the general question of the outfit had been settled. A group of workmates had been kidded into coming along — mostly the secretaries and their boyfriends — and Joan had agreed to come too, on the understanding that she could bring the young one. About the latter there was no alternative, as they had no regular babysitter and Joan's parents were away on a holiday. By four that afternoon, feeling a little unsettled he decided to call it a day.

When he got home Joan was busy giving Jennifer an early feed. She didn't want, she said, to have to be worrying about her dinner just when the play was supposed to be starting. She would try to get Jennifer to nod off in her stroller, which would allow her, Joan, to watch the play in peace. Vic listened, preoccupied, trying not to let a queasy mix of anticipated pleasure and fear overtake him completely.

They arrived at the town hall at six, as agreed, for a last run through. As they had had only one go on that stage it was vital to grab any opportunity to check their cues and positions on stage. Vic's part required him to come on and go off at fairly frequent intervals and he was keen not to muck that up. While he got a handle on not 'tripping over the furniture', as May was wont to say, Joan took Jennifer for a stroll along Church Street. Vic appreciated her not watching him rehearse; he was keen to surprise her with what he, they, had been able to put together over the past few months.

As he waited backstage for the performance to begin, Vic switched between going over his script and peering around an angle of curtain to watch people coming in to take their seats. By 7.15 there might have been twenty-five, maybe thirty. He hadn't given much thought to the question of an audience; he had assumed that if you put on a play people would come. But what did he know? This was an entirely new experience. Things were a little better with five minutes to go — there were maybe fifty scattered around, among whom he could now see Joan and Jennifer sitting at the back; handy if Joan had to retreat because of the baby. The sight of her there, however, compounded his anxiety. He had not considered the effect of her looking at him, her husband, doing something he had never done before. She would be judging him, his performance. Him.

Now came May, hurrying about, hustling everyone to their positions. 'Break a leg!' she said as she went. She sent two of her stage helpers to stand by in the wings — there were no ropes and pulleys, curtains or flies required for this play.

A scattering of applause and the lights came up. Vic entered from one side to begin delivering the Stage Manager's opening speech. He was wearing khaki carpenter's overalls on top of a flannelette shirt, with a hat on his head and pipe in hand. His long speech introduced the play and the location; a country town, one not too difficult to imagine in an Australian form: the grocery store, the school, the various churches, the local cemetery, then on to some of the characters, including young Joe Crowell, Jr — the town's newspaper delivery boy, and Dr Gibbs — the town doctor. Standing to one side, Vic waited while Dr Gibbs and eleven-year-old Joe (played by one of the schoolgirls) had an exchange of minor newsy pleasantries.

Joe exited and Dr Gibbs remained reading a paper, as the play's directions stated. The conceit of the play was that these small events had taken place many years earlier, and it was the Stage Manager's job to tell the audience that the characters were now dead. Vic began his next speech to this effect.

Of Joe Crowell he said, 'But the war broke out and he died in France.'

Something happened as he said those words. He knew he had said them. He heard them as they came out of his head. They sounded tinny and hollow, like an echo you might hear in a factory or a warehouse.

He had only to add: 'All that education for nothing,' but the words dried in his throat. He looked down at the audience looking up at him. Raising his eyes higher, he saw Joan at the back sitting at the end of a row of seats with the stroller in the aisle next to her. Moments passed in which he could say nothing, do nothing. He was struck by the import of what he had said. These words did not carry a meaning to be shared with these playgoers or these amateur actors; they were, he somehow imagined, meant for him and only him. 'And he died …' rang in his head like some great bell.

He heard May muttering something in the background, recognised his next line as she repeated it offstage. But that was not the problem. He knew his lines. He saw Joan stand up, take hold of the stroller with Jennifer in it and quickly push her to the back. She disappeared through the exit. Still he felt frozen to the spot, until some other awareness at last took hold of him. He looked quickly about him, wildly about him. The next character required to speak, milkman Howie Newsome, was still waiting for him to finish his dialogue so that he could respond and they might continue. He heard May say, 'For God's sake, Vic, say your lines, do something!'

There were further whispers, turning of heads down below. Where Joan had been he saw an empty seat. And then everything fell from him. There was nothing to be done but to leave, run, get away. He went quickly to the front of the stage and jumped off, heading directly for the exit. He was unaware of the looks on the faces of the audience; some were so concerned they got up to go after him.

Racing out of the town hall into the night air, he found Joan had gone to their car parked in the street and was sitting inside with Jennifer on her lap. He ran over to them, jumped in beside her. She was looking straight ahead. She seemed to have nothing to say to him. He gripped the steering wheel and put his head on the rim. Then they came. Tears. Words whose meaning he didn't understand even as he said them. Somewhere far off he heard someone shouting his name, a woman's voice. He turned and saw Joan's face, saw anguish turn to terror. He heard the baby start to cry.

He wanted them to stop but didn't know how to make them stop. When they wouldn't, he repeated the line 'died in France' and added, 'That's what happens Joanie, people die. They get killed and die. I killed people too, you know. Me, yes, your Vic ...' He then got out of the car and started walking, somewhere, anywhere.

Vic Stockton was picked up by a police car at around 9.00pm, walking west along the Great Western Highway towards Toongabbie. Joan and Jennifer were in the car with the two officers. Something was said to him which he was never able to recall, but he did later remember that they had put him in the back seat and driven off. Joan seemed to be holding his hand for some of the way.

He was taken to the Gladesville Mental Hospital where the group waited until he could be seen by a doctor. He was asked some questions — his name, where he lived, his wife's and child's names, what he had been doing that night.

He apparently answered them all correctly, or correctly enough. Because he seemed quite calm and coherent again, they let him leave without being scheduled for admission. The doctor asked Joan to come to a small office for a further talk without Vic present. She felt safe enough, if still a bit wary, to leave their daughter with Vic seated in the waiting room.

The doctor asked various questions: how long had he been acting strangely, was he taking any medication, did he drink too much? When she answered in the negative, the doctor gave himself plenty of time and seemed to be thinking of other possibilities. Eventually he asked whether by any chance her husband had been a war veteran. Joan answered yes, at which the doctor nodded and started writing on the pad in front of him.

'Could be war neurosis,' he said at last. 'That can come on years later, you know.'

'What is that exactly?' she asked.

'The stress a man experiences as a soldier, bombs going off all around and what have you, not knowing if he's the one who's going to cop it next, can sometimes "break" him. Nervous shock can make him not much use for anything afterwards. He loses his spirit and becomes depressed, or, more seriously, he might ...'

This did not make much sense to Joan. Even less if he was also hinting there could be worse to come. 'Yes, but he's been fine until now.'

The doctor shrugged. 'It was more common after the Great War and I can't be certain that's what it is in this case — but there is a record of this sort of thing appearing many years after.

I'd like to see your husband again, Mrs Stockton, if he can be persuaded.'

'I'll do my best.'

She left to find Vic holding Jenny's hand. They were both smiling at each other, as if they had just shared some little joke. 'Daddy silly!' Jenny announced to her mother.

When Vic looked at Joan with brighter eyes, she came to thinking that maybe it was nothing more than his being overwrought and nervous about that play and what he was supposed to do. All too much for him. There was no reason to jump to the very worst conclusions.

The police completed their paper work at the front desk and, no crime having been committed and their being no longer required, left Joan and Vic Stockton to their devices. A cab was called and with Jenny nestled between them, they were driven back to their home.

19

Rattiness

Vic went back once more to May Bartlett's drama classes after the debacle to try to explain himself and to make amends. May was most understanding. She cajoled him, very reluctantly, into sitting down among the others ahead of class, and proceeded to make a little speech. Then, solemnly and quietly, she put his behaviour down to stage fright, which could be a terrifying thing and suffered by even some of the great talents. She also asked that everyone try to forget what had taken place and not blame him. Vic was happy to accept May's explanation while the other members of the group seemed to agree it made sense, even if he wasn't so sure himself. Vic gave an apology in return. He was very sorry if he'd let people down, he said, and it was very unlike him to behave like that.

May ended this session by saying it was terribly brave of Vic to even attempt to come back to give an account of himself after so public a disaster. As for the play, no serious harm appeared to be done; refunds had been issued that night and a replacement actor was assigned Vic's role for the remaining performances. The incident of the runaway actor made great copy for the local paper. It might even have boosted ticket sales: the number of seats sold for subsequent performances increased.

In the days that followed Vic tried not to dwell on what had happened, although the events had a way of sneaking back into his consciousness at the most inconvenient times. It also didn't help that the 'stuff-up', as he called it, had been witnessed by a number of his workmates, particularly a couple of the more yappy office girls.

But it was only a bloody play and not real life, he told himself, and others too, if they brought it up and offered sympathy. Aware that the incident was still going around the office a couple of weeks afterwards, Vic even made a little speech in the tea room one morning. There was no need for everyone to keep going on about it, he said. They weren't buying it, he could tell, but felt he had to say something, anything, to end the talk.

Joan was relieved when he came home from the group and told her he had cut all ties, saying that maybe acting wasn't for him after all. She sincerely hoped that Vic's 'rattiness', as she described it to her friends, had come to an end now that his time in amateur theatricals was over.

Vic was soon looking around for other involvements. He saw himself as a man with plenty else to be going on with. He continued to be troubled whenever he thought about the events of the night of the play; he had never been able to explain them to himself satisfactorily. But after a good six months had passed in which he experienced nothing like that panic and distress again, he hoped it was all behind him. It had all been some silly aberration, and anyway, he could call on a simple truth about himself: the more time he had to dwell on things, the less happy he was. The best therapy, should he really need any, was to keep busy.

Vic was therefore most receptive when J. V. came to him with an idea he said might be of interest. J.V. had been approached by certain parties who thought he would make a very good alderman on local council, and had asked him whether he was interested in standing. An independent ticket — or rather a new party with an independent line — was being organised and a man like J.V., someone who knew the local area and community, would be perfect in supporting people's interests. J.V. told Vic that he had been flattered but felt he was getting on a bit in years; this was a job for a younger man. Which was where Vic came in. In fact, he had already put Vic's name forward as a very good potential representative. So what did he reckon? Was he interested in some public service?

They had had this conversation in J.V.'s office one Friday afternoon; J. V. liked to call his most senior chaps in at that time for the weekly ritual of a shared scotch. On this occasion Vic was surprised to see he was the only invitee. The proposition was the bigger surprise: he had only a slightly above average interest in local government affairs, mainly from the point of view of a builder required to deal with council staff and meet building regulations. Apart from minor disputes, all of which had been resolved sooner or later, he had never had any serious trouble with anybody on the council or with any of its functions. It did sometimes occur to him that its responsibilities might be met in better, more efficient ways, and that there never seemed to be enough attention paid to the general amenities available to people in the municipality. On jobs in other areas of Sydney, he had marvelled at what some councils had established since the war: swimming centres, proper landscaped parks, mixed sports grounds.

Now he responded, 'Oh, yeah? Might be ... Depends on what's involved, J. V.'

'Details later, Vic. But that's a yes, I take it? I think you would be an excellent candidate. I've already told them you're an upstanding fellow and fit and presentable. Even if you don't exactly look like Clark Gable!'

'Don't know about that, but I wouldn't mind having a go, depending on the particulars. What happens next?'

'Well, I arrange a meeting and you all talk. They're a good go-ahead sort of crowd — bit of a break from the usual desperados in the bigger parties. I reckon people are looking for something fresh these days, what do you say?'

'Well, they'd want to be if there's any interest in me!'

They both laughed at this, and Vic took his first sip of the whisky.

They *were* a go-ahead crowd, or so Vic thought after being introduced to them the following week. The men he met with, who called themselves the Progress Party were J. V., two blokes from the regional chamber of commerce, a real estate agent and another unaffiliated local businessman. Their belief was that the area needed practical initiatives to improve local amenities and to attract people from beyond Parramatta, as well as improving the meagre facilities available to the residents. One political lot, they said, was in thrall to the unions and only supported union-approved ideas, which never amounted to much beyond workers' rights, wages and conditions, and the other lot never seemed to want to do anything except warm seats.

Vic agreed with their assessment of the major parties as they were involved in the area, and with their views about civic improvements. Under the circumstances, he was happy to take part in the campaign for the forthcoming local government elections and if elected, to serve as required.

He broke the news to Joan only after he felt comfortable with the proposition. He did not know how she would react, but he assumed that he would be allowed a decent hearing. Joan heard him out well enough, but that was the extent of it. All very well to propose getting involved in local affairs, but he had sprung this on her without notice, a habit of his. How was he going to manage his job as well as this new thing? Her parents were growing older and she needed to spend more time caring for them; who was going to help her look after Jennifer if he wasn't there?

He had answers to these questions, and for once had anticipated some of them. He even agreed that he was the sort of bloke who had a tendency to go off half-cocked. But since when had that made him shirk his responsibilities? And this was different. J. V. had agreed to let him have some time off to meet his obligations towards the campaign. And should he be elected, time to go to meetings would be organised during business hours, according to the Progress Party people he had met. Neither she nor Jennifer would suffer as a result — in fact, he was reasonably certain that he would be more available to her, rather than less. And he did believe he had something to offer. He had plenty of ideas to improve things for others, otherwise he wouldn't have entertained the approach at all.

Joan was only partly won over by Vic's arguments. But what he was proposing made a bit more sense, she rationalised, than that juvenile drama club stuff. She tried to put it all in a positive light and the next morning told him over breakfast that she would go along with it if this was what he wanted to do. She even offered to help with campaigning in whatever way she could. Maybe they could work together — she could do leaflet drops with him, or otherwise make herself useful, as she had seen other candidates' wives do during elections. He appeared pleased at this, if rather surprised. But deep down, she was not really convinced this was all a good idea.

Vic began to attend weekly strategy meetings of the embryonic party, held in the Holroyd Businessmen's Club each Friday at lunchtime. He was impressed by some of the work already done to establish policies and the means of promoting them, and felt confident that he had made a sensible decision to take part. For his contribution, he began work on ways to steamline some of the council's by-laws and regulations, to make it easier for new businesses to be established, for new building developments to be assessed with less red tape and — a pet project, this — drew up terms for a feasibility study on costs and possible sites for a new swimming pool complex to be built in an outlying part of the municipality. This was an area he had often visited as part of his work and it always depressed him to see so many kids on the streets with nothing to do, on top of the general barrenness of the place. Vic's initiatives were approved by the other members and were adopted as part of the program to be promoted via letter drop, street posters and newspaper ads in the coming weeks.

And here Joan did come into her own, proving as solid a supporter as Vic could have hoped for. She was a capable organiser, dealing efficiently with the local printer, the newspaper office and so forth. She found she quite liked having a part to play in something outside the home, being taken seriously for a time by people other than her husband. When she learned that his party had come in for mild criticism about where the money to fund their grand plans was meant to come from, she surprised herself by feeling outraged. She even went as far as writing to the local paper in Vic's defence, and fired off a couple of shots at the other parties into the bargain.

At the election, the Progress Party achieved a mixed result. They managed to have three of their candidates elected to the new council, one of whom was Vic. As the conservatives had one fewer aldermen than the other major party, thus insufficient aldermen to control affairs on their own, they entered into an alliance with Progress.

The first year of Vic's involvement in local politics, 1961, was both unexceptional and frustrating. The conservatives, together with Progress, blocked the one or two ideas that the other side put up. But what was more amazing to Vic was to see the conservatives on occasion join with their sworn opponents to block Progress initiatives. Whenever Progress tried to run with something, they could not necessarily rely on the support of any other bloc. His party had, it seemed, only an alliance in the form of a guaranteed Progress vote when a conservative proposal required it: the devil had been in the detail and his group of amateurs had not read the fine print of their letter of understanding on the matter.

Vic's first major idea, for a council-funded youth sports complex, came to nought. His supposed political allies argued that there were already sufficient facilities in the form of a trotting track and a football oval, even though the former was out of bounds to under-age punters and the latter was forbidden to non-club teams (and club teams were themselves few and far between). And all the current talk about swimming pools was just considered 'me-tooism', one council slavishly following another.

As he tried to negotiate the treacheries of the political path, Vic became distant and difficult at home again. On top of his Prestige obligations, he was bringing home council paperwork, sometimes spending hours after dinner reading and re-reading documents. He was so preoccupied that he appeared to forget he had a daughter at all, Joan thought. He also seemed to forget that Joan had ever helped him get onto local council in the first place, for all he ever bothered telling her about what was going on there. He was forever running from one place to another, from work, to council chambers, to meetings with complainers or urgers of one sort or another. Joan felt herself becoming ever more resentful. She grew deeply despondent, and eventually began to ask herself the hard question: whether this marriage had any sort of future at all.

One night when Vic got home late after a meeting, she tackled him directly, asking whether he thought this political involvement was putting any strain on their marriage, because she certainly did. Vic was stunned — there was no other word — to hear her put it like that. He could only come back with the lame response that he had plenty to be going on with — what with learning the procedural ropes for meetings, the rigmarole of agendas, standing orders, motions and minutes, and then the intricacies of dealing with development applications and building approvals. Everything would settle down once he had mastered his role — there would be more time for everyone, he assured her. She just had to be patient with him.

By the last session of 1961 Vic believed he had got on top of most aspects of his job as councillor, becoming especially confident in his own area of expertise. To accusations that he was merely representing the 'developer interest', he responded that he always took an objective, disinterested stance, basing his decisions on technical questions and the greater good, and not on how much money was at stake and who stood to benefit.

But he was not prepared for the curly question that turned up on his agenda papers for their final meeting of December, buried as Item 27 of 34. It was an application for approval to construct a string of fifteen new shops along the retail strip in downtown Parramatta. The application, made by some company named

Nevertire, had been assessed by staff as meeting the technical requirements, and the motion to approve was put by one of his own team, the local real estate agent Bill Drinan. The left said nobody had ever heard of Nevertire; they also said they had some unnamed problem with the application and sought to delay the vote. It went ahead, with Vic voting in support, but the vote was surprisingly lost when one of the Progress Party's members voted with the left. It was held over for further investigation and a report to the first meeting of the new year.

Then the sky fell in. Further council inquiries showed that Nevertire was a shelf company, set up solely to put the application. Its principal directors were J. V. Alderton and Bill Drinan. It then became clear that Nevertire was nothing more than a fudge for Prestige Homes, a fact revealed at a further special session convened to canvas the whole sordid story. The site in question was not untrammelled; indeed, the owner of the present run-down properties, the elderly widow of a long-dead banker, did not wish to dispose of them at all, but had been subject to all sorts of pressure, including visits from strange men. She said that over the Christmas break she had been approached by a council alderman to induce her to sell. When that happened, not knowing what else to do, she called another Progress Party alderman. She called the right man — one of their own who knew more than Vic about what was going on behind the scenes and decided to do something about it. He had subsequently notified the police.

When Vic was made aware of all this, he felt as if he'd been kicked four square in the guts. He could not believe that his boss — and mate, he thought — of so many years' standing had been involved in such shenanigans, even less that he himself had been implicated and used in perpetrating a fraud and a possible crime.

He finally had to accept that he had been manipulated into a position where he could be of advantage to Prestige and some hitherto unknown sidekicks of J.V. Alderton.

After the council meeting when this all became clear, Vic got into his car to drive home, but then thought better of it. He would pay J. V. a visit. Bugger him.

Vic arrived at Alderton's house in Carlingford a little after 9.00pm. The boss had built himself a substantial, modern brick pile, with a sandstone feature on one side of the entrance in a nondescript street of very ordinary houses on both sides. Vic had been there once or twice before but, now that he thought about it, had never felt particularly welcome. Things were starting to make a different kind of sense for him as he got out of the car and marched up the driveway to the front door. He felt dirty, vengeful in a way that he hadn't felt since he last fired bullets in anger at Germans.

He rapped on the door. A few moments later J.V. opened it. He was a bit startled at first and came out to the step, half-closing the front door behind him. He was wearing his dressing gown and slippers — a shiny dressing gown, something like satin, and shiny leather slippers that looked somehow oily. Vic had never seen his boss dressed like this before. J.V. looked like a grub, some cheesy playboy type.

'Vic! What are you doing here, boy? How can I help you?' he said, with no indication he was about to push the door back fully and invite him in.

'Don't 'boy' me, J.V. I think you might know why I'm here, mate.'

'What? What are you talking about?'

'You've sold me down the river, you mongrel, that's what you've done. Haven't you? So much for the politics and what a wonderful bloke I am.'

Alderton began to look a little frightened. He half-turned to consider whether any of this was being heard by his wife, dozing on the lounge.

'Keep your voice down. We can talk about your problem some other time.'

'Jesus, I feel like throttling you, J.V. I really do!'

Vic felt his fists clench, not knowing what he might do next.

'I still don't know what you're on about, Vic. Calm down.'

'I'll tell you what I'm on about! The fact that you and your mates have used me — how dare you set me up like that! — and the fact that I'm quitting. And from the sound of things, you and I are due for a more public punch-up.'

'You're being very hasty, Stockton, and I …'

'Not at all. I won't be made the bunny. It's over between us, J.V. And consider yourself lucky I've been able to control myself here, you low mug.'

Vic spun around and strode angrily back towards his car.

On his way home, Vic concluded that there was a great deal he didn't understand about the world and people. You come to trust men and they turn around and do this sort of thing to you. What in hell was going on? Or was it just that he was an innocent, a trusting idiot? He was buggered if he knew anymore.

He drove up his driveway and into the garage at the side of the house. Sitting in the car alone, he felt devastated. He had no tools ready at hand, he realised, for dealing with this sort of thing. He had taken a bloke at face value, had worked for him for many years, even been favoured and promoted by him. Perhaps Alderton had always taken him for a fool, perhaps it had always been his intention, one day, to use him in such a way. He felt sick at the thought. Then there was a further, no less troubling matter to contend with: what would Joan say? She had been none too pleased before Christmas to learn about the behaviour of the company and the man that had employed him; now she would be even less thrilled about a police investigation because of physical threats against an old woman.

Joan listened impassively as Vic told her he'd obviously been a naïve fool. He should have known better, indeed did know better. He was a veteran after all, he had seen the worst that humans could do — why should he have gone into things postwar with rose-coloured glasses? You could never discount greed. Or the tendency of capital and the profit motive to overwhelm men's thinking and values. He may have been an idiot, he said, but he also believed that he was not naïve by nature.

But Vic did not know just how trusting he really had been. Following the police investigation, charges were laid and a committal hearing took place. There, it was revealed that the two thugs who had gone to threaten the banker's widow had been spotted by her neighbours and their numberplate taken down. But they had been made aware of this, so played a last, dirty card. Vic Stockton, they announced, was actually the prime mover. He had told them to threaten the old lady, verbally and physically; they were simply carrying out his orders. And they had a document to this effect, no less, which their lawyer produced and had tabled at the hearing.

On this damning evidence, Vic was taken away for interview and arrested on charges of aiding and abetting. Joan had the terrible duty of finding him a lawyer to secure him bail and who would defend him against these separate allegations at his own hearing. Vic told her at the station, firmly and directly, that he had committed no crime. That she should not worry as everything would be resolved.

Whether he was to be found guilty or not guilty, Joan Stockton had arrived at a verdict of her own. She would accept he had not broken the law. But she had also decided that it was over between her and Vic.

Joan had lost the ability, the capacity, she didn't know what the right word was, to stand by any longer. She was apparently meant to trot faithfully by his side no matter what. She had done that for what felt like an eternity, she was tired to her bones. Even if he was proved innocent, she would no longer, could no longer care. He had thought only of himself since Jennifer was born. He had been absent. Unavailable. His head was full of all sorts of strange notions that he hinted at on the rare occasions when he did open his mouth. When he started talking about what so and so had done to 'make a million', or his plans for retiring 'by the time I'm fifty' and thereafter just go fishing, she wished he would shut up. She had long since concluded that Vic had never been overly concerned to accommodate her feelings or desires. His interests and needs were, it was somehow assumed, always the more vital. It was no way to be in a marriage. He was not the kind of husband she wanted anyway, or the father Jennifer deserved.

Vic's own hearing took place in a welter of further sensation and imputation. The story was even reported in the metropolitan dailies, with one paper using Vic as an example of the 'new breed of white collar criminal at work'. The paper told its readers that standover men, hired at the local bloodhouse, might be expected to do a job of dirty work, as they had in the case of the Nevertire development. But when the manager of a supposedly reputable building and development firm, a man trusted by vulnerable future homeowners and small-business people could behave in this way, things had come to a pretty pass. Clearly, more and better regulation was required to keep such sharks away from their potential prey.

Vic had to endure these insults and inferences in silence. There was no other option. Joan was not speaking to him in the weeks before his hearing and his lawyer had enjoined him to say nothing to anyone. He had been adamant with his lawyer that there were no such orders as he was supposed to have given because there was no such document. If there was a document, it would have to be a forgery.

Fortunately for Vic, this was proved. Having sighted the incriminatory note — properly typed but in a code lifted straight from the movies, using phrases like 'show her the error of her ways' and 'use whatever means you have to', Vic noticed two things: the letter was typed on Senator Bond quarto, an uncommon paper but standard issue at Prestige, and his name was signed in the black ink of a thick-nibbed fountain pen, one rather suspiciously like the sort J.V. owned and used. Aside from the inanity of anyone actually signing such a letter — its existence suggested only desperation after the event — the attempt at his signature was very poor. All this gave local detectives something easy and enjoyable to chew on. When a handwriting expert was called in, the magistrate had cause to doubt both the evidence and the chance of a conviction. Add to that the unreliability of the accusers — two petty hoodlums with plenty of previous form — and Vic was able to go free. Already under corporate investigation, J. V. Alderton was set to become the next target of the boys in blue.

At the hearing, Vic glanced occasionally at Joan. She was stoic, expressionless. He marvelled at her demeanour and was thankful for her presence, her strength. Vic knew he had a long way to go in making things up to her. She hadn't necessarily been that fair to him, but he must do what he could, was the view he came to. He thought he might start by proposing they all go for a holiday. A proper one, too — perhaps a trip overseas, to England or even Europe. He would suggest it lightly, with a laugh — yes, another of his preposterous ideas, he would happily admit. But there was money to do it and he owed it to them. All she had to do was give it the nod and he would buy tickets the very same day. That would give him, both of them, a chance to clear their heads and start again.

Vic took this plan to the dinner table that night, thinking he would put it forward at a decent moment. But as the meal progressed such an opportunity did not present itself. Joan was in a filthy, silent mood. He decided there could be a better tack: to wait until they had gone to bed.

But over the washing up, while Joan was at the sink and he was drying and stacking, she spoke at last.

'Vic, this is no good. I'm here to tell you I can't stand it, the way things are. More than that, this marriage. I'm … it's on the rocks …'

'What? Why do you say that? Things aren't that …' He had no idea where she was heading.

'I believe we've got to a very bad situation, even if maybe you don't,' she said. 'We're wasting each other's time. You've got nothing to give me or Jenny any more that I can see, not really.'

Vic put down the plate he'd been drying, and turned to stare at her. She did not look at him. But the set of her jaw said it all.

'Worst of it is, I think I was kidding myself, and you've been kidding yourself — you never did, you see,' she said.

'But Joan, things aren't that …'

'Oh yes, they are. I, I think we should separate.'

'Joan?'

She did not reply but turned around and left him at the sink.

Vic carefully folded and hung the dish towel on its foldaway rack and pushed it back under the benchtop.

20
Freedom

Joan continued to insist on a separation and he had no choice but to go along with it. She and Jenny left to stay with her parents and he remained in the house at Toongabbie. He tried to encourage her to give it another go, but she was determined to stay away from him. She wasn't prepared to go all the way to a divorce. They both dreaded that and what it would mean, and Vic hoped that sometime, somehow or another, she would see her way clear to accepting him again. But Joan, to Vic's mind, kept shooting holes in the boat, kept telling him that she had given him his 'freedom', and that from now on he could do as he 'liked'.

Vic was stunned at the speed and completeness of Joan's rejection. He had come to realise how harsh and determined she could be early in the separation when she went independently to see a solicitor and even asked what would happen if she were to seek a divorce. He had tried to challenge her on this but she would not speak to him, on this or any other matter. In Joan's view, he was just lucky that getting a divorce was as difficult as it was; there seemed insufficient grounds, from what she had learned. He had not been unfaithful, not in the conventional way; he had not been violent, or failed to provide.

Vic had much time to reflect on their marriage. From his perspective, their early years had been just fine. They did the things a young married couple did. They had had laughs, fun, they had taken holidays together. The sex had been good — admittedly more so when they were younger than in the last few years. But they weren't lovestruck kids any more, that was to be expected. He was not a bastard, a drunk or a gambler. He had worked to build a home and a family. That was a fair assessment, wasn't it? But maybe he and Joan had never been truly compatible, were two different people looking at things in two different ways.

But despite the rejection, the sense of failure, there were undeniably some advantages to his new situation. Bugger it man, it was great fun being on your own again, wasn't it? You could do anything you felt like, when you felt like it. There were places to go, adventures to be had. Things you could most assuredly never drag the family off to. Such as going camping, as he did on his own one rain-drenched weekend in September in Kangaroo Valley, where he arrived with the realisation he hadn't packed enough food and spent the entire Sunday sitting in his tent getting drunk. Or go to the flicks anytime you felt like it, to see anything you wanted.

Living on his own, with no job, no family and more time than he knew what to do with, Vic needed to find things to do. He began to take long morning walks around the suburb, exploring as many unfamiliar parts as possible, although not so far that he needed a street directory to find his way back. One day, on another of his long and increasingly aimless jaunts, he found himself walking past the Toongabbie Bowling Club. He stood looking through the cyclone wire fence at a patch of beautiful, close-cropped, dead-level lawn dotted with black and white balls.

Various old boys and girls dressed in white stood in groups down the far end. It was a pretty scene in its own way, all neat and quiet except for the occasional clacking sound when balls collided. On a whim, he went through the gate to have a closer look. Once inside, he strolled up to the clubhouse end, where a couple of the nice biddies smiled at him. He smiled back. Then he saw that some of the blokes were hardly older than he was, maybe even the same age.

He soon picked up what they were trying to do. The game had its appeal, more than he might have expected. This seemed like good, harmless fun. All topped off by a pleasant beer or two at the end. His social calendar was hardly overflowing — what the hell, he decided he might give it a go.

Joining the club the same day, Vic was, within a week, down there taking instruction. A week later he played his first game. Right through the winter and until the first of the annual play-offs between the district clubs Vic continued to attend. Then he went along to the meeting before the clubs' competition to be told what was required of him as one of the young bucks on the team, if only a reserve.

He sat close to the window that day, occasionally looking out at the hazy blue sky towards the west. But he found his attention drawn more to the insects flying around the hedge of prawn plants nearest this wall of glass, and with that felt a wave of sadness wash over him. Good and proper. He had been experiencing more of these lately and had begun to worry that his old problem had returned, those feelings he'd had years back and which had led to him being taken to the loony bin.

He heard the club captain droning on, until the words 'I want you chaps, and the ladies too, to go out there as if this is D-Day' struck him and stuck with him. They were absurd, even if you didn't take them as insulting. They were absurd. He was absurd. He got up and walked out. At home he took off his whites, made a bundle of them and threw them into the garbage.

For a good couple of years after the dramas he'd endured there was an important question troubling Vic, and that was work. After the debacle with Alderton, regardless of his innocence, Vic Stockton's name was mud around the district. Even the heartiest of the backslappers, the builders he approached — who acted as if he'd only been involved in a bit of a lark and who told him they would have done the same thing, given half a chance — were suspicious. They were all vague about the facts regarding him, but no amount of explaining himself made any difference to anyone. The slurs had stuck. The best he could get was an irregular job as a quantity surveyor; otherwise it was a matter of having to put on his belt and do the occasional bit of pick-up carpentry. Even that was hard: he was not as young and strong in body as he had been. This period brought home to him that, whatever else, he had arrived at middle age. Perhaps, he wondered in the occasional moments of self-pity he allowed himself, he had done the wrong thing in dumping his bowling gear. What else was he good for at his age?

Vic was not so conscious of other changes. He was having more and more run-ins with the booze, episodes when he would find himself waking up on the lounge at the house of some bloke he had met at a pub, with whom he had wandered home for want of anything better to do. Or he might have to race into his bathroom at home with an attack of nausea, or outright sickness after a bout of drinking alone, usually in front of the TV set, while trying to watch some dumb movie.

Despite hitting the grog too hard at times, as he would readily admit he did from time to time, Vic tried to maintain good order and discipline in the house — or 'pad', as he'd started calling it in line with the 'swingin' sixties' and his gay bachelorhood. He tried to buy and keep food in the fridge; he would put out the garbage, he would mow the accursed lawn, front and back. He was even known to purchase a piece of furniture from time to time — nothing too fancy, a beanbag when they were the fashion, or a coffee table after he had dropped a bottle on the smoked glass surface of the old one.

As company, female or otherwise, was in short supply, and he only had rare visits from Jennifer when her mother would let her off the leash, he had little reason to keep everything too neat and tidy. But he made the effort anyway and the place would have passed muster with any but the most severe of domestic critics. It was a miracle that he was still in the place at all, but he had stayed on after Joan left. Although not obliged to, he had given her the proceeds of their one-time nest egg — a couple of holiday shacks down at Nowra — to help her set up again. He sometimes wondered what she had done with the money; she and Jenny continued to live at her parents' home, even after they had died.

By early winter of 1970, there was some pattern to his life. Maybe not the pattern he might have wished for in an earlier time, but one nonetheless.

Vic had found a permanent job in a hardware shop in a suburb where he was not known. He was grateful for the chance of regular employment again — and even more grateful that he no longer had to do hard yakka on building sites. The only downside was having to wear a silly uniform shirt with a collar and tie. He would finish work, which largely consisted of flogging bits of useless DIY gear and paint to the army of 'home renovators' now appearing on the scene, then drop off at the Glasgow Arms to pick up a half-dozen beers and a meal from the nearby Chinese takeaway before going home to settle down in front of the box.

Life was boring, but it also made some sense. For someone divorced in all but name, this was probably as good as it got. Many other blokes in his situation were often far worse off, having been taken to the cleaners by their wives and hated by their kids. But Jenny didn't hate him, as far as he could tell. And Joan allowed her to come over more frequently as she got older. They would even have a few laughs, share the odd joke when she came over on Saturday afternoons, a strapping teenage girl now. Things could have been worse. And you could never tell when some nice woman might take pity on him. So far female company had not extended beyond a friendly encounter with a bird at work, or else met at a club or pub. But that was an indulgence, or solace, when he was feeling lonely. He took care to announce right at the outset that he wasn't looking for anything serious.

Vic believed he had developed a good enough grip, where someone else might have said he was merely rationalising his situation (when someone did say that, he politely declined to see her again). And one day he would wind back on the grog too, but not yet. Nor was he stuck in a rut, he told himself. New things came up all the time. For instance, he had lately become aware of the history of this district and had set off in pursuit of greater knowledge. He had even gone and joined the local historical society. That Toongabbie was only the third British settlement ever in Australia he found surprising; that a lot of poor bastard convicts had met their maker around here was less so.

One chilly night — as it could often be out here on these plains which, further west, ran right up to the Blue Mountains; any wind from the south or south-west always dropped the temperature a few degrees lower than closer to the coast — Vic went around the house turning on the radiators ahead of settling in for the evening. With two bottles of DA retrieved from the fridge, and with two documents he had received in the mail from the local historical society — the monthly newsletter and a little roneoed pamphlet — Vic set things out on the low table in front of the lounge. The pamphlet told the story of the Battle of Vinegar Hill, apparently the only genuine punch-up between authority and the convicts in the early days, which had taken place not many miles from where he sat.

How sad to think the military of the day had rounded on a few bread and horse thieves and had incarcerated them, then slaughtered them for breaking out. Maybe, he thought, that was just the true history of the world. Some desperate no-hopers trying to get by, while a few others, the powerful, see the very existence of the former as an outrage. Then comes the muscling in, the taking over, the punishment. Who could stop that sort of thing in the end? Governments? Or was it down to heroes and heroines? He would back a hero any time; pity they were in such short supply. As for heroines ... well, he'd known one in his time, he was privileged to think. But where was she, now that he needed rescuing again? The thought brought a grim smile to his face.

He had been sent across the world to be a hero, but in his gloomiest depths he thought he had come nowhere close. Other blokes had been better at that than he ever was, or ever could have been. Not that this was a direction he liked his thoughts to go — and especially not here, not like this, the way he was living now. Maybe he *was* guilty of rationalising. Certainly, he knew that all it took was a cold night on his own and in his mind he was back in places he would do better to forget. But he also found that if he conjured up the image of that beautiful Cretan girl one more time, he would feel better. He did, and he did. Mostly she appeared to him in the simple garb of a village girl, pretty as he recalled that could be. Other occasions he could conjure her as some kind of angel, a woman in a flowing white gown, a goddess … On the other hand, he thought as he took up the Vinegar Hill booklet again, it was just the beer.

Vic tried to go back to reading the story of rebellion and murder and retribution, but was beginning to find it too depressing; he just didn't have the concentration tonight. No longer able to focus on the words while unprepared to allow those earlier thoughts to linger, he took up the second, still full bottle of beer and with his foot pushed the table further away. He would settle back to watch *Homicide* instead.

Vic found himself in a pleasant beery state by 9.00pm, nodding off as the Friday night movie was a little way through. Try as he might not to fall asleep, half-drunk in front of the box, it happened. It happened, too, that this was the night that a billowing curtain caught itself on one of the bars of the radiator, and was set alight. It was also the night that the living-room fire turned into a house blaze. And the night that Vic had had to be rescued from his own home by frightened neighbours who, luckily for him, were able to get him out, kicking in a front window and half-dragging him in his stupor onto the front lawn. They tried to put out the fire with a garden hose, without success.

Vic was sitting on the nature strip, holding his head in his hands, being comforted by neighbours Rhonda and Bill when the fire brigade arrived. But the place was well alight and could not be saved. Sobering up in the deadly light of the fire, Vic understood he had no fight left in him, not to hurl against these flames, not for anything else much either. The only thing he was capable of, it seemed, was disasters. God help him, he thought as he sat in the gutter, that it had all come to this.

*   *   *

That was the end of life in Toongabbie for Vic. The place at least was insured and some money came his way, if not as much as he had expected. When the $10,000 finally came to hand, he began to look around for a place where he could start again. Well and truly start again. Because there was a lot that needed fixing. Staying with the neighbours who very kindly put him up for the period while he was looking, he came across five acres with an old farmhouse at Castle Hill, a district that everyone reckoned was on the rise. He didn't believe such talk at that time, preferring to think that he could do what had been done on that plot for a hundred years past: grow vegetables, run a few cows, a few chickens. A simple and self-sufficient life was the plan. And definitely no more alcohol.

With a goal of new and better times, Vic was as convinced as he could be that this was a right-enough approach. If only his heart didn't hurt as much as it did.

21

A Paddington Reception

1950, the year Vic Stockton arrived at Parramatta to start work for Prestige, was the year Andreas Coroneos left the suburb. He had been working at the Roxy Café since 1946, the year of his discharge. Andreas, or 'Andy', as he had allowed himself to be called there, was by now heartily sick of what he had been doing to get money. It had been more of the same café kitchen drudgery: emptying slops, cleaning pots and pans and dishes, peeling vegetables, all the dreary things he had grown used to calling work in Australia, both before and after the war, from the north of Queensland to central western New South Wales.

He may have been tired of labouring, but the Roxy was without doubt the most pleasant of all the places he'd worked at. It was a popular establishment, had long been doing well for the owners, two elderly Samiote brothers who had arrived in Australia before the First World War — so well that the old boys were easily able to pay their employees something like a normal wage, even if that did rather go against their grain. For Andreas, the money helped ease the humiliation, even if it could not remove the boredom of the past years. Still, Andreas' English had improved considerably during his time in the army and since he had been at Parramatta. And being able to earn reasonable and steady money was vital to his plans.

The Roxy was in the same street as Prestige, some four hundred metres further north on the opposite side. It was known around the Prestige office as the 'greasy Greek's' but, despite the honorific, was well patronised during the lunch break as a place to buy a decent pie or a milk shake or even a sit-down mixed grill at the end of the day. In the year they overlapped, Vic never went, preferring instead to bring lunch from home. The place was something of a landmark, a full-service café and oyster bar, however, with rows of booths along the walls and down the middle, one of the few in the west of the city. At night, with the words 'Roxy Café' lit up in cursive neon above the awning, as well as behind the front windows, and with a team of proper waiters and waitresses in black and white uniforms, the Roxy Café had its own modest glamour. Enough, anyway, to attract a variety of patrons; from courting couples on a night out and those on their way to the fifty-fifty dances at the nearby Royale Ballroom, to some of the better-heeled local businessmen who had acquired the 'continental' notion of eating out.

And eat they did. Andreas was amazed by the Australian mania for meat, a taste well catered for in the menu. As well as the ubiquitous mixed grill with its sausage, lamb chop and bacon, there were steak and eggs, steak and onions, steak and chips, steak and mushrooms, steak and oysters, variations to a total of twenty-four dishes on the main dinner list. In the early days Andreas would sometimes recite the main course menu as he went about his tasks in the kitchen, raising a smile and sometimes a laugh among his co-workers. The owners never found this sort of thing amusing, treating the preferences of their customers as almost sacred. Odd they might seem to Mediterranean palates, but, the brothers would explain, these tastes had made a mighty contribution to their own fortunes as well as keeping their rabble of a staff in more or less permanent employment.

Andreas had his reasons for leaving the Roxy: the old boys' lack of humour for one. It might not have been the most important cause, but he had found tiresome just how sombre those two were and how passive, sometimes plain obsequious, when it came to accepting the peculiarities and prejudices of the blessed Aussies. The greater reason, however, was that he had every confidence he could do what the owners had done: start a business, work for himself, thrive and prosper. He knew about small business, had run one back in Crete, after all. It was only a matter of finding the right opportunity and getting hold of the necessary capital. There was really nothing to stop him doffing his apron and stepping out of the kitchens and backrooms and into the main room. And then into the best spot of all — right next to the cash register.

Whatever the drawbacks of working there, the cafe at Parramatta had brought security. On top of the money he had forwarded to Kalliope for her trip, he had also been able to put aside enough to take a lease and restock a small milk bar on a main road in the inner-city suburb of Petersham. Fortunately, the place had a few rooms behind the shopfront for living quarters and the friendly landlady, once Andreas told her what was being planned, even furnished it with a few basics for the incoming couple.

As he had promised, Andreas was there, waiting, at the dockside when Kalliope's ship was tugged into the harbour to berth at No. 1 Walsh Bay. He was not alone, but one of hundreds of other young men from Greece and the Balkans. The reunion he was anticipating could not be as romantic as he might have wanted. But the day was magnificent. Waiting in the reception hall on the pier, Andreas looked through the glass and saw a crystal Sydney. A north-easter blew in off the sea, the trees on the opposite side of Sydney Cove were green and lustrous, small boats bobbed up and down on the water. Meanwhile around him that entire hall was awash with anticipation and hopes he understood very well and, more than that, shared.

A murmur arose from the crowd as the winches that lowered the main gangplank started. Andreas trained his eye on the gangplank and waited. Soon people, mainly women, began to appear — excited, waving, dabbing at their cheeks. Two or three minutes later, he was able to spot Kalliope, a slight figure in a fawn-coloured coat and light-blue headscarf. He called out to her, but she did not hear him. He waited for her as she headed down the immigration control queue.

Kalliope hesitated when she eventually saw Andreas and tried to go to him but was instructed by one of the many officials that she had to keep moving. When her paperwork was cleared and she was free to enter the main hall with all the other young women, the crowds made it impossible to do much more than identify Andreas and negotiate the crush to try to get to his side.

When they finally met, they could do nothing but hold each other and let their tears flow. Then, after many moments had passed, they looked around for a spot to one side where they weren't at least being jostled.

Once the tumult of thoughts in his head had subsided a little, and enough time had passed for dramatic declarations no longer to seem sensible, Andreas spoke to Kalliope.

'Dear, dear, Kalliope, this is unbelievable … unbelievable …'

'And for me, too, dear Andreas …'

He was pulled up, hearing her say his name like that, her Cretan intonation still intact where his had over time begun to weaken. 'Ha!' he said sardonically, adding, 'Andy, they call me Andy here.'

Kalliope looked at him, so overcome by the occasion that she could not process what she was meant to do about this name.

Andreas met her eyes again, and saw a grown woman. He smiled at her and kissed her. 'Were you able, did you see ... on the ship coming in, did you see the Sydney Heads?'

For a second or two she did not know what he was referring to, but then recalled some mention on board, and then how he had once said something in a letter. 'The heads? Yes! And the harbour, the harbour is as you said it would be.'

'*Omorfo?*' Beautiful?

'*Omorfo, ne!*' Beautiful, yes!

Kalliope felt faint now — tired, overwhelmed, disoriented. Her head fell to his chest and this time sobs, pure and simple, found their way out of her throat. She cried for a mother left behind, for the world left behind, for the fear and confusion she felt.

In the weeks ahead of their wedding, Kalliope would be billeted and chaperoned at the home of one of Andreas' fellow Cretans in Rockdale. The wife was only too happy to look after a sister in such times. The Cretan community Kalliope was introduced to in Sydney was small but energetic, its members intensely interested in one another. The community organised all sorts of activities, social, pastoral and actively philanthropic. Food and clothing parcels were prepared and sent to those struggling on Crete, money was raised for various ventures such as schools and agricultural works. The effectiveness of the organisation was testament to their sense of identity, but also to the reality that there was money to spare, if not much, in Australia.

What the local Cretans didn't have, according to Andreas, was a big chief — in his view a shortcoming. Such big chief as there was in the country, lived in Brisbane, a man by the name of Pavlos Danelakis, also known in the Greek press as 'the richest Greek in Australia'. As Andreas had met and been befriended by him in earlier times, Andreas proposed that he might act as his best man. Danelakis agreed to come down from Queensland, take a holiday and do his duty for the young man. He would do nothing less, for 'we are of one blood', he had emphasised, 'and you are a good boy'. Kalliope left these arrangments to Andreas. She was busy enough merely trying to get used to this place, whose people looked very like the English she had seen in newspapers and magazines, and who spoke the language of the English. She assumed that Andreas knew what he was doing when he invited Danelakis to officiate at their wedding.

The wedding was to be held in a not very Orthodox-looking church in Surry Hills which was apparently the oldest Greek church in Australia. For bridesmaids, Kalliope was assigned the daughters of some pleasant church women who insisted that their offspring would be perfect for the task. Kalliope didn't mind. There was so much that needed organising, and it was so difficult to make sense of everything that was happening around her that she was grateful for anything that came her way. Andreas reassured her that it was best to just let herself go along with things — the community wanted to help, wanted to be involved. She had no argument with that. The hard thing was to put out of mind that she and Marika had once vowed to be each other's bridesmaids. How she longed for her company at such moments.

The church women were very helpful in organising their rooms behind the shop in Petersham. Besides the table and chairs and bed the landlady supplied, there was hardly anything else in the place, as Kalliope discovered when Andreas first took her there. She found difficulty in getting her bearings in these small, airless and dark rooms that ran off a hall from the shop; there was a strange sort of kitchen too, with an upright iron stove which she could not make sense of until Andreas showed her how it worked and used a match to light one of the burners.

'Here, the gas comes out of a pipe, you see!' he announced triumphantly.

Kalliope marvelled at such a facility and was even more grateful when one of the church ladies offered to take her to a place to buy some utensils, pots and pans. And when the same woman introduced her to an experienced seamstress who had run up many a wedding gown for the local Cretan and other Greek girls, Kalliope was happy to be guided in that decision too.

As the day drew near, Kalliope began to fret about her ability to hold in her head everything that needed holding. Here there would be wedding cars, bouquets of flowers a la mode, a professional photographer no less. And all to be followed by a 'reception' — the word for *glendi* that she heard repeated by the others at church, a word she took the trouble to memorise in English.

So busy had she been in the days beforehand that she was not able to reflect for more than a few seconds at a time on anything beyond the wedding. The thousand and one jobs took all available thinking space. But Kalliope was transported to the service in a big black car and somehow managed to get through what happened next without losing her wits completely. At the altar itself, where she and her new husband stepped the traditional three times around, and exchanged their wreaths three times, according to custom, Kalliope could barely breathe, let alone think.

Only at the reception that followed at Paddington Town Hall was she able to gaze out on the scene into which she had been thrust — or which she had chosen, she was hardly sure in the moment — and attempt to make sense of it all. This venue itself was strange. Although it was roughly the same size as the school hall she recalled from Rethymnon, she had never been in a place quite like this before, not one with these odd decorations all around the walls, and pilasters that were somehow faintly Greek but somehow also not. Nor was she prepared for the sheer number of people coming and going at any one time (instead of being seated by family and place as at home), or the casual nature of the proceedings. Back home, the wedding feast had a strict order; here, it seemed a free-for-all, with food before dancing and tables straining with dozens of brown bottles of beer and piles of chicken and meats of one kind or another, and myriad young children running riot everywhere.

Seated at the wedding table, Kalliope looked out on what must have been easily four hundred people. Andreas had said this would be a special day for the community, but as the night went on she had an uneasy feeling about her place in all this. Of everyone here she knew perhaps twenty by name. The speeches that followed, too, were something else. Anyone and everyone, it seemed, was authorised to line up at a microphone to make a speech. She had no problem with the priest, as he seemed a nice old fellow, and he did the normal thing of wishing them well and passing on God's blessing. But there was the president of the Cretan Brotherhood, an Australian politician of some sort, and the woman in charge of the Ladies' Auxiliary, all before any of the official wedding group. Andreas had not given her any hint and she had no idea what any of them was going to say, and she was puzzled by the mention of things that had little to do with a wedding celebration.

Much time was given over to detailing the strides the community had made in recent years; much talk also about how theirs was the pre-eminent among all the regional brotherhoods in terms of numbers and achievements. Andreas translated for her various snatches of what the politician had to say: something about how people 'like the Greeks' were welcome in this fair land provided they played by the rules and didn't try to do things according to the 'old ways', whatever they were.

The star speaker, Danelakis himself, was a large man with what Kalliope thought was a gigantic head on his shoulders. His smile was more of a broad grin, a practised look she considered, perhaps hiding something. To emphasise his less-than-open expression, a sizable gold upper tooth was visible on one side. She had tried to warm to him in the few days he had been down in Sydney, but was conscious of having failed. His words tonight made it more difficult.

'Ladies and gentlemen, you have before you,' he began in a way that suggested he was campaigning for some office, not presiding over a wedding feast, 'the flower of our Cretan youth. Two young people who have come to this country as we all have, in the hope of a better life. Over there, they had nothing ... Over here, they have something, or will have if they continue to work hard. A young man needs to work hard to provide for his family. His wife must support him to allow him to provide. That is age-old wisdom. We all know it. But sometimes failure visits us. Someone will, for whatever reason, let someone else down. Heartache follows. Pain follows. Success does not. I have many years of experience in these matters and I believe I have some knowledge I can pass on. Therefore, I will address my words of advice to our young couple directly and to each ... Andreas, do your duty and treat your woman well. Honour her. And give her the children she deserves and must have to fulfil her role as woman!'

At this there were more than a few titters of laughter from somewhere beyond; Kalliope did not dare look for the source, but lowered her eyes to stare at a point on the tablecloth in front of her. The amused murmurings only subsided when Danelakis began again.

'Kalliope, fine young woman that you are — and I am a good judge, let it be said — you must always have in mind your own duties to your husband. As Father Apostolidis said earlier, you too must honour. And you must obey. That is the mark of a good woman.' Here he paused, looked up and smiled across the crowd, 'while the other kind won't get a mention here!'

At this, there were a few guffaws, from some of the men anyway. It seemed that Danelakis had had much practice with a crowd.

'But the true Cretan woman is a heroine,' he resumed. 'She is strong and fearless — who will ever forget what she has done through our history? Think of your forbears as you go through life, Kalliope. Never forget where you came from. May you bring forth from your Cretan loins the children that I know you would want and that we of course would all want from you ... I am sure that, for his part, your *levendi* Andreas is up to the task! God bless and protect you both! Please raise your glasses!'

By the time Danelakis had sounded his final sonorous notes, Kalliope knew that her face and neck had reddened. She had never heard a wedding speech like this in her whole life. To speak so openly of her bearing children, like so many kid goats or piglets! She was angry, and somehow, in a way she didn't understand, she was fearful too. She wanted nothing more than to be somewhere else, and quickly took herself, with one of the bridesmaids, to the rest room to try to find her equilibrium once more. She could only hope her feelings were not too obvious.

She insisted on the bridesmaid waiting outside while she went into a cubicle. There, she stood leaning her head against the wall, thoughts spinning wildly, but utterly determined not to cry. She would not cry. The man had no idea, obviously, what she and her people had been through, let alone what they had done, on Crete while he had been busy getting fat in Australia. More troubling, she couldn't see whatever Andreas admired in him.

Eventually her breathing returned to something more steady and she was able to leave. She calmed herself further by reminding herself that it was just a speech; words and nothing more. She had no obligation to this fellow; he would be gone again in another day or two. Even if he was to be their *koumbaro*, their best man, he would be out of her life in practical terms because of distance alone. She sincerely hoped that he didn't mean too much to Andreas. As Andreas had hardly mentioned him until recently and then only in the context of their needing a patron, she had no real reason to think he did.

Kalliope went back to the table and sat down again next to Andreas. He looked at her a little concerned and asked if she was all right. Yes, she was, she replied; just a little overcome by all the attention. That was understandable, he said in turn, and tried to pour her a glass of beer.

'*Ohi, Andrea*, if I have another glass you will have to carry me out.'

Andreas didn't think this was such a bad idea at all. 'Well then, you'd better have one!'

But when she touched his hand gently and smiled at him, he saw that thing inside her that he had continued to remember and believed he loved. Kalliope was a woman who knew her mind, but would always be kind to those around her, even in disagreement.

Andreas was gazing at his bride in wonder and satisfaction at the moment Danelakis approached their table. He stood directly in front of the newlyweds and for a long time simply looked down at them, as if weighing something, assessing something. Then there was that grin again.

'You two,' he finally said, ' I think you're going to be all right. You don't know very much, it's obvious. But who does at your age?' His expression slowly changed through another long pause, to one more serious, bordering on grave. This, and his standing there without saying anything, was making Kalliope uncomfortable. Then, he began again: 'Kalliope, let me say to you that you are lucky to have found such a nice young man. And lucky to be here at all, my girl. You should always try to remember what's been done for you by others, if you want to be happy ...'

This was too much for Kalliope. She lowered her head once more and this time could not stop herself from shedding tears.

Andreas put his arm around her, as he looked up at his *koumbaro*.

'She's upset, Pavlos. Anyone would be on such a day.'

Danelakis leaned forward and placed his hand gently on the top of her head. 'There, there, dear girl, don't worry. It's normal to cry on one's wedding day ...'

22

The Baby Business

After the wedding, there was to be a honeymoon. Kalliope was unfamiliar with the idea of such a holiday; her experience had been that a newly married couple wasted no time in moving in with the groom's family and that both would be back at their tasks after a day or two's grace, with the bride also undertaking home duties under the supervision of her new mother-in-law. But in Australia there would be no such thing. Kalliope and her husband would be free to take time off, even to travel if they felt like it.

The plan was that they would spend two weeks out west at Forbes, where Andreas had been stationed in the army and where he had worked just before coming down to Sydney. He told Kalliope that he had made two staunch friends there, a middle-aged Kastellorizian named Lambis and his younger wife, Voula. They ran a garage, and when they had heard of his forthcoming wedding, they had insisted on giving Andreas and his bride a holiday by way of a present. It would be a proper rest after the furious activity of the last few months; a week that would be the perfect introduction to the 'Australian bush', as Andreas, echoing Lambis, explained. Far away as it was, he could not anyway insult them by turning down the offer.

To get there would be no problem. They would drive up in Andreas' recently acquired Morris panel van, a car bought for the business. A trip by car would be preferable to travelling by train, Andreas explained, having been on that line many times and knowing how grinding and uncomfortable it could be.

These details they talked about as they sat in the back of Danelakis' hire car while Danelakis drove them home after the reception.

'If you must go, by all means. As I've said, it would please me more if you came up north!' he called out to them in his large and confident baritone.

When they arrived at the shop, he got out of the car to help them with presents, wreaths and bombonieri associated with the wedding.

'You are generous, *koumbare*, but I did promise those people …'

'Don't worry yourself, next time …' Danelakis said, waving expansively with his left arm.

When it was time to go, he kissed them both, then pulled Andreas aside for a last moment after Kalliope had gone in.

'By the way, my boy … here is a token from your *koumbaro*. Enjoy yourselves, enjoy!'

He handed Andreas an envelope, which the latter put in his pocket without opening, confident as he was about what would be inside.

'Thank you, how can I thank you … We, I, couldn't have done this without you …'

'On your way now — and make sure you do the right thing with that pretty girl of yours tonight, eh?' he said, flashing Andreas what he imagined was a devilish smile. He then got back in his car, tooting as he drove off.

*　　　*　　　*

Kalliope was not entirely in the dark about what was meant to happen on this night. She had been one of a few older girls taken into the confidence of their favourite teacher in Rethymnon — the much-loved *Kyria* Manikakis, whose book of poems she cherished so much she had brought it with her to Australia — and given some instruction on sex and childbirth. Dido Manikakis knew that some of the old heads in the villages didn't like such brazen talk but persisted anyway, with the aid of a serious-looking book that included diagrams. The new woman, she would say, needed to know about these things, to be unafraid, to enjoy all aspects of her marriage. Beyond that, Marika, in her own enthusiastic and provocative way, had always told Kalliope more than she needed to know on these matters.

Kalliope was a little apprehensive, but took comfort in the fact that whatever happened there would not be the obscene and ridiculous business of the sheets being paraded through the village, as had been the custom back in Arkadi until recently. And she was not ignorant about modern practices in preventing pregnancy. They had already agreed they would not try for a child just yet. So when Andreas, now her own Andreas, came to her and helped her through the elaborate undressing required to get out of the wedding gown, all the while taking off garments of his own, Kalliope was very happy to throw her arms around his neck and hold his head in her hands and return his kisses, ardent and hot as they were. When they were in bed together, she was glad he seemed to know what to do. She did not dwell on how he knew what he knew, but the next morning when they lay folded in each other's arms there was a moment when the thought lingered with her.

With the generous wedding gift of £100 cash from Danelakis in Andreas' wallet, and two large suitcases packed (both survivors of their separate journeys to Australia), they set off on the first Tuesday after their wedding to travel the Great Western Highway out to Forbes.

Along the road, Kalliope was constantly diverted by the spectacular ridges and valleys of the Blue Mountains: here a complete cover of unfamiliar blue-green vegetation, there bare ochre and red-brown cliff faces. She took heart that this was the beautiful country her husband had told her about. But once on the other side, verdant ridges turned to sparse woodland, which in turn gave way to an empty, dry vastness of low hills and plains of brown grass dotted with odd-looking sheep. This was land, Andreas explained, that had been cleared for the grazing of a very woolly species of sheep and the growing of wheat crops. By the time they had arrived at Forbes after an overnight stop at a hotel in Orange, she wasn't sure she liked what she was seeing. There was hardly a town or village between the few main stops along the way and the landscape had a forbidding air.

They reached the outskirts of Forbes late on the Wednesday afternoon, with Andreas soon able to point out the right motor garage at one end of the main street. It was a busy place, Kalliope saw, with three or four other cars on the driveway. She was apprehensive about meeting yet more people, all she felt she had been doing since her arrival in Australia. But as Andreas' friends were both outside when they arrived — Lambis cleaning a windscreen, Voula dispensing petrol — Kalliope had at least the advantage of seeing them before they saw her and time to ready herself. Voula was a red-cheeked, vivacious type; by comparison to her own somewhat skinny self, she was a woman all 'curves and handles like a pot' (as she had been amused to hear Andreas describe such a woman in the past). The husband, Lambis, was physically a similar type, round and short, and just as jolly-seeming, Kalliope deduced from his broad grin as he worked.

Andreas honked his horn, to the slight annoyance of Lambis, who turned sharply in the direction of their car. Only when he realised that it was Andreas Coroneos who was acting the goat in that Morris did he drop what he was doing and rush to a tap to wash his hands. He called out to Voula as he went, and she waved her one free hand at them wildly. Kalliope saw her to be very frustrated that she had to finish filling the petrol tank before she could join them. She took the money thrust at her through the window and hurried over to welcome these compatriots who had driven all the way from Sydney.

With embraces and kisses all round, the first encounter with these friends of Andreas went well enough. Kalliope was moved by the warmth and enthusiasm Lambis demonstrated. Voula seemed to hold back a little — she indicated her hands were dirty from serving petrol, but Kalliope didn't know what to make of her desire to get away and inside the garage office so quickly. Kalliope was distracted from what felt like a snub when Lambis took them by the elbows and steered them around the back of the garage. She was impressed to learn that she and Andreas would be accommodated in the main bedroom of the house behind the garage while Lambis and Voula slept in a closed-in verandah at the back. The bedroom itself was more comfortable than might have been expected.

The day after settling in, Andreas took Kalliope to see the sights of the area. As far as Kalliope could establish, Forbes, surrounded by hot and grassy plains, was an oasis because of the river that ran through the middle of the town. She thought the river rather beautiful. Less impressive was the grave site Andreas insisted they go to see, having earlier bored her at length with a story about its occupant, some old bandit named Ben Hall who had been shot dead just out of town. Kalliope was intrigued at how Andreas went on about the fellow, likening him to the best of the Cretan *Klephts*, and even more so — robbing the rich as they so thoroughly deserved to be robbed. 'Had I grown up here, I too would have been a bushranger,' he pronounced.

Kalliope was determined to be as thoughtful as their hosts, helping with meals in the kitchen while Voula was busy in the garage. She thought the extra hands might be welcome, not least because people obviously ate much more here than at home in Crete, and greater quantities of food needed to be prepared. It was no wonder, she thought, that Voula and Lambis were padding out their clothes the way they were.

But much as she wanted to help, the business of preparing food was more fraught than Kalliope expected. She rarely got anything done without Voula dropping in to check what she was doing, then passing comment. Kalliope would chop vegetables one way, to be told that they were chopped differently here. And the cuts of meat were not easy to recognise. One time Kalliope couldn't identify the beef she was told to ready for a casserole, and Voula made a great show of taking it from the refrigerator and waving it in front of her in triumph; then, when she was having difficulty working out how best to slice it, Voula came up beside her at the bench and abruptly pushed her aside. '*Ha! Ise horiatisa akoma vlepo, koritsi mou. Kita, kopse to esti …*' — Ha! You're still the village girl, aren't you my dear. Look, do it this way … — she said, snatching the knife from her and setting to herself.

Kalliope found this behaviour dismaying. Reddening at such moments, she didn't know what she might do or say that was right.

At the table on the first two evenings, however, the tensions seemed to pass. Lambis would tell jokes, the dinners were pleasant enough. Andreas was in high spirits and Kalliope loved to see him laugh.

As the week drew on, however, Kalliope began to feel less and less comfortable at night. It seemed that after dinner and the now obligatory cards, drinking a great deal of beer was what the men most liked doing. Andreas' behaviour, allowing himself to get a little drunk each night, surprised her. Even more surprising was that Voula too was happy to drink glass after glass of beer, to the point of becoming quite silly; one night she launched into some barely coherent tune, which, Kalliope guessed, she remembered from her youth. Over and over she sang the chorus: 'I am burnt, my love, burnt like the ashes of the fire,' until even good-natured Lambis had had enough and shouted at her to stop caterwauling and embarrassing him in front of his guests. At the sound of his angry voice, Voula dropped her head almost instantly, sullen and defeated.

Although surprised at the outburst, Kalliope could find little sympathy for Voula. She had directed one too many sharp remarks at Kalliope — not only her cooking, but her hair, her dress, her quiet voice, all seemed to be out of favour. Kalliope wondered if she had inadvertently offended Voula. But it was also as if she was somehow in the way. Kalliope was more confused when the next day Andreas told her their hosts had planned a small party to celebrate their wedding and had invited others of the small Greek community to join them. There had been no mention of this and Kalliope wondered at the secrecy.

Try as she did on the night, Kalliope could not find the enthusiasm to lose herself in the event. She was moved that their presence had motivated the twenty or so Greeks who lived in the area to get together in their honour, but as a celebration it all seemed so thrown together, so pathetic somehow. The wooden boxes filled with plates of food delivered onto the garage apron were all soggy and lukewarm by the time they were brought inside and all the music came from gramophone records. And oddly, no children had been brought along. She was sorry, finding the company of children joyful, especially the Australian variety who seemed less wary and freer in their play, their style and attitude generally, than children back home.

When Kalliope heard the first of the old-time tunes start up, she went over to look at the collection of records the visitors had arranged in piles next to the radiogram; not one had been produced in the last five years. Later in the evening, after they had finished eating, and dancing was to begin in earnest, she found herself happier to listen to the few American records, 'In the Mood' and 'The Boogie Woogie Bugle Boy from Company B'. Far from the sad old dirges that she had been hearing, these had a driving, lively beat, and even if she couldn't follow all the words, the tunes clearly said joy and happiness rather than misery.

Kalliope eventually checked her watch, a wedding gift from Andreas, and saw it was 11.00pm. It was late, but no one had left and no one even seemed interested in departing.

A few couples had drifted off, some even through the wire gate at the end of the yard so they could stroll around in the paddock beyond. She could hear them shouting and hoopa-ing as they went. Andreas, too, had taken himself off somewhere, leaving her seated alone at one end of the table, content to watch in amusement as an elderly pair attempted some version of a waltz. Kalliope didn't mind being left alone for a few minutes, free of all the cloying attention and stroking she had been subjected to all night. After a time, however, she felt like wandering herself.

Kalliope got up to walk across the yard and around the back of the building towards the garage and the main street beyond. She had the idea that it would be pleasant to see a car go by, some sort of non-human movement anyhow.

No one noticed as she stepped away quietly, rounding one corner of the house. From there she could see the small garage shed where the repairs were done; she could also see Andreas standing next to it, his attention occupied by something she could not see. No one else was around. She was curious and went up slowly in the darkness towards him.

He didn't notice her until she was almost by his side.

'Andreas,' she said quietly as she approached.

Startled, he lurched towards her. He took her arm with one hand, making a shushing gesture with the fingers of the other. Then he grinned at her in a way she had not seen before. Kalliope couldn't read his expression in that instant, but did not like it, whatever it was.

'What is it? What are you doing?'

'Look,' he said, and pointed in the direction of the shed a few metres beyond where they stood. A small window was set into the wooden boards on this side of the building. The glass was dirty, but the inside was dimly lit and it was possible to look in. Andreas moved Kalliope forward.

Smeared as the glass was, she had no trouble making out what was happening in there. Using the end of one of the workbenches, Lambis and Voula were having sex. The sight startled her; more startling was the fact that Andreas had been looking on, apparently amused.

'Andreas!' she said in a loud whisper. 'You, we, shouldn't be here!'

'What are you worried about?' he replied, slurring his words slightly. She understood he was a little drunk. 'They are husband and wife. It's natural! They're enjoying themselves.'

She turned him away and as she did so, he reached out and embraced her. Nothing more, for which she was relieved. But standing there in his arms in the dark she wasn't sure what to make of this. It was troubling, *that* she knew, and she began to pull him away towards the house.

Andreas had been oblivious to the petty-mindedness of Voula over the past few days. Kalliope had let things ride, not wishing to upset him or reject the hospitality they had been offered. Only this morning Voula had let slip a catty remark about how cool and composed was Kalliope, 'not at all like other Greek women one knows her age'. And now for her husband to behave in such a way! Kalliope found herself becoming angry for the first time since joining Andreas in Australia. This was not right. This did not make sense.

Next morning as they lay in bed together, Andreas was sheepish and conciliatory. He leaned over and touched Kalliope on the cheek. 'Kalliope, I did the wrong thing last night …'

She was pleased he had spoken, happy to be in his embrace and indeed to have him as her husband. She rolled towards him, propping herself up on an elbow to gaze at him.

'You have to be more …' she began, but did not know how to continue. 'Andreas, my love, this is a different world for me. I don't know how everything is done here … I'm trying to learn …'

'I should have thought more last night …'

'And you'd drunk too much,' she smiled at him.

'And I'd drunk too much, *ne*.' He leaned across and kissed her again.

* * *

Their last day at Forbes was uneventful, and soon Andreas and Kalliope were back in the city, hard at work — cutting sandwiches and making and selling milk shakes and hamburgers from their new business. The whole exercise struck Kalliope as most peculiar. If someone had once said that across the world, in Australia, people bought and drank so much cow's milk and ate so much beef, she would never have believed them. Cow's milk was heavy, she always felt, and the beef they bought and minced for the meat patties was tough, very tough if you compared it to the kid and lamb she had grown up on. But there was no shortage of customers, young and old. Andreas had been right when he told her that their shop would prove a reliable source of income.

As the till continued to fill each day, the shop was on a sound footing. But with their increasing financial security, Kalliope became less impressed by some of the people who helped provide it. Encounters with customers sometimes had Kalliope baffled and upset. She was still having trouble getting her tongue around some of the new words and their pronunciation: sliced bread please, devon and ham, Worcestershire sauce … Any words that did not have a vowel separating them, sentences that ended in a consonant did not sound right to an ear that knew soft sounds in those places. In the first few weeks she thought things wouldn't be so bad once she had mastered the rhythms and some more vocabulary. She did already have a few words, learned during the war, taught to her by that Australian soldier.

Kalliope had not counted on being mocked by some of her customers. Young schoolboys were the worst: they seemed to actively delight in teasing her, were more transparent in their baiting, especially when they were in a group together. But the more deeply insulting were those men who would snigger in a most adult way — a snigger was a snigger in any language — at her failure to understand their order, or her mangling of their language in response.

The discomfort that went along with each work day was eased a little at night when she and Andreas could retire to the rooms at the back of the shop and prepare and eat a meal together. At that time, they would try to reconstruct some of the things they knew from the old days, even if Andreas had become very Australianised in his eating habits and more than keen on his lamb's fry and chips. They enjoyed cooking with traditional ingredients such as fetta and haloumi and olive oil. To obtain these items required a trip to the one delicatessen in nearby Marrickville that imported supplies for the rapidly growing population of Greeks in that area.

After hours, there was further comfort for Kalliope in socialising with others in the community. The Cretans had a club of their own downtown, in the city, which was always a lively place to visit on a Saturday or Sunday afternoon, especially if there was a special event or meeting. By common consent, the club rooms were divided into separate areas for men and women. The men's was a large room that looked like an old-style city *kafeneion*, with card tables and an elderly gent in the corner whose sole job was to keep the coffees coming. The women meanwhile had a lounge which they made their own for its decent soft chairs and supply of magazines, and the chance to get together to catch up and exchange information or, in the time-honoured tradition, complain about their husbands.

Andreas was less inclined than Kalliope to go along, objecting to the gossip that was traded there and the limited menu in the small dining room. Of greater appeal to him was the restaurant that one of his friends from army days had opened in the same street as the club. Andreas occasionally took Kalliope there for a meal.

On these outings, usually on Sunday afternoons, Kalliope was not so pleased with her husband's tendency to trumpet his knowledge of things Australian — or worse, even to brag about how well they were doing.

In the years they had been apart, he had changed in some ways. This was not a revelation — people changed, that was normal. To his credit, he had explained that he was not the callow youth she might have remembered, but a man who had experienced the world and war and was less sensitive for that. His opinions were now formed, he would say; what should he do but express them?

As for her own experiences of the war, Kalliope had hardly spoken about them since her arrival, believing that the subject had been covered in letters over the years. She said a little more once at the friend's restaurant over lunch, in reply to Andreas' question whether she had ever met an Australian before coming here. She had said yes, she had, and spoke for the first time about a lost Australian soldier. She had not mentioned him in letters, she said, because of her involvement in the resistance and the need to keep some things very secret. Andreas had snapped at her, and cut her off impatiently. 'Yes, yes, but that was years ago, wasn't it? A soldier isn't a good example,' he had said.

Kalliope didn't understand his reaction, and took the censure to heart. From then on, she was wary about mentioning those times. It seemed better to respond only if and when he asked, and he seldom did.

As to her own feelings, she imagined she was less troubled than the people she had left behind. As often as possible she tried not to be overwhelmed by the worry she felt whenever she thought about her mother, her uncle and her friends in Arkadi. The civil strife had intensified since her departure, she knew. The local Greek newspaper reported what was happening overall, but there was rarely any news from Crete itself. Kalliope took hope in the view that she and other Cretans held, choosing to believe that their island would never become a proper Communist stronghold. What they were hearing in Sydney suggested the signs were promising.

Exhausted as she was from keeping shop all day and looking after Andreas at night, she had only been able to bring herself to write one short note to her own people back on Crete; not to apologise or seek understanding but to state in the simplest terms what she had done. She had left for Australia, she had rejoined Andreas, they had married. She had added that, while she was sorry things had happened like this, and she knew it would be difficult for them to understand, she would write later to try to explain.

One Saturday afternoon in the shop, fully seven months after landing in Sydney and unable to put it off any longer, Kalliope took up a letter pad and sat down behind the counter to write to her mother. There was so much she needed to find words for but these would only emerge when she was able to make sense of her chaotic thoughts and impressions.

In the quiet of the shop, she could hear the sound of the refrigerator motors running below the floor. Fridge motors. She had been only abstractly aware that such machinery existed before she came to Australia — there were none where she had come from. And a shop like this, a 'mixed business', as it was termed, was unknown. Here was as odd a gathering of things to eat as anyone could imagine. People came in to look for milk in glass bottles, and exotic fruits like pineapples crushed up and served with ice, and factory-made biscuits of all kinds, which she and Andreas had to weigh and pack into brown paper bags.

Perhaps she could tackle the task from the perspective of dreams. The best of these was that they would set themselves up financially, well enough to bring out her mother. How she would cope in Australia was another question. Kalliope's mother thought the pace of life in their village was becoming too frantic, for instance. She was a nervous person, easily frightened — understandable given what she had gone through in her early days. And she was notoriously picky at meals, unwilling to try anything other than the food she had learned to eat at her own mother's table; Kalliope remembered her once regarding fried potatoes as a daring innovation. If her mother didn't come out, she and Andreas could still possibly return to Arkadi in another five years perhaps, when they had accumulated some capital. If they would be welcome, that is.

Here she turned to the matter of her own behaviour. Would her leaving as she had still be seen as a cruel blow, an abandonment of her own, by those who remained there? She hoped not, but there was always Mattheos doing his best to poison everyone against her.

As Kalliope continued to wonder, she realised she couldn't write this letter yet. So many things remained unsettled, so many things were still unknown and the future difficult to prophesise about. It would have to be enough, for the next few months anyway, that she had let her people know the bald facts. A detailed explanation, the plans they had in mind, these would have to wait.

In time, Kalliope became comfortable with the idea that recreation was possible in Australia — not merely a once-a-year holiday if you were lucky, but as part of weekly, if not daily, life. Andreas introduced her to another of his Aussie-acquired habits:

the movies. Sometimes after closing the shop they would walk up to the local cinema to watch whatever latest Hollywood extravaganza was on offer. Kalliope found the language of these movies difficult, but the way they were made — the simplicity of the stories, the looks the heroes and heroines gave each other — meant she got the gist often enough. In the first year alone he took her to see *An American In Paris* with Gene Kelly and Leslie Caron, *The Third Man* with Orson Welles and Joseph Cotten and, one of his favourites at the time, *Samson and Delilah*, directed by Cecil B. DeMille and starring Victor Mature and Hedy Lamarr. The last she thought was silly, and she was amused and curious to see the impact it had on him while they were watching. Andreas loved the whole idea, it seemed, of a powerful man and a sultry seductress locked together in a kind of combat.

'Don't you think I look a bit like Victor Mature?' he said as they came out onto the street this night.

'Of course!' she said to please him, and sidled up to run her fingers through his hair (the seat of Samson's power, although how she could not see). As she did that, Andreas grabbed her around the waist and pulled her to him to kiss her. But doing such a thing in public was too much for Kalliope, and she pushed him away as kindly as she could.

So much had the movie affected Andreas that, home again, he suggested to Kalliope they might 'play the parts' they had seen. Kalliope didn't mind the idea: presented like this on a night when she felt relaxed and willing, she rather liked the thought of being someone else for a short time. She had come to know her husband as an ardent lover and a good one, even if sometimes his interest didn't seem to have much to do with how she was feeling. Pretending she was still that student of drama she had been so long ago, Kalliope ordered him with the crook of a finger to lie down on their bed as she began to undress in front of him. Much as he tried to hold back, her gesture was too exciting — he immediately jumped up again to try to grab hold of her. As he did so, she pushed him down gently with a free hand.

'*Ohi*. You will do as I say,' she said firmly in Greek, hardly believing it was her own sweet self who was speaking like this.

'Yes, but only because you are my Delilah,' Andreas said in English, attempting his own bit of acting, trying to sound like Victor Mature.

Kalliope felt this piece of play-acting to be oddly liberating. She finished undressing and slowly eased herself down onto him. 'Well, we always said we would be modern people, didn't we?' she whispered in his ear, her own excitement rising with each moment.

Andreas missed her remark and its import, Kalliope saw. He seemed preoccupied, heading elsewhere, his eyes foggy with some other idea. He took hold of her arms and, without looking at her, said, 'But Delilah has bad designs on her Samson and I will not let her overcome me!' then suddenly rolled her over onto her stomach.

'You are jealous of your sister,' he whispered hoarsely into her ear, reverting to Greek, as he could not recall the dialogue in English. 'The woman I wanted and who your people killed. But it was you who killed her!'

Kalliope listened as he lay on top of her. She was beginning not to like the sound of Andreas' voice behind her like this. There was something a little too realistic in the tone she was hearing. What was it?

'Andreas?' she said gently.

'Silence!' he almost shouted through gritted teeth. Kalliope became a little frightened.

'Andreas?' she said searchingly.

'Don't worry, I'm only playing with you …' he whispered. And then, as he began to make love to her with his usual confidence and she began to enjoy the proceedings, whatever discord she felt gradually subsided.

Kalliope had grown used to bringing forth hamburgers into the world, but — as she said to the other Greek women at church on Sundays — she would much rather be giving birth to a child. She often told Andreas they should have a child sooner rather than later, as it was not so easy when a woman was older. Early in 1952 she had firmly said that they should try for a baby, but she was puzzled by his mumblings in response. He was not against it, but he wasn't unconditionally in favour either. She consulted with one or two of her female friends among the community; his ambivalent response, they said, was typical male fear of the responsibility that came with a child, a syndrome that she was advised to accept, and then ignore and get pregnant anyway. That would have been fine except that Andreas was the one in control of contraception.

In late 1956, Andreas relented and soon after the deed was done. That she was carrying a baby was finally confirmed by the friendly Doctor Clarence, whose surgery she had attended on the rare occasions when she had needed any sort of medical treatment over the past few years. Early in the morning of 24 July 1957, after a straightforward labour of eight hours, Kalliope gave birth to a daughter. She and Andreas named her Elefteria, the Greek word for freedom.

Kalliope was elated by the addition to their family. Over time, Andreas also seemed to find the plump little bundle appealing, even if it did put a restraint on his amorous attentions towards his wife. The baby became an object of admiration among their customers, and there was much cheek-pinching and ooh-ing and ah-ing in the early months. Kalliope was able to gain a little time away from the shop each day by hiring a junior boy who helped out with the cleaning and other jobs to give her time to breast-feed and prepare meals. Before long she was able to put in a few more hours behind the counter on weekends, with baby Elefteria at her feet in a bassinet. This suited her and allowed Andreas to slip away for some time off on a Saturday afternoon and — in a not entirely welcome development in Kalliope's eyes — to occasionally visit the local pub for a 'quick one', as he described it, on the way home.

On those afternoons when Andreas was away and it was quiet in the shop and the baby was asleep, if only briefly, Kalliope was pleased to be able to gather her thoughts in a way that hadn't been possible in the past year or more. It was at one of these moments that she was at last able to put pen to paper.

Dear Mother,

I write to let you know that Andreas and I have, after a long time, a child of our own, Elefteria. She is a beautiful little girl and you should know that she is your child as well as mine. Please do give me your blessing. I don't know how else I could have arrived at such a blessed situation — to have married one of our own people after all and to have borne a child — than to have done what I did. I have learned so much through having a child. Realities have arrived that I had little idea about but that you, too, must have discovered as a mother. I am only sorry I cannot be with you to share this knowledge and to show you our beautiful girl.

We work very hard here, but no matter, as it is not an exaggeration to say that had we stayed we would have had barely enough to feed ourselves, let alone any other person.

I hope you are well and please pass on my best wishes to Mattheos. I ask you to forgive me, and as I pray for you I hope that you will for our child. And if you can find it in your heart, please write to me.

Had she ever received any communication from back home, the grinding years that followed might have been easier to bear. These were years of work, work that bordered on slavery. Times grew tougher in the early 1960s, and Kalliope despaired as the shop hours grew longer. Andreas insisted that this extra opening time was necessary. They had taken on a mortgage when the shop was offered to them for sale and they accepted, and further debt for a new car when the old Morris had finally expired. All made worse by rising interest rates that came with a credit squeeze.

By the mid-1960s they were working seven days a week, not only to pay off loans but because supermarkets had arrived and one was set up not four hundred yards from their own place. It did not entirely undermine their business — the new supermarket up the road did not sell hot food — but almost everything else, cigarettes, milk, bread and drinks were all available through such an outlet, and often more cheaply.

Andreas coped by arguing with himself: they can go to Franklins if they want, but who except me is open at 3.00pm on a Sunday afternoon when Mollie or Millie or Jack or Jim has forgotten something? But it was during those Sunday afternoon hours, which she mostly managed herself, that Kalliope began to think their life was not turning out well. Andreas had plenty of words, he would get impassioned and rail against one injustice or another, but nothing ever changed. And he was no longer even prepared to think about returning to Crete, an idea that had once been their ultimate goal, the reason they supposedly did everything they did.

23

A Night Out

The end of 1967 came around with ten-year-old Elefteria announcing almost every day from the beginning of December how very much she was looking forward to receiving her Christmas presents. Kalliope had long accepted the Australian form of gift-giving at this time of the year, a custom unknown where she came from, and was happy enough to put up with the constant refrain. But tempering Kalliope's pleasure in Elefteria's ever-growing excitement was the first news she had heard from Crete in a very long time. Kalliope had given up hope of ever even receiving acknowledgment from her mother that a daughter, her grandchild, had been born, let alone any joy or satisfaction proclaimed for the fact. Instead here was a letter from her, out of the blue, letting her know that Uncle Mattheos had died.

In a scratchy and ancient hand — the hand of *Barba* Yorgos, who must have been eighty-five if he was a day — Kalliope was told that he had been requested by her mother to write as her mother was 'too upset to be able to write herself', *Barba* Yorgos informed her that Uncle Mattheos had passed away of a 'brain insult'. The service had been very sad, but everyone had come from everywhere. There was a long list of the names of sundry long-forgotten villagers and cousins who had attended. And there was nothing more, except the statement that Uncle Mattheos was a good man who had now 'gone to his rest'.

Kalliope read the letter and was at first angry — even in this her mother had yet to write or address her directly. Then she allowed her grief its space and its flow. It might have been indulgent to react like this, but she would not deny her feelings: during the war, before Marika died, the only person who had ever shown her any real gratitude, or real, adult affection, had not even been one of her countrymen, but a young Australian soldier. In the underground the contact had been intense, but it was all work where you were measured, not loved. After the war when the resistance broke up and the suspicions of left for right and right for left had emerged keener than ever and more people moved away, Kalliope had felt a greater loneliness. Her people had talked of obligation, oh how they had talked, and their sense of duty and the strength and beauty of Greek custom that bound them all together. But there was another reality, one she had experienced only too keenly.

As she folded the letter and controlled the urge to throw it away, she wondered how that red-haired boy had done. Had he survived that terrible time? She hoped so. More than once since arriving in Australia she had thought of trying to find out whether he had lived, and if so, where he could possibly be in this vast country. But much as she would have liked to gaze on him one more time, if only to see that he was well and to thank him and wish him all the best, it was not something a married woman could do. Definitely not something a married Greek woman might do and certainly not something her husband would approve of.

Over dinner, Kalliope passed on the news about the letter, but got little in response from Andreas. Later, while he was sitting watching *I Dream of Jeannie* on the television — with a third glass of stout in hand, thinking that his wife needed some cheering up, Andreas suddenly raised the topic. Old people die, and Mattheos was a bastard anyway, he said, getting into his pyjamas. As for their respective families, well girl, he said, you and I were simply destined to draw a bad hand in that regard. There was no use fretting over that sort of thing anymore. Forget the old people, he and she were still youngish, he said, there was still time for them to play. They should go out more often, have some fun. A night out might be just what was needed. Perhaps they could go to the local RSL Club which Andreas had recently joined? He would organise something.

On the Friday evening of the proposed night out, after he had shut the shop, Andreas led Kalliope to their bedroom. He had a surprise for her, he said. Following him in, she saw what he had done — he had got her new clothes for the occasion. Not only had he gone and bought some clothes and shoes, he had gone to the trouble of unpacking them and laying them out on their bed. Kalliope looked at them in disbelief.

Andreas could see she was not impressed. But what was the harm in trying on clothes that you could guarantee would make you look like Sophia Loren? He had other arguments, too. They were a gift after all, he said; had he not taken the time and trouble to go and buy her this blouse and skirt and high heels? Clothes like these, he insisted, would be just perfect for an evening at the club. His urging her to dress up tonight was merely, he said, in the spirit of getting her to try 'something different'.

Kalliope was disturbed. Lea, the babysitter, would already be on her way and there was no getting out of this at such a late stage. She stood in the bedroom looking down at the garments, wondering at the sort of things men found attractive. God knew where he'd gone to get such frippery. He claimed to have detoured one morning when down at the Haymarket, and probably so; she doubted any of this was from David Jones.

Kalliope listened to Andreas whistling as he shaved on the other side of the wall, in the bathroom. Despite his inference that this sort of clothing was right for such a place, it was not as if she didn't know what an RSL club was like. Old Mary Livingstone, who had been buying her bread and milk from them for years, had once invited Kalliope there for company, and out of pity for her age and loneliness Kalliope had agreed. She had sat and watched while Mary nursed her beer and thought what a sad and miserable affair it all was, full of old people getting drunk and wasting their money on the poker machines. The meat and three vegetables meal that Mary had insisted on ordering Kalliope could barely swallow, especially as the place was full of cigarette smoke. And, as for the dancing she saw that evening, what with all those creaky elderly gents and their ladies tripping and bumping into each other, to the sound of a three-piece combo playing in a corner, she couldn't think of anything worse. More importantly, she couldn't remember anyone there wearing any get-up nearly as lively as this.

But it was in her nature to make an effort. She believed she still loved her husband. Amends might be made. She would search for some proper feeling in him again. Encourage that. There had been too many trials, too much work and not a little misery this last decade.

Try as she might to stay with her best impulses, there seemed to be more rather than fewer complications with the passing of the years. Andreas had absolutely refused the idea of a second child:

Elefteria was proving a trial to him if not to her. She had thought that perhaps it was because she was becoming an incarnation of her name — rebellious and independent-minded — but Andreas had claimed that was not so, as he always liked spirited girls. But Kalliope was determined to stay hopeful, on all fronts. She comforted herself that on balance, if perhaps only just, her life, their life, was better than they had had any cause to anticipate twenty years ago.

With much reluctance she picked up the skirt — a bright red cinch-waisted affair — and pulled it on. After that there was no avoiding the wide, black plastic belt she presumed was meant to be threaded through the skirt's loops. Next came the white, low-necked blouse, tight around her midriff, with puffy short sleeves; she looked in the mirror and thought it made her look like a gangster's girlfriend. It hardly seemed the sort of thing that she, a mother in her forties, should be wearing to go out. She felt ridiculous. She would at least put a coat over it all when out on the street.

They arrived at the club and Andreas signed them in — an odd business, she thought again on this occasion, but apparently there were regulations as to who was and was not allowed to enter such a place. There was a bank of tables near the bar in the main room, between the sea of poker machines on one side and the dance floor on the other; Andreas pointed out a table where they would have a view of the dancing. As they moved towards it, Kalliope recalled the layout from her previous visit, the little familiarity reassuring in its way.

'Beer? I'll get us some beer,' Andreas said as soon as they sat down, and rushed off to the bar.

Sitting by herself at the table, Kalliope immediately felt isolated and very much on view, exposed. It was exactly as she had imagined it would be; not a single other woman was wearing clothes anything like hers. By the time Andreas came back she could hardly suppress the dark rage that was gathering inside her like a pack of barking dogs. What were they doing here? This was far from a relaxed environment, let alone a place where people went for pleasure or diversion.

Why, Kalliope asked Andreas when he arrived back, had he joined such a place? For the second time that night Andreas explained his action in the spirit of 'you know, trying something different'. Kalliope frowned, thinking it wasn't much of a reason and Andreas went on. 'Why not?' he said. He, too, was a 'World War Two veteran', and Greece an ally of these 'bloody Aussies' and that they should be welcomed free of charge and with open arms. When she had pointed out that he wasn't, strictly speaking, a veteran as such, he became agitated, raised his voice to say that he had done his bit and more for this country, what with all the taxes he had paid and the hard work he had put in feeding everybody around the place. If anyone was entitled to call himself an Aussie, then he surely was.

Andreas took a sip of his drink, looking preoccupied and impatient too. Glancing around the place, occasionally drumming his fingers, he was obviously waiting for something to happen. But what? There was nothing to do in here but put money down the throats of the machines and perhaps order some food. As for any dancing he had in mind, that idea became less and less appealing with each passing minute. She dreaded the time when the band would strike up, but knew it was inevitable.

After they had eaten a meal of roast chicken in some very bad gravy, Kalliope saw the musicians begin to make their way to the stand. An announcement followed over the PA that they should welcome the Bob Johnson Trio who would be providing 'the evening's entertainment' and 'dance music of all kinds for the young at heart'.

This, it seemed, was what Andreas had been waiting for. As soon as they began their first number, a cha-cha, he jumped up to drag Kalliope onto the floor. No one else had yet to make their way there. She tried to get him to let go of her hand but he had a very firm grip of her.

'*Andreas, ohi*, please … in a minute …' she protested.

'Why? Nobody's there! More room for us!' he replied.

She gave up and followed him out, and one or two other couples also trickled onto the floor. Any relief that gave her was quickly overwhelmed, however, by the mania which Andreas brought to the dance itself. He was pushing and pulling on the backwards and the forward steps, all the while smiling around him in a way that did not make sense.

It was not as if Kalliope was unfamiliar with the dance itself. Latin dancing had become popular among the Greeks in recent years, and it was often danced at various Brotherhood functions where she had picked it up a few years back, or even at the Cretan Ball. But she did not like being wheeled around so physically in such a way. Nor did she appreciate Andreas calling out to her over the music at one point, 'You see? You got the right clothes now!'

What Kalliope thought was that the skirt was too daring. She felt humiliated when the skirt flared up as she moved. She became ever more conscious of fleeting glances, of being eyed, as they danced. The women in particular were giving her second looks. One, she noticed, gave her an expression that was decidedly close to a sneer. She wanted to go and sit as soon as this tune was over, but as the trio immediately launched into another dance number, a foxtrot, she had no opportunity to escape. Andreas insisted that they keep going.

It was while she was trying to follow his steps through this too-energetic piece that she looked up to see a familiar-looking couple a few metres across from them. An older, stick of a fellow with a pencil moustache was leading around a bleached blonde woman, who was plump and flushed. She did not know them by name but was sure she had seen them in their shop. The recognition turned out to be mutual.

'Hey look, Madge, it's the shop lady!' she heard the man say as they whirled around.

The woman grinned at them as they went by; she nodded at Kalliope but said nothing, perhaps unable to say anything due to her exertions. The man had no trouble, however. Next time around, he said, 'Hey Andy! Nice to see you out and about mate!'

'Same to you! Same to you!' Andreas called back.

'And your missus there looks like hot stuff!'

As he spoke, Kalliope could not miss the way he rolled his eyes and then blew on the fingers of one hand as if they were on fire.

She would have let the remark pass, but then when he added directly to her, 'You're a sex bomb, love! No doubt about it!' the moment came crashing down on her. She pulled herself free from Andreas and headed back to the table. She took up her purse and sat still, staring into the distance.

'Kalliope! What's the matter … what are you doing?'

'They shouldn't speak to me like that!'

'They? Who?' Andreas gave every impression he did not know what she was talking about.

She looked up at him, furious.

'Sit. Sit down please, if you want to talk to me,' she said through her teeth.

He sat.

'Do you think it's all right for someone to speak to your wife like that?'

'What do you mean? Bah! He was only being friendly! I know him, you've seen him before.' And then he continued in English, 'He's all right, that bloke, a funny man, that one.'

'Speak Greek, damn you,' she hissed. 'Don't treat me like this.'

For a long time Andreas said nothing but kept staring at his wife. Kalliope would not meet his gaze but, waited for something, she knew not what, to come from him.

At last, with a look of exasperation and finality, he waved his arm as if to call a halt to the whole show. 'Bah! Let's go. You don't appreciate anything I do.' He got up again and left for the exit, Kalliope just behind.

As they drove home in silence Andreas thought that if tonight had not worked out, it was despite all his efforts. Too bad if Kalliope had not enjoyed herself — it was hardly his fault. Some silly old digger had made a remark and the sky had fallen in for his wife. As far as he was concerned he had tried hard. Tried to show her a good time. Just like he'd always tried to keep a roof over their heads. And that was not the end of it either — had he not also given her the child she wanted? God knew, there were far worse men than him around. What did she want? Nothing ever seemed to please her.

Back at the shop Kalliope paid the babysitter and saw her out the door, then, when Andreas mumbled something about going to bed she answered, 'No'. He could go by himself, she was too upset. She needed to calm down. She waited until Andreas was asleep, then changed into her nightgown. She gathered up the clothes she had worn that evening and took them into the shop, then the storeroom, then took hold of the large shears kept there and proceeded to cut the skirt and blouse into small pieces. It took her some time but she was determined. All done, she retrieved the scraps of cloth at her feet, rolled them up into a small ball to stuff them in an empty sugar sack, and put the lot in the rubbish bin.

She was still too agitated to go to bed, so went into the shop to stand at the windows and look out at the night. As it was past midnight, there was no one about and only a very occasional car lit up the area over and above the pale yellow of the street lamps. Her life was *not* better than she had had cause to anticipate twenty years earlier, not at all. How could it be better if she was angry so much of the time? Perhaps anger was the wrong thing to feel. She had let it show tonight, unable to hold it back, but perhaps this anger was something she had not revealed nearly often enough. But if she was angry at anything, it was as much at herself and for the degree of self-delusion she had indulged in.

She moved across and stood at one of the frying vats. Although the gas had been turned off much earlier in the night, these still retained some heat. She put her hand on the metal side and felt the warmth. She recalled the warmth of the village oven, next to their house in Arkadi, and even the years of the war when they were often cold because their meagre wood was always being taken away. They had fought, suffered. Good people had come to help — although it was hard to believe that those men were even of the same race as the ones she had come to know and sometimes loathe here since. Even when they had nothing, even when she was plain hungry or lonely, or when death was threatening all around, she had felt better than this.

Kalliope felt overwhelmed with shame. So many years standing here, muttering the lines from a dreadful script: 'Yes please? What you like? With sauce? No sauce? OK, love, any way you like it, love ...' And then, whenever she got something wrong

— because she was tired, because her mind was on the child, or her schooling, or had flown back to that other world ten thousand miles and a million years away — she would on top of it all be corrected. By her husband. 'Come on Kalliope, the customer wants with sauce! You didn't hear him?' he would say, all the while exchanging winks and nods with some half-drunk old Aussie, waiting there to be fed this tripe. But nobody cared. Nobody had a heart. May God damn this place and what she had become. She didn't care. The only question was how much longer and at what cost she might keep up the charade.

The following week, early on Sunday morning, Kalliope looked through the window of Elefteria's bedroom out into the yard and saw Andreas sitting on a fruit box, reading something. She looked closer and thought he was holding some sheets of paper, perhaps a letter or letters. When he came back inside, she heard him go to their bedroom, come out, and go into the shop. She went into the bedroom. He had taken down a cardboard box of their old letters and memorabilia but had not bothered to put it back in the cupboard. Wondering whether he had been looking at some of these things, in a spirit of nostalgia or remembrance, she thought to open it briefly.

The box was stuffed full, not only with correspondence, but with Andreas' army papers too. On the very top were a couple of envelopes, newly placed there, unusually addressed in English and with Australian stamps on them. She took them up to look at them more closely.

Her own English over the years had improved enough to allow her to read to a simple level newspapers or bills, whatever was needed for the business. She was able to make the first letter out with only a little trouble: it was old, dated a month before

their marriage, and addressed to Andreas from a Miss Gloria
Harrison, 221 River Road, Forbes, NSW.

Dear Andreas,

Thank you for your letter. Yes, it has been a long time
since we last wrote to each other, but things have been very
busy here for me with my bank and charity work taking up
every hour almost. I am happy to hear you are getting married
to that Cretan girl, believe me, and not jealous at all! This
from me who, as you know, was not the marrying kind. But if
you will be in Forbes after your wedding I would like very
much to see you again, if you would like to see me. You say
you do, but I don't know how in the circumstances.

As to other news, nothing much. I see Voula from time to
time at the shops. As ever, she makes too much of me, says
what a lovely princess I am and not like all the Greek girls she
knows. You should hear how she compares me with your
Kalliope! — too favourably I'm afraid — and keeps saying
that *I* should have married you instead ... She wishes we
could still have those Friday night meals at the cafe, as in the
days when you were here and on leave. You and me, Lambis
and her. 'Our little gang' she thinks of us still, I suppose. Well,
you Greeks always were a jolly bunch, I say.

Anyway, it would be very nice to talk about the old times and
about the future. Kalliope, I'm sure, is a good girl from the old
country but I would not talk to her about you and me if you
want my advice. That was all long ago and you have set out on
another life, it seems. Perhaps we can meet in the town if that is
all right, maybe for a coffee in the Blue Bird like the old days?
That would be very nice. Please write to me and let me know.

Your very dear friend, Gloria.

She put the letter back in the case and took up a second. This one was addressed to him too, from the same woman. It was shorter but repeated that she would be happy to see him as he had asked and, yes, they could make a plan to meet some time next month.

This letter was dated only eleven days before. She looked further and found others from various times between.

Kalliope felt as if someone had struck her an almighty blow. It was as much as she could do to reel around and sit on the bed before her legs gave way beneath her. She felt sick. For a long time afterwards she worked to regain her breathing, settle the heaving inside, fight against the urge to fall or retch or hurt herself in some way. And to think she had felt guilty about maybe, perhaps once, trying to contact a long-lost Australian soldier to see how life had turned out for him and to thank him for his bravery!

Was this what it had all been about? Deceit and betrayal, nothing more? But things suddenly became clearer. Whatever these letters meant, for her the world now seemed a much easier place to comprehend. When she was sufficiently in charge of herself again, she retrieved the letters from the box and went out to find Andreas in the shop. He hadn't opened up yet but was still stacking bottles on shelves.

She went to him and as calmly and coolly as possible held the letters up in front of him. 'What are these?' she said in a low voice.

Far from being shocked or surprised, he responded as if he had almost anticipated this happening.

'They are what they are, Kalliope … You must know. You've obviously read them, even if they are not yours to read.'

'I am interested in the letter that says you were going to visit this person in Forbes and quite soon. Next week, in fact, if I'm

270

not mistaken. You didn't tell me you were planning a trip.' She stared at him in quiet fury.

Seeing her standing there before him, so resolved and righteous, was too much for Andreas. However he might have liked to have handled the situation, rage mounted within him. A rage he would not contain because he was, he felt, well within his rights on all fronts on what she was broaching here.

'Why not?' he shouted at last. 'She is a clever woman, works in a bank, not shop people like us, like me, like you! She looked at me like a proper woman, not a country girl. She liked me, yes, me! She talked to me about politics and history. She taught me some English even. And she didn't take everything seriously like you do. Yes, of course I want to meet and talk with someone like that!'

'And to bed her again? Would you like to do that once more? All those visits to see Lambis over the years … ha! You treated me like I was some problem. Now I know why. I was, wasn't I?'

'You were not a problem,' he said, trying to lower the heat between them

'Oh no? Well, I was to those so-called friends of yours, I believe. You were all in it together. They looked after you didn't they, kept your secret. "Let's not upset the *horiatisa*, eh? The village girl. Man's business, after all — nothing for the wife to worry about." And as for that Voula, she was so stupid, she couldn't hide her irritation with it all, with me for existing.

'You're not honest with me,' Kalliope continued. Not now, not ever. I know that now, stupid person that I am, that you say I am. Were you going to tell me this time, or maybe you weren't? Is that it? Were you just going to run away and leave us, your daughter?'

As both understood that some end had been reached, calm returned between them. Yes, they had been close, he admitted, but that was before Kalliope had arrived. It was over by the time of their marriage. And the trip he was planning, he said, was about testing himself, seeing whether he still had feelings for her. If not, he said, he would have been perfectly happy to come back here and 'resume' where he'd left off.

To that final insult Kalliope said, 'Good luck to you, Andreas. Because you would have been "resuming" without me.'

Andreas was silent for a long moment after Kalliope stopped speaking. She looked at him and saw that he did not really have the stomach to fight on, had no answers or words that could mend what had just passed between them. And probably did not want to. She was not at all surprised when he grabbed his keys to let himself out of the shop. Nor impressed when he slammed the car door and roared off somewhere. The shop would not be open today. And if it ever was again, it would not be with her help.

The same afternoon, as she packed a bag for herself and Elefteria, she thought that it was not an old affair that troubled her most; she had long ago come to think he probably had done what single men do. No, it was that he had likely continued the relationship on and off ever since and was planning to see her again; more than that, that he had withheld his true feelings from her. On top of the crudeness that he seemed increasingly willing to show her with the passing years, there was this further reality: his had been an idea about a marriage, not a commitment to one. Always and ever. He seemed to have held her at arms' length, even when they were at their most intimate. The way he had behaved for so long, the absences, the hinting at something that was in him, but beyond their so-called family and home life. So much, so very much now was clear.

Around four that afternoon, Kalliope put a call through to one of her acquaintances, Lina the Italian dressmaker who lived in nearby Leichhardt, to let her know she was leaving Andreas and to ask whether she might stay for a few days until she could reorganise her own and her daughter's life. She had asked Lina because she was not a close friend, but a person who was reliable, kept her own counsel, was kind in her own way. She did not want sympathy, nor did she want to talk to anyone she knew better about what had happened — not just yet, perhaps not ever.

PART THREE

24

A Castle on a Hill

After an hour's drive from Parramatta due to roadworks, the longest it had ever taken him, Vic Stockton pulled into the shade of his carport at Castle Hill thinking, *Castle Hill be buggered*. After a frustrating visit to the insurance office, the death crawl from Parramatta to here had put him in a foul mood. An interminable trip maybe, but useful in a way. It had given him lots of time to scope it all out, really see the muck that had accumulated along that stretch of mongrel road.

Parramatta itself had gone to hell. It was full of those shitty four-wheel drives (no doubt full of shitty car salesmen), that were beginning to appear everywhere else too. Trying to find parking, he had been confronted by whole battalions of them; they took up every square inch of space, each arrogantly dumped wherever its owner felt like. Those phoney mansions lining the sides of the road for mile after mile — grass castles, they used to call them. Maybe, it occurred to him, some of them had been built on drug money, as some had said. Pity he had been responsible for building one or two of them in his day. But he knew better now.

He had been a holdout against the changes around these parts, and for a long time. Since about 1970 all this had been gathering pace; now, in the early nineties, it was an avalanche of so-called development. But he had hung onto his little digs and had had his little wins. Growing choko vines along the side fence and giving his neighbour on that side, Joe Pizzoli, the god-almightys. Keeping chooks in a pen along the other side until the lot next door was built on and they kicked up a fuss. He had objected to that too. They couldn't believe him at the council meeting, one councillor even asking how he, a one-time builder, could in all conscience object to a brand spanking new six-bedroom, three-bathroom Tuscan-style villa on an otherwise useless block of scrub. It was bloody immoral, he was told by the applicant, a remark he could still recall with satisfaction. *Bloody immoral be buggered too*, he thought again today as he clambered out of his Holden Rodeo ute. What was immoral was the way the whole joint had gone these past decades.

What had it all been about really, since the Second World War? Stupidity and selfishness and wasted opportunities. The place might have truly become something, might have become a real beacon, but no — it was now owned and run by grasping mongrels who in another day and age you wouldn't have fed. Well, he'd tried to do his bit, in a one-man band sort of way maybe, and took satisfaction in that he'd done it in his own silly time and not wasted others'. And he'd made sure that when he did get up to have a go, it was only against what the usual crooks were putting about.

In the years after Joan, the years after Toongabbie, he had let go of the bullshit fed him since he was a kid. And begun barracking for anyone or anything that general opinion didn't favour at any given moment. It amused him to think how varied was his contrariness, and how much of a pest he was seen as hereabouts. Especially since he'd become a supporter of whatever the mob frowned upon. Like mosques (this when he'd heard that the local Muslim community were to be denied a permit to build). Like the Saturday market at one of the district schools, objected to by the miserable shopkeepers along the local strip. As to his own 'againsts', the list was long and getting longer: he was against motorways where you had to pay a toll (what were his taxes for?); against 'adventure' playgrounds cluttering up local parks (what was wrong with just swings and the occasional puddle of mud for the kiddies to play in?); against any politician who dared to bang on about 'law and order' (particularly when they were the ones most likely to be offending).

If you asked him, Vic Stockton, aged in his early seventies, long divorced and now retired builder, ex-WWII veteran, ex-member of the RSL for that matter, what he stood for, he would have been happy to tell you. He was all for ordinary Joes and Josephines being allowed a fair go, corrupted as that notion might be. And all for people who believed in something other than lining their pockets. For anyone who was prepared to live and let live and put their point of view without shoving it down the other bloke's throat.

Vic had been pretty busy putting his point of view, he was happy to concede. He had learned to wear funny hats and carry placards on protest marches whenever the government was plotting something, though not so often these days. Still plotting they doubtless were, but his legs weren't up to long hikes or standing on the one spot too long. He would continue to sign any petition that was going, providing it was about something more than one mob's self-interest. Vic Stockton had, in short, become notorious.

Not that this made the slightest bit of difference at the regional office of General Swiss when he went to see about his claim.

Anyone would think he had gone in there asking for the world. All he'd wanted was to be reimbursed the cost of replacing a front fence pushed over by some council idiot in a Bobcat when they had decided to dig up the grass verge and put in a concrete path. His attack on the 'path to nowhere', as he had earlier named it in his sallies against the town planner and his various acolytes, had brought him to general notice more than any other. It had led to his being called a 'nuisance' and a 'troublemaker', not only at council and site meetings but in the *Hills Herald & Messenger* after a prolonged campaign by him to point out that $2 million was proposed to be spent on a stretch of road that no one ever walked along, because it failed to connect anything to anything else.

If it was no wonder the council wasn't prepared to cough up for some fencing, there was another problem: when he'd put in the claim to his own insurance company, it turned out that damage to fences wasn't listed under his policy. He was kicking himself for not having checked, but somehow this afternoon none of this mattered.

As evening arrived, Vic thought it still too hot to worry about food. He went instead to the fridge to get a beer before heading back to sit in front of the box — anything to blot out the day. But all he could find to watch was one of those fix-your-house-and-garden things. He liked the gardening tips, or the colours of the flowers and shrubs they showed anyway; but he was usually offended by some of the so-called building and handyman tips.

Tonight was no different. He had missed the start and the advice of Miss Green Thumbs, and all that was left was the bloke in the squeaky clean overalls with his special project of the week. Vic stared at the screen and listened to him lecture manically on how to repair a wooden chair. Apparently all it took was some Phillips head screws, a drill and the right glue. The right glue being the sponsor's glue of course. To which he responded out loud, 'Yeah, and it'll go again in two days! Wood dowels, high stress resin glue, and at least three days in furniture clamps, if you want it to last, dopey!'

But that was it, wasn't it? Nothing was made to last, everything was rubbish built to collapse tomorrow so they could sell you new rubbish. He turned off the television and sat there, slowly sipping the last of his KB, until he eventually fell into a doze.

When he became conscious again he thought he'd been in his chair perhaps a half-hour or so. Except that looking at his watch it was now ten-thirty, and dark beyond the window. And still humid, he realised, when he got up again to go to the loo. Standing in the bathroom, dealing with the consequences of his ailing prostate, he thought he might as well sleep outside again tonight. In the last few years, on such impossible nights as these, he had given up on conventional sleeping arrangements.

The size of his block meant Vic was still shielded from the prying eyes of neighbours, otherwise he knew this habit of his would count as one more black mark against him. He opened the screen door at the back of the kitchen and went to the shed. There, he pulled out the folding camp bed and an old sleeping bag and headed for the plum tree. Brushing away some of the cobwebs that always hung under it this time of the year, Vic laid out the bag for a mattress and set up a mini camp for himself. He covered his hands in insect repellent from a spray can and, still dressed in his day clothes of shirt and trousers and shoes, finally lay down.

Hoping for a clear sky and some stars, he saw nothing much up above, just the low cloud cover of a warm February night. He watched the patterns of grey, moving north-east to south-west, and began wondering whether he had turned off the TV before coming outside. He couldn't remember for a moment, then it came to him. Wonderful to be losing your memory too.

Turning over to one side he recalled a program from a few nights back. A travel show set in Greece, or some of the islands there. He had not been to any of the islands other than Crete, but Santorini, which they showed in detail, was impressive, to say the least. All whitewashed and beautiful against the blue sky and turquoise sea, lots of little churches with that cross of theirs on top of the usual small dome. Then the show cut across to another island, he couldn't recall which, where they showed the state of repair of some of the old buildings there, including some rural chapels and various historic houses, mostly decrepit or falling down. There wasn't money, apparently, to restore them. Or in the event, hardly anyone left on that island interested or able to repair them — least of all any young ones, who were all buzzing off to the mainland.

Vic woke anxiously, joltingly. He had heard a shell explode somewhere — his first conscious thought — but looked up and saw lightning flashes. *That's what I get for having faith,* was his next thought. Then there was growling thunder and another explosion of sound and light.

He got up to drag himself inside. He stood at the back door under the awning for a moment, conscious that the storm was gathering force. Still groggy, unsteady, he watched the flashes tear across the sky and found himself gripping the door jamb.

He saw again, now, in the half-light of an antipodean night, a brutal assault on an ancient Cretan chapel, saw the flames, those holy men driven off. There were no flames here. The storm began to abate, but the atmosphere was warm and damp still. He felt less afraid. He moved to go inside, was about to pull the door shut, when he began to hear the sound of cicadas somewhere not too far away. That unmistakable buzz of a humid night. He felt some odd relief in that unexpected noise.

Vic wandered up along the side of the house towards the street, to where he believed the sound was coming from. Out the front he looked around for the source, scanned the nearest power pole — maybe those little winged beasts had scaled it in that way of theirs. But there was nothing there. He looked at the electricity wires overhead, sketched out as so many ghostly grey lines against the inky sky. That was it — a junction box up there was crackling. The current had been interrupted by water seeping in, creating an odd and regular percussion. There were no cicadas.

But wasn't there a kind young woman, looking out for him, looking after him, in that other world? If there was, or had ever been, that was far from here. So very far from here. He rubbed at the wetness gathering at the corners of his eyes. Vic Stockton did not want to be a lonely old man — not tonight, not like this — howling at the darkness. But that's what he was. And he knew it.

25

Lavender and Marble

Within a month, come one Saturday morning, Vic Stockton was taking off from Sydney airport.

'Correct me if I'm wrong, love, but I'm on a plane to Greece; is that right?' he asked one of the attendants after take-off.

'Yes, sir. You are on a plane to Greece,' she smiled at him, in a way that suggested she thought he was trying to be funny.

Except he wasn't. Vic Stockton was having trouble believing what he'd done. That he had gone ahead and arranged all this in the first place, let alone that he was moments away from being airborne. An old bloke on a plane going across the world. You'd have to be nuts, wouldn't you? Or maybe he was seen as a sturdy gentleman of a certain age, embarking on a doubtless well-deserved holiday …

He was less certain about his motives today than when he'd begun organising things those weeks ago, but whatever they were doing, holidaying had not been so important in his thinking. All that had mattered was to go to Crete one last time. So he had got his passport in order; out of date since that last holiday with his daughter in Fiji six years ago. He had gone to the Greek Consulate for information — they had given him a lot of brochures and a poster — and to a travel agent for a discounted ticket (although at nearly $2000 he couldn't see where the discount was). And he had ended up with a plan that would mean spending a week in Athens before a trip south and a stay of three weeks on Crete.

After the first five or six hours, time on the plane became a blur. They kept bringing him all sorts of mock food that he was apparently meant to eat, but he would have none of it. Well, only enough so as not to get hungry. But there was an awful lot of peculiar stuff — and definitely too many scrambled eggs, it seemed to him. Apart from the Fiji trip, he'd been interstate a few times on planes over the years, but never on a flight as long as this. There was a stop in Singapore, then non-stop through to Athens, with hours ten through twenty-four a slog of drowsiness and discomfort, and too many visits to the loo.

At some point when the night sky was beginning to gradually lighten, he heard the announcement that he had been anticipating: that they would now commence the descent towards their destination. They were less than two hours out from Athens.

As the pink glow across the horizon became more prominent, Vic began to look around and past the dark-looking chap who'd had the window seat next to him. Noticing him craning his neck, the fellow asked whether he would like the window seat for a while, to which Vic said yes.

Seated there, he looked out and down until some small islands began to appear in the sea below. Little rocky things at first, followed by bigger ones. Dotted here and there with little yellow lights, they were surrounded by waters that were still grey in the early morning light. There seemed to be lots of these islands where he couldn't yet distinguish what might be the mainland. Descending further, they passed over one or two that were much larger, judging by how long it took to cross them. There was no way of telling which ones they were, short of consulting a map or asking the bloke in the next seat. Which he did finally.

'That one you mean?' the fellow checked, leaning over him. 'That one is Rhodes, or *Rhodos*, as we say in Greek …'

'Rhodos,' Vic repeated, attempting to mimic what he'd just heard. And thinking he had made a passable job of it too. He sat back again, playing the sound of that word over in his mind. It was the first time in decades, he realised, that he had tried to sound a word out loud in that language.

After some more of this aerial island-hopping, it was clear they were over the mainland. This was Greece proper. Though still a long way up in an atmosphere that made everything look as if seen through fine gauze, he began to pick out roads and fields. Hints of colour were starting to appear — mauves and lavenders and lilacs. By the time they were on their approach to landing, these had turned to shades of blue: in both sea and sky. Not the same blues he had lived with for decades, but very familiar nevertheless; they seemed to go to work on him.

Vic flushed and felt some kind of slight tremble rise in him, all followed by a twitch in his left eye. For a few seconds he suffered a panicky sensation that this was all too much, too much for an old codger — this trip, the plan, the whole idea. Then, as wheels bumped tarmac, he heard a sound coming from the front of the cabin that he did not at first comprehend. It was the sound of hands clapping; it had commenced somewhere at the front near the cockpit and like a wave was working its way down towards his seat. Everyone joining in. There was laughter and cheering, too. *You've got to love these people*, he thought.

Vic found himself smiling too, more so when his neighbour turned towards him to shake his hand. 'A Greek custom,' he said. 'A safe landing is cause enough to celebrate, yes?'

'You're not wrong there, mate!' he replied.

No longer so agitated, his aberrant eyelid settled at last, Vic wondered whether this might just turn out all right.

Three days later, inspecting the view of construction works from the dirty window of his room in the Hotel Lasselos, Vic Stockton believed the opposite. The city was a dump. Everywhere around his hotel was in uproar. Broken pavements, concrete and cement dust eddying around corners, crowds of pushy people, half of whom were probably tourists. As for his hotel, it was a boiled-eggs-for-breakfast-every-day type of place. He had chosen a three-star hotel as part of the 'package' for this stay in Athens, but had misunderstood what three-stars meant in Athens. In Australia you got more than four square metres of space with a saggy single bed, a cupboard and a bit of a shower, never mind the eggs. And, as for the noise coming up from all those building works below, this third-floor room seemed to magnify it to the point of pain.

All Vic could do was resign himself to putting up with it for a few more days. And why should that be hard, he asked himself. Last time he was here, he was speeding through in overheated lorries, being chased by the Germans.

The day before departing for Irakleion he made the trek up through the Plaka to the Acropolis. Steep as it was, he took his time not only to catch his breath but to stop and occasionally gaze up the slopes of that ancient rock to the crown of its mighty temple above. He also stopped at various stalls to look for souvenirs for Jenny.

That he hadn't told his daughter he had been planning this, let alone the fact that he was now here, was weighing on his mind. The euphoria of 'I couldn't give a damn and will do as I like' had evaporated; now he had to give it some real thought. Not that he was a baby and she needed to be concerned about him or his particular whereabouts, just that she did make contact every few weeks, and that was probably overdue. Letting her know beforehand would have simply led her to worry, and he didn't want that.

At one stall, he quite liked the look of some of the worry beads — the irony was not lost on him — and decided to ask the character behind the counter the price of a small amber set. The bloke grinned a broad grin and said, 'For Aussie, three dollars, that one!'

He was taken by the sharpie's eager expression, and that he had picked his accent.

'All right, let's have them, mate.'

'No worries!' he said. 'That is what you say, isn't it? I been your country many years, you know.'

'Well, well, how about that,' Vic said, pleased with the encounter. 'You blokes get around, don't you?'

'Where you from, mate? In Australia, I mean.'

'Sydney, Castle Hill …'

'Castle Hill? So, you come to the best place for you in Athens!'

Vic wasn't sure what he was getting at. 'Why's that?'

'What mean Acropolis, do you know?'

'No.'

'Castle on the hill, of course!' the worry bead man shouted at him in triumph.

Packing the little parcel into one of the pockets of his backpack, Vic considered that plenty of Greeks had come out to Australia, but plenty had doubtless come back, too. He also thought that he wasn't especially offended by a bloke with a cheeky line trying to make a living by squeezing a quid out of tourists. It struck him as somehow more honest than what some of his own compatriots had got up to — all those corporate crooks and big money men. Villains, the whole bloody lot of them, including people he'd worked with.

He negotiated the final few turns and arrived at the small museum near the steps to the Parthenon itself. He bought a ticket at the counter and headed up and across the limestone perimeter.

Well, this was something. No denying it. He began to walk around the temple of Athena Nike, first along one side, then across and down the other. All beautiful milky marble curves. A very female building, he would have said. And a total mess, what with so much of it having been destroyed. He then stepped away from the structure to get a longer perspective.

Arriving at a low parapet wall twenty or so metres away, he didn't turn back to face the Parthenon, but for a few moments took in the view of Athens below. It was a concrete city if ever there was one, and much of it obviously shoddily built. Maybe there hadn't been a lot of money about when so many of those crummy walk-up blocks had been thrown together, presumably in the sixties. They seemed to fill the entire basin that cradled this city.

Something half-remembered made itself present to him. It was about there where he was standing where that photo was taken: two Nazis raising a swastika, the Parthenon as backdrop. He was trying to get the angle right when the image was supplanted by the sound of raucous voices somewhere behind him. A group of Yanks, all somewhat younger than himself, were chattering loudly as they came his way. For such a small number they seemed to take up a hell of a lot of space; he found himself moving to one side even before they were upon him.

'Will you look at that, Karen?' said one, pointing across Vic and down at the city. 'Now I would say that's something, wouldn't you?'

'Oh yes, oh yes,' came the reply. 'We've got nothing like that back home … have we Frances?' she responded, referring to one of the other women in the party of six.

'Now, I wouldn't know!' this one laughed gaily. 'I have hardly been anywhere in the States, as is well known!'

Another bloke took up the idea. 'You don't have to have been anywhere to know we ain't got nothin' looks like this place, Frances. Only one Parthenon, you know. Only one Athens too, I would say.'

But there's a few more of you than are necessary, Vic thought as he began heading back towards the other end of the site and as far away from this crowd as he could get. They were just like you see them on television, no doubt about it. To bump into them even up here was to realise the Yanks were taking over the world, never mind little old Australia.

He spent the last morning in Athens holed up in his room watching and listening to some indecipherable talking heads on the television. A news program, he knew that much. The footage they cut to from time to time gave him enough of a picture — a bus crash, somewhere mountainous, a wailing woman being restrained from what looked like the covered body of a family member; then scenes of military jets taking off; then a bunch of beauty pageant girls with sashes across their chests. He switched the control off to wait for the call from the front desk that his cab had arrived to take him to the airport. He had considered going down to Crete by ferry but decided his stomach wasn't up to twelve hours at sea. And, although it was March and winter was officially over, he'd been told the weather could still turn.

*   *   *

They did not leave on time, having had to wait for the pilot to show up. Vic, along with the impatient and complaining locals on board, had sat in increasing agitation before the chap deigned to arrive. It took a good twenty minutes after the scheduled departure time before they finally saw him, rushing across the tarmac to their plane, still buttoning his jacket. Luckily, the flight to Irakleion proved to be smooth and uneventful.

Less than an hour after takeoff, the looming mass of Crete's western mountain ranges came into view. In bright daylight the spectacle of the *Lefka Ori*, the White Mountains, was magnificent. Far more impressive than Vic had expected, or remembered. Coming in to land, he wondered why he could not recall them looking as grand as this, and put it down to the fact that there had not been a lot of time or inclination to take in the views back then. But this he knew: he was very, very glad to be here once more. A slight tremble began to overtake his hands and soon he felt his face turning red again. This was different; it was excitement. He could not recall how long it had been since he had flushed for that reason.

Despite the warning of possibly cool weather, Vic found on leaving the terminal that it was warmish. The air, the temperature, was quite Spring-like. And the bus into the city was so overheated that he had to take his coat off and roll up his sleeves.

As for Irakleion itself, what a city it was — a maze of old streets and lanes, medieval walls and fortifications, and a feeling more Middle Eastern than Greek, not unlike the old parts of Athens around the Plaka. Vic peered out the bus window, becoming more and more absorbed in the view. There's something wrong with me, Vic thought: I'm an old man and I feel exhilarated.

The feeling did not last. Settling into his hotel near the Venetian loggia in central Irakleion meant having to put up with the usual nonsense: a lazy porter eyeing him off to work out what he was worth before approaching; confusion about his room (his name had been misspelt); then finding he had been allotted a view of a dank airwell rather than of the 'colourful street scene' described in the pamphlet. He decided he wasn't going to put up with this sort of thing — there were better things to be getting on with. He went immediately to the front desk, to politely and calmly put a case (but anticipating also that he might have to make some noise). To his surprise, there was no problem shifting to another, better room, and the early irritation quickly receded.

The first day, a Friday, Vic spent lying around or familiarising himself with these new digs. He did very little over the next two days either, confining himself to wandering around the nearby streets, dropping in on this or that *kafeneion* or trinket shop; his major expedition was to the local archeological museum, where he renewed a dim acquaintance with Crete's ancient Minoan culture. He was impressed enough, and dutifully read the labels, but tired quickly of so many millennia-old broken pots and jugs.

On the Monday, Vic felt ready to tackle his next stage. He went down from his room to the front desk to ask a question of a pretty, dark-haired girl, so small she stood at about shoulder height to the counter.

'Please miss, can you tell me where I can find a bus that goes to Hora Sfakia?'

'Sir, you would like a bus?' she queried, in gentle accented English.

'Yes, one that goes to Sfakia. To the south coast.'

This was no problem, and the girl came from behind the counter to lead him out onto the street and point the way to the bus stop.

If he needed help anywhere, Vic certainly needed it here. He had formed a plan which he had passed on to no one else, not even — until he had got this far and found he was still in one piece — fully to himself. He was, he understood, on a pilgrimage of sorts. Back to the place where his life had been saved and some other Vic, the one he believed was the best Vic, had for a time wandered the world, alive to his wits and because of his wits. A man whose nerve was intact, although challenged and threatened at every other step.

Vic had returned to where that person had lived his best, sharpest days. And where he had probably died. There had been a different Vic then, no hero but a bloke who, looking back, he thought he liked more than the one he had known these decades past. This self-assessment was his own, agreed, but had been arrived at soberly and quietly, and not just over the last few days either. He was not here to dramatise or for a wallow, but for all the pain he and others had endured on this island, he for one had been alive in a way he had never been since. He wanted to do no more than try to call up the original man, if only for a moment or two. He wanted to remember, at best draw a little strength.

Whatever else he did on Crete, Vic intended to visit once more the monastery at Kastelli to pay homage and give thanks one last time. It occurred to him that the monastery might no longer be there, but it was a thought he didn't want to entertain. Call him a silly old bugger, sentimentalising what was long gone, the time when he too was awash with the usual blood and juices of youth, but what he honestly, sincerely, wanted to do was stand before the place that had provided him shelter and safety.

*　　　*　　　*

The next day Vic set off for Sfakia in the company of what were obviously a bunch of natives. Thin, gaunt-looking blokes in brown suits; a few women in black, some elderly, some with children; and a squad of teenage boys in tracksuits.

No sooner had they left the bus depot than the boys started throwing a soccer ball backwards and forwards and across the aisle among themselves. Vic tried to settle back and resign himself to the idea that this was going to be an uncomfortable journey. He was therefore not a little pleased when the driver pulled up on the outskirts of Irakleion, marched down the aisle and began to berate the teenagers, demanding that they hand the ball over. This he did in such a loud voice and with such a threatening wave of his beefy arm that the leader gave it up to him almost immediately without so much as a squeak.

From then on Vic was free to concentrate on a fundamental truth: that the journey south, but for the fact no one was shelling them or firing at them, was probably no safer or more comfortable than the one he'd been forced to take nearly sixty years earlier. This was as bumpy and upsetting a ride on anything with wheels as he could ever remember. There were corners where he was sure the wheels had hung over non-existent shoulders. Once or twice as they tore into a pretty, quiet village, Vic hoped they might stop so he could take a wander. They never did — he was on some type of express service. He soon decided there was nothing for it but to close his eyes and wait until it was all over.

Some hours after leaving Irakleion the bus began to slow on an uphill drag. The down-shifting of the gearbox suggested they were heading for some difficulty anticipated by the driver, although Vic could not see anything of much concern beyond the windows when he opened his eyes to peer out. A gradual rise to the next ridge was all there was to see.

Then he understood. They had reached the top and the driver needed to prepare for the descent, but he had also slowed to allow his passengers to take in the view.

It was magnificent. Down below, in the sharp-cut ridges of this southern coast of Crete, held in a cleft of dissected rock and bordered by the sea, was the town of Sfakia. Vic scanned slowly and saw green-tipped slopes and hillsides that aproned the town, the little houses with their terracotta or concrete roofs, the occasional white-domed church or chapel. As far away as they were, it all looked glorious.

It was a different view once they were in the built-up parts. He tried to dredge up some image from the past, but there was none. It would be safe to assume, surely, that the town was a good bit larger than it had once been. He excused himself for not being able to recall anything more: how was he supposed to remember anything about the joint when they had arrived under cover of dark, holed up somewhere beyond the general habitation, then raced off a day later?

Much of what he could see from the bus window wasn't very old at all; some small hotels and restaurants, cheap concrete-block built, a mish-mash of this and that. Why did it all look like some kind of staging-post? It took a few seconds and then it came to him: this town was a last stop after the Samaria Gorge, an end point for hikers and backpackers after that walk. Another tourist base. Feeling some disappointment creeping in, he checked himself. He was not here to be a whingeing visitor.

In the town proper he found himself deposited in the street near a tourist information office. Dragging his wheeled bag inside, he came upon a pleasant young fellow who ran him through what was available in the budget accommodation line hereabouts. And no surprise, he also had a driver he could call, someone reliable, rest assured, who could take him to an excellent place not too far away.

Vic didn't mind the offer: it would, after all, to solve problems on a few fronts. And the place, about five hundred metres along the main road, turned out not to be too bad at all. Run by a *Kyria* Frosso it went by the name of L'Avenir, a tidy little pensione of five or six neat rooms where he would be happy to put up for a while, a good base from which to get to Kastelli.

Wandering down for breakfast next morning, Vic stopped to pick up a couple of postcards sitting in a stand next to the doorway of the dining room. One of these had a photo of the Monastery of Kastelli itself. The large main building was there, all whitewashed, and this time as recognisable to Vic Stockton as his own front door. Feeling his heart skip a beat or two, he looked for the nearest chair inside the dining room. He would need to sit down to deal with this.

Finding a picture of the place wasn't the cause; a place like that was always going to be a historical site, something tourists would want to see. Why wouldn't it be on a postcard? Simply being here had brought on a reaction. Getting older, yes, the body more fragile, his head still worked. And if his emotions might trump him every now and then, his head allowed him to understand he had done the right thing in coming here. This felt very right; he would pass over the few drawbacks.

Greece was no paradise, for sure. He recalled the number of hustlers he had encountered here so far — even if they were more open about it and less sneaky than those back home. But no one was fooled. Then they drove like maniacs — you only had to look at all the little shrines on the hillsides and at the top of sheer drops to see the results of that. The food, well, nothing to get excited about, although he could take their nice red mullet, the *barbounia*, with a *horiatiki* salad on the side, any time. But this morning's fare was more typical. He was distracted by Frosso bringing in a basket of hard-boiled eggs, then some hard, rusk-like toast in another basket, then a big jug of orange juice (probably decanted from some even bigger container of orange juice). And that was it, cheap fare if ever there was.

Except there were extras — like the fact that she was only too willing to come over to him, to this old *Afstralezo*, to smile at him warmly, take both his hands in hers as she was doing at this moment, and look him directly in the eye.

'How are you today, Mister Stockton? All right? Yes?'

'Fine thanks, love, thanks for asking.'

'Good!' she said loudly, patted him on the shoulder and went about buttering a piece of toast for him.

Bugger it, but he did have a soft spot for these ratbags. He liked that you knew so readily how they were feeling. Emotional, maybe. But he had certainly come across more than one steel-hearted, flint-eyed type among them, men and women, during the war. He hoped they hadn't all disappeared. As yet, he hadn't seen anyone in the traditional garb he recalled from that time — no breeches-wearing, bolero-topped pistoleros had so far crossed his path. He imagined there might still be some left in the mountain strongholds.

Kyria Frosso spotted the card still in his hand.

'Kastelli, eh? Very nice place! You go there some time?'

'Been there already, *Kyria* Frosso. During the war …'

'Ahh! But you go again, yes?'

'Plan too, yes.'

'*Kala.* But you be careful for the monks, OK? Funny people, them ones.'

'Don't worry, I'm a big boy, *Kyria* Frosso.'

She let out a cackle of a laugh, leading Vic to think she was picking up some meaning other than he intended. The thought of a bunch of old boys trying to jump in the sack with each other was not what he had wanted to convey.

'No, no, I'll be right. Question is, how do I get there?'

'After breakfast, I tell you. And I call them and I say you coming, if you like — or they get upset, you know. Now you eat, OK? Eat!'

'I will, I will … give us a go, for Christ's sake!' he smiled at her. But only when *Kyria* Frosso saw him actually put something in his mouth was she satisfied enough to leave.

26

Descent

When Vic Stockton went by taxi down a narrow gravel road and saw again the main buildings of the Kastelli monastery, he began to feel most unsteady. Crazy that he should feel like this, he told himself, but by the time he got to the entrance he was so overcome that his throat had swelled and his eyes were stinging.

At the gates he was met by some novice monks, spoken to in broken English and, after announcing he was an Australian, taken inside as an honoured visitor and a guest. To be so well received, that he was not expecting. As if nothing had changed since 1941. He asked if he might be let wander around at will for a while and was told that was no problem, and that they would be pleased if he should enter his name in the visitor book in the main office before he left.

Gazing around the main courtyard, Vic saw the two chapels and imagined for a satisfying moment that everything was just how he remembered it. He went and sat on a bench under the old plane tree — still the same one — to better get his bearings for a moment. One of the two chapel buildings seemed to have been tidied up considerably since the war — it was all whitewashed and the trim freshly painted. He presumed it was the chapel of

St George, the one with the great painted screen. Then he looked across at the other smaller and now far more dilapidated structure and realised that this was the more ancient one, dedicated to Saint Nicholas, and it was a mess. A ruin almost.

He got up and stepped over to make a closer inspection. He stopped himself from looking through the gaps in the old doors, which had been boarded up anyway, in case it was even worse than the outside. The wood was rotting, it hadn't been painted in ages, and there were cracks in the walls that were deeper than just the render. What had happened? This was a shame, this was, nothing but a dirty shame. He stepped away from what he saw to look up at the dome and the cross. These were still in one piece, for what it was worth.

Retreating to the shade and the bench once more, he found he couldn't take his eyes off the building. He saw something else from this distance — a pattern of indentations along one side, and then realised what they were: bullet holes. Vic began to sense the place was speaking to him, had something to say to him. He felt it pressing on all his senses and faculties. He could hear the sound of chanting and prayer, smell the burning incense as it soothed and purified. Imagined candles burning defiantly beside an altar. And he could feel something building inside him, rising in answer to it.

But these sensations, now they were calling to him, faded away too quickly for Vic. He was forced to acknowledge instead how tired he was. And how suddenly this tiredness had intruded. He fell to thinking of how strong he had been back then, how he had been able to go for days on end. A young bloke who could go like the blazes, and needed to.

Vic wanted to stay longer, to look around further, but he had begun to feel not at all well. He was dizzy, a touch nauseated but something more than that also. His head had begun ringing and peculiar things seemed to be happening around the periphery of his vision — shapes, phantasms almost, were flitting around and away from him. He tried to catch whatever these were as they disappeared around the edges of the courtyard but could not seem to fix them in his sight. Frightening as they were, they were too quick for him.

It took all his strength to make it back to his taxi. Kostas, the driver, who had been hanging around smoking outside the gates, was shocked to see the state in which he reappeared. He saw Vic stagger, as if he didn't know where he was or where he should go next. Kostas stubbed out his cigarette and went quickly up to him.

'Boss! What's the matter with you? You no look good …'

'I don't feel too good …' Vic managed to get out, then slumped to the ground.

Kostas tried to lift him, but Vic, who was at least able to to sit upright, waved him away.

'No, just give me a minute.'

The taxi driver looked towards the monastery gates and said, 'You wait, you wait … I get help from there.'

This time Vic shook his head. 'No, just help me back in the cab. I'll be right, I'll be right …'

'But you sick. You no right, and monastery people inside,' Kostas said, a little panicky now at how this otherwise lucrative fare was turning out.

'I don't want to cause them any trouble, I just want to go to the hotel.'

'But, Jesus Christ …' Kostas began again, only to be cut off when Vic looked up at him and said, 'Please?'

The cab driver was still not inclined to take this as the end of the matter; it was only when Vic was able to heave himself to his feet again and take a few steps, that he accepted that it might be possible to drive this fellow back to Sfakia without an even greater drama befalling him.

From Kostas' point of view, as he occasionally looked into his mirror, the old boy didn't seem to be too bad. Or didn't look as if he was about to expire anyway. Grateful that nothing worse had happened, Kostas crossed himself more than once on the way back to Frosso's pensione.

Vic had little clue either as to what was happening to him. All he knew was that there were intermittent, piercing noises in his head, the edge of his vision was fading out into white light, and that muffled voices uttering words that he didn't understand in a language neither Greek nor English also kept intruding. An urge to throw up had receded, but he was feeling very distressed. Whatever was going on with him, this was something he had never experienced before. Nothing was making sense.

Vic's last coherent moments passed soon after arriving back at Frosso's. He knew he was being helped out of the car, and knew that Kostas had taken his elbow and shoulder and gently led him inside. He also knew that he felt vaguely pleased, somewhere in the distant reaches of consciousness, that no one was in the foyer to see him in this state or to fuss over him, especially not the manager herself. Having found his room key in his coat pocket Kostas proceeded to let him in, assuring him that he would likely be all right after a rest. Then, with the helpful driver quickly gone, Vic negotiated nothing more than the few steps to his bed. But there, a new agony began.

Over the next hours, Vic Stockton descended into a place he had never known existed. Whatever pain he had known in his life previously, and he believed he had known some, had nothing on this. Unable even to get up to turn the light on or pull the curtain open, he was consigned to an unfamiliar and terrible darkness. His heart began to race, to pound. All manner of images, more distinct and hellish than those earlier in the day, began to appear before him. A truck full of dead men driving towards him, through him somehow. Women, hanging upside down on a clothesline in a suburban backyard. An aeroplane scooping him up from the nature strip outside his house in Castle Hill, then dropping him from the sky. Then falling from another plane, but never landing. Scared beyond endurance, Vic tumbled into some cavernous eternity.

He wanted to call out, scream, give voice to how he felt, but he couldn't get any sound to come out of his mouth. He could not fathom why these things were happening to him, only that they were. He might as well have been strapped to this bed, this narrow single bed with its wooden bedhead, for all his ability to rise up. Pinned down as he was, he yet became conscious of a cold sweat that would come and go, more or less in synchronicity with the rise and fall of the nameless dread that alternately gripped him, then, for a few moments, let him go again. The wetness he felt gradually became greater, stronger, an ocean. He was now swimming in it, now raising his head to look for a shark's fin, watching something dead float past.

Vic lay in bed unable to help himself through the rest of the day and into the night. Sometime in the early hours of the morning, he became aware of a break in the torment insofar as he was at last able to get his throat to make a sound again. He heard his own voice for the first time in what felt like a lifetime, though he couldn't tell for sure what it might be saying.

At four in the morning Frosso, woken by one of the other guests who complained of some terrible sounds — moans, loud whispers, shouts, cries — coming from an adjacent room, turned her master key in the lock of Vic's room door and entered. She had stood outside for no more than a few seconds before hearing Vic Stockton's nightmare-filled voice for herself. The noise of her entry had the effect of startling Vic, if not into a fully waking and sensible state, at least into enough sentience to be able to sit upright and swing his legs over the edge of the bed.

Turning the light on, Frosso saw the expression of someone who might just have seen the devil himself.

'Mr Stockton!' she called out in some alarm. 'Mr Vic! What's the matter? You have the dream, yes? The bad dream?'

There was no response; with his hands gripping the bedclothes, Vic stared straight ahead, half-awake at best. Frosso saw he was trembling and drenched in sweat.

She approached him slowly and eventually was close enough to put a hand on his wet shoulder. Vic looked up at her. He had no clear sense of who she was at first, but a gentle hand on his arm, and a female voice somewhere above his shoulder, brought him comfort of a kind.

He looked away from her and said quietly, 'The good men, love, they all died. It was only ones like me who lived.'

And with that came tears. And with the tears, some relief. Frosso sat next to him, hoping this would help. As she waited, she came to an idea of what he was talking about. These words, or something similar, she had heard said in Greek, too. Phrases her father, a war veteran himself, used to utter long ago.

She replied, '*Ohi, ohi* … everything be all right … no more bad dream … Dream finish …'

Slowly, and though the pain of this night continued to haunt and cling, the torrent eased. Eventually there was no more than a ringing in his ears and a sense of exhaustion. And with that, Vic allowed himself to be gently nudged back down onto the bed.

Vic slept until 12.30pm the following day. He knew that for a fact because that's what he saw when he looked at the digital clock by his bedside when he heard a knock on the door.

Frosso entered in the company of a tall, thin man whom, she announced, was a doctor, though he appeared to Vic too young to be any sort of a medico. Vic listened to him say 'Hello, how are you?' in perfectly good English, and was relieved that whatever took place next wouldn't be complicated by a communication problem.

'Please, you tell the doctor everything, Mr Vic,' Frosso prompted.

'Don't worry. I'm not holding back,' Vic replied. Then began to relate that he might have had 'a bit of a turn, nothing more', and was feeling much better already.

In the pause that followed, Vic waited for a reassuring response from the doctor, and when none was forthcoming he was a little annoyed. But when the doctor began to ask questions about blood pressure, heart disease, strokes, it was satisfying to answer no to these. He baulked, however, when he heard the phrase 'mental problems'. To that he also answered no, and though he immediately recalled an episode or two that others had made a big thing of decades ago, he decided not to say anything.

The doctor wrote something on his pad, then, addressing his remarks more towards Frosso than Vic, said that it would be wise to arrange some follow-up tests, and that his family should be contacted to let them know Vic had been unwell. Vic interrupted him. 'Excuse me, but you're sounding all very serious there. Look, I feel a lot better now. I just reckon it'll pass, whatever it was.' He shot them his best charming smile, then added, 'Probably only need a dose of your good mountain camomile, ay? A bit of a pick-me-up, or a mineral tonic of some kind.'

Vic was very aware of the way Frosso and the doctor looked at him, both obviously weighing up their options, and found their scrutiny a little hard to take. He turned away from them, then said, 'After all, I've been in much bigger stoushes than this. I was in the war, you know.'

At the word 'war', the doctor, like everyone else who had ever lived on Crete in this century, knew what the possibilities now were. He leaned slightly towards Vic and said softly, 'Sir, this sounds like a stress disorder; I think it is possible you are having a nervous collapse.'

Put to bed again and with a sleeping pill, the next morning Vic was packed up and, against his protestations, driven by Frosso herself the thirty kilometres to Hania, the capital of western Crete. There she took him to a Polyclinic recommended by the doctor in Sfakia, which had a small specialist facility for people suffering from mental disorders.

As a tourist, and presumably with access to proper money, it was determined Vic would be assessed reasonably speedily. It did not hurt, either, that he had a Greek-speaking advocate along. But before they were ready to see a doctor, Vic had seemingly entered another state. He was silent and looked profoundly tired. Sitting in the waiting room, he appeared to Frosso to be completely blank and mostly unable to help himself. Which was more or less how Vic himself felt.

Whatever small defiance he had been able to mount the previous day, Vic today had none to show, apparently content to go along with what was being done to him or for him. As far as he could think about it, these people seemed to hold no ill will towards him but on the contrary seemed to want to be helpful. Maybe he had frightened them, he came to think.

When it was Vic's turn to be seen, he was taken into a neat and very white room where a bearded and bespectacled man in a cardigan sat behind a desk. He did not look to Vic like a doctor, but apparently he was. Frosso was kind enough to go in with him to do whatever translating was necessary. The doctor asked him the same questions as the ones the young chap in Sfakia had asked, then turned to his depression. Had he ever been treated for depression, the doctor asked. Had he taken any medication before? Vic answered with what he considered was the truth; he had never been told by anyone directly that he was depressed, and no, no one had given him any medicine for it.

After a long conversation between this doctor and Frosso, she turned to him to tell him that the symptoms he had shown had definitely come from 'in the head' and not 'in the body', and maybe, she said, 'because of the war and because you come back here and you remember bad things. Doctor say it happen many times before — plenty English people have same thing like you ...'

Vic's first reaction was that this was a bit much. He did not like being labelled as some kind of nut case, even if he conceded that things weren't as they possibly should be with him. He was only a little less offended when a course of medicine to make him 'feel better' was suggested. And he reacted not at all when it was put to him that when he returned to Australia it would be a good idea to talk to another psychiatrist there. He didn't react because he was having trouble with the idea that something like this could be the trouble after so long, and because he was reserving his options as to what he might do about how he was feeling.

Vic accepted the prescription for some mild anti-depressants, which he would have to take, so this fellow said, every day if they were to do him any good, and tried to be as grateful as he could to all and sundry, given that they thought what they were doing was for the best. The only injunction that he felt he could embrace wholeheartedly was the idea that he should have a lot of rest over the following weeks, some gentle exercise and a good and proper diet. Frosso promised the Polyclinic doctor that this would be attended to — she never liked to see her guests come to grief while in her 'house', as she called it, and assured Vic she would look after him until he could organise his return to Australia.

Much as Vic believed in the power of exercise to do you good, he felt himself past the stage when he could set off on demanding walks or gym regimes. He knew he had to contribute to his own recovery, but was at a loss as to what he could do without truly killing himself. Over the next days, every time Frosso suggested he might go down to the fitness club in town to 'do some hup! two! three!' as she called it, he would find an excuse. Fortunately, he did have a less than perfect knee, which he would mention to Frosso whenever he was under one of her assaults.

The one thing that drew him out was the waterfront. He found he loved that stretch, and would wander down at least twice a day. Sometimes he did no more than sit at a café table, order a coffee and read an English language magazine; other times he went for a walk — here, miraculously his knee never really bothered him — down one end then the other, before returning to L'Avenir. So satisfying was the sea air, the breeze and ambience along that stretch he would go out whether it was overcast or a day of full sun. He didn't know what the doctors might make of him yet, but after a week of this self-directed therapy, he felt himself gradually improve in mind and body. Certainly there had been no repeat of the kind of nightmare that had landed him in trouble.

27

A Memorial

In further aid of Vic's recovery Frosso organised for him to visit a veterans' group whose members got together in Rethymnon once a month. It was the organisation her own father had belonged to when he was still alive. Having sat through one or two of their sessions in earlier years, mostly involving endless talk of past heroics, infinite elaboration of past glories, bickering over the details of this or that encounter, she had told him they were enough to put an owl to sleep. But she could see the value in them for the poor beggars who had soldiered through the traumas of war.

Frosso's contact among the group was the president himself, Stavros Patrikareas. A young full colonel during the Second World War, he had remained as solid a man as anyone could wish for. He had been her father's closest friend during and after that conflict, and when she told him of the *xenos* who was in residence and the problems he was having, he vowed to personally collect the unfortunate and do what he could. For a start, he told Frosso over the phone, he could take him to visit the newly built and blessed Allied War Memorial situated on the outskirts of the town. Such a stirring site, he told her, would do him the world of good to see, he was sure. It was important to emphasise that what he and other men like him had done was not in vain — ignoring that the battle itself had been lost — and to see something that recognised and respected their involvement. After a visit there, he said, he would take Vic back to their club before returning him to Sfakia.

Colonel Patrikareas arrived on a Thursday morning to collect Vic from the street outside Frosso's. When he first spotted this square-built man of medium height, Vic saw him as someone exceedingly well anchored to the earth. A real specimen and much younger-looking than his years, Vic thought.

Patrikareas strode across the pavement towards him, his hand extended and said in a surprisingly soft voice said, 'You are Mr Stockton, yes?'

Vic took his hand — very strong and at odds with the voice — and shook it. 'Yes, I am. Pleased to meet you.'

'Your hotel lady, *Kyria* Frosso Pantelakis, tells me all about you and ask me to look after you.'

'Oh look, I'm grateful but I don't need much looking after. I don't want to get in anyone's way here.'

Patrikareas smiled, leaned towards Vic, took his hand again and this time put his hand on his shoulder as well. 'Sir, I was senior officer. I know my responsibility. Doesn't matter fifty years ago or today. OK?'

'OK, OK. I appreciate what you're doing, believe me.'

Vic was thankful, too, that, as with so many others he had met around Crete, there was no problem with communication. But then you had to expect that a one-time colonel would be the educated type.

The drive to the memorial site was a little awkward, for the colonel was not an avid talker. He asked questions though: about

Vic's personal story, where he came from, what life was like in Australia. It became easier once they arrived at the memorial site and Patrikareas could talk on a subject he knew intimately. He had, in fact, been active in getting this memorial under way. Vic thought it had been well worth the effort. It was set out at a dramatic point overlooking the sea to the north. A simple thing. Just vertical slabs of rock, two of limestone, one of black granite, and flagpoles — flying the standards of Greece and Australia.

The colonel led Vic out of the car and walked by his side as they approached for a closer look. When they were within a few metres Patrikareas stopped, straightened up, crossed himself, then saluted. Without thinking Vic followed with a salute, then recognised the gesture for its strangeness; he hadn't saluted since he didn't know how long.

'This was made ready last year, Mr Stockton. You should have been here. Big day!'

Vic was perplexed. 'Last year?'

'Yes! Fifty years commemoration — everyone come from everywhere. The black stone is from your country. From South Australia.'

'That's marvellous,' Vic said quietly. He was surprised that such things had been happening without his ever knowing. The question was, where had he been these last decades while others were building such tributes?

Vic continued to gaze at the contrast of colours in the stonework then raised his eyes to follow the occasional lazy fluttering of the two flags on this otherwise still day. It was so very peaceful here. He came in more closely to read the English text on a panel: '*In memory and honour of two peoples who fought as one, for freedom and democracy. Dedicated to the sons and daughters of Crete and of Australia, past, present and future.*'

'The government of Crete make this memorial, with everybody helping,' Patrikareas added.

'With co-operation, eh?'

'Yes, as you say, with the co-operation.'

Patrikareas stood to one side and waited while Vic paced around the site. He seemed to Patrikareas to want to make the most of being here and he took his time. Eventually he came to the low wall that formed a barrier between the memorial and the shoreline not so far away.

Vic returned, nodding his head and deep in thought. 'Thank you very much for bringing me here. Where to now?'

'To our club, Mr Stockton. Plenty more to see there!'

The Veterans' Association of Rethymnon owned small premises not far from the commercial centre of the town. Patrikareas arrived there with Vic in the late morning and pulled up at a doorway on a side street, anonymous but for the sign of an eagle bearing arms hanging above the entrance. A short knock and the door was opened by a weatherbeaten brigand of a man, of the sort Vic hadn't seen in fifty years but whose character he instantly recognised. A killer for sure when the need arose. Patrikareas had to speak to him at some length, it appeared to Vic, before he would let them pass. 'He likes to protect me,' he said. 'So he make me answer questions about you. I tell him you are one of our brothers, from *Afstralia*.'

They entered and the colonel took Vic across a spacious room to a long wooden table. On top at one end were piles of papers in an in-tray and a computer and printer arranged at the other. He bade Vic sit down at the other end and took the seat directly across for himself.

'So, you must tell me about when you were in Crete? We must make the record for the computer, you see.'

Vic was distracted by a glass cabinet behind the table, and hesitated for a moment. 'Hmm ...?'

As Vic peered around him, Patrikareas returned with: 'It's OK, you look if you like ... You were here with a composite brigade, yes? And first position was near the airport at Maleme?'

With that he had Vic's attention. 'Yes, yes! By crikey, how did you know? You've surprised me here!'

'Ha, no surprise. Come around here.'

Patrikareas got up and waved Vic around to his side of the table to the cabinet. When Vic stopped near, he put his hand on Vic's shoulder and pointed at the war memorabilia — the photographs and ammunition, bullet belts and ancient pistols. 'Look, look there ... What you see?'

Vic followed Patrikareas' gesture and couldn't believe his eyes.

'That is your symbol, how you say, insig ... There. You see it?'

'Insignia.'

'Insignia, yes.'

'It is! How on earth did you come by that? I haven't seen one of those in years!'

Vic stood staring at the colour patch, mounted in a photo frame and set alongside a New Zealand and British patch. That they were indoors and in a low light diminished them not at all: to see those twin colour bands like that was to see a distant planet light up. He knew he had never been one for Anzac Days and marches, and the glorification of war was anathema to him, but to have this simple thing brought to his attention in the place where it had all happened was something else. This meant something. This was tremendous.

Vic continued to stare, then turned his attention to another shelf. The Cretan veteran allowed him further time to scan the other contents of the case, then Patrikareas said, 'Some of your boys, they used to write us the letter sometimes. Sometimes send us a few things for the collection we make. As you can see.'

'Our boys? Aussie boys?'

'Yes, Aussie, as you say. Not so much now because many have died, but before, in the old days.'

'That's wonderful, Colonel. I should have done the same. So, which of our chaps wrote to you? I'd love to know.'

'Plenty boys write — we keep the letters, too.'

Patrikareas leaned down to pull out one of the drawers at the base of the display cabinet. 'Look, we keep them here.'

Vic saw a couple of small file boxes neatly fitted into the drawer. Patrikareas lifted the cardboard lid off one of them to reveal dozens of envelopes lined up inside. Patrikareas replaced the lid then lifted both boxes out to place them on the table.

'We ask people from our club if they have mementos and they ask other people and we put something in the newspaper. For the history, we say. And sometimes somebody die and the family give us the English letters.'

'Can I have a look at some of them?'

'Of course. You sit down now, sit.'

Taking out the first of these envelopes, Vic began to feel uncomfortable. It didn't seem right to be looking at other people's letters like this, not something he could recall ever having done before. The yellowing envelope in his hand bore an old Australian stamp in the corner. He casually flicked through some of the others still in the box — all manner of stamps from the 1940s and 1950s and 1960s that he had long forgotten. He overcame the idea that he was about to breach a confidence in opening the envelope in his hand by remembering that these letters had been made available to the veterans' association with the presumption that they would be read by others.

Vic removed the folded blue notepaper and looked in the top corner: 'April 27th, 1951' it read.

Dear Athanassios and family,

I hope this letter finds you and yours all hale and hearty. And I hope old Mr Varvaressos, your English scholar, is still there to read this to you! (Hello to you, Mr. V., if you get to see this.) We have just had our Anzac Day here and I wanted to send a note as 'our' anniversary comes around again — May 21st, and all that. Nothing exciting happening here, I'm afraid. Except that young Terry is now six years old and has started school. He's a bright little chap and loves his alphabet and his sums. Mary reckons he's the sort who will go on to do big things — better than his old man, at least! Speaking of children, have you got anything more to report? How are the girls going? And your good wife, Vicki? Give her our love, would you.

Yours sincerely

Ted Prior ...

It was a touching letter and Vic dwelled on the fact the fellow had also signed off with his unit number. Many blokes he knew had got attached to that sort of military identification, although he couldn't say he was ever one of them. Looking at the efforts so many others had made to stay in touch with the people they had fought for, and who had sheltered them, he began to experience some regret. He had always felt connected to that young woman who had managed his life, who had kept him alive. Other men maintained their own contact, he realised, and in their own ways.

Just then Colonel Patrikareas came over to him with another envelope and letter in hand.

'Look, Mr Stockton, I find the letter from the boy who send us your colours.'

Vic took the letter that was handed to him. This one was typed and dated February 11th, 1964. Again he began to read:

To dear Colonel Patrikareas,

On behalf of all of us here at the Burlington-Campbell Hill RSL Club in Western Australia, please accept this from those of us who remember all that your good people did for us in the Battle of Crete …

Vic went straight to the signature: 'Stan Weller, Secretary'. He tilted the letter away from himself for a moment and thought, *This has got to be him.* He started to read again almost immediately.

Please accept it as a gift for the little museum you tell us you have started. It is not an original but we had it made up as accurately as we could so as to at least give the proper idea.

I hope to visit you there in person in the new year, when we can catch up on old times and, who knows, maybe make other plans for our associations.

With best wishes …

Vic read the name again and this time put the letter on the table.

'Sir? You looking not so good? Are you all right?' Patrikareas asked.

'Just thinking, Colonel. Just thinking … I believe I know this chap.'

Patrikareas was agreeably surprised.

'Is that possible?'

'It's more than possible. I was on Crete with a bloke named Stan Weller. And he did say something about going over to Western Australia for a fresh start, if he survived ... Did you hear any more from him?' Vic asked.

Patrikareas concentrated on the question, trying hard to recall. 'No. I don't believe so. Nothing more. I can look one more time but I don't think so.'

Vic suddenly slapped his hands on the table and felt his face stretch into the widest of smiles. He stood up quickly, so abruptly that the colonel had to step back quickly so as not to be knocked over.

'Sir? Mr Stockton? Everything OK?'

'Oh absolutely. Sorry if I startled you, but I've got to go. Thanks for everything and I'll be back!'

Vic marched energetically across the room, attracting the attention of the grizzled old guard who jumped to his feet as if ready for hand-to-hand combat. With Patrikareas scurrying to catch up to him, Vic was out of the clubhouse and on the street in no time.

'You forget! I supposed to drive you to Sfakia!' protested the colonel.

'Don't worry about it. I'll call a cab from the town centre. I'll be right. Thanks for everything ...'

Vic left Colonel Patrikareas in his wake and headed for the central shopping district. From there he would call Kostas for a lift to Frosso's, but first he felt like a good walk. For the first time in ages he felt recharged and accessing energy that he did not know he still had.

Vic was unaware that Patrikareas had set off after him. The Cretan veteran knew full well that Vic Stockton was having 'veteran's troubles' and was conscious of owing a duty of care to him as well as to Frosso. Breathing heavily, he caught up with the Australian.

'Mr Stockton, wait please … Everything all right?'

Vic wheeled around to face him and immediately spread his arms in reassurance. 'Never felt better, Colonel! Never felt better in my life! I want to stretch my legs. You've done enough for me, believe me. You all have. I'll call a cab.'

'But …'

'Look, if I have any trouble, I'll come back to the club and see you. All right?'

This seemed to reassure Patrikareas. Waiting a few more moments to recover his breath, he said, 'All right. But you call me please when you back in the hotel. OK?'

'Done.'

With that, Vic shook the colonel's hand, and in the next moment came closer and briefly squeezed his shoulders. 'Thanks for today — it was a real eye-opener for me.'

He turned again in the direction he had been heading and began to walk. Gradually, he increased his pace, broadening his strides as far as his worn body would let him.

After another week, the first euphoria at the news of Stan Weller's survival had eased for Vic. At breakfast each morning that past week he had taken his tablet, then sat in Frosso's dining room watching the television and gearing up for his daily constitutional. He felt he was making reasonable progress, getting stronger. At the same time he had set to wondering about the details. How had Stan got off the island? What had befallen him at Sfakia? When exactly had Stan gone over to WA? Was he still alive? The buried unease he realised he had felt about Stan all these years had surfaced and now subsided. He was very glad to have learned that the man had made it through the strife, no thanks to Vic. But if he was relaxing about Stan in one way, Vic found thoughts of his comrade running back at him in a new channel. Stan had gone and done something by way of acknowledging the efforts of these Cretan folks, indeed all their comrades dead and living. What had he, Vic Stockton, done?

The thought troubled him, but for little more than a day. For the very next morning he had an idea about how he might repay some of his own debt. And in order to act on it, he needed to convince Frosso and the doctor that there was no need to ship him out just yet; that he was well enough to stay on. He had no idea whether the pills he was taking were making any difference, but they didn't seem to be doing any harm, he reasoned. And he would need to be in the best possible shape if he was to get back to the monastery. He wanted that, more than ever.

Vic had not given much thought to anything this morning, other than getting here. He was perfectly satisfied to be standing in the monastery grounds, allowing the chapel of St Nicholas to claim his attention yet again. He returned his gaze to this place of worship, built who knew how long ago. A simple long box — limewashed white on those surfaces where it wasn't falling apart — its wall curving with weight and age, and with a domed roof to cap it off. But how small it was in reality. It was the sort of thing you could knock up in a few days really. There was about as much material in it as you might need to put up a shed on somebody's weekend farm or at the back of a big yard. Instead of the limestone with which it was made, all you needed was some concrete blocks, a few mates, a brickie and someone to do the rendering. So why was it in such a lousy condition? Why hadn't it been brought back up to scratch?

He willed himself to look away, try to get some perspective. He stared down at his feet for a time, allowed himself to notice the light, cooling breeze that was coming in gentle waves over the monastery walls. He watched a few leaves rustle around his shoes. But his attention was drawn yet again and inevitably to the chapel, that little sanctuary standing in the corner across the way. He understood now what he was here for, what he was meant to do. And he would do it. There was no choice.

28

The Greek Hammer

Vic Stockton was shuffling along through the Sfakia produce market, trying to juggle all the balls he felt needed to be juggled now that he at last had something of a plan. Someone bumped him as he went. A crush of people he hadn't noticed until then seemed to carry him bodily to one side. He stepped back into an alcove to reorient himself. Appreciating the shade of this indentation between two shopfronts that he currently occupied, he leaned back and steadied himself against the wall.

There was a reason he was not feeling quite so positive today. Somehow Jennifer had learned of his whereabouts before he had got in touch with her. He had certainly been meaning to, but the intention had slipped away from him, what with the disturbances he'd suffered on Crete.

Jennifer had told him over the phone that she intended to come over on the first flight she could arrange. She was worried about him. How could he just up and leave like that when he knew others would be concerned for him? He could not tell her what had happened to him, had only said in reply that he was all right, not to bother, having a good holiday, had things to be going on with. None of this seemed to make a difference.

From the doorway, he allowed his eye to be attracted to the flutterings of some pigeons overhead in the spaces above the market. He watched them circle, then swoop to the ground near a cabbage and marrow stall. Some scraps were tempting them. When the bloke there shooed them away, Vic traced their antic flight again.

Greece was some kind of mad dream; the people behaved as if they were living in one, anyway. They were all explosions, advances, retreats, nothing you could call steady or sober. One minute they were all over you like a rash, next minute they seemed to have the darks with you good and proper. But not for something you'd actually done. More like something that had been done to them, some injustice that had been visited upon them, that they couldn't name but was hurting profoundly, and it was just bad luck if anyone else happened to be in their line of sight at the time. Or maybe it was some sense they'd lost something, or had it taken off them (plenty of that in their history) — and they were having a devil of a job getting it back. Whatever it was, it was pretty close to the surface.

But here was the real question. Why, rather than worrying him as he made his way around this country, this island, did the emotions he encountered here seem all right, acceptable, not a problem? More than that, almost a relief even? Flaws and grievances and all, nothing much appeared to be hidden — perhaps there was a lesson in that.

As for Jenny, she could come over if she wanted to. There was precious little he could do to stop her. He would press on with what he had in mind regardless. It was only people, he decided. All a matter of people. And to find the right ones, those who could help, was only a matter of shoe leather.

He would have to get back to Kastelli and talk to the old

gents, the bearded blokes in black. And he had to find someone who knew about hammers and nails.

This morning Vic decided that if he was going to embark on this craziness, he would have to strike a first blow. On a stroll before breakfast he headed purposefully down a street where he had noticed some building work going on, apparently another typical small apartment block. But while there were indications of activity — a cement mixer was set up, a couple of small trucks parked outside, a gate in the wire fence open — there was no sign of supervisor or workers. Building Greek style, thought Vic, as he came up closer to inspect things. Ramshackle scaffolding, no pretence at neat brick coursework (presumably nobody bothered because everything was eventually rendered over anyway), stuff lying around everywhere ... And men having breakfast and reading papers in the shade.

Two men were sitting on crates in the shell of the bottom storey. Vic had missed them at first, but looking more closely he saw a burly fellow in his mid-fifties or so, and a skinny-looking, long-haired bloke with a sort of wispy beatnik beard sitting next to him. This one proved to be the more alert of the two and noticed Stockton standing on the street.

'*Ti thelis?*' What do you want? he called out, startling the older bloke sitting beside him.

'Can I speak to you?' he replied. And in return heard, 'Oh, English, ay?' as the younger man got up to come across to him. What an odd figure he cut, thought Vic, as he watched him saunter over. He was wearing a vest over a checkered western shirt, sleeves rolled up. Flea market clothes obviously.

'Yes, sir, what can I do for you?' the chap asked, in what Vic thought was an American accent.

'G'day. I was walking past and I noticed the work here … are you the builder?'

'Not me, man. That's him back there. What's the accent I'm hearing by the way?'

'Australian.'

'Oh, well, there you go! Canadian, me.'

He put out his hand to shake, while turning slightly to call out to his colleague.

'*Afstralezos!*' he said loudly in what sounded like good Greek to Vic, adding to the confusion. The Canadian accent and the Greek definitely didn't go together in his book.

The older fellow nodded and seemed to brighten, enough to get up off his crate anyway.

'*Ferton etho.*' Bring him here, the grizzled one said.

'The boss wants to speak to you. Careful you don't break your neck.'

Vic followed the young man across the piles of sand and cement mix and the stacks of terracotta bricks and got a better fix on him. He was somewhere in his thirties and wore a headband that added to the hippie look, but the tattoos on his arms and the jeans he wore placed him more firmly in the bikie camp. He was an odd and confusing mix, whatever else.

'Hello, mister, what's your name?' the older chap asked in a thick accent.

'Vic Stockton. Pleased to meet you.'

'I am Pavlos. This one is Mark.'

'I thought you were American at first.'

'Aw, come on, man. Don't insult me first thing,' said the younger man jokingly.

'He been in Canada,' said the Greek fellow. 'So … you looking for somebody?'

'No, I was thinking to ask … I was a builder myself in the old days.'

Pavlos suddenly looked serious, didn't respond but looked to be deliberating, as if he had been delivered some bad news, as if he was sorry to hear this poor man was suffering a terminal illness.

'Builder, eh? Like me. Bad business, bad business …' he shook his head. 'You builder in *Afstralia*?'

'Yes.'

'I have cousins in Australia.'

'Everybody does, or so it seems.'

To cover the awkwardness he was beginning to feel, Vic cast about for an object of conversation. He noticed an odd-looking hammer lying next to the crates where these two had been sitting. He leaned over to pick it up.

'Now this is a strange-looking thing.' Rather than having a bell head and claws, the hammer was in the shape of a miniature adze — an oblong shape that was squared off at one end but that thinned out and became a curve ending in a sharp edge at the other, and with a sort of keyhole about half-way along the blade.

'What strange?' the older man said.

Mark chipped in, 'He means compared to the hammers back where he comes from, I would guess. Is that right?'

'Ours are sort of round, with a claw part.'

'OK, same as American and English. You're looking at a Greek hammer there. Can you see the advantage?'

Vic stared at the business end for a while, then it came to him. 'Oh, I see. Three functions here? Am I right?'

'Yep, one more than you're used to. It's a hammer, it's a chisel or little adze, and that hole there is for lifting nails.'

'Bugger me but those Greeks are smart, eh, what?' he grinned at them both.

'Design's hundreds of years old, if not thousands. I love 'em. Never seen them in Canada, I can tell you! First one of these I saw was working here for my old man on this,' he said, half-turning to look up at the structure around them.

'Your father, eh?' said Vic, glad that these types were friendly, prepared to talk. For something to say, he asked, 'Is he here, or back in … ?'

'He's here, for sure. This is him standing right here,' he said and made a joke of pointing at Pavlos standing next to him.

Pavlos shrugged. 'What can I do? We live in Canada many years and he become this,' he said, eyeing up and down the apparition that was his son. But with not a little affection, Vic saw.

'Come and sit, *Aftsralezo*,' he said. 'Old man like you, better we give you some coffee.'

There was a Thermos and cup in the mini recreation area they had set up in the back of the unfinished bottom-storey room behind them. Pavlos led Vic to a card table in one corner where he poured some thick black stuff into three plastic mugs.

'So, what you doin' here?' Pavlos asked.

Now Vic felt awkward once more. 'Well, I, it's just that I was looking for some advice. Maybe you can help me. I've got a little building project in mind.'

'Building project?' Pavlos repeated, the second word taking some time to process. 'You want to make some building?'

'No, I want to fix a building.'

'Renovation job?' the son asked.

'Well, sort of. The place hasn't been in good shape for a long time.'

'What kind of building?' Mark asked.

It was clear to Vic that given his better English the younger man was going to do most of the talking, so he turned and faced him directly. He didn't seem such a bad character, vest, beard and all.

'A chapel.'

This seemed to confuse, if not outright stump, Mark. He stared back at the elderly Australian with the weatherbeaten face and dreary blue sports jacket for a long time without answering. His father, waiting for a translation, asked, 'What is chapel?'

'A church, a small church. *Ekklisia*,' said Mark finally.

Pavlos then did what Vic had seen many Greeks do when something was beyond their ken. He spread his arms out wide, tilted his head slightly skywards and rolled his eyes even further, then lowered the corners of his mouth. Having done consulting with the higher power who seemingly had no answer, Pavlos fixed Vic with a narrow squint.

'You want to fix a *church*?'

'Yes,' Vic replied, as if it was a normal enough thing for an Australian pensioner to want to do in Greece on any given Tuesday.

'Why?' the father asked.

'It's a long story.'

'Where is this chapel?' Mark asked.

'At the Monastery of Kastelli. Do you know it?'

At this, Pavlos butted in. 'Kastelli? You want to fix church at Kastelli monastery?'

'I do, yes. But you might reckon that sounds a bit …'

'Crazy's the word you're looking for,' said Mark.

'Oh, well, yes, I suppose crazy. A bit crazy.'

'Very much crazy,' Pavlos added. 'Did you talk to the *kalogeroi*, how you say, the priests in that place?'

'The monks, you mean?'

'Monks, I don't know, yes. The old men there.' Here Pavlos made the shape of a long beard beneath his chin. 'This is big idea for such place.'

'No, not yet,' Vic said, a little embarrassed at the obvious good sense of the question.

Father and son looked at each other quickly.

Vic spread his own arms out a little. 'Look, yes, I don't know if they'll let me. But I want to give it a go. Try and see what happens.'

'Well. Good luck to you,' said Pavlos cheerily, as if addressing someone who was planning to fly to the moon by flapping his arms. 'Nice to talk. But better I start work now,' he said, quickly offering to shake Vic's hand. 'See you some time, eh?'

With this, Pavlos set off for the front of the site once more. Vic was about to follow, but the younger fellow put a hand on his sleeve. 'Stay a bit. You don't have to go straight away, do you?'

'Dunno. Don't want to wear out my welcome.'

'You haven't. Tell me more. You got me intrigued, man.'

'I don't know much more, is the truth. Your father's right. I have to follow this up with, you know, the people in charge there. They might not be interested.'

Mark began moving his head slowly from side to side, a little smile breaking out across his face. He was both impressed and sceptical — especially sceptical, given what he knew about how things were done, or not done, around this part of Crete.

'They might not be, but what a great idea. I mean, what a thing to do for them.'

'I was here during the war, you see.'

'Were you?' he asked. 'Amazing days, I've heard. Maybe you can tell me about 'em. What say you come and have a proper coffee with me when we're done later?'

'Today?'

'Sure, why not? There's better around than what the old man makes, I can tell you. And I'm on Greek time, no matter what he says. Two o'clock and that's it for this slave.'

Impressed and warmed at how this odd bird had received him, Vic arranged to meet for a *metrio* with Mark in one of the cafés on the harbourfront not far from Frosso's place.

29

Filoxenia

As he had requested a further and preferably official visit, an arrangement was made that day via *Kyria* Frosso for Vic to return to the monastery headquarters in two days' time. She had kindly also managed to organise for him to meet the new head, as he had asked if this might be possible also. According to Frosso he was a very clever fellow, someone educated in France and the US as well as Greece; that he apparently knew his ABCs put him a cut above his brethren, she suggested. 'Most of the *kalogeroi* are …' she said, twirling a finger around near her ear, 'how you say, cuckoo … But him, he tries to do modern things there. Not like old days, bam!' she said, slapping her hands together. 'Close the doors!'

In the meantime, Vic would keep his appointment with the young Canadian.

Vic left the pensione to find a brilliant afternoon of cool sunshine. From Frosso's he strolled the few hundred metres down to the water and the Kafeneion Megisthes, where he had come for a coffee once or twice before as part of his recovery regime, and where he waited as directed under an outdoor umbrella for Mark to show up.

The *kafeneion* was situated at one end of the harbour. He looked at the water lapping rhythmically against the breakwater which finished the curve of this small bay, tried to estimate whether the tide was inbound or out. He began to wonder idly whether water understood what it had to do, when to come and when to go. He decided it did. More so than human beings, you would have to say. Maybe it had a memory. The idea pleased him. Maybe each tide had a memory of the tide before, and was driven by what it knew to keep up the familiar beat, the going out and the coming back.

It was quiet at this time of the day, siesta, and Vic had no trouble eventually spotting the young fellow striding nonchalantly down the harbour promenade towards him. Impossible to miss him really — garish multicoloured pants, a different flashy vest and this time some kind of rainbow-coloured beanie. He was definitely no Beau Brummel, thought Vic.

'G'day!' he said, engaging Mark's hand as warmly as he could.

'"G'day" to you too, whatever that is,' Mark responded.

'Oh, that's how we say hello.'

'I had an idea, but your accent …' he grinned sheepishly at Vic.

'*My* accent, mate!' Vic replied.

They took a table with a view of the breakwater and ordered 'Greek coffee'. 'Whatever you do, don't ask for Turkish …' Mark had commanded in a loud whisper when the waiter approached.

'So, Mark, I have to ask you about that cap! What is it? Never seen one like that before.'

'I'm a Rasta. It's what we wear.' Mark knew immediately that the Australian wasn't computing. 'Do you know what a Rastafarian is?'

Vic looked confused. 'No, I don't, as a matter of fact.'

'It's a long story but basically I worship Haile Selassie, Lion of Africa and Emperor of Ethiopia, as my spiritual leader.'

This information made no difference to the blank that was Vic's face. He didn't know where to begin in response. Mark saw the confusion and dropped the subject.

'Tell me more about this idea of yours.'

Mark, whose second name, it transpired, was a mouth-filling Petroyanakis, listened intently as Vic tried to further outline his thinking. But there seemed little more detail than the idea he had mentioned at the site that morning. Rather than embarrass Vic for his ignorance, when an awkward silence occurred, the Greek-Canadian took up the running.

'Hey Vic, wanna hear a hard luck story?' Mark asked with a disarming grin.

Vic began to listen quietly as Petroyanakis junior catalogued the disasters that had befallen him and his old man in the past fifteen years or so.

His Canadian mother had died in a car accident when he was sixteen years old, killed in her Toyota by a prime mover on a Toronto freeway. His father had had to be hospitalised for two months as a result. Meantime, he and his younger sister were boarded out with an uncle on his mother's side. Then, when he was getting on to his senior year at school, he caught some viral disease which laid him so low he completely bombed in his studies and didn't make it to college. As if that wasn't enough, the old man got involved in a succession of small business ventures that went nowhere.

'Nothing unusual so far, Mark,' Vic said for relief. 'I thought you had a hard luck story!'

Mark smiled at him. 'You're right. Nothing to complain about. Best thing my father did was to get us back here, me and my sister.'

He went on to say they had got into the boat rental business, using a converted trawler for half-day trips up and down the coast and for which there were always a few customers during the tourist season. They were based on the north coast, out of Rethymnon at first, and then around various south coast locations before moving here to Sfakia. They had stayed in the boat hire business until the past few years, when they had begun building work on the place where Vic had encountered them.

'See over there, Vic?' Mark pointed to a fishing boat, dilapidated but brightly painted in white, blue and yellow, bobbing gently near the end of the breakwater. 'That is the sum total of the Petroyanakis fleet at the moment ... but we're workin' on further acquisitions even as we speak.'

Vic squinted at the boat in the near distance. 'Pretty. Could have used that once upon a time, myself.'

'I could take you out in it one day, if you're interested.'

The thought appealed. 'Maybe you could ... I'd like that. Took a ride in a boat like that myself, once upon a time. All the way to Egypt.'

Vic saw the look of surprise on Mark's face, and took it as a cue to recount to his new friend his own tale of long ago and of this part of the world. Impressed at the degree of attention he was being paid — not something he expected, least of all here, least of all from someone as different from him as this young man — he was also pleased at how comfortable he felt in his company. Maybe it was the fellow himself, a gentle and enthusiastic sort of kid under all the costume, maybe it was something else, but he realised as he looked around this peaceful scene that he had never really known days like this.

'So, hey, back to before. I always like a guy with an idea, Mr Vic! 'Coz what else makes the world go round? Hey?'

Vic found his equilibrium again.

'Exactly, Mark. You're right there, son.'

Petroyanakis junior added that he didn't know much about the Greek religion, having grown up pretty much a pagan as his father had never been that interested and his mother had been an Anglican. But he would never, he also said, undermine anyone who was a believer so long as they didn't 'try to ram it down other people's throats'. Everyone had to believe in something, didn't Vic agree?

Vic answered with a firm and simple 'Yes.'

'So is that why you want to do the work at the monastery? Faith?'

It was a good question, Vic thought. He took a few moments before answering. 'Faith, no. Not as such. I'm not religious,' he replied. 'I've got other reasons. But you, what about you? Can I ask you to help me?'

Mark Petroyanakis remained silent as he tried to comprehend Vic's motives. He began again by saying he knew little about the Kastelli monastery, except what he had seen looking up from their boat on the occasional trawl past. 'But hey, I've never worked on anything that old. Love to see how it's put together. Just one last question — would there be some pay in it?'

'Of course.'

'Bonus!' said Mark. 'My father never sees much need to hand over any grey folding stuff, sadly, so I'm always looking out for some.

'Don't know about the old man, though,' he added. 'He can be difficult sometimes ... most times!'

Satisfied that this was progress enough for the moment, Vic turned to rattling off his own story of the battle here in '41, a subject which took up the next hour and more. Mark listened with interest. As the talk began to wind down naturally, he told Vic that he was obliged to do some chores towards his present project before the day ended — 'Can't tell you what it's like trying to get materials from the mainland' — and so gave his farewell.

'It's been great meeting an Aussie, Vic. See a few around here during the summer, but I gotta tell you, not all of 'em are as friendly as you!'

'Or as old,' said Vic.

'Correct! Or as old! See ya, pal.'

And with that he sauntered off, pretty much at the same pace as he had earlier appeared. Vic, too, was more than happy to have made the acquaintance.

When Vic next visited the Monastery of Kastelli as arranged, and was ushered into the senior man's office for the first time in over fifty years, he encountered a very different setting from the one he remembered. He was directed by an assistant to the abbot to sit on a swish, modern sort of chair across from a big corporate-looking office desk. He was brought a glass of orange juice by the solicitous junior which he sipped at until the head man was ready to see him. Scanning the bookshelves to pass the time, Vic saw, as well as dozens of indecipherable and heavy-looking volumes with Greek lettering on the spines, more than a few books with English titles: *The 7 Habits of Highly Effective People* by Stephen R. Covey, *Managing the Non-Profit Organization*, by Peter Drucker, and *Corporate Finance and the Capital Markets*, Harvard Business School Press, among them.

Vic was wondering at the meaning of such unlikely sounding books in a monastery chief's library when the door opened again and a black-cassocked handsome young chap, not much older than forty-five, came bounding in with his hand outstretched and a big, fleshy-lipped smile sandwiched between beard and moustache.

'Good morning, Mr Stockton! A warm welcome to you, my dear fellow!'

They shook, Vic surprised at the vigour with which his hand was met.

'I am Gerasimos. And your first name?'

'Vic. Vic Stockton. From Australia.'

'Ah yes, Vic. And I know, from Australia.'

'You do?'

'Yes, and more. You were a soldier in the battle. They told me who you were and that you wanted to visit us, so as always we ask some questions. You are known around here, Mr Stockton. Well known. And there are many — maybe you know how long-lived is the average Cretan — who want to meet you. Not everyone, my God, it's so many years ago.'

'Yes, yes, it is,' was all Vic could think to offer feebly.

'So, you are an honoured guest of course! You have met our veterans' man, Patrikareas, yes?'

'Yes I have. A splendid chap, too.'

'He is. So, now we have some more special people today. Would you like to meet them?'

Would he ever. 'I'll say! Who are they?'

'Come with me.'

Vic could not imagine that a single person on the whole of Crete knew him from back then, let alone anyone who had lived on this more remote part. Probably some mistake, was all he thought as he followed.

Abbot Gerasimos took Vic's elbow and led him into an adjoining room, something like a sitting room and study. Vic saw two women seated on a sofa, with a coffee table in front of them. One was somewhere in her late thirties, he would have guessed, and another around his age, maybe a little younger. They were both dressed in smart business suits, the older a little more sombrely in black.

As he gazed at the older woman, she stood up and stepped around the table to greet him. She was thin and tallish, not much shorter than himself and, despite her age, she had that beautiful skin the Cretans were blessed with, no matter how old they were. She came towards him, her eyes slightly lowered.

And in that moment he knew who she was. By Christ he knew.

Trying for some word, something to say, Vic let out a strangled sound, a deep, guttural noise between a cry of joy and a yelp of pain.

The older woman bowed her head and Vic saw her shoulders hunch as if she was about to be overcome. She did not, however, let out a sound.

Unsteadily, with the abbot by his side, Vic Stockton stepped towards her. As she did to him.

Kalliope stopped. She turned to her daughter and said, 'No, not now. Let me go outside please. I can't do this.'

She turned and moved quickly away, leaving Elefteria scrambling to catch up.

In the open air of the courtyard, she waved to Elefteria to give her some space. '*Mia stigmi, koritsi mou.*' A moment, girl. Please, just to think. I'll be fine, tell them.

Elefteria was uneasy about leaving her mother on her own here and going back inside. She didn't know what else to do but stand and watch her slowly walk across the courtyard.

This is not my doing, Kalliope thought. She would not be here at all had her daughter not driven her down. Nor would she be here had her friend Frosso not dropped the name of her Australian guest, Vic Stockton. A name she remembered yet.

How could she have failed to respond to that name? But at this moment she understood that she had not considered seriously enough what it might mean to sit in the same room with him, a man whose presence could not fail but to bring back a time and events better left buried.

To come here and see Vic in the flesh was all somehow too much, perhaps even wrong. Kalliope thought she had been silly to allow Frosso to prevail over her better judgment, and for a few moments was angry at herself. Vic was an old man, she an old woman. But then what was making her react like this? What was so bad? Two people from opposite sides of the planet and with separate histories seeing each other again was hardly the worst that had ever happened. Was it something else?

She had returned to Crete as a woman in middle age, feeling like a hunted animal with no home, and no idea of where shelter might be found. It had taken a superhuman effort to resettle here, to find work, invariably menial in the first days, settle her daughter into school and a language that she had rarely heard outside home in Australia, and start all over again. These days life was comfortable; there were friends, her relationship with Elefteria was good, and for the first time in her life she had some real money. Australia had been a mistake, but not one she was prepared to entirely blame on Andreas. He had not been strong enough, changed by a way of life that he purported to understand when in truth he had only been seduced by its weaker elements.

She stood outside the chapel of Aghios Nikolaos and slowly began to see things more moderately. It was nobody's fault, not his, not hers. Fate intervenes for each and everyone — one life goes this way, another that. Nothing more needs to be said. What might have been is one thing; what is remains another. Neither Vic nor Kalliope could have done anything but what they did in such desperate times. What was the sense in regrets and wishing for more, for what else might have been?

More important today, she told herself at last, was to show some hospitality, some kindness to a traveller. *Filoxenia* had been bred into her and every Cretan since childhood: when else to call upon that, if not now?

Calmer, she turned and saw her daughter waiting outside the door to the abbot's office, still staring across at her. She began to walk back slowly, measuring her steps, taking time to continue clearing her head. Once back, she nodded at the door.

'I'm all right, I'm all right. Sorry, I needed to get my breath. This is hard, Elefteria. Harder than you think.'

'I shouldn't have …'

'No, I'm ready now. Let's not upset anyone more. They've gone to trouble.'

Back inside, the abbot and Vic were waiting together, anxious that Kalliope was unwell.

'Sorry, dear Reverend, it's nothing,' Kalliope said to Gerasimos. She turned to Vic and took another step closer.

'Are you feeling … ?'

'Don't worry. Nothing. It's nothing. Better now …'

'Kalliope, Kalliope. I can't believe it,' he said.

'Vic. Yes, you are Vic. The soldier. I know. But so long, so many years …' Feeling she had regained a little balance, Kalliope, touched her daughter's arm. '*Se parakalo*, please, this is my Elefteria. *Koritsi mou*, this is Vic.'

Vic nodded at the daughter but immediately returned to gaze at Kalliope and saw her eyes were glistening. She slowly took one more step towards him and Vic rushed across the remaining small gap between them and put his arms around her.

'I can't believe it … You …'

'And you,' she replied, a willing partner in his embrace.

Gerasimos was first to break the spell. He came to them and with much gentleness, gravity and authority indicated they should sit. Elefteria took her mother back to the sofa while the abbot led Vic to one of the two armchairs.

For the next minute and more, Vic and Kalliope could not make much eye contact. Nor could they find words to say. It was difficult to be in this room with each other, after lifetimes, aeons. And what, each of them asked themselves, did they know of the other anyway? Who were they? What had happened?

'Well, well,' said Gerasimos after a decent interval. 'Isn't it amazing? You two people, our heroes from the war that we heard about when we were but children, people who knew each other. And who would know each other today, as we were told …'

'Who told you?' Vic said, at last able to speak again.

'Who? Someone you know, Mr Stockton. She called us and told the whole story. Your story that you had told her. You are Australian, I know that. What you did here we still remember. Cretans never forget such things.'

The abbot had spoken with a sudden flash of fierceness that jolted Vic. This was the stuff these people were made of. He nodded in pleasure and acknowledgment, hardly able to hide the smile that kept wanting to take over his face. He looked across at Kalliope, who was quite red-faced by now. As he did so, she sent him a quick sideways look — a glance sly and deep, and instantly familiar to him — before breaking into a more formal smile he imagined she thought better suited to the gathering.

He reached across from where he was sitting and took her hand.

'Jesus! I would never have … Kalliope of all …!'

'Yes, Kalliope, that's me,' she replied, almost as if she was referring to someone else.

'And you speak English too.'

'Yes. I learned it in your country.'

'Australia?' he asked, with an air that said he couldn't be expected to believe this, too. 'You were in *Australia*?'

'More than twenty years, then I come back. With my daughter here,' she said, smiling at Elefteria with not a little pride.

Afraid that his manners had been too sketchy, Vic immediately launched himself upright again to go over to Elefteria and shake her hand.

'Elefteria. Sorry to be so rude. Pleased to meet you, of course!'

'Me, too.'

'Your English is very good.'

'I went to school in Australia, don't forget.'

'Of course, of course … And a lovely name you have too. Elefteria. Means freedom, if I'm not wrong?'

'Freedom, yes.' She smiled at him.

Vic sat down again and a further awkwardness began to descend. The abbot took hold of matters again. 'Now, Mr Stockton, Frosso tells me you are a good man and I can see that. And I can say, very lovely to see you today with your friend after so long.'

'So it was Frosso, eh? How did she …?'

Gerasimos raised a pacifying hand. 'Ah, easy! Frosso is a friend of *Kyria* Kalliope here.'

'Frosso, she told me one day,' Kalliope added. 'She said an *Afstralezo* from the war time was here. She told me your name.'

'We decided to make a surprise,' Elefteria chipped in.

'You did that all right!'

As Vic was also in danger of being overwhelmed — in his case by the presence of someone who had once been so very dear, but who had been left behind if not entirely forgotten — he thought to pick up a less confronting thread in the conversation. He understood that to communicate sensibly with a woman who had once given so much in the service of his own physical survival would require a little time to organise his thoughts. Not only time, but space, would be needed to do that.

There was something else he might do at this point. He had come here today with a purpose, something he wanted to talk about and still might, however inappropriate it might seem in such circumstances.

After a few more moments, Vic said, 'And maybe I've got a surprise for you too.' Not wanting to come across as a complete fool and urger, Vic took his time before describing the proposition. Given what he was about to say, he wished to sound as convincing and plausible as possible.

He told them he was an old man, he knew that, but that he was not yet dead, and he wanted to do some good for the people who had helped him a long time ago. People he remembered yet. And, amazingly, one of whom was in this room with him. He said it might sound foolish, or impossible, but he wanted to rebuild a chapel. Not any chapel, but the chapel of St Nicholas, Aghios Nikolaos as they called it, situated not a hundred metres from where they sat. It was in a state of terrible disrepair as far as he could see.

At this point the abbot shifted in his seat. Vic understood he was none too pleased to have property that was ultimately his responsibility discussed in terms of disrepair, if not ruin. He added hastily, 'But look, I know the monastery wouldn't have a lot of money. I'm not surprised nothing's been done to preserve it.'

'My friend, no, it's not just money,' said the abbot. 'The chapel you speak of is very important, it is archeological, it is heritage and history. Maybe you don't know but it is something around one thousand years old, the foundation and some of the walls. It cannot be touched without approvals, authorities, and there is a schedule. Unfortunately, it is not time yet. We must wait.'

'Can I say, Abbot sir, that I did know that it's as old as it is — one of your predecessors told me, actually.' Vic said this in a way that he hoped didn't sound like he was being smart, but more like an illustration of his knowledge and concern. He needn't have worried; Abbot Gerasimos was not a man easily upset or rattled. He was, as he returned with some emphasis, a graduate of Harvard Business School as well as the seminary. He was a modern religious, he said, a man always prepared to entertain an idea. He settled back and listened impassively as Vic outlined the rest of the plan. He ignored even the surprise on the faces of the two women, as Vic described how he intended to accomplish this task he had set himself.

Having done his best to try to inspire the abbot, Vic thought a confident conclusion was needed, so he ended with, 'And I think I've found a builder, too.'

At this, Abbot Gerasimos lowered his head to stare briefly at the top of the coffee table in front of them, then just as quickly looked up from under his eyebrows at Vic, his demeanour now decidedly darker.

'What do you mean, sir, you have found a builder?'

'Not one hundred per cent sure, but there's a nice young bloke, Greek-Canadian fellow, and his father who might be right for the job.'

Abbot Gerasimos found he couldn't work up any real anger. The audacity of this old-timer bordered on the amusing. He smiled and said, 'Ah, Mr Stockton, Vic, you move too fast. Please ...' he raised his hand, palm forward, in Vic's direction.

'Too fast?'

'This is Greece. Crete. You cannot do things ...' he now clicked his fingers, 'just like that! And anyway, is today not a day of enough excitement for you already, do you not consider?'

'Sorry. I didn't mean to sound pushy or anything.'

'And not only heritage and history to deal with, as I said before. This is a monastery. Monastery property. We cannot make decisions to do anything without much study, much thought as to our community. What is good for the brothers ...' Confidingly, he added 'And already, to tell you, I make enough difficulties for my superiors — too many new ideas, they have said to me ... And yes, money is a problem too.'

'Oh, look, as I say, paying for it will be my business. I'm confident that I can get money — start a funds drive among the vets here and at home, whatever is needed. I want to do it for the people who died — yours and mine — and not only for them.' He looked at Kalliope again. 'Crikey, for the ones who are still alive! The woman in this room, for instance! Besides, a lovely old building like that shouldn't be allowed to just fall down, should it?'

Kalliope was pleased at the sentiment directed at her but knew the foolishness of what he was suggesting straight away, so tried to avoid Vic's gaze for a few moments. Abbot Gerasimos himself looked extremely doubtful.

'Maybe, maybe. But I can do nothing at this minute, you must know that. I have to discuss your idea with the ones above me. And I have plenty of them, believe me.'

'I understand,' Vic said, trying not to sound disappointed. 'But do you think that will take very long?'

Now the abbot felt his patience was really being tested. He looked quickly at Kalliope, gave her a subtle 'I don't know what to make of this' roll of his eyes, then made to get up. The women, watching his moves and conscious that they were taking up his time, rose almost as one before he did. Vic was the last to get up.

'Let me think, let me think, OK?' the abbot said by way of last remarks. 'I will not say no today, that is all. I will make contact later, if … But now, I am sure you must talk to each other about the old days, Kalliope and Vic, yes?'

Abbot Gerasimos' good humour seemed to return as he came around to usher everyone out of the room. He even put his hand on Vic's shoulder as he said to Kalliope, '*Kyria mou*, my dear lady, please look after our Australian guest. He is one of us, yes?'

'*Ne, Igoumene.*' Yes, Reverend. '*Vevea*, of course, he is.'

Elefteria drove her mother and Vic back to Frosso's place, where it was agreed they would all have some camomile together, a necessity after such a day as this. The trip was difficult for Vic and for Kalliope and they spoke little. Finally Kalliope occupied the silence by turning to how Frosso had got her into this.

Ever since Kalliope had returned from exile, the two would meet for lunch once every two or three weeks. These days, and seeing Kalliope no longer drove, they would get together on a Tuesday, as that was when Elefteria would go to her office at Sfakia and was therefore able to drop her mother in and back. They were having lunch in the *estiatorio* next to L'Avenir when Frosso had remarked on her Australian guest, recalling Kalliope's connection with that place. At the mention of his name, Frosso was then amazed to learn Kalliope knew him.

'Pity he's not here to say hello,' Frosso had said, sipping from her glass of tea. He had experienced some sort of minor crack-up, she said, but was improving. So much so that he had gone off that day to the Monastery of Kastelli, which he seemed very interested in. 'And, you know, he's not bad-looking for an old boy, truth be told ...'

'He is someone I knew, yes, a soldier here during the war, as it happened,' was all that Kalliope had said then, for the sake of the conversation. 'But we saw enough of them then, didn't we? Or maybe I did, you were too young!'

'Kalliope, if you knew him, you should see him!' Frosso practically shouted.

Kalliope remembered watching Frosso break into a smile. She was incorrigible when it came to the opposite sex, had definitely had her share of men trouble. When her own marriage ended, her ex-husband had passed over ownership of their pensione to her and she was able to strike out independently. Lucky for her, she hadn't had to manage the extra trauma of migration to and fro, as Kalliope had been obliged to.

Kalliope had had other demons to deal with — and practical concerns too — that meant she would never allow herself to become nostalgic or sentimental about old times. If there were some good memories of her earlier life or lives, the past was generally something to be kept in check.

Much as Vic and Kalliope might have wanted to talk on this trip, the jarring and bumping of the car along the very basic road back made it hard to get more than a word or two out coherently. But Vic was determined and so tried once more. When did Kalliope return to Greece? 1968. Did she have any other children? No. Vic considered asking whether there was a husband on the scene, but couldn't bring himself to do so. And to the question as to what she had done since returning, the answer ran to a few words. She had sold some family plots, a dozen hectares of largely useless land, and eventually got into the real estate business. At this, Vic was impressed and exclaimed, 'Oh, good on you!' But even had Kalliope wanted to say more, the jolting meant she was only able to add that Elefteria was the boss in their little business these days.

They made it back to L'Avenir safely enough. There Frosso set the pair up at a table in the corner of the dining room, made some camomile tea for them, and with Elefteria withdrew to the kitchen to drink coffee. Sitting with Kalliope like this, Vic had a chance to look at her more directly, and to recall. But how to remember what there was to remember? He thought she looked uncomfortable, uncertain as to what to say. Thinking some babbling on his part might have a positive effect, he started up.

'It's so wonderful to see you again, Kalliope. And good old *Kriti*, eh? Fancy me being back here like this! What are the chances against that?'

'Ah, good old *Kriti*, you say Vic,' she responded, avoiding the subject of herself. 'Changed a lot from what we remember …'

'And so have you, and me. To think you went to Australia. And you speak English.'

'Went to Australia and speak English, yes, that's good. But Australia …' She looked at him for a moment before continuing, wondering just what sort of a person he had become. 'Australia was no good for me.'

Vic was not taken aback to hear the news. He met her gaze and said with some firmness, 'Funny that, Kalliope. Funny you should say that. I don't reckon Australia was any good for me either.'

Now Kalliope became more curious; these were remarks she had not expected. She looked at him more closely. 'You say that, too? Tell me why you say that?'

'Oh, you don't want to hear me complaining, love. This day's too special. Anyway, you lived there yourself; would have been tough as an immigrant. I'd rather hear what you had to say about the place.'

'Me say? I don't want to say anything!' Kalliope replied with a small laugh.

The laugh she intended for cover and deflection. She did not want to go over all that here, and was relieved that he had not so far asked her personal questions. Then she would have to say that she had left behind a broken marriage and a deeply offended husband. And that a difficult divorce had followed, one that took years to sort out because she had left without beginning any formal proceedings, and Andreas was not disposed to make it easy for her. But nor had he been disposed to try and get her and his daughter to stay either.

So troubled and confused had Kalliope been by his behaviour in later years that she eventually gave up trying to fathom him. Something had changed him, or he had changed, and she had found he was a kind of man she had not been expecting. She had only had sporadic news of him since, and nothing that might have encouraged her to try for some amicable, after-the-storm contact. He had gone in search of his long-lost love in the country, but that never turned into anything serious and he had become some kind of playboy gambler, a frequenter of card clubs, with a string of girlfriends and failed business ventures to his name.

Kalliope did not hate Andreas and she had insisted to Elefteria that he was not a bad man. She knew that whatever had happened to him, he was not the type to come after them with a knife or an axe — something known to happen among their people in Australia as well as here. If anything she had felt sorry for him. He, too, had been hurt in childhood and perhaps he was just one of the unlucky ones who could not heal properly, one of the many men who kept patching themselves up but whose bandages would never stay in place.

If Vic ever wanted to know any of these things, there would be time later, possibly. She was pleased when he broke the awkwardness of the moment with, 'That's all right. I know what *I'd* say.'

30

Found

After the first encounter between her mother and Vic, Elefteria had told Frosso it would not be sensible for any contact to take place for a day or two. She had noticed, she said, that her mother was in a strange mood and not a little downcast. She herself would not be coming down to Sfakia from Rethymnon for a couple of days, so there was the issue of transport, as Kalliope did not drive. By the time of her next trip, everyone would have calmed down somewhat and Kalliope would be better able to make a decision. She didn't want her mother overstressed, said Elefteria, at this time of her life. Vic, not content to let things be, kept pestering Frosso for a phone number, having stupidly forgotten to get one at their reunion. Frosso was able to find sufficient excuses and delays.

Occasionally frustrated at not being able to get through, Vic luckily had other things to occupy him. He spent the next days further investigating the local building situation and trying to establish how much permissions, materials and labour cost, and who was responsible for what. It wasn't easy. On the morning of the third day after seeing Kalliope, Vic left his room to speak to Frosso: it had occurred to him that she must know a few tradespeople herself. He found her in the foyer. He also found there, sitting in one of the two cane chairs and with a cup of tea at hand, his own daughter, Jennifer.

She jumped up at the sight of her father and strode towards him in outrage and concern.

'Jenny! What are you doing here?'

'I could ask you the same thing, Dad! Besides, I told you I was coming, didn't I?' she said loudly, her voice filled with scolding and relief. It was the voice of a parent glad to see that her errant six-year-old had made it home from the creek, late for dinner and having worried everyone, but safely just the same.

After repeatedly assuring her that he was all right and scolding Jenny in turn for her needless concern, Vic was marshalled along with Jenny into the dining room by Frosso. She had been there to receive the worried Jenny, had pacified her and told her what the old boy had been up to, and that he was fine. She had added only that ageing, headstrong fathers were always a worry, and it was just as well for them that there were thoughtful daughters in the world.

Vic hugged Jenny before she could launch another barrage at him. It had the effect he sought; she began to calm down as he held her. He sat her down and began to give as breezy an account as he could of all that had happened since his arrival, leaving out that he had had some sort of mental episode and was now on medication. Jenny was not going to let this ride.

'What about what the lady here tells me, Dad? That you had a turn? You haven't mentioned that.'

'No, I haven't because I feel fine. And I don't think it was anything much, really I don't. Jenny, I reckon I'm getting better every day I spend here, you know that?'

Jenny did not answer but waited to see if he had anything more to say. She had many times observed to her mother that you always had to concentrate to get to the bottom of things with him, inclined as he was to ignore or pass over what was important.

Uncomfortable under her scrutiny, Vic started up again. Crete was terrific, much better than he might have imagined. Could she get over his thoughtlessness this once, and take their mutual presence as an opportunity? Could she see her way clear, now that they were both here and she could see he didn't need rescuing, to maybe making a holiday of it together? Shout's on him and no mention of any separate and stupid additional plans on his part?

Jenny thought for a while and decided she could agree to this. He could part with some of his money as punishment. A pleasant break would go a little way to easing the offence she felt at what he had put her through. And he had put her through plenty over the years, busting up with her mother, not always being around. Too bad that she loved him. For what it was worth, he had always loved her.

Vic was about to tell her of some of his experiences so far when he was interrupted by a commotion at the front door. He looked up, and there were Kalliope and Elefteria.

Vic jumped up at the sight of them, knocking over an empty teacup and startling Jenny in the process.

'Dad! Take it easy, will you?'

'Sorry, love, sorry. Look, these people, these are people I want you to meet ...'

Vic grabbed his daughter's hand as if she were no more than a small child and practically pulled her over to where Kalliope was standing inside the door.

'Kalliope, Elefteria, so glad to see you. And a nice surprise, here is my own daughter, Jennifer!'

Kalliope and Elefteria looked at each other. This was an unexpected development, if ever there was one.

Kalliope managed to get out a 'hello', and 'pleased to meet you', when Frosso also arrived to join them.

It appeared to Frosso that the amount of confusion and rising emotion in this room was reaching a point that even she, an experienced hostelier, was unable to manage all at once, so she decided it would be best to eliminate, if only for a moment, the source that was probably most manageable, the daughters. In a loud voice she called out, '*Koritsia, ela!*' Girls, come with me, and led them both, startled though compliant, back into her office behind the front desk at the entrance.

She had a further intention: by calling on the special knowledge of each daughter, she might arrive at a plan as to how to manage these septuagenarians beyond today. Especially now that Vic and Kalliope, it seemed to her — again in her capacity as astute observer of the passing trade — had plenty more to say to each other. It was plain what a complication this Australian might prove to be. Regarding Kalliope's welfare, Frosso was not nearly as concerned as Elefteria: she knew and understood her older friend as someone who, after bitter times, had long been in charge of herself, a woman with an unclouded eye on life and men. Well, mostly.

Between this day and when it was agreed Vic might call Kalliope again, there would be time for further outings with Jennifer. Vic arranged for him and his daughter to be driven north up to the places around Maleme airport in Rethymnon. There he had done his last real fighting, back in 1941. Jenny didn't mind, even if it was war stuff. It was enough that the old boy was still capable of organising anything at all. She had come all this way in the serious expectation of finding a disaster.

At Maleme, however, she began to change her mind and worried that he might indeed be succumbing to something, such was the effect of the flooding, almost overpowering memories triggered by the place. Leaving the taxi to wait, they went for a short walk to stand on a rocky knoll overlooking the main battlefield. She stood close by as he raised his arm towards the north.

'The planes were coming from that direction,' he said quietly, allowing the tears to fall freely. 'Sorry, love, sorry,' was all he could say further.

Jennifer put an arm around him and found it hard not to cry herself. She certainly wanted to: for him, for her, for how things had gone down the years between them. But she knew she couldn't, not here like this. At this moment she diverted herself by thinking about how and when she might be able to get him back to Australia in one piece.

When he had composed himself once more, he turned to her and in all sincerity said, 'I want to do something for this mob, love.'

He then proceeded to outline what he had in mind. Jennifer listened, trying not to interrupt, trying not to pass judgment.

On this rocky outcrop in the north of an enchanted island, she knew he had experienced, was still experiencing, something that was worth her respect. Maybe it was no more than a vantage point on both distant and more recent pain or on his own long-gone youth, but whatever had happened or been done to him, however he had connected with the local people, whatever good deeds they had done him, it was clear his spirit had been called upon in this place.

When Vic finished speaking, Jennifer began to consider her own situation. She let out a long sigh at the same time as she had another thought: she needn't have come over here at all, chasing him like this. Not really. What had she been thinking? To chastise and correct him, save him from himself? When had that worked? Somehow all that seemed pointless, sitting with him here. He had his own plans, as usual. How important was it to get the delinquent back home anyway? He seemed very happy here. What about herself, Jenny? What was *her* reality?

Her father had offered her a holiday — she would definitely take him up on that, and not only because it was free. She felt tired. More than once in her adult life she had asked herself whether she had spent too much time worrying about, trying to 'fix' her parents' damaged relationship. She'd had her share of counselling (for all the good that did), she'd listened to the stories each told about the other and which, in their partiality and reasonableness, were more maddening than if they had been just plain murderous towards each other. But she knew how hard her mother had worked to hold the marriage together, the anger she felt as a result, the fear driven by that, all complicated by her father's up-and-down nature.

And she had concluded they were both wrong. And right.

So where had that left her? Cautious. Too sensitive to other people's feelings. Not nearly strong enough an advocate for her own interests. And also someone who, given the right moment, she told herself here, was prepared to chuck it all in.

So what about her own interests? Maybe she did not have enough of them, or strong enough ones at least. If that was so, and she had an idea in her depths that it was, why not make this her time of change also? She smiled. If she did, the old man would be paying for it, and about time, too. She would stay here for a while. She would take a risk and just see what happened. She deserved a break.

After a time, he asked, 'Can you understand that, Jenny? Tell me you do. It'd make me very happy.'

'I do, Dad. But it's hardly very practical or sensible, is it?'

Vic, relieved, gave her his biggest grin in reply. 'Oh, I know that, Jenny! But when has that ever stopped your old man?'

Vic hoped that would raise a smile, but it didn't. His daughter kept staring out over the smoky greys and greens of the Cretan countryside. She was reminded of something Australian.

31
Restoration

Vic was delighted when he could get through to Kalliope via phone, and even happier when she said she would be pleased to meet again. This time he went to visit her, at her insistence, at their Sfakia residence, a small house a couple of streets back from the main square. They had done all right, Kalliope and her daughter — this was apparently their *other* quarters, a bolthole and office when they weren't in Rethymnon, where they had their main office and a larger house.

He was shown in by Elefteria who, though clearly trying to be friendly, was also obviously a little wary. That he could understand. He wouldn't automatically and wholeheartedly trust some bloke who had suddenly blown into someone's life from across the world either. Her courtesy at the door nevertheless made him feel a little more at ease.

Elefteria asked him to wait in the front room while she fetched her mother. It was a pleasing room too, nicely furnished with folk-style rugs and chairs, but with a neat little desk and phone arrangement in one corner, needed, he assumed, for their business arrangements. He moved in to take a closer look. Above the desk on the wall was a series of photos of houses and blocks of flats, very like those in estate agents' windows.

He heard someone come in behind him.

'Stay there, stay there,' Kalliope said as she went across to join him. 'You like?'

'What are they?'

'Oh, some places that we sold.'

'That's right, you mentioned the property business.'

'My daughter does the real estate, yes. And I help her little bit.'

'I'm impressed, Kalliope.'

'Before many years in Rethymnon, I used to do much more. But Vic, too old now, as you can see! For me Sfakia is, how you say, retirement village!'

'Oh, not too old, girl. Never say that.'

He looked again at the photos. 'Well, how about that. I knew I should have done something about you.'

His last remark sounded vaguely threatening to Kalliope, a little intrusive at least.

'What do you mean?'

Vic heard the suspicion in her voice. 'Oh nothing, Kalliope. Joking … Just that here I am, a builder, and now I find you've been buying and selling houses. We could have teamed up!'

Kalliope had to work to remember the meaning of 'team' and when she did, said, 'Ah!' for the sake of friendliness. 'But not always in the real estate, you know Vic … Only twelve, fifteen years I did that, and because Elefteria, she start in this business after university and I want to help her. Before, not such good days.'

Over some sweet, milky tea, which Vic found a blessed relief after so much of the supposedly helpful camomile Frosso had made him drink of late, he tried to describe to Kalliope in more detail the thoughts that had been taking shape in his head since his return to Greece, to Crete. She listened politely but not with a great deal of enthusiasm, he would have said, as he talked some more about the plan he had announced in the abbot's office.

Rather than tackling Vic head on, by late morning Kalliope had done a very good job of undermining any rosy view he might have had about the commitment and efficiency of Greek builders. They were all villains, or most of the ones she had dealt with were, and she was amazed by the talk currently going round that in a few years' time such people were to be called upon to organise and construct venues for the anticipated Olympic Games. 'Such men, they don't know how to use, how you say it, even the hammer. Talk plenty, but make trouble and never finish until too late … What I have seen, anyway.'

Kalliope tried to judge Vic's thoughts from the expression on his face. He seemed like a boy to her, lacking the heaviness, the sour cast to the mouth, that local men of his generation had. Old as he was, he was not unpleasant to look at. And, despite what Frosso had said about some troubles, he seemed to have some kind of positive energy about him.

'Well,' she started again, 'not all bad maybe … If all bad, we cannot make such places as you see …' She pointed to the photos across from where they were seated.

'Glad to hear it. And you know, the chaps I came across, they're not your typical lousy carpenters, I'm sure of that. They might be right for the job, I reckon. One actually grew up in Canada. His father was from hereabouts in the old days. Apparently they came back.'

Kalliope listened and processed what he said, although she did not receive it as reassuring.

'Vic, some of the ones who come back from America, Canada, come to make trouble. They want to fix everything here, same like back in Canada or whichever place. Believe me, this doesn't work.'

Asking him to repeat Pavlos and Mark's surname, Kalliope could not make any connection. This was odd, as Sfakia was a small town and she knew anyone and everyone involved in the game, such as it was here.

'You sure they are professional builders?' she asked at last. 'Maybe they fix up only the old family place? Sometimes same house in the family many years and they want to, how you say?'

Vic thought he might know the word she was looking for. 'You mean restore?'

'Yes. Do it by themself. Restore.'

Vic felt a bit deflated, foolish. It was not something he had thought to ask about the place they were working on. Maybe they weren't pros at all, just backyarders working on their own place.

'And the abbot, Gerasimos. Vic — you think he can make decision? My God, many more black hats bigger than him, believe me!'

Vic became slightly anxious the more animated Kalliope had got on this subject. He sensed that he had said enough and that the right thing was to not push on at this moment. 'OK, OK, you're the boss, Kalliope. You know more about what goes on here than I do. Just talk at present, but ... maybe you can help me check those boys out at least?'

She smiled at him. He was persistent, if nothing else. But she didn't mind that.

When Vic succeeded in bringing Mark and his father to Kalliope's place at her insistence, she was more reassured. They had demolished an old place that had been in their family for generations but had been allowed to run down while everyone migrated overseas to seek their fortunes and were replacing it with an apartment block. The father, Kalliope thought, did have dangerous leanings — a cheapskate and corner-cutter from the way he talked. But she was taken with the sunny, cheery, open-faced son, bad hair and all. He insisted that he was a trained builder — and maybe he was — and that he was ready for any new project these good people might come up with, including the restoration of a Greek Orthodox monastery chapel, should they so wish.

Even Elefteria, who had had her share of accidents with young Greek males over the years, thought he was all right. More, even. She didn't let on that he'd struck a pleasant note, maybe because they shared a common deracination as children born of immigrants in Anglo countries.

After Vic and the Petroyanakis men had left, and she and Elefteria had cleared up, Kalliope took herself off to her corner desk in the front room. There she sat trying to get some sort of perspective on these various males and the activity they were conjuring up for her. His impractical scheme aside, the reappearance of Vic Stockton, as if someone resurrected, was not easy to process. She tried to dig down through the strata, the layers of her history, to see where he figured, what he really meant.

Kalliope could not easily think of him as what he was, an Australian. To think of him as that was to bring to mind those she had encountered in a life she no longer wished to waste any scrap of emotion on. Old men coming into a shop to buy 'ciggies'. Cheeky young boys taking lollies in front of her face, calling her names, running away without paying. The men she would see through the open doors of the Royal on any weekday as she walked back to the shop from school with her young daughter. Drunk at three o'clock in the afternoon.

She preferred to recall the strapping, sinewy and strong young men of war. Those who, like Vic, had come halfway across the world and so far from their homes, leaving their mothers, their daughters, their sisters and fathers and brothers, with a purpose beyond themselves. Men who would attempt something, or try to do some good. She remembered those men, could see them as clearly as she could see the phone in front of her or the wall beyond. She remembered that life. She remembered him. But what was there now? She leaned forward and put her elbows on the desk, cradled her face in the palms of her hands. She felt the loose skin, so tired and thin, around her eyes, and began to slowly run her fingers in an arc above her cheeks. If only that was enough to make the wrinkles disappear! And the life lived … But she stopped herself. She didn't in truth want to do that.

Returning to Crete had brought pain at first. To go to Arkadi and learn that her mother had died and been buried only a few months before. To go and seek out her grave, and find flowers freshly laid by people she did not know, but who must have cared for her at least a little. Then to realise there were so few who remembered her, Kalliope, or could recognise her. The older generation had been dying out, the younger leaving for the mainland and work, or migration.

As for returning to live in Arkadi, that had never been a realistic possibility: she had to work to support herself and her daughter, and there was no work there. But moving to Sfakia had been sensible, had brought improved prospects. She had found some casual work in a travel agency, where her English — limited as she knew it to be — was a great advantage. She soon understood she was among her own again, even if finding a place in people's hearts would take much longer.

On the occasions she visited her old village, she was required to endure her share of sniffing and sniping — 'Look, the rich auntie from Australia is back!' But then with Elefteria gaining her degree in commerce and going into property, a further move to Rethymnon and a business to involve herself in, Crete had become home a second time. Still, to imagine being a young woman again. What was the harm? Question was whether it was at all possible.

She could definitely still see the dry bread of those days, wrapped in muslin, taken at dawn to a young man, a soldier hidden in the hills. But could it really be the same man? *Was it him?* Memory played tricks and perhaps it wasn't so, wasn't her but someone else who had befriended this old dog. Yet she knew, certainly, it was him. And she knew it was her in the very same picture. They had lived through a time when something mattered, *sto onoma tou theou*, in the name of God, truly mattered.

Kalliope looked up at the wall, at the record of the various projects she had assisted her daughter with over the years, and an interesting and distinct idea came to her. Even if the very next thought was that it was probably beyond them all at this time. But, why not? She would entertain it nevertheless. And maybe share it too.

He comes across with big ideas of his own, does he? Her lonely soldier, whose hair was no longer the red it had been, but whose eyes were as blue as she remembered. A young man in fear then and trying to escape, whom, had she known at the time what she'd learned since of life, she would surely have taken in her arms and held and squeezed as only a young woman could. I'll give him big ideas, the silly old *vlaka* ...

*   *   *

Invigorated by his reunion with Kalliope, Vic wanted nothing so much as to find things to please her with. He insisted to Frosso, for instance, that as he had come to truly love the local Cretan cuisine since being back, why didn't they do a little indulging? Frosso mentioned this to Kalliope when she called to see how the *Afstralezos* and his daughter were doing. And, as Elefteria could see no problem, the idea arose that they might make a day of sampling the native produce, something in which the Sfakiotes still took great pride. They would do the rounds and finish up somewhere pleasant for a picnic lunch.

The coming Saturday afternoon was chosen as the time when everyone would be free and available, and Saturdays were always good for produce beyond what was delivered to the town market. With Elefteria driving, mother and daughter picked up Vic and Jennifer from Frosso's and headed for some of the small outlying villages. It was in those places where everything good was made or grown anyway, or so Kalliope assured her guests. At Limnes they stopped at one of the last real functioning village ovens in the whole district, a wood-fired dome-like structure in the charge of a grizzled and grumpy old veteran — a true *moustakalis*, complete with hanging white moustache and a three-day growth. Looks aside, he baked some of the most beautiful bread Vic or Jenny had ever eaten. The loaves they bought were still warm and one was torn apart there and then by Kalliope who shared out the large hunks among them.

'*Dokimase!*' Taste! she implored.

It was hard-crusted and made from some mix of tough native grains, and Vic thought it an absolute delight. The sort of bread you could actually taste while you were chewing. Then it was off to a local cheese man who sold them some of his best as well as the obligatory fetta.

'This we keep for after,' Kalliope insisted as they got in the car to return briefly to Sfakia for some salad makings they had forgotten to pick up earlier, as well as some of the famed local sausage. From there, the plan was to head across to the monastery. There were trees for shelter and, being close to the sea, a view was on hand just right for an afternoon picnic.

Once they arrived, and though no longer as nimble as she would have liked, Kalliope insisted she was able to trek away from the car to one of the prettier spots overlooking the site, provided Vic and his daughter were prepared to do the same. In the circumstances, nothing could have prevented Vic from playing the ageing gallant. He made a point of giving Kalliope his hand and kicking stones out of the way as they made their way to the cover of some pines. The younger women looked at each other, and with grins and much eye-rolling took on the more difficult challenge of getting blankets, bottles, baskets and folding chairs and table from Elefteria's car to the selected spot some fifty metres away.

The day surely belonged to picnicking: sunny and warmish but with a breeze lifting up off the water adding to the cooling effect of the shade. Kalliope insisted on keeping her jacket on, while Vic made a show of taking his off and rolling up his sleeves, he-man like. Once Elefteria had organised and spread their little folding table with food, Kalliope sprang up to grab some of the cheese on a plate. She moved her chair across to sit with Vic, who had moved his into something of a commanding position, a little to one side of the others and facing directly down at the monastery.

'Vic, you try, OK?'

'Sure.'

He took a piece of this distinctive pale, mellow cheese and began to eat.

'You know what it is?'

Vic didn't know what answer there was other than 'cheese' and, after a couple of mouthfuls said, 'Tasty …'

'Ah, you don't know anything, my friend!' Kalliope smiled at him. 'Do you know the taste?'

Vic thought for a moment and said, 'Yes, now that you mention it. It's familiar.'

'That cheese I bring to you in the war. When you were up there.' She pointed towards the rise above them where, out of sight, traces of the old hut remained.

'This?' His eyes widened. 'The same cheese?'

'Oh, yes. *Graviera*. From Crete only. And from fresh milk, sheep and goats, but free ones … how you say?'

'Free-ranging?'

'Yes, and same family been making it for hundred years, more … only in the months when the grasses and plants are green, to give sweet flavour.'

'How about that.' He leaned towards her. 'If this was the stuff you brought me … you better give me some more, dear, just like the old days,' he said, smiling at her cheekily.

She held the plate closer for him to take another piece.

He looked at her and saw her eyes go cloudy. Realising he was not all that composed himself, he said, 'Steady on, Kalliope, or we'll both fall in a heap here.'

Kalliope wasn't quite sure of his meaning, but sensed she was probably better served concentrating on the here and now rather than talking about the past.

After a sip of the best of Cretan wine, the Mavrodaphne, Vic announced in a loud whisper, 'Jesus, woman, you might have saved me in another place too, if I'd known you were there.'

'What you say, Vic?'

'Oh, nothing. Just what a beautiful view, eh?'

'*Ne*, yes, very beautiful. And now something more I have to tell you.'

'What's that?'

'Well, I talk to Elefteria and some other people, and we have an idea. Do you want to hear it?'

Calling her daughter and Jennifer to join them, Kalliope and Elefteria explained. Elefteria began with the axiomatic: the religious establishment and its various branches in this country were always on the lookout for money, or for means of getting their hands on more of it. This was a rule of life, Greek life anyway. They had assets in the form of real estate, but the drachmas were not so easily come by, or not now that the people were no longer so many sheep adding up to so many flocks. Now there was far more scepticism and cynicism, and the coffers were not nearly as full as once upon a time.

But the idea lay in property. Why not offer to develop the second, older and disused Kastelli monastery quarters as a tourist facility, a low-key, tasteful, resort complex? This could probably be done jointly, in some form of partnership, with the monastery maintaining control through long leasehold and a share of profits or other arrangement. Through her banking associates, Elefteria was very likely to be able to come up with the development capital, if there was any interest or willingness on the part of the religious bosses. They could set up a company together for the purpose.

Vic was astounded at the audacity of the scheme. More than once he asked, 'Yes, but would they go for something like that?' only to be met with sardonic smiles and lovely Greek waves of the hand, the sort suggesting, 'Is the grass not green?' or 'Does not the sun rise in the east?'

'And that abbot, he likes to have the modern ideas,' Kalliope said towards the end. 'This we know about him — he is a terrorist …'

'Terrorist?' Vic was startled. Then he realised what she was driving at. 'Um … I think you mean rebel.'

'Sorry!' Kalliope smiled at him. ' Wrong word I say.'

'If you want to do something, Vic,' Elefteria said, 'this way you really do something, yes?'

'But what about the chapel?' he asked lamely.

'No problem. If we do development, we say to them we fix everything else, too,' said Kalliope. 'We can make a few obligations for them, under the contract, if you like …'

'You bet I like!' were Vic's final words before reaching for the Mavrodaphne and pouring everyone a further drink.

32

Divine Buildings

Vic was told to expect the usual delays, obfuscations, backing and filling from the monastery people here on Crete, and from their higher-ups, who were apparently to be found somewhere in the north of the mainland, although no one seemed to know exactly where. Weeks would go by, months, possibly even years; realistically, Elefteria suggested it would make sense for him to go back to Australia to wait. If there was to be approval the wheels would grind slowly; if the whole thing was to be rejected it could take just as long.

In his euphoria, Vic made no sober estimate as to the time this might take. But he had at least the comfort of an open air-ticket. The extent of his thinking was that he could renew his visa, then draw on his annuity to fund a stay indefinitely, providing he found cheap food and accommodation, which wasn't hard. He had been in Greece going on two months and with no great dent in his pocket. Paying for Jenny would mean a much bigger hole, although he was happy to do that, too, for a while. He wasn't sure what her plans were ultimately, or when she intended to go home, but he was increasingly getting the sense she was content to stay where she was.

Prepared for a long delay, Vic was therefore staggered when the business apparently came to resolution the following Thursday.

That same day Elefteria came into Frosso's pensione to give Vic the news. She found him sitting in the front room with Jenny, sipping a lukewarm tea and reading the English *Athens News*. Elefteria said she had got a call from the abbot saying that, in principle, they were interested and asking for a meeting in two days' time. Vic could barely contain his excitement; Jennifer, though not unmoved, couldn't help thinking of the issues that would need to be faced if this proceeded.

At the Saturday meeting, held in Abbot Gerasimos' own office and in the company of some very sober and besuited Athenian-looking business types, as well as a bishop from Rethymnon, Vic learned that the abbot believed the plan represented an excellent and distinct opportunity: theirs was not a closed order, but meant to be open to the world; the Church needed to welcome the new, reach out beyond the walls. The hierarchy, too, considered this a possibility, if the economies could be made to work, and provided the Kastelli monastery remained the 'principal partner' in the scheme, with rights to hire and fire ('to bind and to loose' were the actual words chosen, in deference to, or borrowed from, the canonical language) any operator chosen to manage the finished resort, on mutual terms and on a ten-year initial agreement. The main points were to be set out in a memorandum of understanding, committing all parties and subject to signature of the final contracts. The usual cooling periods, due diligence, escrow and other requirements would be as per Greek commercial law.

Elefteria translated some of the finer points, but by and large the negotiation — which is what Vic considered it to be — was conducted in English. The business fellows knew the language, and Vic guessed correctly that they had been brought in specifically to deal with 'the Australian connection' as it had already seemingly been designated.

Vic assessed all this as practically astounding, found himself nearly always nodding in agreement at these propositions put to him via Elefteria. Could Vic put up some capital? Yes, he could. Not much, but something. Was he prepared to take a proportionate interest? Yes, he was, in conjunction with his daughter. Jenny was as amazed as he was, and almost as excited at this wondrous idea that they might even be able to make real on the sunny coast of Crete.

Jenny discovered that she was as startled by her own audacity as by her father's, and no less impressed at the ingenuity of her father's friends. She had tried to check and challenge her growing enthusiasm over the past few days, but to no avail. She was ready to take the step. It was not as if she had a partner to return to, or even a pet, for that matter. Against her boring life back home, this was like a fairy tale that was coming true. It was suddenly no leap at all to see herself as a resort operator in southern Crete, actually living a life that she might have only ever imagined. She sat through the meeting wanting, like her father, to say yes to everything: yes to her father, yes to Crete, yes to new beginnings, and the rest could go to blazes. She, too, resolved that the details were for later. She could always sell her flat if she had to.

The meeting ended with agreement that Vic and Jennifer Stockton could stay on, accommodation to be provided by Kalliope and Elefteria, for the next few months until the project details were finally bedded down and, hopefully, the building work could begin. It was agreed that a complicated design process or anything in the way of avant-garde architecture would not be countenanced.

Admittedly the buildings in the old, lower monastery were dilapidated and some even roofless, but they had stood for hundreds of years. Renovation and refurbishment were required and little else. They had an appeal all of their own, did they not, the abbot asked at one stage. 'We believe that if we fix them and open them up to the public, the public will come,' he said. 'Would they not want to come, experience something basic, but attractive? These were once — divine, is that the word? — buildings,' he said, looking towards Vic, perhaps for another adjective.

Vic was happy with the word. 'Divine buildings all right, chief!' he affirmed. 'Too right they are. And they should be kept that way, I agree. Only done up a bit.'

'People today of course, the tourists, will ask for the modern kitchen, the modern bathroom, yes?' the abbot asked rhetorically. He knew very well from his travels and time spent in the United States in earlier days that they most certainly would.

'Don't see how we can get away from that, unfortunately,' Vic replied.

'Hot water and such …' Gerasimos added.

''Fraid so,' said Vic.

'And so these things must be given,' Gerasimos said with an air of finality at one point, and with a stamp of his hand on the desk in front of him.

This gesture seemed to be for the benefit of the bishop, at whom the abbot cast a wary eye from time to time. Perhaps hot water and soft beds were the mark of Satan for him. He seemed to be the only person in the room who wasn't utterly committed to this. Then again, Vic thought, apart from this Gerasimos when did you ever see a happy clergyman?

The meeting had run, with a couple of breaks, for almost three hours. Vic marvelled at Kalliope's capacity to keep up, and that of her daughter too, who seemed to be very much driving the whole thing. He marvelled also at his own offspring, to whom he turned slightly and surreptitiously from time to time in admiration after she had given her blessing. How accommodating she was. What a good kid she was to him — had always been. He had not been mistaken when he detected early on, even before she said anything, that she was largely sympathetic to this. She didn't have to be. She had another life elsewhere, and if she wanted to she could go back to it. He was the one with nothing to draw him back to Australia, except for her. But who wouldn't fall under the spell of people such as these? They were some kind of magicians, no doubt about it. At times mad, at times maddening, but by Christ they could get you in. It was the sheer life in them, he had surmised on other occasions, that drew you to them. And they were just as subject to their passions as he was. On this island, that somehow never felt wrong.

In an afternoon of many achievements, one of the great wins as far as Vic was concerned was the decision to include a restoration of the chapel of Aghios Nikolaos in the main monastery. Having earlier raised it with Elefteria and gained her approval to bring it up here, he had suggested the possibility when some preliminary ideas were put forward regarding builders and contractors for the main work. Again there proved to be no issue. It was agreed that the chapel was long overdue for restoration and contact would be made with the various archaeological and heritage authorities.

But here, in the context of the chapel work, was the only less than smooth element in the proceedings. Vic suggested to Elefteria that his new friends might be candidates for some aspect of the work, accepting that they were talking about a more delicate project than those chaps had ever likely handled. He had put this cautiously to her in an aside, to be met with the only perturbation he had seen so far. She asked for time out and took him to one side. Outside the abbot's office, she gave Vic some home truths: good fellows they might be, but his builder friends were small fry; he also needed to be conscious of the fact, if he wasn't already, that the two big boys in the office beyond were here not for honourable purposes but for what it was worth to them. They would want to minimise risk and would therefore almost certainly want to be in charge of the building works, as appointees of the monastery, and with a big fat percentage as well as fees for their own company. Vic said he would, of course, not compromise any deal. Property and construction had been his life, too. He knew what was involved in a venture like this and understood perfectly what she was saying. But going back inside, he was also able to think of something else those two, or even the young fellow alone, might do for him.

And thus throughout the day the plan acquired substance, found wheels, began to move forward. The thing was as good as real already, Vic was happy to believe. As their little group trooped out to Elefteria's car and prepared to return to the town late in the afternoon, he felt something had to be said. 'Well, girls, fair to say we're going home tired but happy?'

Jennifer managed a wan smile, only too aware that there were a great many unknowns ahead. 'We're tired, Dad, no risk — we'll see about happy.'

Rather than moving in with Kalliope, with all the burdens that would entail, a further arrangement was made to allow the Stocktons to stay on at Frosso's for at least another four weeks. It was Elefteria's idea and could easily be budgeted for, she said, out of an anticipated preliminary development fund she expected to be able to put in place through her banking contacts in the next few days.

No longer in the position of having to rescue an errant, wayward father, Jennifer was encouraged instead by all to stay on as an honoured guest, holidaymaker and potential future business partner. The propositions sat ever more comfortably with her. She liked the idea of this development project they were working on, she enjoyed the company of the Greek women, and she was definitely in no hurry to return to her own insurance company job in Sydney. And when they did return to Australia with the enterprise up and running, she felt confident it could be managed, and well managed, from what she had seen, by these two excellent Cretan women.

Soon, Jennifer was having lunch dates with Elefteria and going on shopping expeditions to Rethymnon and Hania, sometimes to Irakleion too. In her company, she also uncovered a latent interest in archaeology, kindled by a visit to the spectacular palace at Knossos. Without a doubt this Crete was the most beautiful place Jennifer had ever seen.

As was the way with these things, the initial two weeks turned into four, but then contracts were supposedly being drawn up and an anticipated start of works date was put in place for the tourist complex. This was astonishing to Vic and Jenny, less so to Elefteria and hardly at all to Kalliope.

'Who can tell what is going to happen in *Kriti*, Vic? Something can take two weeks, or two years, or maybe never happen ever. And nobody knows which one will be which one. You see, nothing they say about us is true, and everything they say about us is true!'

'Well …' he said uncomfortably as they waited outside the lawyers' offices in Rethymnon, where they had been summoned to deal with the latest developments, 'you keep hearing bad stories about Greeks and organisation … like they don't always go together.'

In mock dismay, Elefteria showed Vic the palm of her hand. 'Stop, please, or you will upset me,' she said with some wryness. 'This country supposed to be getting ready for the Olympic Games, in 2000 or 2004. And we will get ready, you see. And Crete will have many stadiums and sports here. If we can't fix up a few old buildings and paint some walls, *o Theos na mas prosexi,* may God protect us!'

Vic put his hands up, as if in surrender. 'Look, I'm not going to argue. You've won me!'

An hour later, however, Vic and Kalliope and Elefteria exited the lawyers' office with no news on contracts — but a comprehensive defeat. Again, Kalliope was the least surprised of all.

'I can't believe we've just been rolled,' said Vic. 'I thought they genuinely wanted to go ahead with this, I really did.'

'Believe, Vic. Believe. This is the way here. Sometimes yes, sometimes no, and nobody know for sure before the last minute.'

'But …'

'Forget it. We can still do the other thing, and it is a good thing, like we say. Elefteria, take us home, please.'

Kalliope watched Vic stride ahead of them towards the car, looking perturbed. She got in beside him in the back seat, looked out the window to discourage him from too much talk about what had happened; time enough for that later. For a short while she had thought they might make something unusual and good together in this development idea. But if that had turned out to be false hope she did not feel defeated, and would encourage him not to be either. Perhaps he was prone to depression or 'nerves', as Frosso and the doctors had asserted. But what she had seen of him suggested he was also quite resilient, a quality she had learned to appreciate above all others.

She was most heartened, then, to hear Vic start to whistle after a few minutes' driving. Not only that, but he was smiling as well, she saw as he turned to her briefly.

'I'm taking a leaf out of your book,' he said.

'Leaf?' she said, uncomprehending.

'Oh nothing,' he said, and squeezed her hand briefly. 'Just a saying …'

Kalliope was hardly concerned that the thing had gone off the rails, although she knew that Elefteria was not going to be quite so sanguine later. Never mind, she was still young and, though experienced in this game, had plenty to learn yet about life. But the fact that Vic had seemingly taken this rejection so well made her feel even warmer towards him. It struck her that she had not known such men as he in Australia, not as far as she could recall. How could she have, anyway? She had been locked away so completely in the tomb of that shop and that life that she might as well have lived among Martians.

She had thought of this man, it was true, in the years after he had left and in the early years in Australia, but not seriously, not when she had already made her commitment — or thought she had — to another man. And she hadn't even known whether he was alive, after all that horror in 1941, let alone whether he represented any sort of real-life possibility for her at the time. But how *could* he have done in those days? She was a Greek woman, he was an Australian man. There had been some marriages on Crete after the war, between a few of those soldiers who had chosen to return and a few of the braver young women. It was a shame he had not been one of the early ones; pity, perhaps, she had left when she did.

But here and now it was important not to give up, so she would tell her daughter and Vic at home in a little while. Kalliope was not a person easily overcome, and a further strategy was beginning to take shape. What had happened, though unfortunate, might well have opened another door. They were in a perfect position to squeeze whatever guilt there was left in the lemon of the church hierarchy — and she knew they were ultimately behind today's debacle — so as to get out of them one positive result at least: the restoration of the chapel.

Even though the Church had been involved in the negotiations, she surmised that they were probably being led by their financial consultants. And she had a sense that the money men dragged in to advise them were playing a double game. She had an idea they would be on a consultancy fee linked to the proposed sale price, whether the development went ahead or not. They might have concluded the interest rates were too high and the margin too narrow for their lenders in the kind of development being contemplated, let alone all the other issues, and had therefore come up with sufficient negatives near the end.

She was also interested to hear how the religious would explain pulling out like this. The timid, useless Church bigwigs would have needed only the slightest reason to renege, so conscious were they of preserving what was left of their battered reputation these days — but the strain on their own finances, if things went awry with such a project, must have been somewhere in their thinking too.

If that was one side, there was another. A chapel as old and as lovely as that — by what right should it be allowed to rot to nothing? It offended her Cretan spirit to think that someone from across the world should be able to take more interest and delight in it than her own people. She felt a strong urge, call it patriotic, to save some of her own foolish compatriots from themselves, if it was at all possible. Whatever the little church of Aghios Nikolaos should look like after restoration, and disregarding that it was enclosed by monastery walls, it would also belong to those who dared to remake it.

Kalliope watched the countryside stream past as they drove back to Sfakia. Though late this year, Spring had arrived, pushing through blossoms and new greenery everywhere. They were passing an almond orchard, the blanket of snowy pink flowers so thick it was hard to see a trunk or branch.

They owed it to Vic to make that dream come true if possible; or she felt she owed it to him in the circumstances. If approvals were forthcoming, her daughter's company would pay for the work. If Vic wanted to contribute, well and good.

In the days that followed, Kalliope went on to make further representations and another quiet proposal of her own, after which the restoration of the chapel somehow and mysteriously 'moved up the list'. Later again, and as no surprise to her, the go-ahead came through.

33

Sacred and Profane

The monastery of Kastelli had been decked out for the occasion. Coming down by car in the company of Elefteria and Kalliope and his daughter, Vic was pleased to see that the gravel drive had been raked, that the bushes and trees that lined the way had been trimmed or pruned, and coloured pennants had been strung across the tops of the entrance gates. They may not now be in the business of restoring disused monastery buildings and revitalising tourism in southern Crete, but this would do just fine, Vic was happy to conclude.

Abbot Gerasimos had issued a directive that all the monks' cells were to be 'spring-cleaned' in readiness for receiving any of the visitors on the day who might want to take a look. As he had pointed out on previous occasions to some of the recalcitrants who had grumbled at the prospect of having to deal with strangers, it was their duty to be welcoming. The abbot himself had taken the event seriously enough to make sure his best formal outfit was cleaned and ready. This was important. Visitors and dignitaries would come from all over the place to be here today.

Abbot Gerasimos was far from pleased at the way some things had turned out. On the tourism plan, they had been thwarted by a powerful combine: a certain archbishop, or so he'd heard, had alerted another higher up the chain, and once that venerable learned what some bunch of renegades were doing down in Crete, it was all over. The money men had been sent packing and chastisements issued to the various religious involved for 'personal pride and for exposing the mother church to mockery'.

Gerasimos knew better than anyone what the venture might have represented, or at least what he wanted it to represent. A new beginning, an approach that would connect the secular and the spiritual, where people from both sides might mingle and learn from each other — only the best he hoped, though there were risks involved in allowing some of the worldly to occupy the same grounds as his monks. He had tried to explain that the old and the new were to be quartered in two separate compounds, that there would be, as well, a good few hundred metres between them. But in the end the traditionalists were not prepared to buy such a vision.

Still, there was today's occasion to come, marking a separate yet great achievement. There were many thanks to be offered for what *had* found approval. It was no second prize and no small thing, after all, to be able to rebuild a thousand-year-old chapel, given the straitened circumstances of the modern church.

The date settled on for the ceremony, this turning of the first sod, was 18 May, two days before the anniversary of the fateful beginning of the Battle of Crete. In the choice of this day was also the abbot's desire to do something for the old *Afstralezos*, and any other allies who might be around for what had become an annual celebration. The man Stockton had wandered onto this patch all those months ago and somehow, he wasn't entirely sure how, had done more than his share to push at least one brave notion towards reality. He had been here and played his part, then and now; an involvement that he, a worker for God, would be remiss not to honour.

And so they were all here. Two local MPs, an archbishop, the head of the Rethymnon Prefecture Chamber of Commerce, and a woman introduced to him as the big boss of the Cretan tourist bureau (an odd-looking bird, in a tight black skirt and a pair of stiletto heels, and wearing a wig of long straight black hair, or so Vic thought when he was introduced to her). These aside, Vic was very pleased to see that Colonel Patrikareas from the veterans' mob had turned up, with his fearsome sidekick. The latter shook everyone's hands vigorously and Vic, unable to avoid a second look at that monstrous block of a head and scarred brow, and thinking how much carnage he must have wreaked during the war, thought, *Where were you when I needed you, pal?*

Vic took his place alongside the others as they lined up at the ruined entrance to the old monastery. He could not follow the various speeches in Greek, so spent some time instead assaying the crazy tourist lady, and more time trying to catch Kalliope's attention (which he managed quite often, given that he kept nudging her). He saved his best schoolboy grin for Jenny who, on his other side, responded by shaking her head at him firmly, if good-naturedly.

Among the invited guests also, at Vic's bidding and with Kalliope's acceptance, were the Petroyanakis boys. Kalliope and Elefteria had finally relented a little regarding their usefulness and had agreed that they be considered when the time came to start on the chapel work. Kalliope would put in a good word for them, and maybe they could do some cement-mixing or painting, whatever would do the least amount of damage.

Petroyanakis senior had turned up in an ill-fitting suit, and his son had made no gesture towards the occasion except to present himself in a striped T-shirt and jeans, his beard blowing in the wind and hair streaming out beneath that mad cap of his. Vic amused himself by observing the discomfort the older man seemed to be feeling; it was only too obvious that he would have preferred to be elsewhere. Despite the importance this affair held for him — allowing him to call on a little more patience than he would otherwise have had — Vic could sympathise with a bloke who thought shindigs like this were a waste of time.

After the third or fourth speech, there was a break in the talking and clapping and Vic became aware of people turning in his direction. He looked past them and focused more closely on the big shots mustered around the microphone. There he saw the abbot trying to catch his eye, grinning all the while. Then he heard him call his name, and wave at him to come forward.

'Vic, they want you to go. Go. Go on,' Kalliope implored him.

'Go on, Dad, get up there,' Jenny added.

'Me? I'm not talking,' he replied with an air of finality.

'No, they don't want you to talk, silly man,' Kalliope said, and gave him a slight push.

Unsure about what was required of him, Vic slowly manoeuvred his way forward through the fifty or sixty people gathered here, to go to Abbot Gerasimos' side. Now he saw what it was about. The abbot handed him a ceremonial spade.

'Mr Stockton, we want for you to dig first, what is the correct word, for the dirt?' Gerasimos said.

'I think you mean turn the sod,' Vic replied.

'If you say so! You are the expert.'

Laughter and cheers followed as Vic was ushered to a small area in front of the chapel where a ceremonial stone was to be set. He pushed the tip of the spade into the already worked ground and turned over a bladeful of good, hard, dry Cretan earth. There was further clapping and even a distinct 'hooray', in recognisably his daughter's voice.

After that, the official party retired to complete the formalities in the monastery's main office and to end the day with honey-laden Cretan pastries and yet more of that sweet, strong coffee that Vic had recently taken to again, even while it was giving his stomach a devil of a time.

He didn't know how long it was going to last beyond the rebuilding of the chapel — three months, maybe four, but Vic didn't care — the new life would be a delight. To be on Crete, to be able to take in Sfakia and its rugged surrounds and occasionally venture beyond was to be given a gift. And there were others: time surely among the foremost. There was time for a walk, time for a bit of reading, for small explorations, time above all for friends. Vic was making the most of it. Emboldened by his reception, he decided there was more he could do to repay his Cretan brothers and sisters for their kindness and attention. He decided to organise another excursion for them all, and not only for reasons of sociability, for he remained dead keen to get back to his sacred sites as often as possible.

On the morning she was expecting Vic to reappear for this latest outing — he had stepped out earlier on a 'secret mission' and would be back soon, he said — Kalliope was in a reflective frame of mind. She had been watching her daughter go about getting ready for the day's wheelings and dealings, which she was increasingly conducting out of their home office rather than her own agency in Rethymnon. And she didn't mind at all having a man around the house again. It had surely been a long time.

How the world had turned for them both, Kalliope thought. It had not been easy to come back to what was then still rural

Crete. Twenty-four years earlier mass tourism and money were unknown, the place had not yet recovered its identity but was a satellite of the mainland — a lively one in some ways, in others hardly changed since the 1930s. But now there was much more cosmopolitanism and energy — the island's population was growing, getting over the half-million mark. Crete was receiving more people than it was sending out.

But after the first years of trial there was a life to be had. And how much easier because of her daughter — resilient, kind Elefteria, a gift from above. She never felt lonely when her daughter was around and there was work to be done. She herself might not be as active as she had once been, but was content to still have her health and, as far as she could tell, all her brains. Pity she had less use for these now than she had once upon a time.

Kalliope only hoped that all their efforts together — as the mother and daughter real estate team anyway — would leave Elefteria in financial security after she herself was gone. There was every sign she would be. As for the other kind of security, she needed little of that for herself, yet it still hurt that no decent fellow had turned up for Elefteria. Perhaps that was the fate of the Venakis women.

Kalliope was fiddling with her scarf — her favourite, with its splashes of bright orange and teal blue — when she heard a car horn out in the street. She called out to her daughter, 'Elefteria! They're here!' and was immediately struck by the strength and volume she had generated. There was life in her yet.

Leaving the house, the two women were startled to see Vic getting out of a small van of the sort builders used around the area. Less so when they saw the younger Petroyanakis, Mark, at the wheel. Vic came forward to collect them, showed them where to sit. He squeezed them in next to Jennifer and took the last of the five available seats. He would not say where they were going — that was the surprise part — but did say they would first swing by the monastery.

There, Vic engineered a brief chat on his own with the abbot. Mutual condolences flowed regarding the demise of their 'Grand Idea' — too bad that others couldn't see the merit in it — but also reassurances that the chapel project was off and running in most positive fashion, and a reiteration of the great regard that Gerasimos felt for the 'Australian hero' and the role he had played. He had other engagements, he said, otherwise he would have had them all in for tea.

'I'm going to take them up to one of the huts up in the hills, Reverend. For old times' sake. The shepherd's hut that was known as old Manolakis' hut. Do you know where I mean?'

'Ah, yes, I do,' the abbot replied. 'But not much to see there now, my friend,' he added with some sadness. 'It has all fallen down. But you tell me that …'

Vic put his fingers to his lips and the abbot seemed to recall something and stopped speaking.

'Oh, I don't know,' Vic began again with a smile. 'Everyone likes a good Greek ruin, don't they?'

Gerasimos laughed out loud at this, slapped him on the back, and with an 'Always funny, you Australian, you!' stepped away quickly.

Back in the van they set off again. Not much later Kalliope and Elefteria felt a jolt as Mark veered off the road at a point where there was no good or obvious reason to do so. Elefteria asked what he was doing, but Mark had got the van a good way up the rough hillside and still would not answer. He seemed to know where he was going. It appeared to Kalliope that he might have been schooled in this, and she had an idea by whom.

Listening to Vic try to calm everyone and make jokes, she was soon sure she knew where he was heading.

After another few hundred metres Mark stopped and opened the doors for them, grinning all the while.

'What you doing, you silly boy?' Kalliope said.

'Don't worry,' Vic reassured her. 'Can you just come along for a moment …? You too, Elefteria, Jenny …'

Kalliope followed him and the others as carefully and gingerly as she could over such rock-strewn terrain. She was in no doubt now. He was making for the shepherd's hut all right, a place she had not visited since 1941.

They went at the rise diagonally, to reduce the steepness. Now Kalliope saw something that might or might not have been man-made a few dozen metres away. It was indeed the hut, and it was as she might have expected — four stone walls reduced to about knee height, one of them in a half-U shape formed around what had once been the door, and nothing else. Around and about was lying the remaining limestone rubble of its original construction.

'What do you see, Kalliope, girls?' Vic stopped to call out to them.

Jennifer responded with, 'Nothing, Dad! A pile of rocks.'

Elefteria was too distracted to answer, busy making sure her mother didn't have a fall up here.

Vic was conscious that Kalliope didn't seem to be particularly interested in this sight, turning her head and clinging to her daughter's arm. He came back to her slowly, carefully.

'Kalliope, let me take your arm for a minute. Is that all right?'

He looked at Elefteria, who was reluctant to hand over the responsibility of her mother to another elderly person, male or female, on this sloping, loose ground. She decided not to resist Vic's imploring look and relented.

Vic gently led Kalliope to one side, to where he had spotted a low ledge of rock they might both sit on. He waited a while before speaking.

'Do you remember this place?'

She responded without hesitation, 'I do.'

'You saved my life up here.'

Kalliope gave a sudden toss of her head, suggesting that maybe she had but that praise was not required.

'Well, you did.'

Just as quickly, Kalliope replied, 'No, I did not, Vic.'

'Ha, but you did and …'

'Vic, please, *se parakalo* … It was the war and all the people helped.'

'No, not all.'

To that, Kalliope said nothing, merely arched her brows to indicate to him he didn't know what he was talking about.

'Look, I want to do something more. I know things are happening down at the monastery, but I told the abbot that we should do up Manolakis' hut too. He said he had no objection, and it is on monastery land.'

Vic looked for a sign from Kalliope, but none came. Vic began again. 'That's why I asked the young bloke to come up today. He's a decent sort and the other job's too big for him and his Dad, we know that. But this, this is not.' He turned away from her for the moment and shouted, 'Ahoy, Mark!'

Mark swivelled to face him. 'What do you say, Mark? Can you do it?

Before he could answer, Jenny called out, 'Dad! No!' She had already heard from Mark about her old man's latest plan.

Kalliope knew what she meant by that 'No'. The child had clearly had her hands full with Vic over the years, she could tell.

At last she smiled, said, 'Better to listen to your daughter, Vic. Anyway, maybe you doing enough building on *Kriti*, eh!'

Mark thought discretion was the best immediate policy. He didn't know what, but there was something that needed to be sorted out among them here first before he could make his services available.

'Up to you guys,' he said after a moment more. 'But hey, I might just do this myself, for love of my fellow man! We'll see!'

Knowing enough not to push the point any more right now, Vic continued to watch as Mark then took his daughter's elbow and led her further to one side. He was fascinated to see them begin to converse again about something and with so much earnest attention to each other.

'Gee, if you didn't know any better …' he muttered, then turned slightly towards Kalliope. 'Kalliope, you know what's different today, the thing that's missing?'

She looked across at him expectantly.

'There are no cicadas!'

Kalliope smiled. 'No. That's right, no cicadas … You are right. Not summer yet. And never we have cicadas here anyway, only *tzitzikes*! Go on, you say …' she teased him.

Vic tried the word, got tangled up. When that brought forth a soft laugh from Kalliope, Vic felt more than pleased.

As Vic occupied himself with the scene up ahead, Kalliope sat back and surveyed this place again. She had not been back here at all in the years since her return. If she had thought of it at all she would have thought it a site that was about as welcoming as the surface of the moon. A windswept and sparsely vegetated hillslope. But to look more closely today was to see more, much more. For tugging at her now, in this place, was the notion that she could not deny a thing. Not a single thing.

In these hills there had been poverty, hurt, beauty, suffering, anger, joy, a kind of prison, a kind of freedom, a simplicity, a life. But they had given too little of what she had sought, had wanted in her depths. And then she had left it all for a voyage and for a man. But now ... She looked around her at the chips of limestone and the tussocky grass, the wild endive here and there. Here was Crete. Long gone, ever-present Crete. Her home yet again these two decades and more. Her daughter's home, her home.

Then, she felt a touch, lightly on her back. Vic had reached across and placed his hand there. She turned slightly, looked at his face, cheeks red from the effort, the blue eyes, that animal vitality of his shining out. But as his hand came around to rest on her forearm, she saw too an old man's skin and bent fingers.

'Kalliope. You know I love you, girl, don't you,' he said, just like that.

She smiled back at him as if he'd only said, 'What a lovely day this is.'

Which it was for her, and which only required of her that she be present to enjoy it in its clear, spring morning reality and nothing else.

'No, Vic. Don't say such a word, please.'

If he was waiting for something more, she could not give it to him. She had nothing to say to what he had said, but understood it all as a rush of blood, the man's nature at work, a tongue disconnected from sober thought.

Vic waited awkwardly in silence before suddenly dropping his shoulders in a way that suggested he maybe thought he had not said or done the right thing. Then he said, 'Well look, anyway, I've been talking to Jennifer ... Whatever happens, I'm intending to stay. I want to stay on Crete.'

Appearing confused for a second or two, embarrassed at a